金

GUM

MOON

門

A Novel of San Francisco Chinatown

by

Jeffrey L. Staley

Book and cover design: Vladimir Verano, VertVolta Design
vertvoltapress.com

Original artwork on cover and interiors: © *Staci Thompson Adman*

Published in the United States by Jeffrey L. Staley

Author contact:
gummoon.thenovel@gmail.com
on Facebook: Gum Moon: A Novel of San Francisco Chinatown

ISBN: 978-1-7322445-0-4

e-book: 978-1-7322445-1-1

For the Asian women and girls who survived debt slavery, violence, and sexual abuse in San Francisco, 1850-1920; and for their descendants who never heard their stories.

In memory of Marjorie Don Wong, daughter of Maud Lai Don; beloved grandmother of my children, Benjamin and Allison.

Gum

Moon

Chapter One

GOLD
(1898)

Muriel Bailey pushed back her chair, pulled up her skirts and petti-coats, and rested her boots on her desk at *The Morning Call* news-paper building in downtown San Francisco. She picked up Saturday's paper from the corner of the desk. The ink was barely dry. If there were a Dick Custer cigar in her desk's bottom drawer, she would already have it in hand, and she would have bitten off an end, lit it, and taken a few puffs. But except for a box of new pencils, the drawer had been empty for weeks. Muriel tilted her head back and inhaled. Her nostrils tingled with the ac-rid scent of Friday night's potpourri of newsroom tobaccos—a miscellany of cheap, stale cigarettes mingled with her boss's fat, hand-rolled Perfecto cigars from Ybor City, Florida—lingering evidence of copy editors' mad scramble to meet another deadline.

It was eight o'clock in the morning on a holiday weekend—July third to be exact—and except for a lanky Negro janitor clanking trashcans at the far side of the room, Muriel was alone. She opened the paper, rattled it to smooth its center crease, then flipped to page five. The headline at the top read "San Francisco Welcomes *Endeavor Society*." It wasn't an aus-picious sounding start to a feature-writing career. Nevertheless, Muriel hoped the article would mark the end of churning out hundred-word no-tices gleaned from police reports of murders, thefts, and drunken brawls on the Barbary Coast at Pacific and Montgomery streets.

She sighed with relief when she finished reading. She hadn't found any typographical errors, and her editor had made only minor changes in her article.

She had written that the goal of the *Endeavor Society* was to "strengthen spiritual life and promote interdenominational Protestant activities," and this would be the international group's first meeting west of the Mississippi. But the gossip floating around the pressroom was that the big shot city politicians hoped the Convention would boost the state's stagnant economy, still reeling from the effects of the Panic of 1893, five years previous.

Muriel caught her first glimpse of the Endeavorers that morning from the cable car as she rode to work. Flocks of them were gawking, walking up Market Street from the new Ferry Building. Their patriotically colored Endeavor ribbons were blowing in the wind, looking for all the world like the ruffled plumage of tropical birds war reporters were finding in the jungles of Cuba. But San Francisco in 1898 wasn't the Caribbean. And while many of the visitors would think they were teetering on the brink of the known world, apparently some had come early, determined to do a little sightseeing and shopping in the West's largest city. They could wait until tomorrow, the Fourth of July, when their annual Convention opened, to settle into the serious work of saving souls.

Muriel wasn't writing about the *Society* because she was interested in religion. She lost the last vestiges of religious enthusiasm during a second year philosophy course at the University of California, in Berkeley across the bay. When she interviewed for *The Call* position a year ago, her editor told her that on a clear day you could see the university campus from *The Call*'s business offices on the tenth floor of the Claus Spreckels Building. He said if he hired her, he would take her there to see the view. He still hadn't done that, but as *The Call*'s first full-time female reporter, she felt grateful just to have her own desk—even if it was in a windowless corner of the building next door. And she was proud of her desk's scratches and scars. Although she wasn't responsible for them all, she viewed the nicks and scuffs as old friends, as silent witnesses to her predecessors' long hours. Their willingness—like her own—to take any and every scrap of "worthy news" the boss tossed on the cluttered desk. And this article, she felt, was worth at least three or four additional notches.

No one had seemed interested in working the upcoming *Christian Endeavor* story after war had been declared on Spain in late April. So Muriel had suggested a Saturday feature on the Convention, and to her surprise, her editor gave her the job. Muriel knew she could write as well as any man at *The Call*, and this article and the others she had planned for the week ahead would prove it. She was determined to make the most of the opportunity. And so when the topic of future features came up at last Wednesday's planning meeting, Muriel proposed that she interview some of the Christian ladies at the Protestant missions in Chinatown as a follow-up article. She hadn't spent any time exploring the eight-block rectangle of strange sights and foul smells just west of her beat on the Barbary Coast. But she suspected a large percentage of the forty thousand visitors would be taking the dollar Chinatown tours, and an article about the Christian rescue missions would sell papers. A story featuring defenseless Oriental girls and their daring white rescuers would excite the imaginations of the out-of-town guests.

Her editor had grinned across the table and told her it was a splendid idea. In front of all her male peers. Then, after the meeting, he gave her the names of some of the Christian missionaries he had heard of.

Muriel skimmed her article one last time, folded it in half—then again—and stuffed it into her father's well-worn leather satchel sitting beside her desk.

金

Except for the larger than normal number of Americans wandering through Chinatown buying souvenirs and ogling the anatomically intact roasted ducks, pigs, and chickens hanging in grocery store windows, the Endeavor Convention had no effect on Lai Foon and his wife, Muck Shee. With six hungry mouths to feed, they had more pressing concerns than white people's Jesus stories.

Foon had been working in Sacramento for the past year, sending every saved penny to his family in San Francisco. But when he came back to Number One City at the end of Number Six Month, he said he had been visiting a cousin in Fresno, and if he could raise some money, he would take them all there to live.

Foon had crept up the stairs in the dark on a cold June night, long after the children were asleep. The quiet tapping on the door had startled Muck Shee, and when she opened it her husband was nervous and smelled of opium. He said his cousin had offered him a job. Then he told her the bad news that the place where he worked had closed. It was the third job he had lost in less than a year. Muck Shee and Foon argued about money for hours afterwards.

"If we had a little cash, I could buy a partnership in his candy store."

Muck Shee snorted and pulled at the wool blanket, drawing it closer to her body. "You're not going to make a living with a candy store in a place that most people have never heard of and is smaller than Number Two City. If you make any kind of a living there it'll be from selling opium—and maybe some girls on the side. Don't tell me this is about a 'candy store.' You're not going to feed us by selling sugared ginger and red melon seeds."

Foon ignored her interruption. The shadows of his gesturing hands were monstrously huge on the wall behind the flickering candle. "Everyone's having a hard time now. It's not just me. You know I'm not lazy. But there's a class of men who'd spend whatever money they had on a bit of candy before they'd buy rice for their families. And I don't plan on staying in that business—it's just something to get started again until I can open a regular store. I've got money to last a week or so, but that's about it. After that, I don't know. Maybe if we pawned something." His voice trailed off.

"No. Not that." Muck Shee looked into his eyes. She hoped he would hear the anger and fear in her voice, and stop. But he kept on.

"I don't know any other way. We're down to the last grain of rice in our bowl, and the white rat in the corner is trying to get that. I honestly don't know what to do."

"No. You promised." Muck Shee's voice trembled.

Foon slumped over, cross-legged on the floor of their one-room apartment on Jackson Street. Their six children were asleep along the opposite wall, separated from them by a thin curtain. Muck Shee heard the soft breathing, the smacking lips; the rustling blankets as one of the children turned.

Foon raised his head. His eyes reflected the burning candle on the orange crate that doubled as storage for their kitchen utensils. "I'm thinking maybe if we pawned one of the older ones, we could get enough money to buy into my cousin's business. Both those girls are strong and healthy, and either one could do most of the chores expected of an adopted daughter."

Muck Shee listened to Foon ramble on about Fresno and his "candy store" plans, his cousin who said living was cheaper the further you got from Number One City, and the in-and-out breathing of the children. There was always a fear the next breath wouldn't come. She had never quite gotten used to that pause in their breathing. You'd think after the first child was a few years old—

Muck Shee felt eight years old again. She was in Dai Law, her ancestral village in the Pearl River delta of the Celestial Kingdom, looking up at her mother's face twisted and determined, lecturing about family duty and the fate of being a girl in a world ruled by men. It was the last time she had seen her mother.

"You'll know one day," her mother shouted after her, as strangers carried her, arms and legs flailing, across the rice fields. Now Muck Shee was beginning to understand.

Finally Muck Shee spoke. "The lamb has no choice when it's in the jaws of the wolf.

"You say we can pawn one of the older ones—but we'll lose both if you do that. The one we keep will hate us too.

"Those two already can work a little—I've been teaching them to sew buttons on shirts. Oy is getting quicker, and if we didn't have her, we'd lose the money she's making. And from the years we lived in Ross Alley, both those girls know what happens to adopted daughters. I can't live knowing one of my daughters knows—" Muck Shee twisted her fingers in knots— "knows I know about that life, and I still let you sell her." She paused, still working her fingers, then pushed on.

"If you're so set on pawning a girl, why not Chun? Even if we didn't get as much money, we'd probably have enough to start your business. And buy a month's worth of rice—if we're careful. Since she's just a baby, she wouldn't remember us in a year anyway." Muck Shee stopped to catch her breath. She felt as though she was a little girl, straining to keep up with her grandfather on one of his long walks to the hills at the edge of Dai Law village, where he would take her to pick cloud ear mushrooms from the dark sides of dead elderberry trees.

"Chun's small, and the shape of her face—it's the shape that—"

"There's no need to think that way." Foon reached out and touched her shoulder.

Muck Shee pushed his hand away and pressed on, as though straining to reach the hilltop outside her village. "She's so frail. Her three years have cost us more in doctor's bills than the other two girls put together. If my baby's going to die like the other one did, we might as well get something for her now—while she's still living." Muck Shee had reached the hilltop where her grandfather was already searching for cloud ears. Her lungs burned, and she had to stop and catch her breath. "If the baby does survive, and your business in Fresno prospers, we could come back in a few years and get her before—"

"This isn't easy on me either. But I have to think of what's best for everyone—the boys—" Foon put his hand on her thigh. "I can make it up to you— I promise."

Muck Shee pushed his hand away again. "If we have another baby— what then? It'll just be another mouth to feed. And we can't afford it. And if it's a girl, you'll want to pawn her, too."

Foon sighed and blew out the candle, turning away from her in the dark. Muck Shee's breathing was heavy and labored, and the blanket felt raw and wet against her neck.

"You know it's not the Chinese way for the father to arrange the sale." Foon was talking to the wall. "But I'll find a good place for the baby. I'll take it around for those women to look at. It's the least I can do. But you're the mother. You have to be the one who takes it. I'll make all the arrangements. Then you take it."

"Mama?" It was Chun, the baby. Muck Shee could hear her moving, trying to stand.

"Papa came home tonight. Go back to sleep."

"I go peepee."

Muck Shee swore softly. She fumbled for the candle, found a match, and lit it again. "Come here—and try not to wake everyone else." She uncovered the chamber pot in the corner by the door and straddled her daughter over it, squatting beside her and clasping her at the waist.

"Mama. Scary! I sleep with you?"

金

That had been a week ago. Since then, Muck Shee and Foon hadn't spoken but two or three words to each other, and Chun had slept every night wrapped in her mother's arms. Finally, Foon told Muck Shee he had found a woman interested in taking the baby. After consulting a fortune-teller and the *Tung Shing* book for the luckiest day, they had chosen today—Saturday—the day before American boys would be running through Chinatown throwing firecrackers into melon and tomato boxes, for the transaction. And now Muck Shee prepared to venture into Chinatown unaccompanied by a son or her husband. She had lived twenty years in Gold Mountain and could count on one hand the number of times she had been out alone. They were all times before she was married. Respectable married women remained indoors, attending to family matters and household tasks, and left public affairs to their husbands or sons. But today was different.

Muck Shee's hands shook as she dressed her sleepy-eyed daughter in red and yellow good luck clothes. She put a horsehair charm around the baby's neck, then set her in an embroidered pack and lifted it onto her shoulders. She adjusted it three times before she got it right. Just before she left, she tucked a scrap of rice paper in the waistband.

The three year-old's weight forced Muck Shee to bend forward for balance, and she crept through Ross Alley, eyes on the ground, wary of the occasional rotting pear or orange barely visible in the shadows. She cut across Washington Street and entered the narrow, wooden-planked passageway between Washington and Clay called New Spanish Alley—or Spofford Alley, to the Americans.

The morning mist hadn't lifted from the San Francisco hills, and groaning foghorns mingled with bickering seagulls. Muck Shee was the only person in the damp alleyway. She was looking for a Chinese sign that read "Merchant Association Club, Number 11." But she couldn't read, and she had to look twice at the broad, red brushstrokes beside each alley door and compare them with the small piece of rice paper Foon had given her. His writing was cruder than the signs, and she tipped precariously as she bent back and tried to focus her eyes on the marks. After checking one sign outlined in gold for a third time, Muck Shee rapped on the gray weathered door next to it and called for the owner. Her voice shook and cracked, but she called again. She heard a slow shuffling movement, then a disembodied voice. "Who's there?" it screeched.

"Muck Shee." Her voice faltered. "With a daughter."

A stooped old woman stood in the open doorway, squinting sleepily into the morning haze. She clutched a ring of keys and wore a stained, shapeless sleeping garment that looked like it had once been white. A quid of tobacco filled her right cheek and began to ooze over her lower lip.

"Come in, my friend." The woman scratched at her hair.

Muck Shee didn't move.

"So you're Muck Shee. I'm Kim Yook. The keeper here at the Merchant Association Club. Your husband said you'd probably be early, but he didn't say exactly when.

"This is a good house, and I take good care of my girls. Yue Tschi owns three of them. Your husband said he'd heard of him. I've worked in the business for twenty years. Before that I was a girl in a place on Ross Alley, so I know how to handle every type of customer."

Still Muck Shee didn't move. "What did you say your name was?" She wanted to be sure she would remember the woman. When Foon became rich in Fresno, he would bring her back to get Chun. He promised.

"Kim Yook." The old woman wheezed more loudly. "You must have lost your ears on the way here.

"Come." The old woman stepped aside and beckoned with an out-stretched hand. "I keep an altar in the back for the girls to remember their ancestors." Her neck twisted and folds of leathery skin stretched grotesquely. "We've had no sickness here in three years, and no fights to speak of. You'll see the place is clean—but I need a daughter to do the little things I can't. I can't bend over very far anymore. And my eyes aren't good."

The old woman moved the quid of tobacco with her tongue to the other cheek and spit into the alley, barely missing the nose of a scrawny dog sleeping across the way.

Muck Shee watched the dog jump and slink off toward Washington Street and the freshly slaughtered chickens of Wu Chung's butcher shop.

"Friday night's really busy here, so I usually let the girls sleep until noon on Saturdays. It means I don't need to get up quite so early either. But no matter. You're here, I'm up, and that's the important thing."

The old woman grimaced and shifted her weight from one foot to the other. She stared at Muck Shee. The baby burrowed into the back of Muck Shee's blouse. The old woman leaned into the alley, her fingers fumbling with the edge of the baby pack. The old woman nodded. "She's wearing good colors. And a valuable charm. But if that's the same child your husband brought last week, she's smaller and skinnier now." The old woman's eyes twisted their way into Muck Shee's skull, and she couldn't look away. A few crooked, yellow teeth showed. "Come, come. Don't stand in the alley. Careful. There's a step."

The old woman left the door ajar. She turned and disappeared behind a red and black screen protected with two fiery-eyed door gods painted in gold. The screen was positioned a few feet in front of the door and blocked the room's view from anyone entering. Muck Shee knew ghosts could only walk in straight lines. The screen would confuse evil spirits and keep them away from the old woman's business and her new daughter. Muck Shee slipped behind the screen and entered a square room not much larger than the family's place on Jackson Street.

The smell of stale cigarette smoke hung in the air, and Muck Shee stiffened against the side of the screen. A gaslight bolted to the far wall next to a rustling bamboo curtain lit the room—the kind of room she hadn't been in since she was fifteen. Her lungs burned. She breathed out.

A pot-bellied stove with a large, blue kettle on top stood across from her, and beside the stove sat a battered coal bucket. To her left was a table with two chairs and an iron strong box beneath it. Four wooden stools had been pushed against the backside of the screen. The wall to her right was plastered from ceiling to floor with flour and feed sacks. The old woman seemed to like ones with bird pictures. More stools lined that wall, and above the stools were pegs for customers' winter coats and hats. There was a stack of newspapers by one of the stools. For customers to read as they waited for the next girl.

Foon's business troubles had brought them to this. Muck Shee had made Foon promise on their wedding day not to sell her back to a brothel.

No matter how bad things got. And he hadn't. But Foon had never promised he wouldn't consider pawning a daughter to one.

Muck Shee's skin grew cold and prickly. Except for the owner, it could have been the same place she had been the first year she lived in Gold Mountain.

Muck Shee wanted to turn and run. She wanted to take her baby and get as far from the place as she could. But the old woman reentered the room, waving her hand through the bamboo curtain. She gestured toward one of the wooden stools beside the screen. The sleepy baby sniffed and burrowed into the pack. Muck Shee couldn't make her feet move.

Her eyes fastened briefly on a small niche above the stove where she could see the vague outline of a stove god figurine. But then, against her will, her eyes moved to a crude wooden shelf that hung above the table. It was lined with an odd assortment of clay jars. They would be full of herbs and things for preventing pregnancy. Probably the old woman's "store." Whatever the girls took, the old woman would charge against their accounts. Muck Shee remembered the rules.

"Please. Sit. The paper's ready."

Muck Shee took the nearest stool. The old woman kicked an open bedroll under the table then pulled a chair beside it.

"I've decided to take the child for one hundred dollars. Just like your husband and I agreed." The old woman licked her lips and tapped her fingertips together.

"Foon said you promised two extra dollars if I brought some papers." Muck Shee sat on the edge of the stool, untying the embroidered baby pack and setting it on the floor. She lifted the little girl out and held her on her lap. She took a packet from a pouch hanging around her neck. "These say she was born in the year of the sheep. Snake month. The astrologer said it was a good combination. One hundred and two dollars."

The old woman swore under her breath. She banged her gnarled knuckles on the table and glared at the baby. The baby shrank back against Muck Shee's breast.

"I never told him anything like that. You mothers are all alike. Ready to close a sale and then trying to squeeze one extra penny out of a poor woman—a woman with no husband or son to protect her in her old age.

If your husband was here I'd tell him to poke his skinny stick up a rat hole and stop wasting my time."

"My daughter's not much trouble. She's a fast learner. She already knows how to spread her legs—"

The old woman stood and seemed ready to tell Muck Shee to take her business elsewhere, when the door swung open wide, illuminating the niche above the stove. A young man strode into the room and then stepped back in surprise.

His queue was freshly tied and his loose cotton pants were clean and pressed. A faint smell of chicken fat lingered beside the screen. He was about the age Foon had been when he first came to her in a place like this—perhaps twenty years old—certainly no more than twenty-five. Muck Shee wondered if he had a wife and children in the Celestial Kingdom, like her Foon—like so many other men—all unable to bring their families to Gold Mountain.

金

Kim Yook studied the man. Her gaze moved from his eyes and jaw to the small package pressed against his side. It was wrapped in butcher paper and tied with red string.

"Mr. Leong. It's good to see you. You're early today. But I suspect Yet is awake. I'll take you up and unlock her door."

"I have a new job, and I have to start earlier on Saturdays. I saw the door open, so I thought—" The man started for the bamboo curtain at the back of the room.

"You know the rules, Mr. Leong. All gifts go on the table. I'll give it to Yet when you leave, after I enter it in her account book."

Mr. Leong glared at Kim Yook, but he set the package down. "Just make sure it goes on her account."

Kim Yook led Mr. Leong behind the clattering bamboo at the far edge of the room, ignoring his last remark. There was a shallow alcove with two doors behind the curtain, and a small, rough-hewn wooden stand with the ancestral tablets of Kim Yook's distant family members. She made sure to add the names of each new girl's ancestors to the tablets on the altar—if they gave them to her—so the girls would feel safe and part of the family.

The scent of half-burnt joss sticks and moldy lotus fruit wafted upward as Kim Yook opened the door on the left. Mr. Leong thumped behind her jangling keys through the darkness and up the steep, creaking stairs. There were two sharp turns, and then at the top, a thick door with a heavy lock: A surprise to new customers or unwanted visitors. The latter came only at the end of those months Kim Yook was late in paying the Chinatown police squad. The door was already unlocked, and as Kim Yook pushed hard against it, it grudgingly opened.

A narrow hallway with five small doors on the side facing the alley lay before them, and now the tang of human sweat along with the lingering stench of dirty chamber pots hung in the air. Each door had a small cutout in the center at eye-height, for the keeper, with a wooden slider that could be opened or closed from either side. A dirt-stained window at the end of the hall let in just enough light to frame the doors. Kim Yook limped down the passageway, unlocking each one as she came to it. She tapped on the slider at the third door. She heard Yet's muffled "Yes?" and unlocked it.

Kim Yook had nicknames for each of her five girls. She rarely said them aloud, but when circumstance required, she would use them. Yet's nickname was "Pretty One." It was simple and accurate. And because Yet was vain, there were occasional business situations when Kim Yook needed it.

Like all her workers' cribs, Yet's room was rectangular; just long enough for a narrow cot. A shuttered, cross-hatch iron-barred window about one-foot square was opposite the door, and Yet had already opened the shutter, letting in the coal-filtered sunlight, the salty morning air, and the muted sounds of the alley. The window was close to the floor so the girl could sit on the edge of her cot and call to prospective customers passing below.

Yet's room was neat, unlike the other four. Kim Yook had been trying to convince the other girls they would make more money if they kept their rooms clean, but Yet was the only girl doing anything. She had been keeping her room clean long before Kim Yook realized there might be a connection between neatness and more money in the strong box.

Across from Yet's cot was a small steamer trunk that held her belongings. Above it hung a shelf with various oils, medicinal herbs, sponges, and cleansing agents in vases and jars of all shapes and colors. The largest of these was a porcelain ginger jar a customer gave the girl long ago—and Kim Yook had let her keep it. For some reason it seemed to make Yet work harder. On its side was a painting of a girl. The girl sat cross-legged beside a river, beneath a mulberry tree, with a lute on her lap. Sometimes in the mornings when Kim Yook unlocked the door and peered in, Yet would be lying on her cot, staring at the jar with a distant look in her eyes. At those times Kim Yook thought Yet might be remembering her life before she came to Gold Mountain. But she didn't ask about life before the brothel. It was better that way. If a pretty jar could keep a girl working, that was all that mattered.

Kim Yook knew Yet kept her special combination of ginseng, powdered deer tail, and Queen Anne's Lace seeds in the porcelain ginger jar. Kim Yook mixed these together in careful proportions and sold it to the girls. It had the right balance of hot and cold to prevent pregnancy. A small plain dish next to the jar held dried hawthorn berries. The girls were supposed to take a few each morning to balance their bodies' *chi.* Kim Yook asked them each day about their supply of herbs and berries—whether they needed more, and if so, how much. She rarely checked what was in the other jars, since most girls simply kept perfumes and lubricants in them. But Kim Yook was adamant that her girls use her mix of herbs after each customer, and she would look in her account book to see when a girl was likely to need more.

Next to Yet's trunk stood a covered ceramic chamber pot with a towel and mirror on top. A pitcher and basin of water were on the trunk beside the chamber pot, and alongside that, a stack of rags. Kim Yook had the cleaning girl bring fresh ones each day. The girls were supposed to put them under themselves when they had customers. Boys, especially, had a tendency to leak, and customers preferred dry beds. A bright red abacus hung on a nail behind the door. It helped track how many days were left before Yet's next monthly bleeding.

"I need the money from last night." Kim Yook surveyed the crib approvingly. "By noon. And don't forget this is police protection day. I'm taking an extra dollar out of what you owe me for that. We don't need any of those Jeezachrise-hollering women around here thinking they can come and throw you girls in jail—or something worse—because we didn't pay."

Kim Yook paused and looked into Yet's eyes. Then she left Mr. Leong in the room and locked the door—more out of habit than anything. She had learned over the years always to be careful, no matter how good the customer seemed. She unlocked the remaining two doors, then made her way back downstairs to the table.

Kim Yook untied the red string from Mr. Leong's package, and a sheer silk, jade-green cheongsam fell out of the butcher paper. She looked over at the mother sitting on the stool where she had left her. She had pulled up her blouse and was nursing the baby.

"What's that girl going to do with this?" Kim Yook held the dress against her body. "I tell you, some customers' brains are smaller than an alley dog's. But that man's a regular. He comes in every Saturday before the others so he can have Yet to himself.

"She's my top money-maker, that Yet." Kim Yook set the dress back on the table. "Beautiful face, strong legs. Never sick. But she's headstrong, I tell you. I have to watch her like a beady-eyed rat." She grinned, but the mother's eyes seemed focused on the sucking baby.

"She'll rob me blind, if I'm not careful. If I ever lose her, half my business will be gone. Poof!" Kim Yook snapped her fingers in the air with a flourish, as if she was a *Cai Dan* clown actor in a Chinese opera at the Red Cassia Theatre on Waverly Place. The mother finally looked up.

"I know I'll never be rich. My other girls barely bring in enough money to pay for their rooms and the rice in their bowls. I just want to make enough to get back to the Celestial Kingdom and my ancestral village, then die in peace." Kim Yook scratched at herself and coughed hard, her body doubling over in pain.

"If I live that long. Jeezachrise." It was one of two American words Kim Yook knew. The other was "wharsahorbitch." A white devil who frequented the Merchant Association Club a few years back called her girls that name. Kim Yook loved to use the words on the Jesus people who played loud American music in the alley on Saturday afternoons. She had no idea what the words meant, but they seemed to make the Jesus people angry when she said them. And more importantly, shouting the words made the people go to the other end of the alley to drum and sing, ensuring more customers for her.

"So, let's talk business." Kim Yook clenched her teeth and sat next to the table. "Come here." She patted the chair beside her.

金

"I said Chun already knows how to spread her legs and squat to pee in a pot. No one will have to teach her that." Muck Shee put her little finger in her daughter's mouth and broke the suction on her nipple, then sat at the table. She moved the baby to her other breast.

"Well that's worth something, I guess."

"So one hundred and two dollars." Muck Shee clamped her jaw and looked straight into the old woman's eyes. "That's what Foon said. We may be poor, but my husband's word is good. He doesn't lie."

"I don't want to hear about your family problems. I have enough of my own. And look at your child." The old woman reached over and pulled the baby's head away from Muck Shee's breast. "She's as scrawny as a rooster hanging in Wu's butcher shop. I swear I heard her sniffling when you came in. I'll be lucky if she lives to be five. This isn't an easy life. You know that."

Muck Shee felt her cheeks grow hot and she turned her face away from the old woman. Out of the corner of her eye Muck Shee saw the woman bend and spit into a rice bowl under the table. A fat rat scooted across the floor.

"Tobacco's cheaper than opium, and not as bad for you," the old woman laughed. "Of course I don't know what it does to rats."

Muck Shee sat stiffly on the chair, her ribs lifting in rhythm with her daughter's shallow breathing. She leaned forward to hear the woman's words.

"The white devils' immigration laws keep getting tougher and the inspectors keep getting meaner. You have no idea what it's like to run a business when the devils' laws make it impossible to import fresh girls."

"One hundred and two dollars," Muck Shee hoped the woman couldn't hear the quaver in her voice. "Here's a picture of her and the paper from the building that keeps birth records. Chun was born at 614 Jackson Street—upstairs in that place at the back of the Globe Hotel.

Foon said you might be interested in that." Muck Shee spread the papers on the table.

The old woman's eyebrows arched. "Let me see those."

"You can see the paper has American words on it." Muck Shee smoothed it and pointed. "Foon says that's a good sign."

The old woman stared at the paper and picture for a long time, tapping her fingers on the table. "This paper—if it says where the child was born—could be worth something." She handed them back. "So, two extra dollars, you say?"

Muck Shee nodded.

"Well, you've got me in a bind. Your husband knows how desperate I am for an adopted daughter—I need someone to care for me and clean around here. Girls like Yet get a few regular customers and they think they're too good to empty their own piss pots. And the other girls won't even make their beds after a customer's gone. The competition in the alley's getting fierce. Men don't like to come to a brothel that's dirty when there's a cleaner one for the same price next door. And I need a girl or two to make sure my business will be around in ten years. If I live that long. Life isn't easy for me. I'm not like you. I'm old and don't have a man to care for me like you do." The old woman farted and spat again.

"Well, let's get this deal done. Give me the girl—and the picture. And the paper."

"I'll take the payment in gold coins, and I want a red paper."

The brothel keeper cursed. She took one of the keys on her ring and holding on to the edge of the table, knelt to unlock the strong box.

Chun wriggled a hand free from Muck Shee's grasp and slid it up Muck Shee's long sleeved blouse. The baby found a bracelet on Muck Shee's wrist and began to tug on it. It was gold and jade—Foon's brother had given it to her at her second son's red egg and ginger party, when he was one month old. The day he received his formal name. Muck Shee had worn the bracelet as an amulet every day since then. And not one of her children had died since she put it on six years ago. Now Chun twisted the braided chains more tightly. Muck Shee felt the soft skin of her inner wrist pinch, and she slapped the baby. Chun yelped and buried her face against Muck Shee's neck. Muck Shee pulled back her sleeve to look at her arm. Even in the dim light she could see the twisted braid bracelet had raised a welt along the width of her vein. She swore and made an angry face at Chun.

"Now you're being bad. And in front of a new auntie. If you don't stop crying, demons will jump out and get you tonight when you're sleeping." Muck Shee made a throaty hissing sound. She put the baby on the floor.

The brothel keeper was sitting again at the table, now with a stack of gold coins in front of her. Muck Shee gasped. She had never seen so much gold.

The keeper shuffled the coins from one hand to the other, all the while staring at Muck Shee. The coins went clink, clink, clink. The sound spoons made in rice bowls—rice bowls that would be full from now on.

The keeper studied the baby, but didn't lose count of the coins. "So you say she won't be much trouble? I ought to keep this twenty-dollar piece for myself after seeing her hurt you like that."

"Mama. Mama. Uppee." Chun clung to Muck Shee's knees.

The keeper kept counting. "So here's sixty dollars, and another twenty. Jeezachrise." She reached down the neck of her bedclothes and pulled out a red silk bag. She poured out a pile of silver coins.

Muck Shee pushed her baby toward the keeper. The old woman sorted and counted out eight silver coins. She pushed five gold pieces and eight silver ones across the table. Muck Shee counted them and gripped them to her breast. They were heavy. They weighed her down.

"Take her—and the paper and the picture." Muck Shee felt a crushing pain rising in her bowels and willed it down with difficulty.

"She's yours now. She'll be a hard worker when she's older."

Standing abruptly, Muck Shee turned toward the screen. But Chun clung to her legs. Muck Shee pried her daughter's fingers loose and again pushed her toward the keeper. Then she remembered the receipt.

"I need the red paper."

"Oh yes, the receipt." The brothel keeper found an ink brush on the table and added two straight lines for the two extra dollars. "And I'll take the child's pack, too. The girls can carry her around like you did. Maybe it'll make her happy." The keeper held Chun's arm. But the baby began to scream and tried to pull away.

Muck Shee took the paper from the keeper's hand, untied the embroidered pack from her back, and put it on the table. She stumbled toward the screen. The alleyway. The outside world. She shut the door and leaned against the red and gold sign. An otherworldly sound started deep in her belly and made its way up through her throat, like the afterburn of vomit. She forced it back, but she couldn't keep it there. The heavy coins weighed her down, and she sank onto the rough board planking of the street. She pulled her thighs to her chest the way a woman might if she were in labor. Strange men passed by and stared. And the sound started again.

金

Muck Shee heard Foon's voice and felt his hand on her shoulder.

"Did you take it—the baby? Did you get the full amount and the receipt?"

She shrank from his touch. "Here." She thrust the red paper and the heavy coins in his face. "One hundred and two dollars. I got two extra dollars for the papers.

"Where are my children? What did you tell them?"

Foon helped Muck Shee to her feet. He smiled grimly. "I said we're leaving the baby with Uncle Yong on Clay Street until we're settled.

"We have to hurry. We have a ferry to catch if we're going to make the late morning train to Fresno. Wing's keeping Ho, Oy, Moon, and Gum at the dock."

Although Foon pronounced each child's name slowly and carefully, Muck Shee had difficulty deciphering the sounds coming from his mouth. She felt hot, like she was suffocating in a smoke-filled opium den. She had borne the man seven children. One was already dead. Now one was sold. It might as well be dead. She might as well be dead. Opium would be good. It would take the edge off the pain. She would get some from him. Later.

"The children took everything. There wasn't much to carry.

"On the way over here I bought some sugared ginger for you. Here, try some. It's good."

Muck Shee pushed Foon's hand away and stumbled ahead of him toward Washington Street. The man continued to talk gibberish at the back of her head.

"With those extra dollars we'll eat well tonight. We'll celebrate our new life in Fresno. You'll see. It's the right move."

"I'm not hungry." She walked faster.

"You'll be hungry soon enough. But don't worry. With this money I'm going to open that candy place in Fresno and sell some merchandise. From now on we'll have enough to eat. And when we've saved some money we'll come back and get the baby. I promise." Foon was beside her now, but Muck Shee couldn't bear to look at him. She shoved him away again and moved into the morning light. Out into the sounds of clopping and whinnying horses, the creaking drays. The shouting merchants of Washington Street.

Foon stepped around her, and they turned toward the Ferry Building. A group of white people with bright colored ribbons pinned to their coats forced them against the vegetable boxes outside a grocery store, and Foon shielded Muck Shee from the Americans' rudeness. The two of them ducked under a broken awning and into the store, waiting for the white people to move. The shop owner yelled something about a wagonload of fresh long beans and bok choy from Santa Rosa. But then a tall white boy wearing a round green hat with writing on it stopped in front of the store, and the group of white people crowded in close. He faced the street and began to shout.

"What's he saying?" Muck Shee tugged at Foon's sleeve. She caught a strong whiff of opium on his shirt, and the tang of oranges, garlic, and ginger from the stacked wooden boxes beside her. "And why won't they move out of our way?" Foon had been to a Mission ABC school when he first came to Gold Mountain, and Muck Shee knew he understood American.

"Those white people with the ribbons paid that boy with the green hat a dollar each to bring them to Chinatown to look at us," Foon told her. "And the boy with the green hat says that girl looking out that window over there works in a slave den and is locked in chains all day."

Muck Shee watched the white boy with the green hat give two small silver coins to a Chinese boy lounging in front of the grocery store. He straightened and ran across the street to hand one of the coins to an old man waving from under the iron-barred window. The boy put the other coin in his pocket and sauntered back to the grocery store with a smirk on his face.

The crowd of white people finally moved away from the store and up Washington Street. "Take me to Fresno. I never want to see this city again." Muck Shee rubbed her nose, but couldn't get rid of the white people's sweet sweaty stink, or the sour smell of horse manure and urine from the street. Her belly began to heave again. Her throat burned, and she started to wander blindly down the cobblestone street toward the bay.

金

Back at the Merchant Association Club in New Spanish Alley, Kim Yook was yelling upstairs. "Girls! Come here. Toi has your rice ready in the kitchen. And I have a surprise for you."

How Ming was the first to slump into the room. At twenty-five years old, she was the oldest of Kim Yook's five girls. She was pudgy and had a smallpox-scarred, "heavenly flower" face. She was always tired. And as usual, she looked cross. Kim Yook's secret nickname for Ming was "Ugly One." Kim Yook kept Ming for boys who couldn't pay much. She rarely received a dollar for her work, but if boys only had enough money to look or touch, she could make almost as much money in a night as Yet. That's because she would have twice as many customers.

Ming stank and needed to wash herself, and Kim Yook guessed she was still angry about her last customer—a loud, drunk boy barely sixteen, who was celebrating his winnings from a lucky lottery ticket. He used Ming twice but only paid her once, claiming the first time was so fast he didn't owe her anything. Kim Yook had to send a message to the alley watchman to make the boy pay in full.

"Look, Ming," Kim Yook grinned. "A new wife-of-a-thousand-husbands in training." Kim Yook picked the sobbing girl off the floor and held her as high as she could. "Wooo, Wooo. Money in my strong box."

Ming rushed to the child as three more girls made their way into the room. "Let me have her." Ming snatched the child from Kim Yook's arms and rocked it, making soothing, clucking sounds.

Kim Yook laughed as the other three girls crowded around Ming. "She's beautiful," exclaimed Chon Moy, the stupid one. She was nineteen, but still forgot her numbers and prices. Moy lifted one of the child's arms and inspected its tiny hands. "What long fingers!"

"And perfect pink little nails," said Low Hoy, the boney one. "And the smart mother left her with a good luck charm, too." Low Hoy pulled on the horsehair charm dangling around Chun's neck. "She'll need it if she's going to stay here long."

As usual, Chow Jun, the silent one, simply stood and stared, with her mouth open.

"What's her name? How much did she cost?" asked Moy.

"Chun. Her name's Mei Chun. And a hundred and two dollars," grinned Kim Yook. "It was a good purchase. The parents were desperate. And they left me a photograph and birth paper too. The paper should tell me the month and year she was born, so I'll have to find someone who can read American and help me figure out her two zodiac signs. I don't trust what the mother told me.

"If the child dies, I can sell those papers for at least a hundred dollars and import another girl on them. But if she's lucky and we keep her alive until she's twelve, we could sell her to another keeper for over two thousand dollars. If any of you are still with me then and can help me keep her out of the hands of those Jeezachrise-hollering people in the alley, I'll give you part of the profit on her sale."

金

The only girl who had ignored Kim Yook's call was Yet. She had just finished with Mr. Leong and was pushing him off her body when he began to talk.

She had her rules about talking men. Some girls loved to hear their customers talk sweet to them—and those girls usually ended the night with barely enough money to pay their *kwai po*. But not Yet. When her customers started to talk, she tried to get dressed quickly and call to the keeper to unlock the door. Talking men cost more in time than they made up for in tips. And they always thought their tips were generous and would be appreciated. But she knew her arithmetic, and she knew for every ten minutes of talking, the customers would have to pay double to make it worth her while.

"I've been thinking." Mr. Leong sat up, but moved his index finger in a circle, resting it on Yet's inner thigh. "I want to buy out your contract and get you away from this place." He blurted the words, and the passion she heard in them surprised her. He wouldn't look at her, but simply stared at his finger making smaller and smaller circles on her thigh. She poked his hand away.

"If you want that, it's going to cost another dollar."

"I can afford it." He pulled his hand back. "I'm a partner now in Jew Ho's grocery store up on Stockton. I have a merchant card, so I won't be picking vegetables in Santa Rosa anymore."

Mr. Leong's artlessness brought a trace of a smile to Yet's face. For her, his new job would simply mean a different smell when he came on Saturdays—and eventually, softer hands. Like most of her day-laborer customers, Mr. Leong's hands were rough and calloused, and often left her skin red and raw. She could guess most customers' occupations by their hands.

Yet sat up and began to brush her tangled hair. Later in the morning when she washed it, it would hang almost to her waist. But now it was sticky and smelled of a week's work. She wound it around her fingers. She looked into the mirror across the room, then pinned it above her right ear. It was the traditional hairstyle for Chinese girls and made first time customers think they were lucky enough to get a virgin—or at least a fresh girl. Mr. Leong knew better, of course, but Yet did it out of habit.

Yet wrapped a blanket around her shoulders. Although she was curious about the source of Mr. Leong's financial success, she stifled the urge to ask him how he had gotten the money to buy into a partnership. Most of her customers were having difficulty making ends meet.

"Mr. Leong, it would take you ten years' wages to buy me out. I had a plan to do that once, but I could never save anything. Every time I try to get my owner to tell me my value, his price changes. It always goes up. Never down." She smiled and moved away from the calloused hand inching back to the blanket wrapped around her. She held out her hand for his payment. "One dollar, Mr. Leong. And ten cents for all your talking."

Mr. Leong put $1.25 in Yet's palm and pulled at his pantaloons. "You can keep it all. I'm not as poor as you think. And I left a gift for you downstairs. It's on the table—if your keeper doesn't sell it before noon."

As Mr. Leong stood, Yet reached over and slid open the small window in the door. She yelled for the keeper. She listened as the keeper came limping up the stairs and unlocked the door. After the customer left, Yet uncovered her chamber pot and forced herself to pee. She poured some water from the pitcher into the basin on the steamer trunk. She crushed a pinch of *kwai po*'s herbal mixture and stirred it with her index finger, pressing the leaves against the sides of the basin until the water turned a pinkish brown. She moistened a linen rag and put it inside herself, washing carefully. Once. Twice. Three times.

金

Muriel exited *The Call* building and strode briskly up the two blocks of Market Street to Powell, carrying her satchel with Saturday's paper sticking out the top. She caught a crowded cable car headed toward Chinatown and her ten-thirty interview with a certain Miss Margarita Lake at the Methodist Mission. It was a sunny summer morning, and Muriel's mood matched the day. She felt as though she had been invited to a lunchtime poker game with the other *Call* reporters on the floor, and if she played her cards right, she just might clean them out.

門

Chapter Two

DOOR

It was an unusually quiet Saturday morning in the four-story Methodist Mission House on Washington Street at the edge of Chinatown. But with forty thousand Christian Endeavorers due in the city—at least that's what the papers were saying—Margarita knew the coming week would be hectic. When the Endeavorers found the Chinese Methodist exhibit at Mechanics' Pavilion and learned how close the Mission was to downtown, it would be inundated with well-meaning guests.

Margarita knew nothing about Muriel Bailey beyond the information on the calling card she had received earlier in the week. The front of the card now stuck in the mirror on her bureau pictured the new Claus Spreckels Building with three lines below it that described Muriel as "*The Call*'s first female reporter," and "B.A. English, University of California." On the back the reporter had scrawled a hasty note saying she wanted to interview Margarita Saturday morning about her "Ch-town rescue wk." The reporter thought with so many visitors in the city, it was the sort of article that "should attract readers." Margarita didn't doubt that. But she hoped to talk about more than simply the rescue of Chinese slave girls from "shameful dens," as the papers called the brothels of Chinatown. Two years of mission work had taught her that corruption and exploitation were problems not limited to the eight-block section of the city outside her window.

Margarita had been trying to get caught up on correspondence—the *Woman's Home Missionary Society Board of Managers* had to send her reminder notes every quarter that her reports were overdue—when she heard the doorbell ring. One of the two windows in her third floor Mission House room above Washington Street was open. She got up from her desk and stretched, then walked across the narrow room to the window. She looked below just in time to see the hem of a woman's skirt slipping inside the Mission House door.

Margarita opened the small red and black lacquered Chinese jewelry box that sat on her bureau. It was empty except for a simple jade bracelet and the small gold cross she had received when she graduated from the Chicago Deaconess Training School. She was proud of her two years of religious education. Her framed diploma hung above her bed. Margarita took the cross and pinned it on the breast of her pleated plain black dress. She straightened the white cuffs and the large white neck bow that took the place of a dress collar. Lastly, she put on the simple bonnet that matched her dress, tying it under her chin. She stared at herself in the bureau mirror. Her mother, Kate, disliked this dress, saying it made her appear thinner than she was. But Margarita was pleased with its fit and with her image in the mirror. She debated whether to wear the gloves that completed her Methodist deaconess uniform. Since she wasn't planning to go out, she left the gloves in the bureau drawer.

Margarita took Muriel's calling card from the mirror, then hurried downstairs and through the darkened chapel, where two of the Chinese pastor's girls played quietly beside the piano.

Thirteen year-old Laura Chan stood in the parlor foyer, talking to an attractive, smartly dressed woman—about Margarita's age—but a full head and shoulders taller. The woman's lips were pursed in a manner that suggested a degree of nervousness, and her strikingly green eyes narrowed when she turned toward Margarita. The woman's auburn hair was combed up in a fashionable French-braid pompadour, and topped with a mannish dark green trilby. The freckles across her nose and cheekbones reminded Margarita of her cousins who spent their summers romping in Oregon hayfields. But this woman's tight-lipped smile and a straight-ahead, levelheaded gaze bespoke business rather than pleasure. She clasped in one hand a worn, leather satchel with a newspaper half falling out of it.

"You must be Miss Bailey." Margarita stretched out her hand. "I'm Deaconess Margarita Lake, in charge of visitation for the Methodist Rescue Asylum—or Home—upstairs. Please come in."

"Yes. I'm sorry I arrived a bit early. I set my watch a few minutes ahead to make sure I wasn't late." Miss Bailey pressed Margarita's hand. "I'm excited about the prospects of this interview, Miss Lake, and I'm looking forward to hearing about your Chinatown work. I've read articles in the papers about the missions, but I've never visited one.

"This young lady has been telling me all about the building." Miss Bailey smiled down at Laura then looked over Margarita's shoulder.

"Is there a place where we can chat?"

Margarita pointed toward the room on her left. "Why don't we sit in the parlor? And please, call me Margarita.

"Would you care for a glass of water—or perhaps some tea?"

"Water would be fine, thank you." Miss Bailey leaned forward and rummaged through the satchel she had set on the floor beside her chair.

Margarita caught a fleeting image of the Endeavor arch and the masthead of *The Morning Call* before Miss Bailey managed to push aside the newspaper and pull out two sharpened pencils and a legal-sized note pad.

"Laura, are you still there? Will you come here, please?" Margarita peered into the darkened chapel.

"Yes, Miss Lake. We're trying not to disturb you and your guest." The girl tiptoed into the parlor.

"You girls are fine. But I was wondering if you would run downstairs and fetch a glass of water for Miss Bailey. And be careful carrying it up the stairs."

The girl grinned broadly, apparently thrilled to have an errand that would bring her into the parlor. She pranced off, leaving instructions with her sister on how to behave while she was gone.

門

"I know shorthand." Muriel turned to face Miss Lake who still stood in the parlor doorway. "So don't worry about talking slowly. Pretend it's a normal conversation—perhaps like after Sunday church." She watched an

Oriental girl slip into the parlor and walk gingerly toward her. The girl was trying hard not to spill the glass of water, but it had apparently already lost nearly half its contents. Muriel took the glass, murmuring a thank you.

"Laura, you and your sister can keep playing in the chapel—as long as it's at the back, away from the front door." Miss Lake guided the girl toward the chapel. "The girls won't be a problem. They're the Chinese pastor's children, and they're quite well behaved." Miss Lake smiled and sat beside Muriel, next to a large ornately painted Oriental vase.

Muriel set the glass on the mahogany lamp table beside her, and found the object of her search. It was a delicately engraved, silver-plated pocket watch, a college graduation gift from her grandmother. She set it on the table. "My editor wants me back at the office by one, if possible, and he's hoping I can fit in at least one other appointment this morning. This is my first real interview for *The Call*, and he's more than a little worried about me. He's afraid a woman can't interview another woman without it turning into a two-hour front-porch gossip party." She rolled her eyes. "So I apologize if I seem a bit rushed. If things go well, I do hope I'll be able to come back for a follow-up story or two." Muriel smiled and wiggled her gloves, pulling carefully at each finger. The gloves were sea green, a few shades lighter than her trilby, but they accented the fancy work on her skirt. After what felt like minutes, she finally removed the glove from her left hand. Her diamond engagement ring caught a ray of sunlight, sending dancing colors around the room.

"So, let's begin with a little personal background." Muriel crossed her legs at her ankles, exposing the edge of a finely polished, brown leather boot. "What specifically is your work, Miss Lake—Margarita? How long have you been in it, and how did you get started? I realize that's three questions in one, so feel free to answer in whatever order you wish."

"I'm a consecrated deaconess in the Methodist church, and I'll remain so as long as I'm unmarried. It's the closest thing to ordination for women in our denomination."

A religious pledge of virginity seemed more Catholic than Protestant, and Muriel frowned, wishing she paid more attention to her relatives' animated arguments about religion. She had an uncle and aunt who were Methodist, but when they started accusing her Episcopalian parents of popery, she always found excuses to exit their conversations.

"I spent my childhood in Oregon," Margarita was saying. Muriel scribbled on the legal pad, trying to catch up with the deaconess's story. "My father died when I was a few months old—so I never knew him, and my mother never remarried. My mother says I was a delicate child, and she hired a Chinese house servant to care for me while she was away teaching. She claims that man's care saved my life."

Muriel underlined "man" and kept writing. Her editor would probably challenge the word choice and ask her if Margarita really said "man" instead of "boy" or "Chinaman."

"Even though I don't remember the man—times were hard, and Mama had to let him go when I was two or three—I've always felt deep down I owe my life to him—to his race. So when I finished Deaconess Training School, I decided—I felt God's call—to go to China as a missionary. But the Deaconess Board had other ideas. They chose to place me here in San Francisco for a few years before sending me overseas. My mother and I have worked here now for two years.

"A month ago I was asked to take over some of Mrs. Ida Hull's responsibilities. She's the senior missionary in the Rescue Asylum or Home—we use both words to describe our work—and she teaches kindergarten, besides planning most rescues. You really ought to talk to her." Margarita smiled, and her uniform seemed to lose some of its severe plainness. Muriel guessed the woman was roughly her own age—perhaps twenty-five. "She lives on Leavenworth—I can get you her address when we're done, if you'd like. I'm sure she'd love to talk to you. She's been in this work a lot longer than I—for about ten years, I think."

Muriel studied her open watch on the lamp table. "If I have time, I'll try and get over to talk to her, too. I—and the entire city, really—have heard a lot about her rescues of these Oriental prostitutes—"

"Miss Bailey, we do not use that word here to describe our girls." There was an edge to Margarita's tone that made Muriel swallow hard. She took a deep breath to refocus her attention and took a sip of water.

"I'm sorry if I offended you." Muriel's words felt rushed and insincere. She forced herself to speak more slowly. "I certainly didn't mean to. Working as I do in an office surrounded by men—I sometimes forget my audience. So please, go on. I really am interested in hearing about your rescue work."

Margarita ran a finger down a pleat of her uniform. Her eyes seemed focused on the girls playing in the other room, even though Muriel could barely hear them. Muriel waited nervously, her pencil poised on the notepad. She heard the far off ticking of a pendulum clock, and the clatter of horses and buggies on the street below the parlor windows. Finally, Margarita spoke.

"I don't know much about American women in the brothels on the Barbary Coast or their circumstances—the Salvationists mainly work down there. But we have good reason to believe most of the thousand or more girls here in Chinatown are kept in brothels—really slave dens—against their will. Many have the ripped and scarred flesh to prove it. You can see the effects of the slavery upstairs, later, if you wish—if Mama—Mrs. Lake will allow visitors. Meeting strangers can be stressful for our girls, as you can imagine—even when we give them our word that the visitors can be trusted. After two years here, I still—" Margarita paused. Her jaw tightened and tears began to well at the corners of her eyes. "I'm sorry."

"I probably won't have time to meet any inmates today." Muriel hoped her tone expressed the sympathy Margarita and her mother deserved. "And anyway, I'm quite sure my editor would prefer one of our artists accompany me if I come back. But if my editor approves, I would very much like to meet your girls. I think sharing their stories—with an appropriate drawing or two—would really help our readers understand what you're fighting. Perhaps you could tell me—"

"I'm sure my mother would want advance notice if you were to bring an artist." Margarita seemed to regain her composure, and she continued on in a more matter-of-fact tone.

"The girls upstairs trust Mama. And most of our girls—even the brothel girls on the outside—are quite virtuous. That's why I objected to your choice of words before. It seems so unfair to use that word after all they've been through."

"I am truly sorry, Margarita." Muriel could already hear her editor's shrill tirade if she lost this, her first Chinatown contact. "As you were saying, 'The girls—?'"

"These girls are sold against their will—some for over two thousand dollars—others are simply kidnapped." Margarita's hands were shaking.

"We know most would choose a different life if given the opportunity. And that's what we try to do here—provide them with the opportunity. Of course, we hope they become Christians, too."

Margarita's voice began to rise, and she leaned forward, fists clenched, as though she were a pugilist preparing for a prizefight. "It doesn't matter whether American people are religious or not. So long as their shirts and skirts are clean and pressed cheaply, they don't care what goes on behind the barred doors of Chinatown. The less they know, the better, they seem to think. But we believe the girls here are as much in the image of God as American girls, and if we can teach our girls to sew, cook American food, and clean, then they might have different futures.

"Some of our inmates go out as house girls, others leave here as wives. We try to ensure that the men who court them are reputable, but not all are. And some of the girls, sadly, return to 'the life.' That's what they call brothel life. And that's the term we prefer to use. We're never happy with those who return to the life, but at least those who leave our Home and go back to their former ways do so freely."

Muriel chose Margarita's sermonizing as an opportunity to change the focus of the interview. "So tell me about this Chinese slavery, and about your rescues. I'm sure that's what our *Call* readers will want to know about." Muriel toyed with her pencil and smiled encouragingly. "I suppose the rescue stories bring in the donations to keep your work going?"

The deaconess's eyes narrowed. Her body tensed as though it was about to absorb a sharp blow. "We have a girl—Ying, who's been with us for about four years now. She was rescued from a second type of Chinatown slavery. The first I already told you about—girls sold against their will directly into brothel life. The second kind is what the Chinese call a *mui tsai*, or 'little sister.' The phrase really refers to debt slaves. Like Ying, they're usually girls of poor parents. The family that purchases the girl—or 'adopts her,' as the Chinese would say—raises her as a domestic in their home. It's somewhat similar to the old American custom of indentured servants. The adopted daughter is then married out when she's about sixteen. But when a *mui tsai* is young, she's often abused by the family that adopts her. Ying was one of these *mui tsai*—sold twice before coming to San Francisco, where she was mistreated after being blamed for the failure of her adopted father's jewelry business.

"Mrs. Hull found the girl a little over a year before I came to the work, when Ying—or Grace, that's her new Christian name—was about eleven. She had been a doorkeeper in a brothel for a number of years at the time of her rescue. Her adopted mother beat her regularly, and after one particularly severe beating, Ying fell down a flight of stairs and badly injured her hip. The Chinese doctors never set the bone right, and as a result she walks with a limp to this day."

Margarita's simple summary of the slave girl's life left little for Muriel to build a story around. And without specific details of the girl's rescue or abuse, Muriel's editor would crucify her. Muriel was poised to ask Margarita about the girl's rescue and medical care—she had heard rumors that most American doctors wouldn't treat Orientals—but Margarita's next remarks seemed to render any follow-up irrelevant. Muriel pushed her question aside and kept writing.

"Miss Bailey, I want you to know—and your readers to know—that we do very few of these rescues on our own. There are some Chinese men—most are unknown even to us—who risk their lives to give us names of girls that wish to be rescued—where they live, and how to get them. Sometimes the men want us to get the girls just so they can marry them, but we don't ask a lot of questions. We feel any life outside is better than a life inside such shameful places.

"Then there are our own rescued girls like Ying—Gracie—who lead us back to the very places they've escaped from, to help their friends get out. You can imagine the bravery it takes to do that. There are also the societies for prevention of cruelty to children. Mr. Moulton of the *Eureka Society for the Protection of Children,* and others like him, help us gain entrance to the brothels. From time to time we have a lawyer who will work for free, helping us in habeas corpus and guardianship disputes. Occasionally, even a policeman will help. But as I said before, that's unusual. So you see it's not only us. The Chinese who give us the names of girls, and the girls themselves, literally risk their lives in helping.

"We're rarely the ones in danger—although we're often verbally threatened. As you no doubt know, there's an automatic death sentence for any Chinaman killing a white person, and for hurting a white woman—well, Chinatown would be burned to the ground when word got around the city. So the slave owners won't risk harming us. Besides, they have many ruses—less dangerous ways—to get their lost merchandise—or girls. The simplest is through money paid to American lawyers."

"I'm sure not all American lawyers are so easily bribed." Muriel thought of her own fiancé who had recently finished law school. Although she didn't have much respect for lawyers in general, she knew her Harry to be an extraordinarily honest man.

"You're right. Not all lawyers are disreputable. There are a few trustworthy ones who've helped us." Margarita paused and stared out the parlor window, as if recalling a particular courtroom experience.

"I'm afraid I've rattled on. But you need to know that in the two years my mother and I have been here, you're the first reporter who's actually been over to talk to us. Our rescues are in the papers occasionally, but no one's ever taken the time to print our point of view on Chinatown slavery."

Muriel put down her pencil and notepad. She closed her watchcase. "You've been most helpful, Margarita. And thank you so much for your time. You've given me a lot of material to work with." Muriel took the newspaper from her satchel and set it on the lamp table, then picked up her gloves. "And before I leave, I'd like Mrs. Hull's address, if you don't mind. From what you said earlier, I do think I should visit her too."

門

Muck Shee had no idea how she came to be on the boat that day. She had a panicky feeling it was her first time, long ago, when she came to Gold Mountain from the Celestial Kingdom. She clung to the railing with her eyes closed because she had forgotten the rolling motion of water. She wondered what it would be like to let go and slip over the side, sinking slowly beneath the waves, never to come up.

The summer sun shone brightly, but it was cold and windy on the water. Muck Shee's children clung to her pantaloons, pushing their bodies against her to stay warm. They chattered about the blue water, the green trees speckling the golden hills in front of them, and the tall buildings of the gray city behind them. A gust of wind whipped the sleeves of Muck Shee's loose blouse, and she opened her eyes. There was a welt on her wrist, near her bracelet. It was the mark Chun made when they sat in the brothel. How long would it remain? She rubbed it, then let the sleeve fall.

"Mama, look." Her oldest daughter, Oy, pointed to a peaked island in the distance. "That looks like a giant jade dragon rising out of the water. And look over there. Papa says that's *gum moon*—the golden gate to Gold Mountain. It looks like the dragon got lost inside and can't find its way out."

"You have a wild imagination, Oy." Muck Shee braced her legs against the railing and raised her hand to shade her eyes. She peered across the sparkling waves. Her lips brushed across the sleeve hiding the welt on her wrist. It was the closest thing to a prayer she could conjure.

"Mama, Papa said he would go back and get baby from Uncle as soon as he's got enough money. It won't be long. Don't look so sad." Oy's forehead wrinkled with concern.

Muck Shee sighed and leaned into the wind. All five children were shivering. She stooped and straightened their denim jackets.

"It's cold up here. Let's go below and find your father and Wing. Papa said he bought some sugared ginger for you."

門

Margarita sat at her desk, trying to write a letter or two before going out to play her cornet with the Chinatown Salvation Army Corps. She bumped her cup of tea with her elbow and spilled it on a half-finished letter to the *Board of Managers*. She sighed. She would have to start the letter again.

Muriel had sent a note over yesterday—Friday, telling Margarita the "good news" that the paper had received a large number of calls about the Chinatown missions article, and that her editor wanted her to write a couple follow-up articles. Margarita had bought a copy of Thursday's *Morning Call*—the day the article was published—but the paper lay on the floor beside her desk, still unopened. The past week had been incredibly busy. She had been at the Mission booth every day, talking to people and handing out literature all day long. And then she would come back to the Mission to find Endeavor people everywhere—in the parlor, the chapel, and in the fourth floor Rescue Home sitting room. By Wednesday she was sneaking in the Mission's back alley entrance by the outdoor privy, and taking the stairs to Reverend Chan's flat. She would ask whoever was home if they would let her through to her room by way of the Chan's bedroom, since they had an extra door that opened to the back end of the third floor hallway. She would undress and collapse on her bed—then start the routine again the next morning.

Margarita stared at Thursday's newspaper on the floor and decided the spilled tea was a divine sign telling her to stop her afternoon letter writing. She put down her pen and picked up the paper. Endeavorers had been stopping at the Mission booth to tell her how wonderful the article was. How it described perfectly the heart of the Protestant Chinatown missions. But Mama hadn't been quite so complimentary.

Margarita had been much more hesitant to read Muriel's article after Mama expressed her opinion. Margarita doubted whether anyone could ever say anything about her that would match Mama's protective love. But this time Margarita had the feeling she could trust Mama more than the opinions of any number of Endeavorers—even if all forty thousand disagreed with her mother.

Muriel's article was on the first page of the second section—a section usually devoted to local news. There, just below "Thursday, July 7, 1898" was a large drawing of a rescue led by a white woman wielding a hatchet. The woman was surrounded by a group of fiendish-looking "Chinamen," and the caption read "If they will not let me in after pleading and coaxing—and they don't like to—why, I take my hatchet and let myself in." The full page headline was: "San Francisco Has the Bravest Women in the World." Margarita shook her head in disbelief and skimmed the article for her name. The first column was about "Mrs. Ida B. Hull" and the trusty hatchet she used to break down the doors of "places" where girls were rescued from "lives of shame."

Apparently after leaving the Methodist Mission, Muriel had spent time with Mrs. Hull. And Muriel—and obviously her editors at *The Call*—had found Mrs. Hull's stories more to their liking.

There was also something in the second column about the Presbyterians, and Miss Donaldina Cameron, the young lady helping Mrs. Culbertson. Finally, in the last column, Margarita found her name—alongside a somewhat garbled definition of "deaconess."

Muriel's article said nothing about Gracie's bravery, nothing about the child saving societies such as the one Mr. Moulton worked for, and nothing about the problems the Mission had with city police and unscrupulous lawyers.

Margarita tossed the paper onto the floor and toyed with the handle of her now cold teacup, She had read enough newspaper articles about the filth of Chinatown, its secretive, wily Chinamen and tong murders, to know that about eighty percent of the stories were sensationalism—exaggerations to sell more papers—but still, the tenor of Miss Bailey's article surprised and angered her. Was it wounded pride in not finding her name more prominently displayed? Or the fanciful Molly Hatchet-like drawing of Mrs. Hull? Margarita picked up the paper once more and flipped through the other sections without reading anything. Finally, she threw it on the floor again. She was certain her anger wasn't due to pride. Although she hadn't been interviewed before, she had seen her name in the papers enough times to stop clipping the stories for her scrapbook. What angered her, she decided, was that Muriel's article was no less simple-minded than any other. And Margarita had hoped—and thought—she had given Muriel enough background to show her the rescuers weren't the real heroes; that the Chinese people weren't simply helpless or evil.

Margarita stared out her window at a line of sparrows pecking at each other on a telegraph wire. There was a light tapping at her door.

It was Dr. Landon from across the hall. He leaned into her room in an annoying manner, and so she stood in front of him, trying to block his view of her desk.

"I'm sorry to interrupt you, Miss Lake, but there's a woman downstairs who wishes to see you. She says she's the woman who wrote that article in the paper the other day. She brought over some extra copies. I told her to leave them on the table, but she insisted on seeing you."

Margarita found Muriel standing in the downstairs foyer, twisting her gloves in her hands. Her satchel lay at her feet, a roll of newspapers jammed into its side pocket. Muriel looked up and bit her lip as Margarita walked toward her.

"I'm so glad you came down." Muriel took a step forward but didn't give Margarita a chance to offer a greeting. "I know you've had a busy week, but I wanted to give you some extra papers—"

"Quite frankly, my mother and I were appalled at what you wrote, Miss Bailey." Margarita could feel her neck and cheeks flush. The stress and exhaustion of the week suddenly overwhelmed her, and she felt her knees weaken. She took a deep breath and straightened her spine.

"We're not the heroines in this place. I thought I made that perfectly clear to you last week. It's the girls." Margarita's entire body was shaking now, and she leaned against the chapel doorframe—half in the light, half in the darkness, clenching and unclenching her fists.

"'The bravest women in the world?' You have no idea. I— "

"Miss Lake, please. Let me explain." Muriel's lips trembled. As she took another step toward Margarita, Margarita could see small beads of perspiration lining the roots of the woman's auburn hair. "I really came to apologize for the article—probably not even half the words are mine. I turned it in like I always do, expecting my editor to come back to me with a draft we could talk about, but he wanted to print it while the Endeavorers were still in town. So he did his own editing without ever showing me his work. Look at the byline. He couldn't even spell my name correctly." Muriel's words tumbled over one another in a torrent, her eyes still searching the darkness. "You should have heard the argument we had when I saw what he had published."

"I came here to give you these anyway, as promised." Muriel stooped and pulled the papers from the satchel. "I know we can do better, and I think my editor and I have come to an understanding. I'm hoping you'll allow me to come back—" A lopsided smile played at the edges of Muriel's clenched jaw, and she offered Margarita the handful of newspapers.

Margarita snatched them from Muriel's fist and shook them in the woman's face. "I really don't care whose words they are. I'm so tired of reading the trash your papers print about the Chinese people and us! You can keep these and do whatever you want with them." She threw the newspapers at the woman's feet. "I'll tell you what we usually do. We use them for wallpaper in our outhouse."

Muriel stiffened and stretched to her full height. "Miss Lake, I said I came to apologize for my article. But I see you're in no disposition to hear what I have to say. I'm surprised you think it's easier for me to work in a man's world than it is for you."

The reporter spun around, leaving the newspapers swirling on the floor. In two quick steps she was in the entryway. "And I can see myself out without your help." The door slammed so hard behind her, the parlor lamp nearly fell off the table.

Chapter Three

ALLEY

Muriel stepped off the Powell Street cable car at Washington Street one warm afternoon in late September, a few weeks after returning from her honeymoon near Lake Tahoe. This wasn't her first visit to the Mission since that tumultuous afternoon in July. For much to Muriel's surprise, a few days after Margarita had thrown the "Bravest Women" newspapers at her, Margarita had sent a note over to *The Call* apologizing for her "unchristian" actions and asking Muriel if she'd like to meet some of the girls in the fourth floor Rescue Home. Margarita had even suggested Muriel bring along one of the paper's artists.

Muriel had worked at *The Call* long enough to develop what her editor called "a healthy dose of cynicism," so she wasn't convinced the deaconess's religion had motivated the change of heart. It seemed just as likely the Rescue Home Board members had pressured Margarita when they saw how much public interest Muriel's article had generated. But regardless of the reason for Margarita's reversal, Muriel's editor had her back at the Mission within the week—with *The Call*'s best artist in tow.

Ironically, Muriel's—or better, her editor's—"Bravest Women" article, along with her subsequent visits to the Rescue Home, spawned a lengthy series in *The Call*. Muriel's editor told her Mr. Spreckels himself noticed her articles in his newspaper had sparked competition over which paper could get the most salacious interviews from the different missions. So initially her editor was happy to have her keep churning out the reports.

Her final three focused on Kuan Ho, a ten year-old girl who had been left to die in the "Chamber of Tranquility"—the name the Orientals gave to their only mortuary. The girl was a hunchback—the result of having been beaten by her owners—and Muriel's stories aroused such sympathy, the Methodist Rescue Home was inundated with donations.

Muriel's husband, Harry, chided her good-naturedly after the second article was printed, saying her emotions were beginning to undermine her professionalism. She was biological proof, he said, that women should never have careers. She told him he was biological proof men were the only species that could speak out of both ends of their bodies at the same time.

Finally, after two weeks of Chinatown stories, even Muriel's editor began joking she was taking herself and the Mission workers a bit too seriously. "If you're not careful, you'll soon find you're a Methodist—or worse, a Presbyterian, and you'll have to give up your Sunday bicycle rides in the Berkeley hills for stuffy sermons and starched bonnets."

There were other features she could be working on, he said, and suggested something dealing with the exotic peoples of the newly acquired Philippine Islands. She told him somewhat tartly that if he paid her way to the Far East, she would be happy to write a month of articles. That exchange marked the end of her Chinatown series. The Endeavorers were long gone by then anyway, so it didn't much matter from that standpoint. The following week she was back writing summaries of drunken brawls on the Barbary Coast.

So when Margarita sent Muriel a message saying Kuan had been released from the Children's Hospital and inviting her over to the Mission to see the girl, Muriel pounced. Muriel was fairly sure she could convince her editor that her readers would be delighted with a sympathetic update on Kuan.

巷

An Oriental girl stood waving from the Mission House steps as Muriel approached the building. "Miss Lake told me to wait here for you. She's down the street with the Army people." The Oriental girl reached out and took Muriel's hand just like an American girl would. "I've seen you talking to Miss Lake and Mrs. Lake before. My name's Gracie."

The girl's English was impeccable, and despite her halting limp in descending the Mission steps, she spoke with an easy, impressive confidence that complemented her stylish plaid American walking skirt. "I'm almost fifteen, and when I finish grammar school I'm going to go to Normal School. I want to go back to China and teach children the Christian way."

Grace pointed at the dull glow of the paper globe lanterns hanging from balconies and strung across the Chinatown alleyways that intersected Washington Street. "It's the Moon Festival," she said.

Women and children were wandering about in festive clothing of the brightest and boldest patterns. The small, garishly bright costumes were evidence there were far more families in Chinatown than Muriel had supposed. She could count on one hand the number of families she had seen in her previous weeks of walking down Washington Street. Now there were children everywhere, and wearing the queerest hats she had ever seen. The girls' caps had dangly beads that bounced in their eyes as they walked, which they kept brushing out of their faces. The boys' caps seemed to be made of crushed velvet and had owl-like ears with tufts of feathery threads falling from them.

"To scare away ghosts," Grace said, apparently reading Muriel's mind.

Down at the corner of Washington and Spofford was a different scene entirely. There a crowd of black-smocked Chinamen had gathered like a band of crows pecking at a pile of overripe fruit. The men's clothing contrasted with the children's bright, pajama-like costumes. The figures in black blocked the sidewalk, making it impossible to get around them without stepping out into the filth of the cobblestone street.

Their queer cylindrical pill box-like hats were pulled over their long-braided queues, and some held bright colored fans to shield their eyes from the sun. As Muriel and Grace approached them, Muriel caught the first wave of their distinct odor. Opium, tobacco, ginger, garlic, and a hodge-podge of other scents she couldn't identify. She pulled a handkerchief from her sleeve and waved it in front of her nose.

"Americans smell too." Grace glanced sideways at Muriel, a crooked smile playing on her lips. "You don't know it, because you're around them all the time."

An invisible band burst into a loud, march-like tune, drowning out any response Muriel could make. A couple of cornets chimed in with a large bass drum, and then the crowd parted as if a prizefighter were approaching a boxing ring. There were navy blue uniforms at the far end of Spofford Alley. It was the Salvation Army—and apparently Margarita was somewhere in the midst of the human menagerie.

"Jeezachrise, wharsahorbitch!" A scrawny old Oriental woman stormed out of a doorway barely twenty feet away. Muriel nearly dropped her satchel as she fell against a fat Chinaman who had pressed in behind her. She regained her composure, but she wished she had out her notebook. She would have to rely on her memory if she was going to write about the bizarre events unfolding before her eyes.

"Jeezachrise, wharsahorbitch," the old woman screeched again. The woman held a long iron spoon in one hand and something like a large frying pan in the other, and began furiously banging them together.

"Miss Lake's over there," Grace shouted, standing on her tiptoes and pointing. Muriel spotted Margarita—the only player in the band who wasn't in Salvationist attire. As Margarita played her cornet, a handful of people in blue uniforms began to sing tentatively, warily watching the old woman at the edge of their half-circle.

"What can wash away my sin?"

The woman waved her iron spoon and frying pan in a bizarre antiphonal response:

"Jeezachrise, wharsahorbitch. Jeezachrise, wharsahorbitch."

The group sang louder. "Nothing but the blood of—"

"Jeezachrise, wharsahorbitch!" The old woman marched up to the Salvationists, taunting the singers and clanging her makeshift drum in their faces. She bent over and began to prance, rump in the air, pencil-thin legs exposed nearly to the knee.

"We are in a war!" roared an American evangelist in an opening volley. He stared right through the woman and motioned for the band to stop playing. A Chinaman dressed in a Salvationist uniform complete with flat-topped cadet hat stepped forward and began to translate.

"Wharsahorbitch. Wharsahorbitch." The slit-eyed, Oriental hag wouldn't let up. But neither would the evangelist, who was warming to the confrontation. "Great Jehovah has declared war on Satan's dominion here in Chinatown, and we're claiming this alley, and Clay Street back there, and Washington Street over there, and this woman here, and all of Chinatown for God and his holy angels. In Jesus' name." The evangelist's arms punctuated the air like giant exclamation marks as he strode in ever-widening circles. The interpreter walked behind him, mimicking every motion.

"This is an idolatrous festival of wicked superstitions. Do you think you can find salvation by burning a few joss sticks in that temple over there to a fat-bellied grinning god, or to a red-faced angry demon? Let me tell you, there's only one God. And Jehovah is his name." The evangelist shook his finger heavenward, exposing a bony forearm under his tight-fitting jacket. "And you won't find him in there." He circled the band, hunched over, pointing at every alleyway door as he came to it. "Hallelujah, sisters? Captain Thomas, an amen? Ensign Bankes? Can I hear you?"

There was a smattering of shouted hallelujahs and amens from the crowd.

A little Oriental girl scampered out into the alleyway from the same door the old woman had exited. The girl, who appeared to be about two or three years old, wore only a short, ragged smock covered with soot; her legs and arms a mottled gray.

"Let me hear another amen," the evangelist shouted.

The little girl screamed. Tears ran down her cheeks, smearing the coal dust into a bizarre, two-tone war paint. Her arms were outstretched. She spotted the old woman and chased her around the Salvation Army circle, fingers working madly in what Muriel assumed was every culture's sign language for "Gimme, gimme." Nothing slowed her wild run around the circle. Her screams grew shriller—a staccato matched by the beating pan. But the old woman was too engrossed in her pounding to notice the child.

Another Oriental woman came racing out behind the little girl and grabbed her, putting a hand over the child's mouth to quiet her. The girl struggled in the woman's tight embrace and screamed more loudly. Finally, the woman capitulated and set the child down, watching her protectively from the alley doorway.

"What can make me whole again?" The band picked up where they had left off, and this time the chorus sang with conviction. "Nothing but the blood of Jesus."

"Jeezachrise, wharsahorbitch."

A group of opium smokers from the den across the alley laughed uproariously, waving their long bamboo pipes as if they were censers at the Church of St. John the Evangelist where Muriel spent most Christmas Eves. "Wooohooo." One who spoke English began shouting, "Preesh Jesus meester. Preesh Jesus."

As if to oblige the Chinaman, the Salvation Army evangelist yelled even louder. "We're in a war! Breaking down Satan's walls of sin and self-destruction. Turn away from your idolatry!"

Muriel knew about Salvationist work, the hellfire street sermons, the women in their broad-brimmed, wide-ribbon hallelujah bonnets, and the loud brass bands, but she had steered clear of them in the past. She couldn't imagine why Margarita would spend any time with fanatics like this.

"Look at that baby." The evangelist wiped his frothing mouth on his sleeve, and pointed at the soot-covered girl weaving in and out of the crowd. "Someone bring her up here to sit with these other street arabs."

Muriel couldn't see the children the evangelist was speaking of—apparently a group was seated on the other side of the big bass Army drum at the end of the alley. The evangelist continued his boisterous appeal. "She's a neglected, half-naked child from that sinful den over there. But Jesus said, 'Blessed are the children,' and 'Suffer the little ones to come unto me.' That Mongolian heathen child is loved by God as much as any of us. She needs to be washed in the blood of the Lamb and the waters of baptism, and put in Sunday school, where she can be cared for and learn the story of Jesus' love. Do I hear an amen?"

"Wharsahorbitch!" The old woman could be a Persian whirling dervish, Muriel thought.

"And look at that old woman there still trying to disrupt God's holy work." Someone handed the evangelist a Bible, and he held it high in the air. "Like the one Saint Paul met in Philippi—a heathen 'possessed with a spirit of divination' if there ever was one. Well, we can put our own Mary Magdalene up against her any day, and prove the Christian God is more powerful than heathen, shameful slavery, or opium, or lottery tickets— or anything else the Devil might throw our way." The preacher shook the Bible again. "Lassie Mary, put on your hallelujah bonnet and come testify at the drum. Tell this woman and the rest of those dark-hearted, opium-smoking Chinamen what it means to be saved from the life."

Another old Oriental woman—this one in full Salvationist garb, pushed her way through the men to the middle of the crowd.

"Testify, Sister Mary. Let's all fire a prayer volley for her."

"Holy Moses. Sweet Miriam."

Muriel had never seen an Oriental woman like this one, in American clothes, shouting out in Chinese what must have been a Christian message of hellfire and damnation. Muriel glanced down at Grace, but the girl seemed unaffected by the two-ring street circus. She was standing on tiptoe, her eyes glued on the musical band gathered at the end of the alley.

In the midst of the fearless Salvationist woman's raucous haranguing, the Jeezachrise-hollerer spied the younger woman who had followed the baby out into the alley. The old woman swore what must have been a tirade of Oriental curses, and the young woman shrank back in fear, running toward the open door with her arms covering her head. The old woman chased after her, swinging the frying pan. The little girl—arms outstretched and still screaming—stumbled in step behind them. The old woman stopped at the door, shooed the baby inside, then slammed the door shut.

巷

Leong Ti heard only the tail end of the commotion in the alley as he walked up Washington Street to the ABC school in the basement of the Methodist Mission. After two and a half months of learning English, his language skills were already bringing in a few white customers to Jew Ho's grocery store. He would stand on Stockton Street with fresh cut oranges and peaches, handing pieces to tourists walking by. Most were afraid to take anything from a Chinaman and simply stared at his hands in disgust. But he would smile anyway and say to them, "You tie. Velly good." A few white people were beginning to frequent the shop, and the owner had begun to take notice.

Leong Ti looked above the crowd to see if Yet's iron-barred window was open. It wasn't. He wondered if she had a customer. She wasn't the first girl he had ever paid for, but from the moment he had seen her five months ago, he had known she was different. Maybe it was her room—how clean and organized she kept it. He had never seen a brothel room like that. Or maybe it was the way she stared at the jar on her shelf when he was with her. But something kept him coming back. And when he negotiated with the keeper to come early on Saturdays to be with the girl, she had seemed pleased to see him. When she saw him now, she would almost always smile. There were things he wanted to tell her, but he didn't know how.

He turned back toward Washington Street and Mr. Gardner's ABC school. Learning English to sell more fruit and vegetables was good. But he wanted to learn to read and write so he could join Ong Lee's *Chinese Society for English Education* over on Commercial Street. He knew some of the men there helped girls get out of brothels.

巷

The old Oriental woman stood in front of the closed door with a smug smile, brandishing the frying pan-like utensil. The Salvation Army band marched out on to Clay Street with its accompanying crowd and regrouped. The excited chatter of the opium smoking Chinamen, still in the street, replaced the fading strains of *Onward Christian Soldiers*.

By the time Grace and Muriel waded through the crowds on Dupont Street and dodged a cable car on Sacramento, the Salvation Army band was breaking up. A group of children knelt in prayer around the large bass drum, and men and women in Salvationist uniforms were passing out *Pacific Coast War Cry* newspapers to curious bystanders. Margarita was engrossed in conversation with a tall, spindly-thin, mousy-haired woman. Muriel stooped to search her satchel for a pencil and notebook, and when she straightened, Margarita was waving and walking toward her.

"If it isn't the new Mrs. Monroe." Margarita hugged Muriel—notebook, pencil, satchel, and all. "I thought I saw you with Gracie over in Spofford Alley. I was lamenting to Miss Davis here about my lack of time to practice those Salvationist songs. I'm not familiar with most of them.

"Mrs. Monroe, this is Miss Carrie Davis. It's Miss Davis's first visit to a Chinatown street meeting—her brother works at the Customs House, and she's recently become interested in our Chinese work."

Miss Davis was a severe looking woman whose askew, smudged glasses and plain muslin walking dress—about ten years out of fashion—made her appear downright owlish. Her hat, more practical than fashionable, was a simple straw sailor's. Muriel guessed the woman was at least forty years old, and probably hadn't laughed since 1885.

A woman in a Salvationist uniform hurried toward them. "Maggie! Did you see her? That little girl in the alley? The one all covered with soot? That's the one I was telling you about." The woman turned toward Muriel without giving Margarita a chance to answer. "I don't believe we've met. I'm Captain Thomas. I take it you're a member of one of the downtown Methodist churches. We're always so happy to have new folks come out and join the battle."

Captain Thomas seemed to be about Margarita's age—mid-twenties, a slim figure, a bright smile, and light brown hair pulled back tightly in a bun under her bouncing Salvation bonnet. Her cheeks were a blushing pink from singing in the brisk evening air, and Muriel thought she would be quite pretty if it weren't for her plain Army coat.

"I've wanted to meet you for some time," Muriel said. "Margarita's told me a lot about your work with street arabs. But I'm not Methodist—just a reporter for *The Call*." She waved her pencil and notebook in the air. "And I'm sorry to say, not particularly religious. When I attend church—usually at Christmas—it's Episcopal. I love the pageantry, the poetry, but—"

"You can tell we Salvationists have an entirely different kind of pageantry than Episcopals." Captain Thomas had an easy, disarming laugh. "We have music, sights, and smells all right, but these folks wouldn't feel comfortable in a church building. So we try to meet them where they are—with what they need: soup, soap, and salvation. And in that order."

"You certainly attract crowds. Even little children." Muriel set down her satchel and flipped open her notebook. "I'd love to talk to you about your work with the children of the Chinese quarter."

"They're what I like most about our work." Captain Thomas peeked around Muriel's shoulder. "Take the half-naked child who was out running around in the alley." She pointed off in the direction she had come from. "If you were over there earlier, you must have seen her."

Muriel nodded. It was a Chinatown image that would stay with her awhile.

"Well, the folks there call her 'Chun.' They say she's the daughter of Kim Yook—that's the old keeper at Number 11 who was banging on the big wok and causing such a ruckus. But if that's her daughter, Kim must be related to Sarah or Elizabeth of Bible fame." Captain Thomas's eyes twinkled, and Muriel assumed there was a touch of humor in the allusion. But she had no idea who Captain Thomas was talking about. She jotted down the women's names anyway.

"Kim looks far too old to have a child so young." Captain Thomas seemed oblivious to Muriel's lack of Bible literacy. "The girl appeared in the alley a few months ago, and we're always suspicious of those situations. We think she's probably a slave girl. But we're not sure. Sister Mary—that's the Chinese Salvationist lady who was preaching in the alley—is trying to get Kim to let the girl come to our Saturday school. Girls like her pine so for a little love and attention. I feel sorry for them. Miss Davis here heard some of our children sing last week at our Saturday school and says no Methodist child could sing louder."

Miss Davis seemed ready to respond, but Muriel spoke more quickly. "I'd love to talk to you more about your work, Captain Thomas. I'm wondering if you're going over to the Methodist Mission? I promised Margarita and her mother I'd stop in to see one of the Oriental children I've been writing about." Muriel scanned the dwindling crowd for Margarita and the two Mission girls. They had wandered over to the large Army drum, and were talking to the few street urchins still gathered there. "Perhaps we could chat on the way?"

"We're not going there, but you can walk Miss Davis and me up to the Powell Street cable car. If it's not too much out of your way." Captain Thomas stooped down. "Why don't I carry that? I can't believe you can walk and write at the same time. And there's absolutely no way you can carry a satchel and take notes—unless you're hiding a third arm somewhere." Captain Thomas's remark elicited the trace of a smile from Miss Davis.

The street lamps were being lit as the three women said their goodbyes to Margarita and Gracie and turned up Sacramento Street, still jammed with gaily-colored Moon Festival throngs.

"So tell me about your Salvationist work. Quite frankly, I've always been a bit put off by the uniforms and the kinds of crowds you attract. So I've never actually talked to one of you before."

Captain Thomas laughed and squeezed around a happy Oriental family—the children were holding hands so as not to get separated or lost, just like American children would. The mother walked with the gentle, teetering sway of a foot-bound woman—marking them as well-to-do. "Even we think Salvationist outfits are a bit queer sometimes. But they help mark us out to people in the streets. They see our hallelujah bonnets and immediately know they can trust us."

Fog from the bay was fingering up the steep cobblestone street by the time the three women got to Powell. There were fewer people now, and all were Americans. This was the San Francisco Muriel was familiar with. She loved these fall evenings—the tang of salt in the air, the distant bass of foghorns. It was once again a typical, workaday evening, with late-working commuters hurrying home to their families.

Muriel said farewell to the women and walked back down toward the Mission. Thanks to her developing skills at writing on the run, she had managed to jot a few shorthand scribbles on the way up the hill with Captain Thomas and Miss Davis, and she hoped she would be able to transcribe them later, on the ferry ride home. She knew if she didn't have a draft of the article on her editor's desk in the morning, she would catch hell for wasting the afternoon in Chinatown. And she wasn't about to give him free rein with her notes.

巷

Muriel rang the Mission's side entrance bell on Trenton Street, making sure to hold out Margarita's calling card and stand far enough from the door so the person on the other side could see her through the peephole. The doorknob was painted white—a policy Reverend Gibson had begun in the 1870s so girls escaping from brothels could find it in the night. Jennie Lee, the mixed-blood thirteen-year-old girl from Chicago, opened the door.

In the background Muriel could hear someone struggling to play piano scales. The sound magically stopped the moment Jennie said, "You're the newspaper lady who talked to me before."

A girl with a piano book peeped from behind Jennie's waist. Muriel thought it was Siu, but she wasn't sure. All the little Oriental girls looked alike when she began her interview series at the Mission House, and although she was now almost always able to distinguish one girl from the other, she hadn't seen any of them in over a month.

"Miss Lake isn't in right now. She's down on Waverly, I think." Jennie scowled down at the smaller girl beside her. She attempted to push the girl away from the door but failed. "She's with Gracie and the Salvation lassies."

"Actually, I'm here to see Mrs. Lake. But didn't I interrupt someone's piano practice? Was that you—Siu?" Muriel set her satchel by the door and smiled at the girl still half-hidden behind Jennie.

The girl grinned when Muriel said her name. "Yes. Miss Lake gives me lessons. But I'm done."

Muriel heard footfalls overhead as she followed Jennie and Siu up to the sitting room. "Done practicing already, Siu?" Margarita's mother, Kate, was wiping sweat from her forehead and gasping for air as the two girls and Muriel entered. Kate had folded over a red-checkered apron and tied it around her ample midriff, and her plain white shirtwaist—at least one size too small for her bulging body—looked like it was about to burst its middle buttons. "Who was at the door, Jennie?

"Oh Muriel, it's you. Maggie said she sent her card over, telling you Kuan was back. Come sit down—if you can find a place. Siu, can you help me clear off that settee? Just put the sheets on the floor for now.

"September can be so hot up here. We've had the windows open all afternoon, but when the evening fog starts rolling in, it can cool down fast." Kate pushed hard against a cracked window frame, trying to close it. "No satchel today?"

"I left it at the foot of the stairs," Muriel laughed. "I wasn't sure if I'd be able to see Kuan at this late hour, so I thought a pencil and notebook would be enough."

"Things are a mess up here since Kuan came back." Kate shook her head. "We wanted to give her a room to herself, but with having to temporarily house two new girls before they're deported, we're really short on space. We had Kuan lying out here for a while today. It's cooler here than in the girls' rooms.

Kate turned toward the girls. "Thank you Siu. Could you girls see if Kuan's still awake? I think Muriel would like to see her."

"I'd like that very much." Muriel peered down the hallway.

"I don't know if Maggie told you, but Dr. Worley diagnosed Kuan with consumption, and that's why we had to bring her back. The Children's Hospital is overcrowded and they needed the space for emergency cases. And since Chinese aren't allowed in the city hospital, she couldn't go there. She'll get more attention and more rest here, anyhow.

"We're fortunate to have such loving women like Dr. Worley to care for her. And Minnie—Dr. Worley—promised to stop by if we get desperate. Otherwise I don't know what we'd do. There are very few doctors who'll treat Chinese patients." Kate paused and wiped her neck with the hem of her apron.

"I've forgotten my manners!" Kate clapped her hands and leaned forward. "Congratulations on your marriage. Mrs. Monroe is it now? Maggie and I saw the announcement in the *Evening Bulletin* a few weeks ago. You're getting quite famous. Not only announced in your paper."

"My mother insisted it should be in all the papers." Muriel laughed and shook her head. "I thought that was extravagant, but my father said if I didn't know before, it should be obvious by now that the wedding was about the mother of the bride—not Harry and me. Truer words were never spoken. But I'm glad all that's behind us, and we can begin to get back to a normal life."

"So where have you decided to set up your new home?"

Before Muriel could answer, Jennie appeared in the sitting room doorway. "Mrs. Kate, Kuan's still awake—and I told her she has a visitor."

巷

Muriel had done her more recent interviews—if you could use that term for the give-and-take of translation and the groping for appropriate words—in the Asylum sitting room. But she had never been down the hall. It was long and narrow, and dimly lit. If it weren't for the fact it opened into another windowed, parlor-like room at the far end, it would be difficult to see anything. But even in the dim light Muriel could tell the wallpaper had lost whatever color it originally had. It was peeling and its diamond pattern was barely discernible. All the doors stood open, and as Muriel passed by, she noted each room was the same. Small windowed alcoves under the eaves, two or three white painted iron beds, lumpy mattresses with mismatched but nicely straightened spreads, a bureau—or a trunk on the floor—and framed Bible verses on the walls.

"We keep the youngest girls in the room closest to my mine, at the end of the hall." Kate spoke as though she were leading a tour she had given a hundred times before. "We try to pair one of the older girls who's been here awhile with one of the newer inmates, to help them feel less afraid."

In one room two girls sat on beds, quietly sewing buttons on blouses. But the other rooms were empty. Muriel was about to ask where the girls were, when Kate answered her unvoiced question. "Most of the girls are in the basement finishing up their English lessons and getting ready for supper."

Muriel could hear Kuan's labored breathing before they came to her room. Shallow, panting breaths; tense pauses; then hacking coughs.

The girl lay on her side, facing the opposite wall. The top sheet was half off the wrought-iron bed, and her nightclothes were soaked; twisted around her thighs, exposing spindly legs.

"We put her here because this room has the best ventilation." Kate shook her apron. "Dr. Worley thinks fresh air is the best thing for consumption. The other side of the house gets so much coal dust and smoke from across the street I sometimes think we'd be better off never opening the windows. But then it gets so awful smelling I can't stand it."

Open window or not, the room reeked of sarsaparilla, alcohol, and urine.

"Jennie, can you please empty the chamber pot? And be careful on your way down." Jennie made a face, but picked up the enamelware pot and headed out the door. "You're going to have to dump it in the privy off the back stairs," Kate shouted. "Miss Lake said the toilet on her floor is stopped up today too."

Kate moved over to reposition Kuan on the bed. She turned the girl on her back and propped a pillow behind her.

There was no place to sit, so Muriel bent down, patting Kuan on the arm and trying not to breathe in the stagnant air. The girl wasn't much more than a yellow skeleton. Her skin—despite the warmth of the room, was cold and waxy. Muriel felt more at ease around these Oriental girls now—even a sick one—and although she knew Kuan couldn't understand her, she spoke anyway. "You're quite the famous girl now, you know. My readers will want to know how you're doing."

The excitement started Kuan coughing. "Sometimes the best thing to do is just hold her tight." Kate bent over the girl. "It seems to relax her and ease the coughing. The fits weaken her so."

Muriel moved toward the faint breeze in the hallway. "I can see she needs rest. I should leave her alone."

Kate kissed Kuan on the cheek and changed the position of the pillow one last time, then rose to face Muriel.

"I'm glad Margarita told me Kuan was here," Muriel said. "But I'm not happy about the circumstances. It's shameful our American doctors won't treat these people. Does Dr. Worley think anything can be done for her, besides keeping her comfortable and giving her as much fresh air as possible?"

巷

"Kuan's so sweet," Kate murmured as she plopped into a sitting room settee opposite Muriel. She dabbed her eyes with her apron. "You can't believe how a human being can go through the torture she has and still be cheerful. And the older girls are convinced God will heal her. What can I tell them? I worry as much about the girls praying for her, as I do about Kuan herself. I don't know how they'll take her death—which is sure to come. I only hope it's sooner than later. I think that's partly why Maggie invited you up to see her. Maggie thinks it'll be soon."

"I'm glad Margarita told me Kuan was back. To think just a few weeks ago Margarita and I had that awful row, and I didn't care if I ever saw this place again. But Margarita was right. Girls like Kuan are truly the brave ones." For a few minutes Muriel's pencil on paper was the only sound in the room. She jotted down her immediate impressions of Kuan, thinking of how she might deal with the tragic quality of the Oriental girl's life, while still giving her readers a sense of the feelings she had for the girl—that she was as much a human being as any American.

When Muriel looked up from her notes, Kate was once again the composed matron of the Rescue Asylum. Kate smiled and wiped her brow. "Before we went down to see Kuan, you were going to tell me where you and your husband are living."

"In Oakland." Muriel was grateful for the change in conversation. She set her notebook aside and pushed her pencil through her French braid. "Harry finished Hastings College of Law in June and we've decided on the other side of the bay for the time being. We both love the hills for riding our bicycles. And the ferry to the city is quite pleasant. We both get a lot of reading done on the ride over and back."

Kate dropped her head and began to pull at a loose thread on the hem of her apron. She looked up at Muriel and her brown eyes narrowed. "I don't think Maggie told me your husband's a lawyer. The world—including San Francisco—could use a few more honest ones."

"I know this may sound like I'm a young married woman head-over-heels in love." Muriel smiled, recalling the accolades her husband had received at his recent graduation. "But one of the things I admire most about Harry—and one of the reasons I fell in love with him—was because he has such integrity."

"I wish we had a lawyer like that." Kate's eyes searched Muriel's face. She paused as a ball bounced in the hallway. Girls chattered excitedly.

"Mrs. Kate?" Jennie stood at the entrance to the hallway, jabbing her index finger in the direction of Kuan's room.

"Yes, Jennie?"

"It's Kuan. She's coughing again."

"Tell her I'll be there in a few minutes." Kate sighed. "You can change the position of the pillow that's against her back, like you saw me do. That usually helps."

"If you'd like, I could mention your work to Harry," Muriel said. "He's started looking for a permanent position, and any experience would prove helpful to him."

"Muriel, you've been around here enough to see we can't afford to pay much of anything—anything—for legal advice, and the Board would have to approve—"

"I understand. But I think Harry would at least be interested in meeting with your Board and exploring possibilities. As you can imagine, I've told him a lot about your work. Even if he doesn't read every word I write, he's at least heard my stories."

"Feel free to mention us to him then, if you wish." Kate smoothed her frayed apron.

The girls in the hallway were chattering again, and there was a rustling by the doorway. "Mrs. Kate?"

Siu, and Sau—who could have been her twin—poked their heads into the sitting room, one atop the other. "Can me and Sau play jacks?"

"Pardon?"

"I mean, may Sau and I play jacks in your room?"

"Yes, you may. Remember, it's 'May I.' Not, 'Can me.' 'Can me' is if you want to be put in a pickle jar."

The girls giggled. "Mrs. Kate, we're not pickles." It was Sau, the bashful one.

"I know. You're the wrong color—not green enough, and a bit too big."

The girls giggled again. "Mrs. Kate!"

"Just be sure you find every jack when you're done. The last time you played in there you forgot one, and I stepped on it in the dark. It's a wonder my yelp didn't wake everyone on the floor."

"Those girls are darling." Muriel watched them disappear down the hallway. "You would hardly know they weren't American." Muriel picked up her notebook. Straightening her dress, she stood to leave. "Thank you so much for letting me see Kuan today. And for letting Grace take me down to see Margarita. I saw her with the Salvationists in Spofford Alley a little while ago, and had a chance to interview Captain Thomas about the Army's rescue work. It seems quite different from yours. To be honest—" Muriel searched for words she hoped wouldn't offend Kate. "It was quite a surprise to see Margarita surrounded by all those uniformed people shouting hallelujahs and amens."

"It's true Maggie's not given to their type of religious enthusiasm." Kate laughed somewhat nervously, but remained comfortably seated. She seemed oblivious to Muriel's attempted leave-taking. Muriel felt awkward and sat down again. It was clear Kate had more on her mind. "But she believes Jesus when he said, 'He that is not against us is for us.'" Kate paused and looked down, twisting her apron in her hands. "We've had arguments over those words."

"That's not so unusual for mothers and daughters." Muriel thought of her relationship with her own mother—how she had all but decided to elope and forego her wedding after a lengthy fight about her choice of reception venue—until her father stepped in to mollify her mother.

"I think Maggie cares so much about her work and these girls," Kate was saying, "that she doesn't see the trouble that can come from working with different kinds of people—each with their own purposes. It's not that Maggie doesn't understand people. But she's young and so dedicated. And there are groups—like *God's Regular Army* here in Chinatown—that dress like Christians and pretend to help, and you think they're on your side, then you find they use little children to beg and sell subscriptions, and every penny they collect goes into their own pockets. It reflects badly on all of us, and makes our work harder. I just don't want to see Maggie hurt. And people can be so hurtful."

"I know." Muriel nodded. "But you need to give yourself some credit for the way you raised her. She's a strong and independent woman. And she's certainly not naïve."

"I suppose you're right. 'Once a mother, always a mother,' as the saying goes." A brief smile touched the corners of Kate's mouth, but then her jaw reverted to its earlier rigidity. "But she's been talking recently about inviting a Catholic man—a Mr. Kane—to help with our rescues. He's in the papers from time to time. Maybe you've seen his name. He's the Secretary of the *Pacific Society for the Suppression of Vice*—I think that's it. Miss Cameron, Mrs. Hull, Maggie, and I are so well known by the brothel watchmen it's hard to get to the girls. But Maggie thinks Mr. Kane will be unknown around here. He has a police deputy star, too, and lots of experience getting into places. But I don't know. I don't think he's ever worked with the Chinese. Working with Salvationists is one thing. But Catholics are so—so different. They have so many queer ideas about things."

"They certainly do." Muriel stood once more and took a step backwards toward the stairs. Some of her Methodist relatives had gotten into a row with her father at her wedding reception, arguing the only difference between Catholics and Episcopalians was Latin. To them, Episcopalians like her father were simply English-speaking Catholics. Muriel had no interest in continuing this particular turn in the conversation. "Kate, thank you again for your time, and for letting me see Kuan. But I really must be going if I hope to make the next ferry."

巷

The following Saturday Leong Ti was at the Merchant Association Club at his usual early time. An old Chinese woman dressed in a Jesus uniform was sitting at the table when he entered, talking to Kim Yook. Chun crawled about with a bowl in her hand, scraping it across the floor. The girl seemed different somehow—then he realized it was the first time he had seen her with her face clean. The girl's mouth dropped open as though she recognized him, so he smiled at her. He put his foot under her bottom and scooted her toward the stools by the ghost screen. "You'd better be careful. I almost stepped on you."

The cook walked out from the kitchen carrying a large steaming bowl. It smelled like jook, the rice gruel he usually had for breakfast. The cook spotted the child and scolded her. The girl stood, chin quivering, with the dirty bowl tipping dangerously in her grimy hands. She scampered to the table and hid between Kim Yook's legs.

The keeper snorted and pushed Chun under the table. "I'm sorry, Mr. Leong. My daughter's not very well behaved. I'm just beginning to train her. I'm paying the girl next door to teach her how to pick up rice bowls and chopsticks after meals. It helps get her in the habit of work." Kim Yook stood and tapped the tabletop with her knuckles. She grinned at the Jesus woman seated beside her. "Excuse me while I unlock one of my girls' doors."

巷

"So what's the story with Chun, the little girl who lives downstairs under the table?" Leong Ti tugged at his pants and fished in his pocket for a dollar and a tip.

"What do you mean?" Yet turned away from him and pulled her sleeping smock over her head and shoulders. She knelt and took a cloth from a pile underneath the bed and wiped a wet spot on the blanket. Her boyish calves were suddenly exposed. Her skin was the color of moon glow, a pale gold dust. Ti saw the mole behind her left knee—the one he had touched earlier—and he trembled. Yet's thick hair was slung over one shoulder and fell to the floor. She sat back on the edge of the cot and threw the cloth across the crib to a rag pile between the small, canvas-covered steamer trunk and the chamber pot.

Ti pulled out a handful of coins. "That Jesus woman who yells in the alley was downstairs when I came in, talking to your keeper about Chun. I think the Army woman is trying to get her to their place on Sacramento Street. How old is she?"

"Chun? About three, I think. We don't know for sure."

"Where'd she come from? Is she a neighbor—or the daughter of that cleaning woman I've seen around?"

"Why should you care?" The girl stared at something over his shoulder, and Ti knew it was the jar on the shelf behind him. There was a needling in her tone.

"I was just wondering. She was out in the alley last week with Kim. And with that old girl down the hall. She chased your *kwai po* around those Jesus people. It was funny."

"You saw all that?"

"I was on my way to the Mission, to the ABC school. I'm learning American, and how to read and write Chinese." Ti was proud of his language skills, and he wanted Yet to know he was smarter than most customers. "Anyway, she seems to be fearless. Like she was born in January—the ox month."

"I don't know about that. But it's nice having a little girl here. Her mother stopped in a few months ago."

"You mean the mother left her here?"

"No. The baby's yours. I just never had a chance to tell you." Ti felt a challenge in Yet's voice, a thrusting knife. He winced and closed his hand around the coins. Why should he pay her?

"Don't tell anyone I told you about her." There was a pause as Yet's eyes briefly met Ti's. The soft pleading he saw there belied her earlier response. "*Kwai po* says we're not supposed to say anything about her, or we'll get in trouble. She's the mother now. Chun's another adopted daughter—like the rest of us."

"I don't think I could do that."

"Do what?"

"Give up a child."

"You might surprise yourself. I've heard lots of men say that. But when it's a matter of giving up one to keep the rest of the family from starving—" Yet bent forward on the cot, pulling her legs to her chest. She wrapped her arms around her knees. Her sleeping smock was tight against her thighs, exposing her small, narrow feet. Her toes were delicately formed, and they curled over the edge of the cot like a baby's tight-fisted fingers.

Ti stared down at the top of her head. He was close enough to touch her hair. He had never realized how black it was against the milky-white line of her scalp. "I still don't think I could give up my own daughter."

"I'm not saying you would. But men are the ones who decide whether to sell or not. Then the women have to do the rest." Once again, Yet was staring at the wall behind him. Her eyes, steady, unblinking. "I'm sure I'm not telling you anything new—unless you're more stupid than most men. When your brain's shriveled and stuck between your legs—" The girl shrugged and stood, pushing the cot hard against the wall.

"Is that what happened to you?" Ti stalled, not wanting to leave.

"Maybe. What do you care?" There was a harshness in the way Yet emphasized the last word.

"I'm sorry. I really didn't think—"

"Now you know." She faced him now. Her eyes, a few inches from his shoulder, cut into him again. Her hands clenched. "It happens all the time. We all have the same story. The same as what Chun's will be in a few years. We're happy adopted daughters, wives with a thousand husbands, working with our legs in the air until they drop off. And loving every minute."

She looked at the floor, her voice quavering, but determined. "Now you'd better stop wasting my time, or you'll owe another dollar."

Ti stared out the iron-barred window, his mind drifting somewhere far beyond Yet's room—he didn't quite know where. He wanted to tell her he cared about her, that he had a plan to get her out. But he knew he couldn't say those things. Because he had no plan.

"So, did your *kai po* give you the cheongsam I bought for you a while back?" He hoped mentioning the gift would show something.

"What?"

"Remember, I told you I brought you a present."

"Customers tell me all the time they're getting me things. And usually I don't see a thing. So I don't trust what anyone says."

Ti dropped his head and counted his coins. He had no way to reach the girl. "Here's what I owe."

She didn't take the money or call for the keeper. "I did ask *kwai po* about the thing you said you bought—because you seem to be more honest than most men. And no, I don't have it. She said she didn't have time to enter it in her books. She needs to see how much it's worth, anyway, if I want to count it against my debt."

"I knew she was a thief." Ti kicked the leg of the cot, nearly causing it to collapse. "All the keepers are. Well, I can tell her how much it cost."

"It wouldn't make any difference." There was almost a touch of kindness in Yet's voice. She eyed the coins in his hand. "She thinks you stole it. She said she'll have to check around to make sure it really belonged to you. That takes a while."

Ti snorted. He held out a dollar and an extra quarter.

"Two dollars today, Mr. Leong. You need to remember to keep your mouth shut until your pants are buttoned." Her voice was unsteady. She didn't look at him.

Ti felt his face grow hot. He knew some men hit girls when they talked like this. He felt his hand turning into a fist in his pocket—but then it touched a coin, and he pulled out another three quarters.

"*Kwai po*! The customer's done." The girl was at the door, shouting, her mouth next to the open slider. And Ti watched as her shoulders shook.

巷

When Kim Yook and Mr. Leong got back downstairs, the Jesus woman was standing, ready to leave. Chun pranced around the Jesus woman, grinning, with a stick of candy squeezed in her fist. "So if I come by here next Saturday in the afternoon, you'll let Chun come with me to the Army place on Sacramento?"

"I suppose." Kim Yook pushed Chun off toward the bamboo curtain and the kitchen. "Maybe I'll send Ming along to keep an eye on her. That girl's practically useless anyway. She's getting so ugly most men see her and turn and run out of her room. They won't even pay for looking. Chun's too young to read and write, but if I find you're teaching Ming anything, I'll beat them both so badly neither one will ever want to go anywhere with you again. Girls learn to write, then they pass notes to men to help get them out. And Chun's my daughter, the only child I have. I need her here to help me in my old age."

奴

Chapter Four

SLAVE

After an unusually warm and dry fall, San Francisco's weather turned unpredictable in late November. The first storms of the season slammed into the city with their strong winds and driving rain. A few days later the skies would clear to a brilliant blue. Then the winds would pick up, bringing a bone-chilling cold, and the dripping dampness would return.

Unlike the fickle weather, Leong Ti was a creature of habit. He was as regular and punctual in his brothel visits as he was at his job at Jew Ho's grocery store. And he expected the same behavior of everyone around him. He was at the Merchant Association Club at nine every Saturday morning, Kim Yook always had the door cracked open for him, and she was always sitting at the table, keys in hand, waiting to lead him upstairs.

So when he stepped inside the door one wet, foggy morning in late December and hung up his dripping coat and hat, it seemed peculiar that there was no one in the room. And it seemed even more peculiar when he called for the keeper and there was no response. The kettle hissed and popped on the pot-bellied stove, and Kim Yook's bedroll still lay in the corner of the room as though she had recently gotten up. Ti thought she might be in the back heating a pot of jook for breakfast. He called for her again.

A stack of newspapers—*Hua Mei Hsin Pao*—*The American and Chinese Commercial News*—lay on the floor, so he sat on a stool near the screen and picked up the top one. Ti was learning to read, and he searched for words he recognized. He found an advertisement for Jew Ho's store. "Best price on broccoli" he read out loud, pleased with his ability. His evenings at Mr. Gardner's school in the basement of the Methodist Mission was time well spent, even if there were nights when he could barely keep his eyes open after long days at the store.

Ti heard a rustling sound and looked down. Chun was squatting under the table, next to Kim Yook's safe. "Chun, what are you doing down there?"

"I make breakfast."

"Making breakfast? For what?"

"I make breakfast Mama rat."

Ti set down the paper. Chun was filling Kim Yook's improvised spittoon with what looked like the remnants of a meal. "You mean the one always sniffing around that bowl?" Ti dragged the girl from under the table and tried to stand her on the floor, but she screeched and pulled her legs to her chest.

"No, Uncle Ti."

"Suit yourself, then." He sat her on the floor, a bit harder than he intended.

"Owie." Chun's lower lip began to quiver.

"You don't need to feed that thing. Rats are smart little animals and can find food on their own. They bring good luck. Look at me. I was born in the year of the rat."

Chun stood and faced him. Her arms were folded across her chest and she thrust out her lower lip. "He my friend. Ming say so."

Ti had little experience arguing with three year-olds, and this one had already exhausted his patience. "Suit yourself." He wiped his hands on his pantaloons and shouted again for Kim Yook. "Chun, where's your mama?" Ti's time with Yet was precious and he didn't want to be late to work. The keeper knew his schedule.

"With Yet. Yet have owies. Yet crying." Chun's lower lip quivered again. "Mama mad."

"What do you mean?"

"Yet has big owies. Yet cry all night. Me have owie too."

Chun tugged at her smock, but Ti's eyes were focused on the bamboo curtain at the other side of the room.

"Yet! Kim!" Ti stepped around Chun and pushed aside the bamboo curtain. He ran up the stairs, two at a time. The hall at the top of the stairs was almost as dark as the stairwell, but the girls' doors were open, and above the sound of his pounding heart he heard fragments of a muffled conversation. The girls huddled by Yet's door.

Ming guarded the hallway, facing Ti. "*Kwai po*! You have a customer. It's Mr. Leong." Ti tried to push her aside, but the other girls formed a wall behind her, refusing to budge.

Through Yet's open door he saw the top of Kim Yook's head and heard her shrill staccato "Jeezachrise." Ti's eyes jumped crazily from shape to shape, searching for the one body he knew. But he couldn't see her. Then he heard the sharp intake of breath followed by shallow exhaling groans. He had heard these sounds once before, and now his legs began to tremble like they had then. When his brother fell off the neighbor's water buffalo and was trampled.

"Please. You have to let me in." This time he pushed his shoulder hard against Ming. His hands gouged her waist. She cursed and fell into the girls standing behind her.

"*Kwai po*, it's Mr. Leong. Mr. Leong's here." Ming shrieked.

"Let me out!" Kim Yook fought past the girls, into the hallway, where she faced Ti. Sweat dripped from her forehead, and her eyes were red and bulging. She held a bloody rag in her hand and she pushed it into Ti's chest, trying to force him back. "You know the rules, Mr. Leong. No customers upstairs—no one, unless I bring them." She pulled Ming to her side, and they stood, legs spread; solid as roots of an ancient tree. "Ming, take him downstairs until I call you." Kim Yook pressed her body into Ti, swinging a fist at his abdomen. "Now get out."

"Yet!" Ti grabbed Kim Yook's fists, forcing them to her throat. Taking a step forward, he thrust his knee into old woman's thigh. "Yet! It's Mr. Leong. I'm here!"

Kim Yook hissed, struggling for air. The smell of her rotting teeth was strong and hot. "Mr. Leong, don't do anything you'll regret later." Her words were the only cue her girls needed. All four came at him, scratching, gouging, screaming. He felt as though he had fallen into a thicket of thorns, and he covered his face and backed toward the stairs. When he dropped his hands to feel for the door, he found Ming alone facing him, steely-eyed, her nose inches from his chin. There were streaks of blood on her cheeks and sleeping smock. "Downstairs, Mr. Leong."

"Just tell me what happened. I need to know." He tried to force his way past Ming one last time, but it was no use. He was in the doorway and the girls had come forward again, pushing Ming ahead of them.

"I'll tell you, when you get downstairs." Ming grabbed his arm.

奴

Chun was still squatting under the table, whimpering, when the girls shoved Ti into the customers' sitting room. She crawled out, sucking her thumb. She stared at Ming and Ming picked her up. "Sit down, Mr. Leong."

Ti couldn't find a stool. He stood, bewildered, in the middle of the room. "*Kwai po*'s taking care of things," Ming said. "Don't make it worse. You're not the first customer who's tried to get upstairs without her, and believe us, if you want to see Yet again, you'll stay here until *kwai po* says it's all right to bring you up."

"What happened?" Ti's eyes regained their focus, and he found a stool near the coal stove. His legs were shaking. His face stung from the girls' scratches.

"It was earlier this morning." Ming sat at the table, across the room from him, with Chun on her lap. "The man wasn't a regular. He pounded on the door, saying he had lots of money and wanted the best. *Kwai po* thought he might have been drunk, and she usually doesn't open after hours for new customers, but business has been slow lately. When she told him he would have to pay double because of being closed, he said that was no problem. *Kwai po* said he showed her a handful of gold coins, so she let him in and then went to wake Yet."

Chun put her hands over Ming's mouth. "Stop talking!" Ming took Chun's hands and held them, wrapping her arms around the child.

"Yet wasn't happy," Ming continued. "She started yelling at *kwai po* for waking her. That's when we all woke up. They had a big argument, but *kwai po* made Yet take the customer anyway. When he was done he started shouting at Yet. Maybe he thought she was still angry. We don't know. Anyway, he said he wasn't going to pay the full amount. And you know how Yet can be. She doesn't stand for men who try to do that. She kept telling him he had to pay full. Then he started hitting her. *Kwai po* had to call the watchman."

"How is she?" Ti felt a stinging in his throat, like he was going to vomit. He forced the sour taste back down.

"*Kwai po* will probably let you see her." Ming set Chun on the floor. The girl began crying and raised her arms to be picked up again, but Ming shoved her under the table. "Stay there," she scowled.

"You've been a good customer, so she won't want to lose you." Ming turned again toward Ti. "Just be patient. I'll be back."

奴

Kim Yook sat on the cot beside Yet, pressing a damp rag to the pretty one's left cheek and eye. She glanced up when Ming entered the room, but then ignored the ugly one. The pretty one needed her full attention at this moment, and with her condition, the business was in a precarious position. If she lost Yet's earnings, there would be no way to make them up. Neither the ugly one standing in front of her now—nor any of her other three girls—could make up the loss. Kim Yook knew Yet's owner, Yue Tschi, always made keepers pay for lost profits on his girls. That was the rule she agreed to when she took the job, and that's why she always paid the alley watchmen what they demanded. Every keeper in the alley knew Yue Tschi's ways, and Kim Yook trembled when she thought about him.

Yet's normally neat crib was in shambles, and that made Kim Yook angry. Yet's mirror was broken, and shards of glass lay everywhere. She couldn't trust Chun to clean the mess. The pitcher and basin of water were overturned, and the floor was wet and treacherous to walk on. Gold and silver coins were scattered in puddles everywhere. Kim Yook would have to pick up those herself, and it was painful for her to get on her hands and knees.

"Where does it hurt most?" It had been years since a customer had attacked one of her girls, and Kim Yook didn't know what words would get the girl back to work.

"All over," Yet mumbled. "I want to lie down, but I don't think I can even do that."

"That's why I tell you girls not to fight with unhappy customers." Kim Yook tried not to sound like she was scolding. "It's not worth it. And with some men they get even more excited when you fight back. That's what they want."

"*Kwai po*, Mr. Leong wants to see Yet. You need to go talk to him." The ugly one was standing in the doorway.

"Tell him she's fine." Kim Yook scowled at the girl's pudgy, pox-scarred face. "I'll be there in a few minutes."

"You know house rules," Kim Yook said when Ming left. "You can take a sick day, if you want. But I'll have to add a month to your contract for each day you say you're too sick to work."

"I know. But I don't think I can work tonight." Yet's eyes were closed, and her entire body shook.

"I'll get Dr. Wong Him in later to give you something for the pain. If you want, I can make sure you don't see as many customers for a few days."

Kim Yook lifted the rag from the pretty one's cheek to see if the bleeding had stopped. She had seen many beatings in her early years as a keeper, and she recalled face wounds usually looked worse than they actually were. This wound didn't seem deep, but it could be weeks before the swelling and bruises were gone, and that made Kim Yook fearful.

"Some customers like to see women black and blue—they won't hit or kick a girl, but they'll pay extra for looking and touching. You might make money that way—and hardly have to work at all."

The pretty one opened her eyes and stared at something across the room. Kim Yook knew what it was. The only unbroken thing in the room. The porcelain ginger jar, sitting precariously on its shelf—with the girl under the mulberry tree, still staring down at her lute.

"Try and get some rest, my Pretty One." Kim Yook patted Yet's knee. "You have a few hours to think about things before we open. It's not even ten." She paused to let her words sink in. "Ming said Mr. Leong's downstairs." Kim Yook stood and repeated Ming's words to see what effect Mr. Leong's name had on the girl. "If you want to see him, I'll bring him up. He knows what happened." Kim Yook watched Yet carefully. But Yet didn't move, and the empty expression on her face didn't change. Kim Yook plunged onward. She wanted to know what the pretty one thought of the man. Whether she should be concerned about the girl's loyalty. "You don't want to lose Mr. Leong as a customer. He's your most regular one, and you'll need to keep him through all this. He might even give you sympathy money without expecting much in return." Kim Yook paused and listened to the girl. Her breathing was still ragged and deep. "But be careful with him. After what happened he might try to take you away from here." Kim Yook thought she detected a slight change in the set of Yet's jaw—a brief straightening of her shoulders. But she wasn't sure.

"There's no place in Gold Mountain that'll treat you better than I have." Kim Yook bent down, took the pretty one's chin in her hands, and turned her face toward her, as she would with Chun. Yet winced, but wouldn't meet Kim Yook's eyes. "Look at me, my Pretty One. If at any time I think someone's trying to take advantage of you and trick you and take you away from me, Yue Tschi and the Hop Sing tong will find you, and things will be even worse. You know I've kept you safe all these years, and this is just one time. The watchmen will make sure that customer never comes into this alley again.

"I've always been good to you." Kim Yook smiled down at Yet. "And little Chun loves you—Ming too. You're like a big sister to Chun—a mother, almost."

The pretty one seemed to be listening now, her breathing more regular. Perhaps the worst of her muddled thinking was in the past, and the beating wouldn't result in financial loss.

奴

Ti stared at Yet. She sat hunched on her cot, head down, knees pulled to her chest. Her hair fell in stringy sweaty knots across her face, her arms, and her thighs, but her left cheek was visible, and it was swollen. Purple. Tear-stained. The girl held a bloody rag in one hand. Her ripped sleeping smock was falling off her shoulders and had scrunched up under her buttocks, fully exposing her calves and ankles. Ti could see everything. Where the customer had been.

The girl rocked back and forth, whimpering in a strange, high-pitched way. Dark welts and long scratches crisscrossed her arms, her breast, her back.

"What happened?"

Ti knew what had happened. Ming had told him. But she didn't tell him how badly Yet had been beaten. And now, when he saw the cuts and bruises—the blood and tears—he remembered how a few months earlier his own hand had formed a fist in his pocket when Yet made him angry. His mouth wouldn't shape the right words. So he repeated himself, foolishly. "What happened?"

"Nothing. Just get me out of here." Yet looked up, and the fire in her eyes and the anger in her voice were more terrible than the mottled color of her skin.

"What do you want me to do?" He was surprised to hear himself say this. He had thought about this moment many times in the past; what he would say to Yet when he had a plan. But the words that came out now were spontaneous, unrehearsed. And his hands were suddenly wet and shaking.

"I don't know. Just get me out." Yet's shoulders heaved. Her head fell forward and rested on her chest and knees, her breath rising in shuddering gasps. "If you're not going to do anything, then get out." She hurled the last two words at Ti with such force, he fell back against the door. Something fragile crashed and shattered on the floor.

Keys jangled in the stairwell, and Ti heard a slow limp on the stairs. There was a pause, and the sounds grew louder. He watched Yet. She didn't lift her head from her knees.

"What's going on in there? I heard something break. Are you all right?" It was Kim Yook's voice.

"It was that jar on the shelf—it fell—that's all." Ti shouted over his shoulder. "It's all right. We don't need you."

The girl didn't move. Ti stood still, barely breathing, hoping he had permission to stay.

"Are you all right, my Pretty One?"

"Yes, *kwai po.*"

"It's not that easy." Ti whispered, listening as the muttering and limping faded down the hallway. "It takes planning. But I know what to do. There's something for men called the *Chinese Society for English Education*. They probably can help. And maybe the Jesus people—but there are so many different ones. They're all confusing—I don't know which is best." Ti talked fast and disjointedly, trying not to look at Yet's swollen face, the purple welts on her back and breast. He had loved the golden, translucent color of her skin—soft as the summer sunlight that only a few months ago had bathed her little room on Saturday mornings. But he had never thought about what was below her skin. And now all that was visible. Now he saw the pain and suffering there. That it wasn't just about what he wanted from the girl.

"So how old are you?" He knew next to nothing about her. "The Americans have laws—"

奴

It felt strange, hearing the man talk like this. Like she was sitting at her window, overhearing a conversation in the alley below about someone she thought she knew—someone she had once met—but couldn't quite place.

The pain came in waves, sharp and piercing when she breathed, followed by a vague, slow pounding dullness. She willed the pain away—she could do that. She did it every night when the men came. She would stare at the magical jar on the shelf and think of the girl with the lute under the mulberry tree and be taken to a far away place. And if a man tried to get her to look at him, she would turn away. Sometimes she would turn her cheek to someone who paid extra for a kiss, but she would never look at him. She would just stare into the darkness of the far wall.

There was another sharp burst of pain, and Yet gasped. She focused all her attention on the words coming from the man standing in front of her.

"I don't know—maybe sixteen—I'm not sure."

"All the keepers tell their girls to say that," he said. "But I want to know the truth. How old are you, really?" The man stepped closer, and she could feel his eyes moving over her skin, pointed and piercing. She lifted her head from her knees, but refused to look at him. She pulled at her sleeping smock to cover her breast. "Maybe seventeen now. I think I was fourteen when I started working." It hurt to shape the words in her mouth. Her lips moved slowly, and the words sounded strange, as though they were coming from somewhere else in the room.

"That's close enough. An American who knows the laws here in Gold Mountain told me if you're sixteen and don't want to be in a place like this, you don't have to stay."

Finally Yet turned her head toward the man. She remembered it was Mr. Leong, and she remembered how he had been with her in the past. No one had told her about not staying, but it didn't matter, because Mr. Leong didn't know about Yue Tschi and what he could do. "*Kwai po* told me if I didn't say six—sixteen—"

She fought again to control the pain in her chest. She had stopped her head from turning any further, but she couldn't stop the shallow panting. And the panting brought more pain and a panicky, suffocating feeling. "She said bad Americans would come and take me away and beat me."

"That could be true. I don't know." Mr. Leong was dabbing a long red scratch on his cheek. He looked at his fingers, and then at her again. She turned away. "If you're under sixteen, the keeper can say you're her child. If you're over sixteen, Americans think you're here only because you want to be."

And no one had told Yet this. She felt a great rush of air leave her body—as if her *chi*—her life force was departing, and she was watching it leave.

"Didn't you tell me once you were born in the Celestial Kingdom?"

"Yes."

"That could be difficult. The Americans will want to send you back, since you probably didn't come in the right way."

"That's all right. Anywhere is better than this place."

"No, it's not. Look at me, Yet. It's not all right."

She lifted her head and looked into Mr. Leong's eyes. She held on to them with all her strength. And for a moment, the pain subsided. She stared more intently, and she saw in his eyes the two-room house where she once lived in the Celestial Kingdom. Behind the walls of the house were her father's eyes. And her mother's. Her grandfather's. Her grandmother's. In his eyes was an entire village on New Year's Day. Firecrackers and dumplings and new bamboo pushing green shoots through the spring mud behind her parents' home.

"Are you all right?" It was Mr. Leong's voice, but it sounded like Ming's sometimes did when Chun cried and Ming tried to comfort her.

"I'll be fine. Do whatever you have to. I just don't want to die here."

"I'm going to leave now, but I'll be back tomorrow if I can."

"Ti." She had never called him that before. And she knew instantly she should have swallowed the name and buried it deep in her belly.

Mr. Leong stopped and turned in mid-step, the sound of porcelain jar fragments crunching under his shoe. "How do you know my name?" There was a sharp edge to his tone that bit into Yet's ribs. "Don't ever call me that."

She turned her face away from him, a hot stinging in the welts on her cheeks. She could no longer hold the pain inside, and it finally came out, spilling over herself.

"I'm sorry—Chun told me—I thought—I mean—"

"I mean, don't use my first name here." Once again it was Ming's voice, talking to Chun. "It could be dangerous for both of us. Your *kwai po* will be suspicious. When I get you away from here, you can call me Ti as much as you want."

She raised her eyes again. She wondered how his cheek got scratched. Was it because of her? She thought she had heard his voice earlier in the morning, calling her name. But that seemed long ago, and right now she wasn't sure of anything. She whispered, "Mr. Leong, I was going to tell you. *Kwai po* gave me that cheongsam."

"What?"

"The cheongsam. The one you said you bought for me awhile back. *Kwai po* gave it to me a few days ago. She said she found out who sold it to you. That you came by it honestly. It's in my trunk over there. Under that mess." Yet smiled as best she could, but she knew it wasn't the smile she wanted to show him. "I tried it on. It fit perfectly."

"I want you to wear it for me one day," Mr. Leong said. "But not in this place. Never in here." Yet nodded, and a great rush of air entered the room. The life force that had left her body earlier returned, and she knew it would stay with her until she saw him again.

"I'd better go now." He came to her and touched her shoulder.

Her hand found his hand. His hand was warm and pulsing. Full of life. She clutched it hungrily.

"You need to rest. Here's a dollar," he said.

"I don't want it."

"You need all the money you can get." He pulled his hand away and took a step backwards, toward the door.

"Mr. Leong, I don't want your money."

There was a stir of air in her lungs now, and when she looked at him, his eyes reminded her of the porcelain eyes of the dreamy girl beneath the mulberry tree—fragments of the ginger jar now lying scattered across the floor.

奴

"That was fast." Kim Yook shoved the customer out of Yet's room, toward the stairs.

"He only wanted to look at me." The pretty one turned away.

"I told you that's all some men would want to do." Kim Yook remained in the doorway, watching Yet's shoulders. Listening to her labored breathing. "How much did he pay?"

"A dollar."

"Good. Like I said, you might make more money this way than the other way."

Kim Yook pondered the coins scattered on the floor. "My mother once told me a story, and I have never forgotten it." She paused and kicked at a large, sharp fragment of the porcelain jar. "I've told it to some of the other girls, but I don't think I've told it to you. Here's what she said: 'Because of its special trees, the mountain weakens itself. The bark of cinnamon trees can be eaten and so people cut them down. One type of tree has mushrooms that grow in its roots, and people sometimes accidentally kill those trees getting the delicacies. Varnish trees make things last long, but people make deadly cuts in them to get their sap. Everyone knows the advantage of being useful, but not many understand the advantage of being useless.' Look at Ming. She's the oldest and ugliest worker in the house. I often think she's survived so long because she's practically useless. No one really wants her, but they can't afford anything else. So she's the tree that lives on." Kim Yook paused for effect. "That's why I think I've lasted so long." She watched Yet hunched on the cot. "Do you understand?"

The pretty one's face didn't change. Her body didn't move. Kim Yook sighed and turned, then limped slowly downstairs.

Her other four girls were sitting at the table, eating their morning jook and watching Chun try to coax the rat out from its hole in the wall. "I think Yet will be fine, " Kim Yook told them.

"Look at me, girls. She'll be fine." Kim Yook opened her mouth and stuck out her tongue. "Is my tongue still in my mouth?"

"Yes, *kwai po*." The girls responded in unison.

"What about my teeth?"

The girls never lifted their heads from their breakfast bowls. "No *kwai po*. Half of them are gone."

"So, my tongue's still there because it's soft, but my teeth are gone because they're brittle and hard. Isn't that right?" She waited for the words to sink into their thick skulls. But nothing happened, so she finished the lesson herself. "Just remember. To survive here, you must be willing to change and be molded. You cannot be a tooth, brittle and hard—bitter and rebellious."

奴

It was about noon when Ming heard a light rapping at the door: Tat tat, pause. Tat tat, pause. Tat tat. It was the secret way the Jesus woman—Old Mary—had for telling Ming she was outside. That she was there to pick up Chun and her for Saturday Army School.

Ming opened the door and the Jesus woman went straight to the pot-bellied stove to warm her hands. A puddle formed around her scuffed leather shoes. Ming knew Kim Yook would leave the water on the floor until they returned. Wiping up spills was one of the chores Kim Yook was teaching Chun.

"It's raining again." Old Mary rubbed her red hands above the hot metal. "I hope you have something warm for Chun to wear."

"I do." Ming held up one of the girls' old buttonless, shapeless black smocks she and Yet had worked on recently. They had folded it in half to shorten it, and then re-sewn it into a crude winter jacket. "Chun, come here. Auntie Mary is here, and we're ready to go."

The girl crawled out from her place under the table and smiled shyly at the Jesus woman. "Candy day? Sing day?"

Ming knelt down, and before the child had finished speaking, Ming had pulled the homemade jacket over Chun's head. The girl giggled when Ming made big eyes and said "Oh, there you are."

"Yes, there'll be singing—and some big surprises too." Old Mary smiled at Chun. "But where's your mama? We need to tell her we're leaving."

"*Kwai po*'s talking to the alley watchman." Ming picked up Chun. "We had some problems last night and one of our girls got hurt. *Kwai po* wants to know if the watchman got the customer's name or knows where he lives. If she can find out, she'll make sure he never comes back."

"You know we help girls who want to get out of this life." Old Mary spoke in a low voice. She reached into her uniform pocket and pulled out a small stick of red and green striped candy for Chun. "I used to be in the life too."

Ming leaned forward to catch Old Mary's words. "I know, but we hear bad stories about those Jesus places. They're worse than being here."

"That's not true." Old Mary put on her Jesus bonnet and tied it. "Look at me. And think about the people you know at Saturday school. Do we look like we're afraid?"

Ming heard someone at the top of the stairs, and her back stiffened. "Can we go now?" She saw a customer had left an old frock coat hanging on a peg above the row of waiting stools, so she took it—not so much for herself, but to keep Chun warm and dry. "*Kwai po* knew you were coming and said we didn't have to wait to tell her."

"Remember." Old Mary paused in the open door. "If you ever need help, we'll do whatever we can."

When Ming and Chun got to Sacramento Street there were sheets hanging in the Army storefront windows. Old Mary grinned and opened the door. "Look."

There was a quick, warm rush of winter smells Ming was familiar with from the brothel—damp cotton and wool, sweat and coal soot. But mixed in with everything was something else—a scent Ming recognized from her childhood in the Celestial Kingdom. Fresh pine needles. Ming stood in the storefront doorway with Chun wiggling in her arms, and as a Jesus man turned to welcome some American ladies, Ming and Chun stared, their mouths agape. "That?" Chun finally asked, pointing across the room.

"It's a tree." But it was the strangest tree Ming had ever seen. It was as though the Americans had taken ornaments from the Chinese Lantern Festival and the Moon Festival and hung them together on one thing. Instead of paper globes, tiny glass balls of all colors—reds and blues, greens and yellows hung from its branches; and gold and silver ropes draped around it, shimmering in the glow of the gaslights. Oranges, apples, candy, and little bags of nuts had been tossed haphazardly beneath the tree and lay atop stacks of small red and green wrapped packages.

"I don't know why the tree looks that way," Ming whispered in Chun's ear. "But it must be for some sort of magic."

Chun struggled to get down. "I see. I see."

Old Mary gave Ming a gentle push toward a table on the far side of the room. "Take Chun over there. She can sit with those children, and you can sit behind her—by those American ladies."

奴

Other than the skinny Christmas tree, the Salvation Army storefront room was quite plain, Muriel noted. The walls and windows were bare. There were a few tables and chairs in an "L"-shape on two sides of the room, facing the tree, but the only decorative elements on the tables were red paper tablecloths. Large steaming pots of soup and platters of bread sat at the ends of each table. Perhaps fifteen Chinese children were in the room, seated in small chairs around short-legged tables. The only children dressed in American clothes were the five Margarita had brought from the Mission. They wore starched white dresses, and Margarita had told Muriel they would be singing some Christmas carols later on.

Margarita and Captain Thomas sat on either side of Muriel—black pleated deaconess dress on one side, navy blue Salvation Army uniform on the other—and Muriel's auburn pompadour topped with a low crown, ivy-green felt hat sandwiched between. She had seen the millinery trimmed with holiday red and gold in a Union Square store window a few days earlier, and couldn't resist it.

A couple of other uniformed Salvationist women whom Muriel didn't know were on the other side of Captain Thomas. But surprisingly, the tall, dour-faced Miss Davis whom Muriel had met in Spofford Alley several months previous, sat opposite Muriel, with her back to the Christmas tree. Miss Davis had a sprig of holly protruding dangerously from a buttonhole—just as Miss Thomas did. Apparently holly was the one mark of the holiday season both Salvationists and Methodists could wear without giving offense.

These women were the only Americans in the room. The rest were Chinamen—and, incongruously, two Chinese women—one, the Salvationist Muriel recognized from the Spofford Alley menagerie in September, and the other, a scared, scar-faced woman—perhaps thirty years old—wearing a man's old coat. Muriel wondered what the woman was doing there, surrounded by men who kept eyeing her suspiciously.

True to what Muriel remembered from her September conversation with Captain Thomas, the Salvationists were starting their Christmas celebration with soup. It remained to be seen how the Army would deal with the "soap" part of their trinity of "soup, soap, and salvation." Muriel guessed the small rectangular packages under the tree were the soap part. The "salvation" segment of the afternoon was rather obvious, and was the reason she was there. Margarita and Captain Thomas had invited her to watch the children of Chinatown celebrate an American Christmas.

"I see you don't have your satchel, Mrs. Monroe. Did you bring a sleigh instead—to match the season?" Margarita's teasing made Muriel feel like a best friend, even though she hadn't been to the Mission in over two months.

"You sound like your mother." Muriel laughed and tasted the soup—watery and salty—heavy on noodles, light on what she assumed was chicken. Would it fill a stomach enough to bring salvation to a needy Oriental soul? She doubted it.

"Believe it or not, I don't take the satchel everywhere. Actually, I'm not planning on writing anything today. My editor thinks my articles are beginning to sound too Progressivist for *The Call*. And, as a matter of fact, I doubt if I'll be writing any more Chinatown stories for the paper." Seeing nothing that resembled a napkin on the table, Muriel reached into her coat pocket for a handkerchief. "I'm here today strictly on my own time." She dabbed the corners of her mouth, then set the handkerchief on her lap, pretending it was the appropriate cloth. "A few weeks ago I had an argument with some of our artists over the outrageous Chinese caricatures they've been drawing lately. They were as awful as anything you would see at a vulgar, blackface minstrel show." Miss Davis, who was listening attentively, nodded in agreement. "Well, my editor called me into his office afterwards, and lit into me. The bottom line is, I'm hoping to move to another paper."

While Margarita and Muriel were talking, Captain Thomas got up from the table and walked to the center of the room. She waved her hands and shouted. A Chinese Salvationist, acting as interpreter, moved forward to help quiet everyone.

"We'll have some special music shortly." Captain Thomas repeated herself three times before everyone quieted.

Margarita nudged Muriel. "That's our cue," she whispered. "Captain Thomas wants us to pass bells out to the children—except for the girls who came with me." She pulled a wooden box from under the table near Captain Thomas's chair.

"I wanted to tell you how sorry I was to hear of Kuan's death." Muriel squeezed Margarita's wrist before taking the Salvation Army bell Margarita handed her. The bell was sized perfectly for a child's fist. "And I'm sorry I haven't been up to give my condolences to your mother. This holiday season's been so busy—being our first as a married couple and all—and now I can't get over to see you or your mother on company time either."

"Kuan's death was hard on the older girls," Margarita nodded. "Christians like Gracie think if they pray for a little one to get well—one that's also Christian—then God's obligated to make them better. So the last month hasn't been easy."

"Yes, I remember your mother telling me the religious part might be the hardest for them." Muriel skipped the row of Mission girls dressed in white, and moved with Margarita to the last children's table. "Kuan was so sweet, and bore her pain so patiently. Seeing her lying there, and knowing the city hospital wouldn't take her because she was Oriental, broke my heart. It makes you wonder about God and—"

"No, it doesn't make me wonder." Their eyes met briefly, and Margarita turned to the next child, who grabbed the bell from her hand.

Muriel handed her last bell to a shy girl who was perhaps three years old. The girl was frail, and wore a crude, handmade jacket that didn't look like it would keep her warm on a cold, rainy day like today. But the child's eyes shone when she received the bell. Muriel straightened and surveyed the growing cacophony. "Handing out these bells early may not have been the best idea, Maggie." She avoided Margarita's eyes. "And I don't think it was a good idea for me—of all people—to be talking to you about religion. You know I care about you and your mother—and your girls. You do amazing work. Sometimes I just—"

"It's all right." Margarita shook her head at one of her girls who had picked up a bell to test it. "We're both headstrong people, wanting to do the right thing our own ways. You're the reflective writer. I'm the impatient doer. But deep down we're not so different." She smiled and copied Muriel's earlier gesture of sympathy, pressing her fingers on Muriel's forearm. "Captain Thomas is trying to get our attention. We'd better sit down."

Muriel wanted to add the rejoinder, "True, but writing is a form of doing, too." But for once she kept her mouth shut, smiled, and did what Margarita suggested.

奴

"As I was saying," Captain Thomas shouted above the children's not-so-furtive bell-testing. "We'll have some special music in a few minutes. So children, please set your bells down and don't touch them until I say. Now children, I want to tell you why this tree behind me is so important."

Like the children fidgeting with their bells, Muriel soon lost interest in Captain Thomas's attempt to connect Jesus' death on "a tree" with the decorative thing in front of them. Instead, Muriel's attention focused on the woman to her right, dressed in the traditional Oriental baggy black pantaloons and jacket. The woman leaned forward on the edge of her seat and seemed to be the only person listening to Captain Thomas's translator. But Muriel doubted whether any Oriental mind—child or adult—could make sense out of Captain Thomas's interpretation of a medieval tree tradition, something no more Christian than the pagan temple around the corner on Waverly.

"Thank you for waiting so patiently." Captain Thomas could barely be heard above the children's giggles, the clanging bells, and the old Chinamen jabbering. "And now, we have a special Christmas song for everyone." Captain Thomas motioned for the Army children to come forward, and then she arranged them in the semblance of a straight line.

"The song the children are singing today is called *I Would Be*," Captain Thomas shouted. "And little Chun here is going to sing a solo. Chun's been with us only a few months, but already she's impressed us with her talent. You're in for a treat." To Muriel's surprise, Captain Thomas pointed at the shy, frail girl to whom Muriel had given the last bell. Captain Thomas turned and knelt in front of the ten children. She shook her fist, and the performance began.

"I would be a Christmas bell—" the children sang in unison. Mimicking Captain Thomas's arm motions, they shook their bells in ragged time.

"Ringing, ringing for Jesus."

Captain Thomas took Chun's arm and pulled her forward. In a loud, clear voice the little girl sang—precisely on key, the bell in her little fist keeping a near perfect tempo.

"All around, good news to tell, Ringing, ringing for Jesus."

The room erupted with cheers and foot-stomping. The children grinned and seemed pleased with themselves, but Chun ran to the corner, to the Oriental woman wearing the man's coat.

"That little Chun's an amazing singer," Margarita exclaimed.

"Yes, I truly believe she could sing the entire song herself." Captain Thomas flushed with excitement. "Were you watching her, Muriel?

"Yes, I'm the one who gave her the bell." Muriel was still watching Chun, who sat on the Oriental woman's lap, pointing at the Christmas tree. "I didn't think she would have enough courage to shake the bell—let alone sing. But she seemed to know all the words, and sang louder than everyone."

"She has a natural singing voice and is a great mimic." Captain Thomas laughed and pushed the bell box under the table with her foot.

"Are you saying she doesn't know what she's singing?"

"I'm quite sure she doesn't understand a word." Captain Thomas shook her head, her hallelujah bonnet flopping like one of the children's bells. "Most of our children know only a smattering of English. That's why we use the translator. But they love to sing. And we don't think the word of God will return empty, regardless of the language barrier. Whatever happens to them in the future, these songs and Bible verses will remain in their hearts a lifetime."

The final event of the afternoon was what everyone had been waiting for: the gift-giving. The leaders of the Salvation Chinatown Corps stood on one side of the tree handing out gifts to the adults, and Captain Thomas invited Margarita, Muriel, and Miss Davis to the front on the other side of the tree, to hand out gifts to the children.

In between her smiles and her, "You did a wonderful job," compliments, Margarita told Muriel a resolution had been passed at Wednesday's Home Board meeting to invite Harry to become an ex officio member.

The Mission girls were in line now, and Muriel was pleased to hear Siu and Sau squeal "Mrs. Monroe! Mrs. Monroe!" when she gave them oranges.

"Harry should be getting the formal letter soon," Margarita said. "And I hope he accepts. We think there'll be a change of Customs Collectors, and if so, we'll need all the legal aid we can get."

Muriel handed the last orange to a little ragamuffin about to cry—clearly afraid there was nothing left for him. She smiled and patted his head. "I'm sure Harry'll say yes," she said to Margarita. "He's told me more than once he'd like to help you and your mother in whatever way he can."

奴

Ti pushed open the door of the Merchant Association Club on Saturday morning and heard Kim Yook's girls talking in the sitting room.

He hadn't been able to stop by to see Yet on Sunday, as he had promised. And when he came by Monday evening, Kim Yook said Yet was with a customer, and that there were already three men waiting for her. She was doing much better, Kim Yook told him. Then she reassured him with the observation, "Head wounds always look worse than they really are."

Finally, she said Yet would be waiting for him on Saturday, at their regular time.

Ti believed Kim Yook—because he wanted to—and because he needed the extra time to think of a plan to get Yet out. He thought the two of them could surprise and overpower Kim Yook when she came to unlock Yet's crib. He hoped he could get some Mission people to wait in the alley outside the brothel door, then he and Yet would yell to them. When the Mission people heard them they would come in and help. There were still some details he hadn't yet gotten straight. For example, he was worried Ming and the other girls might try and help the keeper, and that would cause more trouble. And he didn't know what to do about the watchmen. So Ti waited until his regular day—and his regular time, to tell Yet.

The girls' voices were barely audible, and the ghost screen leaned at a peculiar angle. It was cracked badly on the right side. Someone had tried to fix it, but had done a clumsy job.

Joss sticks were burning, and the room was thick with the pungent odor of sandalwood and cinnamon.

"What happened to the screen?" Ming and Moy, and the other two girls were sitting at the table, but didn't look up. Ti spoke louder. "You shouldn't leave the ghost screen like that. It should be repaired. You've had enough trouble this week. You don't want to encourage ghosts."

"Let them come." Ming's voice was husky and deep, and sounded as though she hadn't slept in days. She didn't raise her head. "We don't care. And if you're looking for Yet, she's gone. That's why the screen's broken. She did it."

Ti felt unsteady, like he was standing in Jew Ho's empty produce wagon while it was moving. He searched for somewhere to sit. "Where is she?"

"Yue Tschi sold her the other day. The new owners came yesterday and took her," Ming said.

Ti tried to form a prayer to the stove god grinning from its perch above the pot-bellied stove, but no words came. He found a stool and pulled it to the table. Finally Ming raised her head and looked at him. The other three girls sat with their shoulders slumped forward. Their hands hidden, their heads down. "What house has her?"

"We don't know," Ming said. "*Kwai po* thinks maybe she's on her way to some other city with lots of Chinese. Maybe that cold place where the Americans found gold."

Ming's eyes narrowed and her jaw worked as though she had a mouthful of food. But there were no bowls on the table. "Yue Tschi was really angry when he came. But Yet didn't care. She fought like a tiger. She knocked over *kwai po*'s ancestral altar and broke the ghost screen when they dragged her out. But it was no use. The men took her anyway. They didn't care how badly she was beaten. Then Yue Tschi hit *kwai po*, too. He said since she couldn't protect his merchandise he would have to take it to someone who knew its worth."

Ti heard the word 'merchandise' and felt his hands turn into fists. The girl had a name. She wasn't a thing to be bought and sold like vegetables in a market.

"Yue Tschi brought the new girl in a little while ago, but she's not broken in yet."

Ti pulled his stool closer to the table. His hands were tight balls. His nails cut into his palms. He thrust his hands into his coat pockets. "What's her name?"

"Lin."

"No, I mean Yet. What's Yet's last name—her ancestral name—clan name. She never told me—and I never got a chance to ask."

Ming stared at him, her mouth open. But no words came out.

"We don't know—Tam, I think." It was Moy mumbling. But one of the other girls shook her head. "No, no, I think it was Kam—I'm sure she told me once. I think Kam."

How would he find her now? No one could even tell him her name. He would have to take his chances with the keeper, and somehow get it from her.

"Where's Kim Yook?"

"Upstairs with the new girl." It was Ming again.

"Where's Chun?"

"Next door at Sing's place. She hasn't been sleeping well since all the screaming. *Kwai po* sends her over there at night."

Ti heard Kim Yook's shuffling on the stairs. The bamboo curtain began to rustle.

The new girl pushed aside the bamboo, and Kim Yook limped in behind her, cursing and holding the girl's sleeve. Kim Yook's left eye was purple and swollen shut. She squinted into the room.

"Mr. Leong, it's good to see you." She shoved the girl further into the room. "I thought maybe you heard Yet was gone and decided not to come back. This is Lin. I think you might want to try her. She's a virgin."

The girl was thinner and shorter than Yet, but Ti couldn't tell how old she was. Her thick black hair was coiled tightly and pinned over her right ear. The girl's face was pointed at the floor and she shook like a mountain ash in a winter storm. Ti thought of Yet and wondered if she had a new *kwai po* who was doing this same thing to her.

"You can have her for a reduced price." Kim Yook grinned at Ti through her swollen lips. "Some customers will pay extra for one like her. Especially Japanese. But I can't wait for one of them. So you can try her. You'll need a new girl now, and you can train this one to do whatever you like."

There was a long silence in the room. A dog barked in the alley. Like Ti, the four girls stared at Kim Yook's purple eye and at the new girl shaking in front of the bamboo curtain. Finally Ming whispered, "I remember the first time. That's the worst part. Everybody remembers the first time. After that, it's all the same. But the first time, you never forget."

"Don't listen to her." Kim Yook waved at Ming to be quiet. "If you were as ugly as she is, customers would treat you badly, too. But you're young and beautiful, and customers will want to keep you that way. Isn't that right, Mr. Leong? Like the way you kept Yet? Even buying her expensive presents? You'll treat this one the same way, right, Mr. Leong?"

奴

After Mr. Leong left and Kim Yook had taken the new girl back upstairs, Ming motioned to the girls to move in closer. They leaned forward at the table, their heads nearly touching. "Something happened last week at the Army place where I take Chun," she whispered. "I didn't want to tell anyone, but I'm going to tell you now, after all the bad things this week.

"The Jesus people had a big tree there. I haven't seen a tree in a long time, and it was different from any one I've seen around here. But I knew immediately what it was from the smell." Ming peeked over her shoulder at the bamboo curtain, then bent forward toward the girls again. "The tree was beautiful. It had all kinds of bright glass things like fruit hanging on it. And there were packages and food under it. Chun had never seen a tree and wanted to touch it, but the Jesus man was guarding it. I saw a small branch lying on floor, and when he wasn't looking, I picked it up. I thought if I brought that piece home, it might bring good luck to Yet." Ming reached into her smock pocket and pulled out a small pine sprig and laid it on the table. The three girls gasped and reached out to touch the needles, but Ming pulled it back. "I gave the biggest piece to Yet, and this is all I have left." Ming paused, and closed her fist around the green thing. "But I'm thinking now maybe I should throw it away."

"Why would you want to do that?" Moy's eyes got small and thin. "You were meant to find it. You can't find that tree anywhere around here, and if you keep it, maybe Yet will live long, and Mr. Leong will stay loyal to her and find her again."

"That's what I thought too. That's why I took it." Ming leaned forward again, her voice growing taut. "The Jesus man told a story once about an ancient tree long ago that had a precious fruit on it, and the first man and woman ate it. But because the Jesus god wanted to protect his most precious thing he put fiery demons around the tree so no one could get at it.

"I thought maybe if I brought some of the Jesus tree back here and gave it to Yet, it would keep her safe. Since Yet was beautiful and useful like that tree, maybe the Jesus god would put his demons around her and protect her too. But now I think I was enchanted by the tree, because I forgot something else the Jesus man said. He said the tree was beautiful now, but later it would turn into something evil. It would turn into a tree of death. The one Jesus would hang on. I think I've done that to Yet. The good luck charm I brought to protect her has become something terrible. This tree has brought bad luck to all of us."

"I don't know." Moy shook her head. "The tree you have there has always been a good luck charm for Chinese people. Maybe it only changes into evil for Americans." The other girls nodded in agreement.

There was a loud snort behind Ming, and the girls sat up straight. Ming was so engrossed in her story she hadn't heard the keeper enter the room. The girls looked at one another, then at the thing in Ming's hand. Ming's body grew cold, and she closed her hand over the piece of the tree, slowly withdrawing her hand from the table. She slipped her hand into her smock pocket.

"I told you not to believe those stories. They only get you in trouble." The keeper put her hand on Ming's shoulder and dug in her nails. "The only Jesus story I heard and thought might be partly true is the one about a girl who never had a man, but had a baby anyway. In that story, a god comes down to earth and climbs inside a virgin and gets born as Jesus." Ming remained perfectly still, her eyes flitting from girl to girl. The keeper's grip relaxed. But the pain, like sharp little needles, sunk deeper beneath Ming's skin.

"When I heard that, I said to myself, 'It sounds like how I get my girls.' Like how I got Chun—and now Lin. No man grunting over me. Everyone comes downstairs, and poof, there's a new sister. That's what you have now. Another Jeezachrise-magic sister."

The girls laughed nervously.

"Now give me that charm, Ugly One." The keeper's nails clawed into Ming's shoulder again, and the other hand thrust into Ming's pocket. Ming cowered and gasped, waiting for the hard slap across her face. But it didn't come. Instead, the keeper took the pine sprig and broke it into tiny pieces. She dropped them onto the table in front of the girls' widening eyes, then scooped them up and limped to the door. When she returned to the table her hand was empty. Ming and the girls sat with their mouths half open, staring at their keeper. She wiped her hand on her smock and rapped her knuckles on the table. "I think you're finished taking Chun to the Jesus place on Saturdays," she said to Ming. And then she hit her.

奴

Ti entered Yet's room and took a deep breath. Although the new girl stood in front of him, naked, he couldn't look at her. He could still smell Yet in the room—her oils, her herbs, her body. He glanced up at Yet's shelf. Then he remembered the vase was in pieces on the floor the last time. He looked down at the steamer trunk. But it was smaller than Yet's, and the canvas covering its wooden frame was faded and worn. Ti wondered if Kim Yook had emptied Yet's trunk and kept the cheongsam for herself. Finally he turned toward the new girl standing beside Yet's cot. The girl stared at the floor, shaking; her hands covering herself in shame.

"Do what you're going to do." The girl whispered, her lips barely moving.

"I just want to know how old you are."

"Sixteen." The girl still wouldn't meet his eyes.

"No you're not. Tell me the truth. I won't hurt you or tell anyone."

"That woman said I have to be sixteen, or bad men will come and beat me and take me away." Ti had to strain to hear her words.

"You can tell me." Ti still made no move toward her.

After a long pause, the girl replied. "I'm not sixteen. A lot younger. Now do what you're going to do."

"I'm not going to do anything."

Ti didn't mean for it to come out that way. What he meant to say was he wouldn't hurt her—but the other way was also true. What could he do? He had been in many brothels before, and he had had girls like this one before—always, without thinking about it—about them. Only about what his body wanted. He knew Yet—that she was a fighter—but he didn't know this girl. And he wasn't prepared for her.

Who would he tell? Today was already too late. This girl would be used by someone tonight—by many men tonight, all without thinking. And tomorrow the same—and the next day. He was one person against how many? He didn't know. There was the girl's owner—and others who were probably partners in the cost of her body and labor—a tong perhaps. Then there were the watchmen and the American policemen in the street. Beyond that he had no idea. But he knew there were still others. The members of the Chinese *Society for English Education* sometimes talked about the Americans who owned the buildings in Chinatown, and about the mayor's relatives who pretended the buildings were used for lawful things. Who was Ti against all this? He was nothing. There was only one person he wanted, and he had failed to save her before he even had a plan.

Ti stepped toward the girl. "Do you want to be here?" Again, it was a stupid thing to say. He knew the answer before he asked.

"No." The girl gulped the word. She forgot her shame and rubbed her fists in her eyes.

"You're going to have customers here in a few hours. I can't do anything about that tonight, but I know some people who can help you. You'll have to be brave and patient." He knew he was giving the girl false hope. But even false hope was better than no hope. And he had seen the despair in Yet's eyes when he told her what the Americans thought—that if you were sixteen, you were here because you wanted to be. And he knew Yet had been thinking about all the years she might have run away if someone had given her hope.

"I know what the men are going to do. I heard it downstairs. And that woman told me." The girl's voice was barely a whisper, and Ti had to lean forward to catch each word.

"I won't be the first one." But then the thought came to him that perhaps he should be the first. It wasn't because he wanted her. He didn't. But because he knew he could be gentle and because he understood the girl's pain and because he could tell the girl what men liked, and it might save her from more pain later. But all this was a fleeting thought—gone almost as quickly as it came. Instead, Ti said, "Your keeper will want to know how much I paid for you, so here's a dollar and twenty-five cents. Tell her the extra quarter is because you're a virgin.

"Now, put your clothes on. I'll shake the bed for a few minutes, and then you can call the keeper. If she asks how it was, say 'He didn't hurt much. He was gentle.'"

Ti wanted to ask the girl about her family, how she got here, and that he knew people who could help her. But he said nothing. He kept coming back to the fact that he was in Yet's room, and that Yet had once been like this girl, and now she was gone.

Ti sat on Yet's cot, closed his eyes, and rocked back and forth. He could smell Yet's skin—her hair—as if she was still present in the room. He stopped and opened his eyes. Next to the leg of the cot was a fragment of the porcelain ginger jar that had been on Yet's shelf. He leaned down and picked it up. He turned it in his hand.

On the fragment was part of a tree branch, a few leaves, and part of a girl's face with one half-closed eye. This is what Yet always stared at, he thought. His heart lifted imperceptibly, like the slightest rustling of mulberry leaves at sunset in the Celestial Kingdom. And Ti thought that if he kept the fragment, he would have Yet's eyes on him—wherever he was. And whenever he looked at the fragment, his eyes would be on her—wherever she was. Without thinking anymore about it he dropped the broken thing in his pocket.

奴

Kim Yook limped down the hall, cursing Yue Tschi with each step. Ti followed the keeper, still not quite believing a new girl was in Yet's room.

"How was she?" The old woman grimaced and paused at the top of the stairs, breathing heavily.

"She was fine."

Kim Yook turned to let him pass, and in the dingy darkness her blackened eye clung to him. Ti stumbled past the evil eye and smelled the stale tobacco. Her dried sweat, her flatulence. Her contempt. As the old woman started back toward Yet's room, Ti vowed he would never hear her sounds again: Her step, rest. Her curse. The step. The rest. The curse. The unlocking and shrill scraping of Yet's door.

Ti heard the girls talking in the kitchen when he reached the bottom of the stairs. But he didn't want to see anyone. He gathered his belongings quietly and left.

Ti stood outside the door of the Merchant Association Club for a long time, his coat and hat in hand. He kicked at the old stray dog lying in the shadows, but it sensed his mood and moved out of harm's way. He walked toward Washington Street as though he was a ghost, looking back at himself. He knew he should be going to work, but he felt lost. Without thinking, he headed toward the Mission. It was raining again, and he put on his coat, turning up its collar and pulling his hat over his queue. He would tell the people there about the girl, about Chun, and tell them they had to do something quickly.

He felt his spirit enter again into his body. But there was still an empty space inside him, one that hadn't been there in a long time. It was like the hunger he remembered from childhood, standing with an outstretched bowl, waiting for the first rice harvest after a long cold spring of starving.

奴

"Not many men are as nice as Mr. Leong." Ming carried a large serving bowl of hot jook from the kitchen to the table. She was talking to Moy who was right behind her, bringing the teacups and soup bowls. Ming peeked at the pegs on the opposite wall. Mr. Leong's hat and coat were missing. "I wonder if he'll be back now that Yet's gone."

Chun followed the two girls, carrying a handful of spoons to the table. She was barefoot, and her oversized shirt hung almost to her ankles. Her hair, crusted over and tangled, hadn't been washed since before Army Saturday School. "Uncle Ti nice to me. He give me candy." Chun set the ceramic spoons down hard on the table, and Moy and Ming frowned at her.

"Uncle Ti gives you candy?" Ming spooned jook into the girls' bowls too quickly, and rice gruel spilled on the table. "Like Old Mary does?"

"Mama going to hit," Chun whispered, staring at the puddle. Her lower lip began to quiver. "Mama going to hit now." She sat down and began to wail.

Ming flinched and used the sleeve of her smock to wipe the table. "Shh, Chun. Mama's far away. She can't hear us. So Uncle Ti gives you candy?"

"Yes. Like Old Mary. And Mr. Fong too. When I be nice."

Ming stiffened. "When you're nice?"

"Yes. I be nice and do things. For Mama. I clean table and peepee pot with Mrs. Sing. And I do nice things for Mr. Fong."

"What kind of nice things do you do for Mr. Fong?" Ming set down her teacup and searched Chun's face. "What kind of nice things?"

奴

"Just as I suspected." Kim Yook poked her head through the bamboo curtain at the bottom of the stairs, and sneered. "Mr. Leong didn't do a thing to that girl. She lied and told me he did, but I checked her and there wasn't any blood." Kim Yook waved her fingers at the workers around the table, but not one lifted their head. All four were cowering, hunched over their bowls. Only the worthless baby looked up.

"No hit, Mama. No hit."

Ming held the child tightly on her lap and clamped her hand over the girl's mouth. "Hush, Chun."

"I'll have to make sure there are extra watchmen in the alley to protect the house. Jeezachrise! I don't have time for this. And we'll need someone to paint a different number on our sign. That'll confuse the stupid white devils for a while."

As soon as she said these things, Kim Yook realized no precautions would be enough to keep Lin in her place. Mr. Leong knew the girl was young, and he would try and get the girl out as payback for what happened to Yet. Kim Yook shook her head. Her black eye ached, and a knot began to grow below her belly. She couldn't let it get too large, or it would show in her voice, and the girls would know she was afraid of something. She paused for a moment and gathered her anger in one place, pushing down the knot of fear.

"I'll have to tell that Jeezachrise wharsahorbitch Yue Tschi to move Lin somewhere else. Lin's not safe here after what Mr. Leong did. And Yue Tschi will make me pay her moving costs from your wages." Kim Yook curled her fingers into a fist and shook it in the girls' direction. "I'm glad I told Yue Tschi about Mr. Leong. I knew that customer was growing fond of Yet. Ones like him only bring more trouble to a house after their favorite's beaten."

Kim Yook let the rattling bamboo curtain fall back into place. The girls weren't looking at her anyway. "Let that customer be a lesson to you all. Never—under any circumstances—trust what a customer says. Do you hear me? Never."

And without waiting for their responses, she turned and limped into the kitchen. Her stomach was growling, and she needed to put something in it before she opened for business.

Chapter Five

RAT
(1900)

Kim Yook sat in the doorway of the Merchant Association Club in month two of the Year of the Rat—March 1900 by American counting—staring across the alleyway at one of the strangest things she had seen in all her years of living in Gold Mountain. Business had slowed over the past year, and in the last month she had begun sitting out front, soliciting. Occasionally she enticed a potential customer inside for a free look at Pon—the newest girl to replace Yet. But Pon was no Yet, and business had suffered since Yue Tschi took the brothel's best girl. Repairing the damaged ancestral altar and ghost screen hadn't helped either. And so Kim Yook would drag out a stool and sit under the badly faded sign that advertised her business. She didn't even have enough money to hire someone to repaint it.

The old dog Kim Yook spat at every morning when she unlocked the brothel door had finally died. And that's what the commotion was about. The dog barely moved when she opened the door yesterday, and there had been a dullness in its eyes. She thought maybe someone had beaten it. But when she spat at it this morning and it didn't move, she knew it had died in the night.

Kim Yook had been trying all morning to find someone to remove it. The corpse would be stinking soon, and she didn't need more bad luck at her end of the alley. Finally someone at Sing's place promised to do something. But what Kim Yook hadn't expected to see in the alleyway was a white woman and a white man dressed like the American army. Kim Yook recognized the woman as the American doctor who worked in Chinatown. Now the doctor and the bald-headed army man hovered over the dead dog like it was a victim of a Hop Sing tong feud. The Americans had notebooks and pencils in their hands, and there was a burlap bag on the ground beside them. They talked excitedly. Kim Yook watched warily as the doctor walked toward her. The doctor smiled and said something that sounded like it was supposed to be Chinese. But it wasn't.

"The dog died last night, I think." Kim Yook made a guess at the doctor's gibberish. Then she added, "It didn't belong to anybody. So take it away before it brings bad luck."

The doctor seemed confused, and said, "Ah Quai." Then she said an American word. "Old Mary?" She lifted her hands over her head, making the shape of something Kim Yook guessed was a Jesus woman's big bonnet. Then the doctor added the American word, "Jesus."

Kim Yook supposed the doctor thought the dog belonged to the Jesus woman, so she pointed down the alley to where the Jesus woman lived, repeating the name "Ah Quai" and "Jesus." Once more Kim Yook told the doctor the dog was a stray, and no one was to blame for its death. The doctor finally stopped pestering her and went off in the direction Kim Yook pointed.

鼠

"Those crazy Americans out in the alley yesterday said they'll pay a dollar for every dead rat we find," Kim Yook told her girls the next morning at breakfast. "They say don't touch them or move them. To call the Jesus woman, and she'll get the American doctor to come get them. Jeezachrise. Just when I think I'm beginning to understand white people, they do something so stupid I feel like Moy with her first customer. Maybe you girls would have an easier time collecting rats instead of customers. Especially you, Ming." Kim Yook glared across the table at the ugly one, wondering how much longer Ming's owner would keep her at the brothel. She hadn't brought in enough money in the past two weeks to pay for the rice in her bowl. "You could start right now by crawling under the table and killing Chun's rat. That might at least pay for a meal or two."

"No Ming. Don't hurt my rat." Chun crouched and peered under the table.

"Hush, Chun," Ming whispered. She poked the child. "Eat your jook."

Kim Yook laughed at her joke and scanned the faces of her five girls, hoping to find some evidence they had grasped her meaning. She had been talking like this for months to make them work harder. But as usual, they sat there looking stupid. Their eyes were focused on their bowls, and they said nothing.

Two days later Kim Yook knew why the American doctors were so interested in dead animals. A Chinese lumber salesman in the Globe Hotel on Dupont Street had died from a disease that looked suspiciously like *yi*—the plague. The Americans circled Chinatown in the middle of the night, roped it off, and posted policemen all along its perimeter. No Chinese person could cross the line for any reason. They would be beaten if they did. The morning after that, the Americans set smoking sulfur pots all through the Globe Hotel. They threw the dead man's belongings out into the street and then set them on fire. A giant stinking prayer pyre to appease angry demons.

鼠

Muriel was working the Chinatown beat for *The Examiner* when she received the tip about the Chinaman's corpse. She had spent a lot of time developing her contacts during the ten months she had been with the paper, and it was beginning to pay off. But if it hadn't been for a cocktail party celebrating Harry's appointment to a prestigious San Francisco law firm—where she happened to meet an *Examiner* editor—she would still be at *The Call*, writing about boxing matches, baseball scores, and horse races.

Muriel put a call through immediately to Dr. Kinyoun at the Angel Island quarantine station asking for an interview. He said he was expecting a steamer the next day, and if she could get onboard, he would be pleased to meet her at Hospital Cove where she could watch his plague tests.

鼠 Rat (1900) 鼠

The following morning Muriel stood on Angel Island's badly weathered wharf, staring up the hill at a poorly whitewashed house and a dilapidated clapboard building Dr. Kinyoun had described as his laboratory. She had been the only passenger on the steamer, and the captain said if she weren't back on the dock by two-thirty, she'd be staying on the island the rest of the week. "We don't have much reason to stop here except to drop off supplies and pick up mail," he warned.

The box-shaped cove was sheltered from the prevailing wind by high hills on the west, and the only sound was the outgoing tide, washing against the pebbled beach. Muriel took off her jacket and draped it over her satchel. Since Dr. Kinyoun wasn't there to escort her to his laboratory, she decided to walk up the hill alone.

鼠

Muriel perched on a tall metal stool in the cluttered laboratory next to the doctor's windowed office, staring at two foreboding syringes. They lay on white cloth, on a tabletop in front of a small menagerie of animals in terrariums and cages stacked two and three high—frogs, rats, hamsters, guinea pigs, rabbits, and monkeys. The morning was unseasonably warm, and thankfully, the windows were open. But the lab still reeked of slightly moldy oranges, formaldehyde, and animal feces. Muriel couldn't imagine the laboratory stench on a more typical dreary March day, with the windows shut.

Dr. Kinyoun told her one syringe held bacteria from a Spofford Alley dog, and the other held bacteria from the Globe Hotel Chinaman. The bespectacled doctor picked up a glass slide and slid it under the metal clamps on a microscope. He motioned for Muriel to step toward the lens. "You see the rose-tinted rod-like things?" When she nodded, he continued, "That's the plague bacillus. If you know what you're looking for, it's easy to identify.

"Now, you may not want to watch this next step. I'm going to inject two rats, two hamsters, and two monkeys with the bacteria—one set of animals with the dog bacteria, and one set with the Chinaman's bacteria. So if you think you might be squeamish, you can step outside. I'll come get you when I'm done."

Muriel was grateful for his warning, and left him alone with his test animals. She walked part way up the hill toward the house to get her bearings, but since the lab windows were open, she knew precisely when he injected the monkeys. The pastoral setting was punctured by their yowls and screams, and they were still scolding the doctor when Muriel went back inside.

Dr. Kinyoun seemed oblivious to the monkeys' shrill chattering. He spun his chair around to face her in the drafty laboratory and shouted above the angrily screeching animals. "Now that that's over, we have nothing to do but wait. I'll call *The Examiner* office and leave you a message as soon as I know anything. I told Lizzie—my wife—we'd have a guest for lunch." He stood; apparently ready to escort her up the hill to the house. But Muriel sat down on a stool opposite him and took a notepad and pencil from her satchel.

"Perhaps you have time to answer a few questions before lunch?"

"Sure." Dr. Kinyoun leaned his elbows on the rust-stained table and adjusted his eyeglasses on his nose. "But I'll warn you. The city politicians and newspaper editors don't think much of my plague theories."

"I know." Muriel smiled, thinking of her own editor's eye-rolling when she told him where she was going. "But I'm much more interested in what you think than in city politics and economics. The people in Chinatown won't take this man's death lightly. We may not know his name, but he was a human being as much as we are—despite what some of the other papers might think. So, what exactly do you think he died of?"

Dr. Kinyoun opened a lab table drawer and pulled out a small humidor and silver cigar cutter. After inspecting each cigar, he chose a Dick Custer. He sliced off an end, lit it, and began puffing; rotating it deftly between his fingers and thumb.

Dr. Kinyoun took the cigar from his mouth, examined it, then turned to face Muriel. "I'm pretty sure the Chinaman died of the plague." He paused, puffed a few more times, and looked beyond her, out the window. "The dog, I'm not so sure. There seem to be plague-like bacteria in the vial Dr. Kellogg and Dr. Worley got from it, but I doubt that's what killed it. Dr. Worley said dogs rarely die of the plague, and she's right. But if the Chinaman died of it, I'm going to recommend Chinatown remain under quarantine until the Orientals have the Haffkine vaccination."

The monkeys' high-pitched yipping didn't subside, and Muriel found it difficult to concentrate. She held up her hand to stop Dr. Kinyoun before he went further. "From what little I know of the Chinese philosophy of medicine, they're not going to accept your vaccination plan. If you could convince them you extracted the serum from a chrysanthemum flower, their response might be different. But taking fluid from a corpse isn't their idea of medicine. That's more like witchcraft. Everyone in Chinatown knows about the Honolulu fire. They'll think the vaccination's a white man's trick to kill them all instead of burning down their quarter."

Dr. Kinyoun turned away from Muriel and took two old army blankets from the stack on the table, then draped them over the monkeys' cages. Surprisingly, the monkeys quieted almost immediately. "I can have ten thousand doses of the vaccine here in a few days." Dr. Kinyoun turned toward Muriel again. "And what happened in Honolulu could never happen here. The entire city would go up in smoke if the mayor tried to burn any infested buildings in Chinatown. The hills and shifting winds would make it impossible to control the flames. Besides, there's no need to destroy anything if we can convince the Orientals to get the vaccine." The doctor arched his eyebrows and tapped his cigar on the edge of a petri dish, already half-full of ashes. "Maybe you could help."

"Me? How?"

"By working with the Mission people. If the missionaries got vaccinated, then maybe the rest of Chinatown would too, and I could lift the quarantine before it does any economic damage—which is the only concern the city politicians have."

Muriel closed her notepad. "What if you gave me the vaccination before I leave this afternoon, and then I write about the experience for the paper? If I can get Ng Poon Chew to translate my article for his new Chinese newspaper, it might work. If anyone could convince the Chinese to take the vaccine, it would be him."

鼠

Muriel waited until after supper to tell Harry the day's events. She lay on the overstuffed sofa in the parlor of their two-bedroom bungalow; her notepad and pencil nearby on the corner table. From her position she could see through the little dining room to the kitchen where Harry washed the dishes.

"You did what?" Harry's neck muscles bulged. He slammed a plate into the drying rack and turned to face her, dripping dishrag in hand, water stains on his white starched work shirt and black suit pants.

"Harry, please be careful—you'll break a plate. And look at your clothes."

"Good God, Muriel, you're worried about plates and pants, but not your own health. You've become another one of Kinyoun's guinea pigs. I can't believe you had that vaccine without talking to me."

"It's really quite safe." Muriel propped herself on an elbow. "Dr. Kinyoun himself has had the vaccination—and more than once. And despite what the papers are saying, I'm convinced Joe's right. The Chinaman died of the plague. So someone's got to convince the Chinese they need the vaccine."

Harry turned back to the sink and began to scrub furiously. His back was taut, and Muriel could tell by his tone he was speaking through clenched teeth. "I thought we had agreed—actually you told me—we were going to make all serious decisions together. We would discuss them and sleep on them, then decide—together." He turned to face Muriel again, wadding the dishrag in his fist and shaking it. His cheeks splotchy red. "Now here's a life-and-death decision—one you made on your own—all for a spectacular spread in *The Examiner*. You're always complaining about sensationalism in the papers. And now you're acting exactly the same way. And without a thought to your health, or me. Damn you, Muriel."

"Jesus, Harry. Dr. Kinyoun gave me the vaccination hours ago. It was a pinprick. My arm feels tingly, that's all. Which reminds me, I'm supposed to be taking notes on this." Muriel sat up and reached half-heartedly for the pencil on the corner table. The motion of sitting made her dizzy, so she set the pencil down and rested her head on the back of the sofa. Her eyes were half-closed, but she could see Harry as he went back to work on a pot soaking in the sink.

"A lawyer married to a newspaper reporter." Harry lifted his head toward the kitchen window. "If we survive five years together, we'll be lucky. What am I saying? If you survive the night—" Harry dried his hands on the dishtowel, draped it over his shoulder, then came to sit beside her.

"You can be so impulsive sometimes." He put his arm around Muriel's waist and drew her close. "Take it from a lawyer. Impulsiveness isn't a virtue in the courtroom—or in life. If I were a Methodist I'd call Maggie and have you put on a prayer watch."

"You're giving me a headache." Muriel pushed his arm away and stood gingerly. "I think I'll go to bed."

Harry followed her to the bedroom. "Do you want me to call a doctor?"

"No, I'm fine. Just dizzy. It's been a long day. Ferry rides, a university science lecture, my first vaccine, and a courtroom debate. It's all a bit much."

She let down her hair and put the hairpins in the dish on the bureau. She unbuttoned her dress, took off her petticoats, and dropped them on the floor. "Can you help me with my corset?"

Harry nuzzled the nape of her neck and moved his hands up from her waist, toward her breasts.

"Harry, not tonight. Really, I don't feel well. I'm sure it's just the long day, but I have to take notes—and not even *The Examiner* would print a story of what you're thinking of doing."

Harry sighed and moved away. "All right. Can I do something else? Maybe get you some water?"

"That would be nice." Muriel sat on the edge of the bed, elbows on knees; hair spilling between her legs. Pain shot up her arm from the point of the injection, across her breast, and up her neck to her head. She was having difficulty breathing. When Harry came back she lay spread-eagled on the bed.

"I brought you some *Pinkham's* instead."

Muriel closed her eyes. "I don't think *Pinkham's* will help. Can you unlace my shoes? I think my feet are swollen. They hurt."

"Honey, you look feverish." Harry touched her forehead with the back of his hand. "Christ, Muriel. What the hell have you done? I'm calling the doctor."

"These are all symptoms Dr. Kinyoun said I'd have." She started panting shallowly to control the pain racking her upper body.

"Harry, my shoes. Please." Muriel's shoulder muscles constricted into hardened balls. Her ears were ringing, and the thought of turning over made her squeamish.

"Will you lie here with me?"

鼠

Muriel awoke in the morning, feeling as though her body was once more her own. She poked at the needle prick in her arm. Only a small pink bump remained. She turned over and nudged her husband.

Harry yawned and stretched. "How are you feeling, honey? You certainly look better."

"Fine, actually—which is exactly how Dr. Kinyoun said I would feel. But you never can be too sure. Maybe I died in the night and went to heaven." Muriel rubbed her toes against her husband's leg. "You might be in bed with some sort of angelic creature." She smiled and loosened the drawstrings on her chemise.

鼠

Muriel sat at the table, her chemise still untied, madly scribbling her memories from the night before. She glanced at Harry who stood at the kitchen stove in his undershorts and undershirt, turning pieces of bacon in the frying pan. "I wish I hadn't fallen asleep so quickly last night. *Pinkham's* tastes like it's half alcohol. Maybe that's what makes it work. But now I don't know when the pain in my chest and neck started to subside."

"Maybe you should have Dr. Kinyoun give you another vaccination today so you can keep better notes this time." Harry smirked as he set the hot bacon on the front page of the Saturday *Examiner*. "This, in my estimation, is what newspapers do best. Sop up bacon grease."

"You could have at least put the bacon on the part I already read." Muriel scowled and shoved the greasy paper to the other side of the table, nearly knocking it on the floor. "And I haven't heard you complain about the money I bring home each week. If it weren't for newsprint, you wouldn't be eating bacon at all."

鼠

The Chinatown quarantine remained in effect for the next few days. Since no Chinaman could cross the rope barricade to a job in a white neighborhood, the Chinatown gambling houses and brothels were bursting with business.

"As far as I'm concerned, this nuisance can last awhile," Kim Yook said to the men waiting impatiently for the next girl. "I've had more customers these past two days than all last month."

A scraggly-whiskered man and a schoolboy, whose hair was cut short in the American way, poked their heads around the ghost screen. The man pushed the boy into the room and then disappeared. "Nothing wrong with introducing a young man to the finer things of life." Kim Yook sniggered as the boy stumbled toward the customers. "But if any Jeezachrise people saw you come in, I could be in trouble."

Kim Yook circled the boy slowly, putting on a show for her customers by inspecting him from head to toe. She poked at the breast pocket of his rumpled shirt and pulled lewdly on the drawstring of his pantaloons, pretending to peer down the front. "All my girls are busy right now, but tell me what you want. I think I have one about your size."

The boy twisted his fingers around the long braid on his black silk skullcap. "I'm looking for my sister." He spoke in a nervous, high-pitched voice.

"We don't allow that here at the Merchant Association Club." Kim Yook grinned wickedly. "Almost anything else—but not brothers with sisters. You have to go to a Japanese place for that." Kim Yook surveyed the room, arching her eyebrows as if she was a painted *Cai Dan* clown actor on opening night at the Red Cassia Theatre. Her customers snorted, enjoying the boy's discomfort.

"No, no, I'm not looking for that kind of girl." The boy stammered and dropped his head. "It's my real sister—she would be about five now. My mama brought her here—maybe two years ago."

"You mean the little one who runs around doing chores?" A bored customer joined in the conversation.

The lad squared his shoulders and smiled broadly.

"I don't think anyone's with her right now," the man teased. "I'm getting desperate, and I was thinking about taking her for myself." He laughed uproariously. "She's got a pretty face if you can ever see it. But she spends most of her time under that table when she's not working. Take a look—she's probably there now."

"That's my daughter you're talking about." Kim Yook shook her finger in the man's face. "And I keep her there so twisted men like you can't touch her. You'll have to wait eight years for a chance with her."

In the middle of Kim Yook's lecture, Chun pushed her way through the bamboo curtain and set a basket of dirty rags beside the keeper.

"By then your skinny little stick will probably have fallen off and you'll be senile. But I'm willing to start a waiting list, if you're really interested. You can put down a dollar to hold a spot."

Chun scooted under the table as the other men in the room broke into raucous guffaws.

The boy stood helplessly in the middle of the room, his eyes darting from customer to customer. "We're from Fresno—my father and me. We're here on business. But we can't leave because of the American doctor's rules. And my mother wanted me to check on my sister—to see if she—to see how she was."

"Chun, you dropped something." Kim Yook pointed toward the coal bucket near the stove. The girl darted from under the table to pick up the rag. "You mean that girl?" Kim Yook jeered.

"Chun! Do you remember me?" In two quick steps the boy was beside her. He knelt and tried to give her a hug. "You're so big! I'm your brother, Seu Ho."

Fear flashed in Chun's eyes. She screamed and kicked at the boy, trying to break his embrace. "No! Just big girls do that."

"That's exactly what I taught my daughter to do to strangers." Kim Yook glared at the boy. "Now stop pestering her." She grabbed Chun by the shoulders and pulled her away.

"But she's my sister." The boy pleaded and clung to Chun's sleeve. "I used to hold you at night when you were afraid. When people shot off firecrackers in the street. Don't you remember?"

"Leave me alone!" Chun tried to kick him between his legs. The boy finally let go and stood, shaking his head. "I'm your brother," he whispered incredulously.

"Tell your mother the girl is fine." With one hand Kim Yook shoved the quaking Chun toward the bamboo curtain, and with the other she dug her fingernails into the boy's shoulder and steered him toward the ghost screen. "Now you'd better leave before a policeman sees you. They're swarming like fleas in a dog's ear. I don't want to have to pay because you're underage."

鼠

On Wednesday, Dr. Kinyoun left a message for Muriel at *The Examiner* telling her the animals injected with the Chinaman's bacteria were either sick or dead. And all of them had dark, swollen lymph glands—telltale signs of the plague.

For San Francisco's business community, the specter of a lengthy quarantine was a disaster in the making. Despite Dr. Kinyoun's scientific results and Muriel's personal account in *The Examiner* about the effects of the Haffkine vaccine, the city fathers were not convinced that they faced a potentially serious health problem—especially with the state's economy at risk. Although the Chinatown newspaperman, Ng Poon Chew, had the vaccine and persuaded fifty other Chinamen to have it, only about two hundred Americans were vaccinated—and most of those were people connected to the Christian missions in Chinatown. Since there were no more publicized Chinatown deaths, people went about their affairs as if nothing had happened.

Muriel was still convinced Dr. Kinyoun's analysis was correct: The bubonic plague was a real threat to San Francisco. But by late May, even Muriel's editor had lost patience with her pigheadedness. He called her into his office for a chat. "Look, I've given you a lot of leeway on this plague issue," he told her. "But you have one more week. Then you've got to move on. We're the only paper in the city still covering it, and I need your expertise elsewhere. You just have to learn when to give up on a thing."

鼠

"Mama, come here!" Chun's anxious voice broke through the early morning silence on the second floor of the Merchant Association Club.

Ming stood in the doorway of her room, sleepy-eyed, a full chamber pot in hand. She frowned and peered downstairs. "Chun, I have something for you. And why do you always have to yell in the morning? What's so important you have to wake the entire house?"

"It's my rat. He's not moving."

"You woke us all to tell us that? Leave it alone. Now come up and do your chores."

"Please, Ming. I can't find Mama."

"She's up here working. What you should be doing." Ming sighed, knowing she wouldn't be able to go back to sleep. "I'll be down in a minute. Just stop yelling, or you'll wake everyone in the alley."

"See?" Chun was under the table, poking the rat with a chopstick when Ming got downstairs. "I gave him my leftover rice yesterday but he didn't stay to play. And now he won't move."

Ming put her hands on her knees and bent down. "Don't touch it."

Chun scrambled out and hugged Ming's legs. "You scared me. Did you kill my rat like Mama said?"

"You know I wouldn't do that." Ming knelt beside Chun and wiped the girl's tears with the sleeve of her blouse. "We need to talk to *kwai po*. You might have a special rat the American doctor wants to see. Maybe they'll give you money for it."

"If they give me money, I'll have to give it to the Army people. They always take my money." Chun thrust out her lower lip in a pout.

"Are you still singing with them? I told you before I don't think they're good."

Chun pulled away from Ming and crossed her arms. "You don't like anything I do.

Uncle Ti said rats are good luck. And now you killed it."

"I didn't kill your rat." Ming stood. "And you can't always tell if a thing is good or bad by the way it looks."

The girl glared at Ming. She was pale and barefoot and she wrung her hands. Her smock fell half off her shoulders. "Mama always tells me to clean under the table first. If I leave my rat there, everyone's going to yell at me and Mama will hit me."

鼠

Kim Yook remembered the crazy American doctor. That she would give a dollar for a dead rat. Which was as much as Ming got for two customers. So when Ming told Kim Yook about Chun's rat, Kim Yook sent one of Sing's girls from next door to find the American doctor. And she told the girl to bring the Jesus woman, too.

When the American doctor and the Jesus woman got there, it was late afternoon, and a customer was upstairs. Kim Yook wanted to get the American doctor out before the customer finished. Any white person in her place would start people talking and might make the police come.

"The rat's under the table," Kim Yook said to the Jesus woman. "Tell her."

The American doctor put on a pair of gloves, stooped, and peered beneath the table. She picked up the rat by its tail and dropped it into a bag. Then she plunked a silver dollar on the table. Kim Yook stood by the stove, shaking her head incredulously.

"Did anyone touch the rat?" The Jesus woman spoke for the American doctor.

"I don't know. My daughter may have. You can ask her. The rat was her pet." Kim Yook smirked and shouted for Chun.

There was a quick pitter-patter on the stairs, then Chun pushed the bamboo curtain aside. She poked her head into the room and jumped when she saw the Jesus woman. "Are we going to school today?"

"And who's this?" The American doctor spoke more gibberish to the Jesus woman, and gave Chun a big smile.

"This is Chun. The keeper's daughter." The Jesus woman answered in American gibberish. "I've been taking her to Saturday classes at our place for a few years now."

"That keeper looks too old to have a daughter this young. And the girl's obviously neglected." The American doctor turned toward Kim Yook and her eyes narrowed. She continued her rude gibberish. "You should tell Miss Lake about her." The American doctor reached into her coat and pulled out a stick of candy. "Here you are sweetheart. I'm sorry your rat died."

Chun stared at the candy, and then at the bag. "Did the white lady take my rat?"

Before the Jesus woman could answer, the American doctor started talking gibberish again. This time the Jesus woman translated for Kim Yook. "She says your daughter looks unhealthy. That you need to make sure she gets three meals a day, takes baths regularly, and gets fresh air. She says if your daughter gets sick or starts acting peculiar, to tell me. I know how to find the American doctor, and she'll come check on her."

"You tell that crazy American my daughter doesn't have time to go outside." Kim Yook waved a finger in the Jesus woman's face. "This is a hard business, and she's my only help." The creaking overhead had stopped, so Kim Yook pushed the Jesus woman toward the door. But the American doctor stood in the way. "Sometimes I let her go out walking with the Jesus people. That's the best I can do."

鼠

The next morning Kim Yook was seated at the table with a stack of receipts and a pile of coins from the night before, when one of Sing's older girls peeped shyly around the ghost screen. "Hello. My mama says Chun can't work today."

"Jeezachrise." Kim Yook slammed her fist into the table, making the pile of coins jump. "Can't you see I'm counting? Now I have to start over." She put down her brush-pen and paper, and glared at the fidgeting girl.

The girl licked her lips, stared at her bare feet, and rubbed a dark spot on her pantaloons with her foot. "Mama says when Chun woke up she was real quiet. And then Chun said she was hot, and started taking off her shirt. Mama felt her skin and looked at her eyes and says she's sick. She says maybe it's *yi*—that disease the Americans are talking about."

Kim Yook scowled, and the girl took a step backward. "Tell your mother to keep Chun over there today. But I don't care how sick she says she is. Tomorrow she has to be here at the usual time. If I have to come get her, everyone in the alley will hear her screams."

鼠

That evening Muriel was in her office, reviewing her final article on the plague when Harry called. He was at the Methodist Mission for a meeting with the Oriental Home Board. He sounded as agitated as when she had first taken the Haffkine vaccine.

"Muriel, you won't believe what's happening. After we finished our meeting, there was a commotion below us, on Washington and Stockton. We looked outside and there were at least a hundred policemen putting up fence posts and rolling barbed wire down the streets. It must be another Chinatown quarantine. You've got to get over here right away. There's a huge story here if it's really the plague."

"I don't know, honey. My editor said no more plague stories, and I don't want to make the same mistake I made at *The Call*—"

"I've already talked to Maggie, and she says she can put you up for the night on the floor in her room. You've got to see this. The police have already put a stop to Chinamen trying to leave the quarter. Only white people are getting out. I have to go. Hurry." Harry hung up the phone before Muriel had a chance to raise another protest.

By eleven o'clock Muriel and her *Examiner* escort were off the cable car and walking down Washington Street. It was a chilly, moonless night, and Muriel pulled her woolen shawl tight around her shoulders. It felt more like February than May.

The Mission House drapes were partially drawn, and the parlor gaslights lit the sidewalk where the streetlight missed. Harry's face appeared at the window, and when he saw Muriel, he opened the front door. He took her elbow. "Look over there. It's like something from the Boer War. Picket lines and men in uniform—they're only lacking cannons. I can't believe the city's doing this again. Maggie and I just talked to one of the officers. He said it's a clear case of the plague this time. A Chinese laborer died last night, and the city coroner confirmed it."

"If it's the plague, then why haven't the police cordoned off all of Stockton? Shouldn't those buildings be within the barricade?" Muriel pointed down the street, to her right. "They're in Chinatown too, aren't they?"

"Maggie's pretty sure those buildings are owned by Americans. So we're thinking the officers are only quarantining Chinese properties."

"So the city's going to tell us in the morning only Chinese buildings can be plague-infested? A building owned by white people, no more than six feet from a Chinese-owned building, is immune? You're right. This seems really crazy."

Muriel shivered and Harry pulled her close. "I guess you'll have to unravel all this tomorrow. I hope you brought a score of pencils and notebooks. You'll be using everything in your satchel this time."

"Harry, why don't you invite your wife inside, out of the cold?" Margarita appeared in the doorway behind him, rolling her eyes at Muriel. She led Muriel into the parlor. "I'll take care of your wife. But if you don't hurry, you're going to be spending the night here too. Now go home and get some sleep."

"And don't forget my clothes and things." Muriel gave Harry a quick kiss and pushed him toward the steps. "See you in the morning."

鼠

"Mama and I usually eat breakfast with the girls." Margarita led Muriel down the two flights of stairs to the Rescue Home dining area. "The fare is decidedly not American, but I've grown to like it."

The basement room was damp and cold, and thin shafts of morning light filtered through two dirty windows barely above ground. Muriel recalled her first visit to the room a year or so earlier. The feeling she had then was of entering a Midwest storm cellar. She felt no different now, and she still marveled that the uninviting space doubled as the girls' classroom.

"About the quarantine." Muriel swallowed her first tentative mouthful of fried rice with Siu and Sau grinning at her from their places at a nearby table. "I'm curious. Do you know any Chinese in the stores close to the barricade? I'd love to get their perspective on what's going on."

"There's a man who works at Jew Ho's grocery store on Stockton, right next to a white store owner, and I suspect the American store is outside the quarantine line." Margarita balanced a green leafy stalk of something on her chopsticks, then plopped it in her mouth. "The Chinese gentleman learned his English here, at Dr. Gardner's night school, and he's a member of the *Chinese Society for English Education*. He could probably help you."

"This is actually quite delicious." Muriel smiled at Siu and Sau who had finished their meal and were watching her intently. "Next time maybe I'll try chopsticks—like the rest of you."

Muriel and Margarita were on their way upstairs when the doorbell rang. "I hope that's Harry with my change of clothes," Muriel grimaced.

鼠

Muriel had no time to fret over the bizarre ensemble her husband brought. For almost as soon as she and Margarita stepped outside the Mission, a burly, blue-coated policeman confronted them. A barbed wire and log post fence ran through the middle of Stockton Street two blocks north and south of a hastily constructed gate on Washington Street. Guards were stationed along the inside of the four-block barricade at what Muriel estimated to be twenty-foot intervals. They faced in opposite directions— one toward Chinatown, apparently to keep the Chinese from trying to escape, and the next facing outward, away from Chinatown, apparently to keep curious Americans at bay.

The policeman spread his legs wide and stretched his arms, blocking the only access to Chinatown. "No one allowed beyond this point, ladies. Orders of Mayor Phelan."

"I'm a reporter for *The Examiner*." Muriel pulled a calling card from the side pocket of her satchel. "Chinatown's my beat. We don't intend to cross the line. I merely wish to interview a Chinaman about the new quarantine."

"Why would you want to do that? These Chinks ain't going to tell you anything we don't already know." The policeman brushed aside Muriel's card and stepped forward, trying to force the women back to the sidewalk on the west side of Stockton. The women didn't move.

"They don't like being fenced in, I can tell you that." The officer laughed nervously. "And they may be making trouble later at Portsmouth Square. That's the latest news. Now, why don't you ladies go back home." He waved his arm as though he were a harried father, shooing his children outside to play.

"Please." Margarita smiled up at the officer. "Just pass this card to the man in that dray." She pointed down the street, and Muriel's eyes followed Margarita's arm; her curiosity aroused. A group of black-smocked China-men stood about twenty yards away, gesturing wildly at someone lifting crates from the back of a horse-drawn wagon.

"Tell the man Miss Lake from the Mission wants to talk to him."

The policeman took Margarita's calling card, nodded, and tipped his hat. "So you're the lady who's done the rescues of Oriental slave girls from those dens? I'm pleased to make your acquaintance."

"Yes, this is she," Muriel interrupted. "And I'm the person who wrote the newspaper articles about her. Now, if you'll take her card over there to that man—"

The officer scratched his cheek and ran his tongue across his teeth, still pondering Margarita's card. "Well, I can't leave my post, and no Chinaman can cross this line." He looked down the barricade. "If you re-ally want to talk to him, maybe another guard could take him the card. But you'll have to conduct your interview over there a ways, across the barbed wire. I can't have you standing here, blocking the gate." The policeman tapped the card on Margarita's shoulder. "But I'm warning you two, if my captain comes by, he'll chase you away. We have orders not to allow folks to loiter at the barricade."

"Talking there will be fine." Muriel set her jaw and crossed her arms, clasping her satchel close to her breasts. "I've conducted interviews in stranger places."

The policeman rubbed his nose and wiped his hand on his pants. "Hey Joe! Take this card to the Chinaman in that dray. This woman claims she's a newspaper reporter, and she thinks the Chink knows more than we do."

Margarita thanked the policeman, then, tugging on Muriel's satchel, turned and started down the barricade line toward the Chinaman.

"I suppose that was your Christian charity at work back there." Muriel fell in stride beside Margarita. She couldn't hide her anger. "If I had opened my mouth again, I would've destroyed any chance of an interview. So I appreciate your cool-headedness." She squeezed Margarita's arm, and paused to watch the guard approach the dray.

"I've had four years of experience working with city police." Margarita stopped alongside Muriel. "And I use the words 'working with' quite loosely." Margarita's voice changed. There was a hard edge to it that seemed closer to Muriel's churning fury. "I haven't yet resorted to bribery—which is the way most of the city works with the police—but I must confess, I've been tempted. Thankfully, my deaconess salary is too small to make bribery a serious option. So mostly I just swallow my pride and pray for patience. That works—sometimes."

The Chinaman whom Margarita had identified dropped his last wooden crate onto the sidewalk, and a group of men pressed forward, grabbing at the boxes, shouting and shoving. The Chinaman was hatless, and his hair, minus a queue, was slick and shiny. A gust of wind caught his black shirt and pantaloons, briefly exposing his muscular arms and calves. The Chinaman jumped down from the dray and took Margarita's card from the guard.

Margarita waved as the Chinaman warily drew near. "Mr. Leong, I want you to meet Mrs. Monroe. She's a reporter for *The Examiner.*"

"Miss Lake tells me you speak English." Muriel took a notepad from her satchel and used it to shade her eyes from the mid-morning sun. She squinted across the tangle of barbed wire and fence posts. The Chinaman was a few inches shorter than she, with hair trimmed and parted in the American way. Muriel judged him to be about twenty-five years old. But there was a depth in his eyes Muriel hadn't seen in other Chinamen. They seemed to bear the weight of something heavier than the day's stress.

"Can you stay for a few minutes to answer some questions?" Muriel waved her notepad. "I'm hoping you can give me a Chinese perspective on this latest quarantine."

Mr. Leong wiped his hands on his pantaloons and came closer to the barricade. He smelled of onions and cantaloupe. "Sorry, ladies. No time to talk.

"No vegetables today." He scowled and peered over Muriel's shoulder, in the direction the guard had gone. "I get back, or boss mad. He not protect the store hisself."

Margarita was right, Muriel thought. This Chinaman might be perfect for what she wanted—and his English seemed adequate for carrying on an extended conversation.

"I unload everything." The man turned and pointed toward the wagon. There were crates piled beside the dray, and tilted empty bins lined the awning of the sidewalk produce stall. A bright red sign with Chinese characters and the English words "Jew Ho Grocery, Best Price" hung above the gaggle of Chinamen—now squabbling with a fat, angry-faced man wearing a black skullcap askew a traditional queue. Muriel assumed the fat man yelling and shaking his fists in the air was the owner.

Mr. Leong turned toward Muriel and Margarita again, his mouth twisted sideways as though someone had hit him in the jaw. "Nothing but old bean and onion—and soft melon. When gone—" he paused and drew his index finger across his neck. His eyes clouded.

"Come back one hour. We talk then."

鼠

"Hey you! Stop!"

Muriel spun in the direction of the shouts and saw the guard who had given Margarita's calling card to Mr. Leong, running alongside the barricade. He brandished his nightstick and lunged forward to pull a Chinese woman back from the barbed wire. The woman stumbled, and her hallelujah bonnet tilted precariously across her forehead.

Muriel recognized the woman immediately. It was 'Old Mary.'

"Miss Lake!" Old Mary struggled to catch her breath. She pushed her bonnet out of her face. "Miss Lake, I have something for you." She panted and waved a calling card at the guard. "The American doctor said give this to Miss Lake when someone gets sick."

The guard grabbed the Salvation Army woman under her armpits, lifted her off the ground, and carried her back from the barricade. "Jesus holy shit ghost. What's with you people and calling cards today? Do I look like a telegraph messenger boy?"

"It's Chun. Miss Lake. Take this." Old Mary's legs flailed against the guard as if she were pedaling an invisible bicycle. She waved the calling card in the air.

"Let go of that woman this instant." Margarita's voice was cold and authoritative—the tone Muriel imagined Margarita used when conducting brothel raids. Margarita strode to the edge of the barricade and reached through the barbed wire. "I know this woman. She's a Christian, and so am I. Now give me that card."

"It's Chun." Old Mary said again. "Remember her?"

The guard set Old Mary in the street and handed the card to Margarita. "Here you are ma'am." He tipped his hat. "Sorry about my language. I didn't see the cross on your lapel. But Christian or not—don't expect me to do this for you again."

"Of course I remember Chun." Margarita took the card without thanking the guard. "She's the little girl with the marvelous voice. I've seen her out lately with *God's Regular Army*." Margarita smiled at Old Mary across the barricade. "What seems to be the matter?"

The guard stepped back from the barricade and tucked his nightstick into his belt, warily watching the women from a few paces. "Look ladies, I'm sorry about all this, but you need to understand we're under strict orders to keep the Chinks away from the fence. There's already rumors flying about a demonstration planned for later today. And we can't make any exceptions." The guard cleared his throat. "So if you have anything more to say, do it fast, because if the captain sees you, that'll be the end of it, and I'll have hell to pay."

"Chun's sick." Muriel saw the fear in Old Mary eyes and heard it in the sharp rise of the Salvationist's voice. "Dr. Worley wants to know when someone gets sick, and she told me to find you and tell you. She said you knew how to get ahold of her, and maybe you could do something too." Then, as an apparent afterthought, Old Mary added, "And yesterday Dr. Worley took a dead rat from the place where Chun lives."

"That's it. I'm going to break this up. Now." The guard stepped between Old Mary and the barricade and pushed her back. "You heard me. I told you to stay away from the line."

Muriel turned just in time to see a police officer marching determinedly up the street toward them.

"Be back here in an hour, if you can." Margarita shouted at Old Mary. But Muriel wasn't sure the woman heard.

鼠

At eleven o'clock Muriel, Margarita, and Mr. Leong were back at the barricade, standing a few yards from Jew Ho's grocery store. The policeman they had met earlier was still on duty, and he told Muriel he would allow her fifteen minutes to conduct the interview. But if they tried anything, he would have them all arrested—Chinaman, missionary, reporter—it didn't matter. There would be no exceptions.

Muriel wrote as quickly as she could, her shorthand getting sloppier by the minute. Mr. Leong was in the middle of an animated explanation of his quarantine theory: That it had nothing to do with illness, and had everything to do with money. "Just one more way to burn Chinatown and chase us away. Ho Yow think so, and Ng Poon Chew say the same thing in newspaper. Maybe everyone need think hard about all bad thing blamed on us. When bad thing happen someplace else, do American blame Chinese there too? Do American think only Chinese make sickness?" Mr. Leong paused for a moment—Muriel wasn't sure why—perhaps it was for rhetorical effect. Or perhaps it was exhaustion due to carrying on such a complicated soliloquy in English. "I don't know if one Chinaman idea will count," Mr. Leong said finally. "I don't know what make sickness, but I think American or Chinese—make no difference in getting sickness."

"Mr. Leong, thank you for taking the time to talk to me today—on what is clearly a difficult occasion for you and your people." Muriel looked down the line of barbed wire and policemen—at the way the barricade looped in front of the American business next door to Jew Ho's grocery, ensuring it was outside the quarantine—and wondered how long the Chinese could endure the prejudice. She understood now why they felt the quarantine was simply a strangulating economic blockade. "I think my readers will be interested in what you have to say." She stooped and picked up her satchel, preparing to put away her pencil and notebook. "My readers usually only hear things from the Consul or the Six Companies. Never an ordinary Chinese merchant's voice. You've given me a lot to work with, and I'm wondering if you have anything else to add." Muriel scanned the barricade, waiting for Mr. Leong to collect his thoughts.

Margarita had slipped away during the interview—apparently to find Old Mary—for now the two of them were walking toward Muriel in parallel lines—one on each side of the barricade. Unlike Margarita, Old Mary had to navigate through a growing crowd of disgruntled Chinamen, and she had difficulty keeping up. The Chinamen stared menacingly across the quarantine line, sending shivers down Muriel's spine—despite the warmth of the late morning sun.

"I know her." Mr. Leong pointed down the line. "Her name Old Mary. She Jesus woman." As Old Mary approached Mr. Leong, opposite where Margarita and Muriel stood, the two began an animated exchange in Chinese.

"Mary told us earlier about a little sick girl in a brothel." Muriel spoke to Mr. Leong in an attempt to insert herself into the bewildering Chinese conversation. "She wants Miss Lake to find an American doctor who can check on the girl."

"So sorry. It's Chun." Old Mary answered in English, apparently wishing to include Muriel and Margarita in what she had to say. "You remember her, Mr. Leong?"

"Yes. But I not see her in long time."

"You know the girl?" Margarita and Muriel responded with simultaneous surprise. Then, before Old Mary could answer, Margarita added. "The little girl in Spofford—New Spanish Alley?"

"Yes—that one." Mr. Leong dropped his head and began cleaning his fingernails. He put his hand in his pocket and seemed to search for something. He pulled out a pottery shard. He scrutinized it for a moment; then, as if caught in an act of thievery, he looked up with reddening cheeks. He dropped the shard back into his pocket. "There was a girl. I used to see her where Chun live." Mr. Leong licked his lips and focused his attention again on the backs of his hands. "One time I ask her about Chun. She say Chun not keeper's child. The girl I see there say she there when mother bring Chun and sell her." Mr. Leong was watching Old Mary's face—almost in a game of cat and mouse, Muriel thought. "Three year pass, I think. I going to tell Mr. Gardner—but forget."

Old Mary and Margarita stared at each other through the barbed wire, their bodies taut; tension evident in the lines of their lips. Margarita glanced over at the policeman, and Muriel followed her eyes. The man was preoccupied with two Chinamen shaking their fists and yelling in broken English.

Muriel wasn't privy to the wordless conversation—the cat and mouse play between Margarita and the two Orientals across the fence. But she knew Chun's story had taken a dramatic turn. She just wasn't sure how mentioning Chun's sale to a brothel keeper years ago connected to Old Mary's concern for Chun's health now.

"We'll need evidence the keeper's not the mother, if we want to get Chun out." Margarita's voice rose to match the increasing tempo of her words. "And Mr. Leong, what you told us is important, especially if you're willing to testify in court to what you said. Are you willing to do that?"

"I think about that little girl for long time." Mr. Leong wiped his knuckles across the front of his shirt, and faced Margarita through the barbed wire. Muriel sensed that the weight she had seen in him earlier had somehow lifted. "If I do something to help, I know I do good."

"For the sake of the law, we'd need to get Chun when she's in the brothel," Margarita said to Old Mary. "That'll make it easier to get custody. If I can get hold of Dr. Worley quickly, maybe we can do something this afternoon."

It suddenly dawned on Muriel that Old Mary's request to find a doctor had turned into something much more. With Mr. Leong's revelation, Muriel had become an unintentional witness to the planning stages of a Mission rescue. The mousetrap was being set.

鼠

The policeman pulled out a pocket watch and swung it back and forth as he walked toward the four of them. "All right ladies. Time's up. You have to find some other way to conduct your business with these Chinks, because I have no more charity to dole out."

"Be at the barricade gate at three-thirty and wait for me," Margarita said to Old Mary. "Now go."

Margarita and Muriel thanked the policeman for his patience, and Muriel slipped him one of her cards through the barbed wire. She told him if he got into trouble with his superiors, he should call her at *The*

Examiner and she would have her editor straighten things out. He winked at her and said he already had something that needed straightening.

Muriel stiffened. Her cheeks burned. She clenched her satchel and pulled it tight to her breasts.

"Ignore him, Muriel." Margarita grabbed Muriel's arm and pulled her back to the Stockton Street sidewalk. "We may need his help again before the end of the day."

When they were out of earshot of the leering policeman, Margarita continued. "I know you need to get back to your desk, but could you stop off on your way—at the *Society for Suppression of Vice*—and see if the Secretary, Mr. Kane, can get over to me as soon as possible? Tell him there's a rescue we need him for—a neglected, underage Chinese girl in a brothel. He'll understand. His office is at 14 McAllister."

"I know where it is." Muriel slammed her satchel on the sidewalk, surprised at her physical response to Margarita's request. She knew she wasn't simply reacting to Kane's name. It was a combination of things, beginning with a poor night's sleep on Margarita's floor and the strange Oriental breakfast. But then there were all the emotions of the morning mixed in—the excitement of interviewing Mr. Leong, glimpsing the Chinese perspective on the barricade, and the insight into how spontaneous rescues could be. And, of course, topping it all off—the obnoxious behavior of the quarantine policeman.

When they reached Washington Street, a cable car bell clanged loudly. Muriel waited for the car to move on before she continued. "I'm not sure Mr. Kane can be trusted any more than that policeman." She waved in the general direction of the quarantine line. "Not long before I left *The Call*, a reporter did some articles about his work for that *Society*. As I recall, he runs it more as a business than a charity. If a person slips him a few dollars on the sly, he tends to work more quickly."

Margarita stopped on the Mission House steps and turned to face Muriel. "I need to get that girl out of the brothel as quickly as possible. Mr. Kane may not be a saint, but under the circumstances, he's the best hope I have. He has a uniform and a deputy's star, and he's unknown in Chinatown. And if he's available and the rescue's successful, we may need that policeman's help to get the girl across the line." Margarita paused, her eyes scanning Washington Street. "The first thing is to get her out of the place before she gets any sicker. We don't have time to go searching for angels."

"I'll do what I can, Maggie." Muriel sighed and put her hand on Margarita's shoulder. She was surprised at how thin it was. She felt nothing but bone. "You know far better than I, who you can work with and who you can't. But I don't have as much patience with men's bull-headedness as you. If you hadn't steered me clear of that officer, one of my satchel straps would have ended up wrapped around his neck—barricade or not."

Margarita laughed. "Now I know why you carry that thing. Policemen have their nightsticks. I have prayer, and you have your satchel."

"Well, it's also good for carrying a change of undergarments," Muriel smiled. "Which reminds me—I'd better come in and collect my things from last night. And please, let me know if the rescue is successful. I remember Chun singing at that Salvation Army Christmas party a couple of years ago. Some articles following up with her life here—beginning with her rescue—would be of interest to my *Examiner* readers."

鼠

By three o'clock, Margarita sat with Dr. Worley and Mr. Kane in the Mission House parlor, putting the finishing touches on the rescue plans. "Why don't you repeat them, to make sure you have it straight?"

Mr. Kane's jaw tightened as though annoyed at Margarita's request, but he nodded. "Here's what I have: Dr. Worley and I stand near that butcher shop on the corner while Old Mary looks for the girl. If the girl's not in the brothel, Old Mary walks towards Clay, and we won't attempt the rescue. Dr. Worley and Old Mary try and find the girl and attend to her physical needs, and I simply return here alone." Mr. Kane paused and ran his fingers along the crown of the bowler hat sitting on his lap. "But if the girl's in the brothel, then Old Mary should tell her a *God's Regular Army* man is coming in a few minutes to take her singing. When we see Old Mary leave the brothel and walk toward us, we'll know the girl's there, and I'll go get her. Since the girl knows Old Mary, I'll need her beside me as soon as I get outside the brothel, to calm the girl, if she's afraid." "Is that it?" Mr. Kane didn't wait for Margarita's response. He rubbed his knuckles on his blue topcoat's shiny brass star, unpinned it, and stuck it to his shirt instead. Then he took a small silver cross from his topcoat pocket, and put that where his six-pointed deputy's star had been.

Mr. Kane smiled at his reflection in the parlor window, straightened his coat, and put his hat under his arm. With his one simple change, the Secretary had become a member of *God's Regular Army.*

Margarita led her two co-conspirators to the Mission House door. "I'll walk with you as far as the barricade gate. The policeman on duty's the same one Muriel and I talked to this morning, so he shouldn't give you any trouble."

She took two calling cards from her pocket. "Take these, in case I'm not there when you return. God willing you'll have Chun with you, and you can tell the policeman you're bringing a sick girl to the Mission."

鼠

Chun was stacking papers when the door opened. She was sweaty and tired. Like she had climbed stairs all day, carrying pee pots. But all she had done was clear the table twice and collect papers. She had even been too tired to get mad when a customer said he would take her upstairs. There were only two of them in the sitting room now. They were old and fat and sat far away from Mama's table. They didn't look at her when she straightened the newspapers and they didn't look up when the door opened. They just kept on talking angrily about American policemen not letting them go anywhere.

Chun was surprised to see Old Mary.

"School today?" It didn't seem like the right day.

"No, just a singing day. But I can't take you." Old Mary patted Chun on the head and asked how she was feeling. Chun wanted to tell Old Mary Mama had yelled at her and hit her when she left a dirty spoon on the table. But before she could answer, Old Mary said an Army man would be by in a few minutes to fetch her. "He's a tall white man with a blue coat, like all the other Army people."

Chun didn't feel like going out to sing. She wanted to lie under Mama's table and sleep. But she was afraid to say anything.

Chun was putting one last paper on the pile in the corner of the sitting room when the white man came in. He was dressed in blue like Old

Mary said. He was tall and thin and his eyes were shiny black. He had whiskers like her pet rat that died. The whiskers began to twitch and he yelled in American. Then he opened his coat and pulled at a shiny thing on his white shirt. Chun was afraid and ran across the room to Mama's table and hid underneath. Close to Mama's metal box and the rat hole. She scrunched up small like she always did and rested her chin on her knees to watch what would happen.

"Raid! Police! Raid!" The customers shouted and tipped over the ghost screen when they ran out.

Mama stood by the bamboo curtain and Chun screamed when she saw her. Her face was fat and purple and her eyes were big and red like the fire-hot coal in the stove on a cold day. Chun crawled out from under the table and tried to follow the customers out the door, but the white man grabbed her and picked her up. He showed the shiny thing on his shirt to Mama and yelled and waved his arm. Then he turned and kicked the ghost screen again and again, breaking it to pieces.

The white man smelled like tobacco and his coat was damp and scratchy like rat hair. Chun screamed and tried to kick the rat man in the belly. Then she saw the American doctor who gave her candy. And Old Mary was in the alley too. And Chun remembered what Old Mary said. That the man had come to get her.

Chun looked over the rat man's shoulder and saw Mama limping behind them. She was angry and shouting. Crying and kicking. "Aaiiee! Jeezachrise. Wharsahorbitch. Aaiiee! My baby. My baby." Mama pulled on the arm of a man smoking a pipe in a doorway. "Help me. Stop them," she said. But the man just laughed and turned away.

Chun's head felt heavy. Like a pee-pot that was full. She didn't know why Mama was yelling at the rat man, but she didn't care anymore. She put her head on the rat man's shoulder and the tobacco smell on his coat made her feel like throwing up. She closed her eyes and squeezed her mouth shut.

"They'll take you and lock you in a room and drown you," Mama shouted. "I'm an old widow minding my own business. That's my only daughter. She's all I have."

Old Mary and the American doctor were talking to Chun but she put her hands over her ears to try and make Mama's voice go away. Mama just yelled more.

"Chun, listen to me. Those people will put you in hot water and boil you. They'll cut you into soup bones and feed you to the other girls they stole. Tell those people you don't want to go with them.

"Aaiiieee! The white devils have cast a spell on my baby. Demons have bitten off her tongue. It happens every time they steal one."

Mama's voice wasn't as loud now, so Chun lifted her head to see where she was. Old Mary and the American doctor were walking fast beside the rat man, and Mama was far away, by the butcher shop, waving her arms and stamping her feet.

Chapter Six

GUARDIAN

It was almost four o'clock when Mr. Kane and Dr. Worley crossed the quarantine line and met Maggie. Mr. Kane carried the trembling girl into the Mission House and set her down in the foyer. "Well, folks, I wish they were all that easy." He unpinned the silver cross from his topcoat and dropped it back into his coat pocket. "I'm going to run down to Superior Court and see if I can get temporary guardianship papers before the building closes. If I get there in time, I'll bring them by tomorrow morning when I check on her."

The two women thanked Mr. Kane for his help, then turned toward the girl.

"Maggie, if you don't mind, I'd like to check for signs of plague before you take her upstairs." Dr. Worley knelt beside the girl. "We found a dead rat yesterday at the brothel where she lives. We haven't been able to test it yet, so we'll need to watch her over the next few days to see if she develops any symptoms."

Maggie stood looking down at the frail, tangle-haired waif and simply nodded in assent. It was the girl's eyes that got to her—it was always the downcast eyes. The Bible's term "bowels of compassion" expressed perfectly how she felt when she saw a *mui tsai*—a debt-slave child—on the streets of Chinatown. It was a wrenching—almost retching in the pit of her stomach.

Over the past four years Maggie had had two girls die in her arms. No one should have to watch a child take its last breath—much less battered girls who had barely begun to know the love of God and family. And she vowed to God and to heaven, and to whatever—whomever—that no lamb would go to the slaughter on her watch if she could prevent it. And so "Not this one," was always her first, silent prayer.

Dr. Worley spoke a few Chinese words to the child and pulled a peppermint stick from her jacket. The girl took the candy, popped it in her mouth, and grinned. "Sugar," announced Dr. Worley, smiling at Maggie, "is a doctor's best friend."

The doctor felt the girl's neck and probed under her arms. She pressed the girl's abdomen. Maggie saw the child flinch and her eyes grow wide. It didn't seem to be a reaction to pain—but rather one of fear. Had the girl been abused? Please, God, no, Maggie prayed.

"She doesn't seem to have unusual swellings anywhere, so that's good news. Swollen lymph glands would be a sign of something serious—typhoid or the plague, perhaps." Dr. Worley peered into the girl's eyes and felt her forehead. "However, she does seem to have a bit of a fever." Dr. Worley stood and smiled down at the child. "I'll come back tomorrow afternoon and examine her more thoroughly. She's been through a lot today, and I don't want to put her under any more stress." Dr. Worley paused at the door, hand on the knob. "A good night's sleep and a full stomach will probably do wonders."

護

Miss Lake lifted Chun and carried her into the creaky darkness. Miss Lake sometimes talked to Old Mary, and Chun had seen her playing a loud shiny noisy thing with the Army band in the alley. One time Miss Lake had given her candy. Just like the American doctor. And now Miss Lake was carrying her. Chun buried her face in Miss Lake's neck and shoulder and breathed in. Miss Lake smelled sweet. Like opium. Only better. Miss Lake held her tightly and Chun wasn't so scared. She hoped Miss Lake would hold her for a long time. The ka-thump ka-thump ka-thump sound in Miss Lake's shoulder made Chun yawn. She closed her eyes.

Miss Lake spoke and Chun lifted her head. They were in a big room. It was like the Army place where Old Mary sometimes took her. And Miss Lake was walking toward a tall, wooden box-like thing. Chun knew what it was even though its white teeth-like things weren't showing. The Army place had one too. It had a special name but she couldn't remember it. She wished she could hear its sounds. She wished she could open its mouth and put her fingers on the white teeth-like things and make songs come out of it. Miss Lake saw her looking at it. She pointed and smiled and said something in American.

There was another door and then lots of stairs. Lots more than at Mama's place. But there was no altar by the stairs. No smoky smell of incense. No grinning god with a bowl full of moldy fruit for Miss Lake's ancestors.

At the top was a room the size of Mama's place. But there was no ghost screen to protect anyone. And Chun trembled when she thought of what could happen. How there were big windows on two sides where ghosts could get in.

There were soft-looking bench-like things to sit on. Probably for customers. And on one wall was a big picture of Jesus with children like at the Army place. The room smelled almost like outdoors. There was no dead rat stink. No tobacco smoke. No opium. Only a nice smell like sweet rice mixed with coal dust.

"Mama, I have someone for you to meet."

"You must be Chun." The fattest woman Chun had ever seen came into the room and smiled at her, making lots of nonsense American sounds. "Maggie's told me so much about you. She says you're a great little singer. Gracie, can you come here please? We have a new girl, and I need a translator."

Chun saw an open door and heard voices coming from somewhere down that way. Big girl voices like at Mama's place. But little girl voices too. The little ones must be cleaners. Like me, she thought. Just like at Mama's place. And she was afraid.

A big Chinese girl in American clothes came out of the doorway and smiled. "You're going to like it here," the Chinese girl said. "There are other little girls here just like you, and they like to sing too. They were once *mui tsai* like you, but not anymore."

"Maggie, can you stay for a few minutes longer?" The big fat woman was making American nonsense sounds again. "I'll start the bath and then maybe you can find her something clean to wear. I'm thinking some of Siu's old clothes might fit."

Miss Lake carried Chun across the room. Her head felt heavy again and she rested it on Miss Lake's shoulder again. The Chinese girl standing beside Miss Lake told Chun to look out the window. At first she didn't want to but then she did.

Chun had never seen so far in all her life. She was high up in the sky. As high as birds. Much higher than Mama's place where Ming and the other girls slept. There were big buildings everywhere. The biggest ever. Going way up into the sky.

From the girls' rooms in Mama's place she could only see across the alley. Not above everything like here. The sky was blue and the hills far away were green. Like pieces of jade that customers sometimes gave Mama.

"What's that?" she said to the Chinese girl. Her voice sounded squeaky and strange. Like it came from somebody else.

"It's water—the ocean. And those are boats floating on the water." The Chinese girl pointed. "Over there are hills with grass and trees. I've been there lots of times. Maybe someday you can go there too. But right now we're going to get you cleaned up before supper."

"There's the doorbell. Gracie, can you take her?" Miss Lake set Chun down.

When Miss Lake left, the fat white woman and the Chinese girl took Chun down the dark hallway. There were lots of rooms just like at Mama's place. But the doors were open and she didn't see or hear any men. Girls poked their heads out of the rooms to look at her as she went by. Some were big and some were little like her. Some were dressed in American clothes and some were dressed in Chinese clothes. All the little girls smiled at her. But only some of the big girls did.

They came to a small room with a big long thing full of water and the Chinese girl told Chun to take off her clothes. But she said no.

"We're going to put you in the tub to get you all clean. Here, put your hand in the water. Isn't it nice?" the Chinese girl said.

Chun let the Chinese girl take her hand. The water wasn't hot enough to cook her like Mama said. It was more like the rice tea Ming sometimes gave her in the morning. The Chinese girl stood her in the tub and this time Chun let the girl take her smock. The water came to her knees. Never in her entire life had Chun been in so much water. Then the Chinese girl said to sit in the water. But Chun was afraid and held her tight.

The Chinese girl and the fat white woman pushed Chun's legs out in front of her and set her down. But still she held on to the Chinese girl. There was warm water all over herself. At first it stung her bottom and she bit her lip. After a while she felt like she was sitting next to Mama's coal stove on a cold day, and she got sleepy. Her legs floated to the top of the water and she pushed them down. They floated up again. Chun thought she was dreaming and that her legs were wings and that she was a seagull like the ones she saw sometimes in the alley. She was a seagull flying far above and away from everything.

The fat white woman knelt beside her and began to scrub her skin with a rough rag the way Ming sometimes did. Then Chun woke up.

The fat white woman stopped scrubbing and began to poke at Chun's body. The fat white woman touched a black line on Chun's leg where Mama hit her and Chun closed her eyes. It was from spilling Moy's pee-pee pot on the stairs. When Mama stepped in it before Chun cleaned it up. The fat white woman saw the other black spots on Chun's body and looked sad.

The Chinese girl said the fat white woman wanted to wash between Chun's legs but Chun said no. She pushed her legs together and wouldn't let her. Like Ming said she should do if a man wanted to do that.

護

"That was *God's Regular Army.*" Maggie came huffing into the bathroom, gloves and deaconess bonnet in hand. "They said they have a rightful claim to the girl, and they accused us of stealing her from her mother."

Maggie watched as her mother inspected Chun's body. The little girl had bruises on her legs and back—but only the one on her upper left thigh seemed recent. Most were long and thin—perhaps from being hit with a stick or cane. Her mother clucked soothingly and shook her head.

"What do you think Mama?"

"Compared to some of the girls you've rescued, she doesn't look too bad. She's malnourished, for sure—look at her ribs. But I don't see any scars or abnormal swelling anywhere." Her mother pushed herself up from the tub, grunting loudly. The girl ducked and covered her head with her arms.

"Mama, you scared her. You've got to be more careful with your animal sounds."

Her mother wrung out the washcloth and wiped her hands on her skirt. "Gracie, tell her I'm sorry, and that no one here will ever hit her.

"I can't tell if she's been abused in other ways." Her mother's eyes were rheumy, and strands of gray-flecked hair were plastered to her forehead and cheekbones. She picked at them as if they were cobwebs on a winter coat. "She won't let me touch her privates. She seemed quite fearful when I got close, and that worries me. Who knows what she's seen and heard in that brothel—or wandering the streets with *God's Regular Army*—that can't be good either. You know what the papers have accused those people of."

Maggie heard the exhaustion in her mother's voice. She suddenly felt guilty for bringing another needy child to the Mission—to the Home—adding to her mother's already heavy workload. It was likely neither of them would sleep much tonight—or during the next week—if the girl were here that long.

Rescues affected Maggie differently than they did her mother. Maggie's monthlies were often irregular, and sometimes she would miss one or two bleedings before they would resume. Her Uncle Ben, the doctor, thought her female problems might be the result of stress and anxiety. Her mother, however, had a different theory. She half-jokingly suggested on more than one occasion that the rescues caused Maggie's body to feign pregnancy. "After all, they're your babies," Mama would say.

"Gracie, maybe you could talk to her when she trusts us more. You were so good with her a few minutes ago in the sitting room." Maggie took the washcloth from her mother and hung it over bathtub faucet. "And Dr. Worley said she would do a complete physical in a few days." Maggie paused. "After she gets the lab results on the rat she found in the brothel."

"Dr. Worley found a dead rat there?" Her mother's chin dropped to her chest. "You didn't tell me that."

護

Miss Lake disappeared again and now the Chinese girl knelt beside the tub and began to wash Chun's hair.

"Look for lice, Gracie." The fat white woman was speaking more American gibberish. "We might have to cut her hair short, if you find anything."

"Mrs. Kate, I think I've found something." The Chinese girl was pulling hard on Chun's hair. Chun squeezed her eyes shut and bit her lip again but didn't cry.

"I'd better get the kerosene and scissors, just in case. Hopefully there's no infestation."

Chun heard footsteps and opened her eyes. The fat white woman was back in the room and had a small can and scissors in her hands. Chun thought maybe what Mama said was true after all. That this was when they would cut her into pieces for eating. She began to whimper and whisper. "No, no, no!"

The Chinese girl said not to be afraid. That they wanted to cut some bugs out of her hair. Chun said only the Chinese girl could use the scissors, so the fat white woman gave them to the Chinese girl. The fat white woman bent over and put something bad smelling in Chun's hair, and the Chinese girl washed it again and again and again. Finally, they took Chun out of the water and dried her off with a big fluffy cloth. They looked at her hair one last time and cut out a small patch and showed her the hair with the bugs in it.

Then the Chinese girl told her to open her mouth. Before Chun knew it the fat white woman stuck something like a chopstick in and rubbed it on her teeth. Chun gagged and spit the bad taste on to the long cloth wrapped around her. She began to cry. She looked up at the Chinese girl, and the Chinese girl smiled at her and told her not to be afraid. And when Chun looked at the Chinese girl the sick feeling in her belly went away.

Miss Lake came into the room with a pile of clothes. She had short white pantaloons and long black pantaloons and a long-sleeved smock with a big red-flowery pocket on it. And soft pretty slippers. And the Chinese girl said they were for her. All for her to wear. Chun couldn't believe it.

A bell rang and Miss Lake carried Chun down, down, down. When they got to the bottom of the stairs, Chun knew there was a kitchen close by because she smelled rice and other things cooking. She hadn't eaten since early morning and with all the things happening she had forgotten about food. But now her belly ached to have something in it. She felt her smock to make sure the pocket was still there. Now she wouldn't go hungry because she could put some rice in the pocket when no one was looking.

Miss Lake took her into a room full of long tables. Big and little Chinese girls—many more than at Mama's place—were quietly sitting at them. All the girls looked up and smiled at Chun when she came in. Every girl had a bowl and chopsticks and a teacup. And each bowl was full to the top with rice and vegetables.

Miss Lake sat Chun on a chair next to the fat white woman with the Chinese girl who told her things, on the other side of the table. A girl brought her a bowl of steaming white rice, and she was just about to eat it when the Chinese girl across from her said "No, we always pray first."

Chun knew Jesus prayers from the Army place but she could hardly wait for the prayer to stop. Her nose was in her rice bowl and she could smell its deliciousness and her belly was aching and empty. She finished her rice and vegetables before anyone. But she forgot to make a rice ball to put in her pocket. She was tired and began to cry again. But the girl who brought her the rice bowl at first brought her more. Chun couldn't believe her good luck. And she thought maybe this was going to be a good place. Where she wanted to stay. Even if there wasn't a ghost screen anywhere to protect her.

護

"Here's your room." The Chinese girl and the fat white woman took Chun back upstairs after eating, and now she stood in the hallway looking into a room that was like Ming's. Only lots, lots bigger. "You get a bed all to yourself, here with Siu. And with Sau. They'll be your friends and keep you safe," said the Chinese girl. And then she left.

There were two girls in the room. Ones that Chun saw downstairs in the eating place. The girls were bigger than she was and they were sitting on a bed looking at pictures in a book. Chun knew what it was because she sometimes saw books at the Army place. The room had a window close to the floor like at Mama's place. But there weren't any bars on it. Anybody could get out if they wanted to. Even she could. There was a big wooden box with knobs on it by one wall and she wondered what it was for. On either side of the big box thing were pictures of smiling American children.

The fat white woman said something in American, and the smaller chubby girl went to the big wooden box thing and pulled out a smaller sliding box and took out another smock. "For sleeping," the girl said, and she handed it to Chun. Chun didn't want to put it on because only big girls wore different clothes at night. Nightclothes were for customers to see and Ming told her if someone wanted her to do a big girl thing like that she should tell her. But Ming wasn't here and there was no one to tell, and Chun couldn't trust these girls because they were already wearing nightclothes.

Chun stood in the middle of the room. She was shaking. Her hands and legs hurt and her head was hot and all she could say was "No, no, no."

The fat white woman looked sad and said something in American. And then the Chinese girl said she could sleep in her day clothes if she wanted to. Chun said yes.

The fat white woman said something again in American and this time the two girls got on their knees beside their beds and closed their eyes. Chun knew what was happening because it was the same thing the Army people did. It was like being out with the Army people. Except inside.

Everyone was talking to Jesus at the same time but it went on and on, and Chun didn't know any of the strange American gibberish. She said nothing but just stood in the middle of the room and let the sounds float around her.

> "Father we thank thee for the night,
>
> And for the blessed morning light.
>
> For health and food and loving care,
>
> And all that makes this world so fair.
>
> Help us to do the things we should,
>
> And be to others kind and good.

In all we do, in work or play—

To grow more loving every day.

Amen."

The two girls climbed into their beds, but Chun didn't want to get into the other one. Only big girls had beds. And after that the men would come and pay their money. And Ming told her not to let men do that.

Chun wanted to sleep on the floor like little girls should, but the fat white woman lifted her into the bed and tucked the blanket around her. Then the fat white woman put her lips on Chun's cheek and made a smacking noise. Sometimes men did that to Moy and Ming. The fat white woman smelled like sweet bean cake. Like Old Mary bought sometimes on the way back from singing.

The bed was soft but Chun was afraid of it. She held on to the fat white woman and tried to sit up. The fat white woman said something and one of the Chinese girls told her this was her bed and not to be afraid. Then the fat white woman pushed her down again. But not in an angry way. The fat white woman did something and the room got dark. Then she went away and shut the door.

Everything was quiet. A sound of quiet Chun never heard before. She lay perfectly still in the darkness, barely breathing. Her body was still prickly from the bath and the new clothes. She listened for the sound of men shouting in the street below the window. For footsteps on the stairs. For men's loud laughter. For the fat white woman angrily jangling her keys in the hallway. For doors unlocking and creaking open. For girls arguing with customers. For beds squeaking and men grunting. The sounds she knew would come sooner or later. But try as she might she didn't hear anything. There was nothing. Only a strange tick tick tick noise coming from somewhere. And the other girls breathing and whispering. And the clanging of something outside and far away.

"When do the men come?" Chun whispered to the girls. She was shaking again and she curled into a ball like she did when Mama beat her.

"Men never come here at night—and almost never in the day." Chun thought it was the tall thin girl.

"And men are never allowed in these rooms." Chun thought it was the small chubby girl. "They're just for girls."

"Just for girls? And no men?" Chun couldn't believe what she was hearing.

"Yes. Only for girls."

Chun lay awake for a long time hoping what she heard was true. She listened as hard as she could. But all she heard was tick tick tick. And a clop clopping horse, and a squeaking wagon in the street below.

When the girls were breathing noisily Chun pulled the blanket off her bed and crawled onto the floor. On the hard cold floor she heard more strange noises. There were creaks and cracks and Chinese voices below her. But she didn't hear any footsteps in the hallway or on the stairs. She didn't hear any men laughing. Or any jangling keys. She didn't smell any burning joss sticks. She didn't hear curses or screams or loud grunting or painful breathing.

Chun thought about Ming and wanted to see her. She wanted to tell Ming what had happened today. She wanted to tell Ming she was still alive. That no one boiled her or ate her. That she had nightclothes and a bed to sleep in but that she didn't wear the nightclothes and only stayed in the bed until the fat white woman left. Because she didn't want a man to come in and do the things Ming said shouldn't be done to little girls. She wanted to tell Ming she would stay awake and listen to the strange sounds until she knew what they were. She wanted to tell everyone she had a bath and she saw the water that went all the way to the Celestial Kingdom. And that she ate two bowls of rice. And that no one yelled at her or hit her.

Chun lay awake on the hard floor for a long long time. She listened to every strange noise and wondered if they were ghosts. She waited to hear the sounds she was sure would come. But she didn't hear anything like that.

When Chun awoke in the morning she found herself back in the bed, and the fat white woman smiling down at her.

"Good morning," the fat white woman said. In Chinese.

護

Frank Kane stood at the Mission House door at eight-thirty in the morning, with a sheaf of papers under his arm. He twisted his black handlebar mustache nervously.

"It looks like you got to the courthouse, after all. You must have run all the way from the Market Street cable car," Maggie smiled. She had just finished the morning Bible reading with the girls when Ethel told her the downstairs doorbell was ringing. Maggie set her worn, leather-bound Bible on the lamp table in the entryway and took the papers Mr. Kane offered.

"You see I signed my name as 'temporary guardian.'" Mr. Kane took off his bowler hat and ran his fingers over its crown. "I found Judge Coffey's clerk as he was leaving, and it seemed the wise thing to do, under the circumstances." He coughed and cleared his throat. "I didn't get a chance to see your Asylum yesterday. I trust your arrangements are much like the Presbyterian place over on Sacramento?"

Mr. Kane's voice was low and measured, and it turned into a half-question at the end of the sentence. When Maggie looked up, he was peering over her shoulder into the darkened chapel. "Please, come in. May I get you a cup of coffee for your trouble?"

"No, I'm fine." Mr. Kane continued to fondle his hat. "I stopped in at *The Cold Day* on the way over. The girl—how is she? Did she sleep any?"

Maggie tapped her finger on the last page of the document, where Mr. Kane had signed his name and printed in large letters underneath: "*Secretary of the Society for the Suppression of Vice.*" She never slept well after a rescue, knowing the new inmate would probably keep her mother and the other girls awake for much of the night. Sometimes the family would fall asleep just before dawn, when her mother's labor would begin again. And last night had been no exception. Maggie had lain awake long after her mantle clock struck one, her nightgown uncomfortably bunching and twisting around her thighs as she tossed and turned, endlessly reviewing the events of the day.

When Maggie untwisted her nightgown one last time and finally fell asleep, she dreamed she was climbing over the quarantine barricade into Chinatown. Her skirt caught on the barbed wire, and when she reached down to untangle it, she saw huge dead rats hanging from the fence— like the Indian salmon she used to see as a child, drying on racks along the banks of the Columbia River. She screamed and fell forward, into the grasp of a drunken policeman who laughed and pawed hungrily at her. She fought to get out of his arms—waking herself just as the morning light bathed the corner of her room.

Maggie tried to focus on the document Mr. Kane had given her. She shook her head to clear her mind. She had arranged yesterday's rescue and brought the girl to the Mission—so why had Mr. Kane named himself as "temporary guardian?"

"The girl—how did she sleep last night?" Mr. Kane repeated his question, still peering into the darkness behind her. He snorted impatiently, then stepped past her, searching the empty chapel. "I've listed this place as her temporary residence." He stumbled against a wooden chair. "As you know, I've made successful rescues for Miss Cameron at the Presbyterian Mission, and if you don't mind—my Board always wants to know what the living arrangements are like for the children I place—even if only temporarily."

Mr. Kane's quick movement caught Maggie off-guard, but she told him their Home Board had funds for a new building and they hoped to purchase a lot soon. "So we consider our Rescue Asylum as temporary as well." She picked up her Bible from the lamp table and followed the man's vaguely defined form into the gloomy room.

"There's an aisle here." Maggie straightened the chairs behind the Secretary. She hoped he caught her undertone of disapprobation. "It would be easier if you let me lead the way. As you can imagine, we don't usually have men upstairs on the women's floor." Mr. Kane stepped aside to let her pass. "You may have to wait on the landing for a few minutes for my mother—Mrs. Lake—to clear the sitting room. No one's expecting a visitor—especially this early in the morning. And I'm sure you understand we don't allow men beyond the sitting room, into the girls' rooms." Maggie glanced over her shoulder, but Mr. Kane didn't appear to be listening. His head was bobbing left and right, up and down, like a frustrated fly on a windowpane.

護

The girls were well into their lunch of vegetable soup, home-canned peaches, and freshly baked bread when Maggie finally made it downstairs a few hours later.

"It's been a busy morning for you." Kate pulled out a chair.

Maggie scanned the room nervously, searching for Chun. She saw Grace standing at the corner of the children's table with the new girl scrunched low beside her, still wearing the clothes Maggie had picked out the evening before. "That girl's so small—I'm afraid we're going to lose her if we're not careful." Maggie sat down and shook her head. "I'm sorry Mama. Yes, the morning's been hectic. I had other visitors after Mr. Kane insisted on going upstairs." Maggie smiled over at Chun, who was noisily slurping her soup. "And in between them I barely had time to call Muriel and tell her about the rescue. She was glad to hear it went smoothly—but of course her editor and her *Examiner* readers aren't interested in rescues like yesterday's—they want danger, violence, and hair-raising escapes."

"Maybe it's my nerves or lack of sleep, Maggie. I don't know." Kate swirled her spoon in her soup, then rested it on the edge of her bowl. Her mother's voice had a pensive edge Maggie recognized from childhood. But at twenty-seven years old, she found the concern somewhat cloying, and she looked away. "You spent a good deal of time yesterday with that Mr. Kane." Kate rested her fingers on Maggie's wrist, but Maggie moved her arm. "And I have to say he made me feel very uncomfortable this morning—the way he scrutinized the room upstairs. It was like he was taking notes in his head. He said he wanted to see the Home for his Board, but I got the distinct impression he had other motives." Kate paused, and Maggie waited for her mother to slap a trump card on the table. Mama always kept her strongest arguments for last.

"And I really don't like the fact that he signed those temporary guardianship papers himself. You've always done that. It's not like he planned the rescue or had any prior knowledge of the child's situation." Kate finished her soup and surveyed the room before delicately patting the corners of her mouth with her napkin. "Harry should change those papers as quickly as possible."

Maggie swallowed a spoonful of home-canned peaches, then set down her utensil with a clatter. "Mama, you don't like him because he's Catholic. But Miss Cameron trusts him. And you've never doubted her judgment. Besides, he's seen the Presbyterian mission, and that place isn't much better furnished than ours. Anyway, Mr. Kane wasn't my only worry this morning. No sooner had I shown him out and turned to go upstairs, than the doorbell rang a second time. It was those *God's Regular Army* folks again, saying Chun was their little 'ringer and singer for the Lord.'

They started yelling that we were 'demons disguised as angels of light,' and would have to answer to God for 'kidnapping innocent Chinatown children' and 'stealing their sheep.'"

Kate snorted. The chatter at the children's table stopped, and a wide-eyed Chun turned to gape at the two women. "I'm sorry girls." Kate pulled a handkerchief from the sleeve of her shirtwaist and dabbed her eyes. "Go ahead and finish eating. Miss Lake is full of stories today, and I couldn't keep from laughing. But I was too loud. You should 'do as I say—not as I do.'"

True to her word, Dr. Worley stopped by the fourth floor Rescue Home later that afternoon. The doctor told Maggie and Kate the good news that the lab results on the Spofford Alley rat had come back negative. It had none of the rose-tinted, rod-shaped bacilli that were the tell-tale signs of plague. And after checking Chun thoroughly, Dr. Worley was quite sure the girl didn't have the disease either.

護

Judge Coffey refused to schedule Chun's guardianship hearing while Chinatown was under quarantine. "The Chinese mother needs to be given the opportunity to appear in court," he wrote in his first letter to Maggie, explaining the delay. "Along with any other witnesses she or her lawyer may wish to call."

But when the quarantine was lifted on June 15th, the earliest date Judge Coffey could propose for Chun's hearing was August 10th. The backlog of Chinatown court cases was that large. As soon as Maggie received the Superior Court citation she telephoned Judge Coffey's office to tell him she would be gone most of the month of August, and she hoped the hearing could be scheduled for early September instead. His secretary said he would check the court calendar and get back to her in a few days.

If the hearing couldn't be rescheduled, Laura Williams, the Oriental Bureau Secretary and Home Board President, would represent the Rescue Home at Chun's hearing. And Maggie didn't want that. Laura hadn't yet been apprised of Mr. Kane naming himself Chun's temporary guardian—a possible complication Maggie wished to keep from Laura as long as possible.

Maggie was becoming less and less enamored of Laura and her Home Board leadership. It wasn't that Maggie didn't respect the woman for her twenty-five years of work with the Rescue Home. She did. After all, the woman was one of the two still-living founders of the Home. And her connections with former inmates were crucial to Maggie's Chinatown work. But Laura often made decisions about the Home without consulting either Maggie or Mama, and without considering the day-to-day impact those decisions had on the workers. Like when Laura fired the Home's English teacher and then announced she was adding teaching to Mama's regular Home responsibilities. Mama had no say in the situation, and now she spent half of each day in the classroom downstairs—on top of everything else she was doing—and all without any additional pay. So who was supposed to watch Chun and help her adjust to Home life when Mama was teaching? Mama couldn't leave Chun upstairs alone. And it wasn't fair to make Grace responsible for Chun—hours at a time—especially when Mama didn't know how the girl would respond to new situations.

No one on the Home Board ever raised objections to what Laura did. And if Maggie or Mama tried, the other Board members simply smiled, patted them on the arm, and said condescendingly, "Well, you're still new to the work, dear," and "In time you'll learn how things are done here." But all that meant was, after four years, she and Mama were still the "new ones in the work." And they were feeling more and more estranged from Laura and the Board.

護

The day before Maggie was to leave for Oregon and her annual vacation, she found another Superior Court citation in her Mission House mailbox. Thankfully, the court clerk had rescheduled the time and date of Chun's hearing. It was now set for Tuesday, September 10th at 2 PM.

Mixed in with the rest of Maggie's mail was a letter from May Thomas, the *Salvation Army Chinatown Corps* Captain. Maggie had written her hoping to discover more about Chun.

"Dear Miss Lake," Maggie read.

After receiving your letter of a few weeks ago, I asked some of our Chinatown friends what they might know about Chun, and here is what I have been able to determine. When Old Mary first knew Chun, she was at Kim Yook's place at #11 Spofford Alley. That house was known to be disreputable. And Kim Yook was then the keeper of the house.

As to Chun's parents, I know only what Old Mary told me recently. She did some detective work of her own and found the parents sold Chun to Kim Yook for about one hundred dollars. She didn't know the exact sum. Apparently the parents haven't lived in San Francisco for some time.

Mary thought they lived in Fresno, and that the family name was 'Lai.' But she wasn't sure.

I hope this helps.

Praying God to make you victorious.

I am yours for the Master,

Captain Thomas's letter confirmed what Leong Ti had said—that Chun wasn't the brothel keeper's child. This knowledge, along with the fact they had rescued the obviously neglected child from the brothel itself, should make the guardianship hearing little more than a formality. Judge Coffey had presided over numerous Presbyterian and Methodist guardianship cases and was sympathetic to the missions' causes, so Maggie was confident the judge would grant guardianship of the girl to the Home. But having Mr. Kane's signature on the temporary papers could add needless court hearings to Maggie's already heavy workload and jeopardize her delicate relationship with Laura Williams. If Mr. Kane retained custody of Chun, he could take her from the Home whenever he wished, and Maggie would have to resort to legal means to keep the girl. She hoped it wouldn't come to that.

Finally, Maggie was worried about being away from the girl for nearly a month. She had reminded Gracie to tell Chun she would be back in a few weeks—but it was one thing to tell the girl that, and something quite different for the girl to believe it—or to even know what the word "return" meant. Abandonment was something these little slave girls understood only too well. And trusting an adult was a bewilderingly new notion that would take years to nurture—and it could be easily shattered, with devastating results.

護

The new place was different from Mama's place. Mainly because Chun was surrounded by girls all day and all night. And some of them were no bigger than she was. There were lots of girls too. Lots more than at Mama's place. There was Sau and Siu who had the same room. Then there was a new girl Haw who came only a little bit after Chun did. But then there were girls with funny-sounding American names. There was Gracie and Caroline. And Helen and Ethel and Jennie and Lily. And there were big girls too. Ones who got scared and talked about men like Ming and Hoy and Pon and Moy and Jun did. But the men never came to see the girls "upstairs" in "the Home." Just like Siu the chubby short girl said. So no one laughed at Chun about being with a man or asked her how much she cost.

And "The Home" was one of the first American words Chun learned. And "upstairs" too. Those were after "Miss Lake" and "Mrs. Kate." "The Home" was where she was living. And "upstairs" was the highest part where she could see everything. "The Home" was on "Washeendon-Street." And all the girls told her she should remember that big American word too. "TheHomeonWasheendonStreet."

One man Chun saw lots was Mr. Chan. He yelled at everybody on Jesus days like the Army people did out in the street. But he yelled indoors in the dark room downstairs where the sound bounced off the walls. Where she had to sit on a hard chair that bit her bones instead of just walking in and out of the crowds on the street where the Army people yelled. But no one downstairs yelled back at Mr. Chan or laughed at him like the people outside.

Most of the time Chun didn't listen to what Mr. Chan said. But sometimes he talked about a ghost that Jesus people had inside them. A ghost that was strong and good. And those times Chun listened. And she wondered if a girl like her could get that good ghost too. A good Jesus ghost to keep her safe all the time. That's what she wanted. And she knew that was why "the Home" didn't need ghost screens or altars by the stairs. It was because it had the powerful Jesus ghost floating inside it.

Miss Lake "played the piano" in the downstairs room too. That's what Siu said the sound-making was called. And everyone would sing after Mr. Chan stopped yelling. And Chun would watch Miss Lake's fingers going up and down and dream of "taking piano lessons" like Siu and Sau. That's what Siu and Sau called it. "Taking lessons."

Another man Chun saw from time to time was Tsang Wan, the sweaty fat cook with crooked fingers. But Mr. Tsang never looked at her or the other girls. He was too busy stirring pots and scraping woks over the hot stove. And because he already had two girls. Ruby and Pearl. And sometimes Chun saw them on Jesus days and sometimes in the kitchen with Tsang Wan.

But then there was Ti. And he was the biggest surprise of all. Ti came to see Chun one Sunday soon after she got to "the Home." Miss Lake wanted her to sing. And so she stood in front of everybody just like on the street with the Army people. And she sang the song she knew best. The Army *At the Cross* song. And Ti was sitting right there in front listening. And when she was done he smiled at her and said, "You sing beautiful."

Then Ti gave her money to give to Miss Lake. It was like when she sang for the Army people. And he said, "Do you remember me? Or the girl I used to visit at your place—Yet?"

And Chun said yes. And when he said "Yet" Chun almost remembered her too. How she hardly ever had to clean the girl's room because the girl kept it almost perfect. Except for the last time when there were broken things and water all over the floor. And after that Chun never saw Ti again. Until now in "the Home."

And Chun wondered why she was seeing him now after so long. If there was maybe a big girl at the Home he wanted. Then one day Ti said "From now on I'm going to give you the dollar I used to give Yet. It'll be for what it costs for you to live here." And Chun thought then for sure Ti would take her out of "the Home" after he gave Miss Lake enough money. Because Siu and Sau said a man could pay money to Miss Lake and Mrs. Kate for a girl and if they liked the man and thought the man wouldn't beat the girl he could have the girl after one year. So Chun always found Miss Lake and gave her the shiny money Ti gave her. And Miss Lake always smiled, and said, "Thank you." So Chun would look for Ti every Jesus day in the dark room downstairs. And it made her happy when she saw him. And she knew Miss Lake liked Ti too.

And another thing about "the Home" was that every day had a plan to it. Mama's place had a plan too. But in Mama's place Chun worked by herself and was always listening for Mama yelling or watching for her hitting. But at the Home all the little girls did things together and no one yelled or hit. At first Chun didn't know what to do without the yelling and hitting. So she just followed the other girls from one thing to another thing and from one place to another place and hoped she was doing the right thing.

They all got out of bed when they heard a bell. Then they all got on their knees beside their beds and said prayers in American to the Jesus god. Then they all marched downstairs to eat. Then they marched back upstairs to make their beds and clean their rooms and listen to Jesus stories. Then they studied American things. That was the morning. Then after eating again the little girls had quiet time in their rooms. And then they learned Chinese things and played the piano and sang. And then they ate again.

Every day they ate three times. And almost always there was enough. But sometimes the food was strange and Chun didn't like it. And she had to learn how to use the new American eating things. And each one had its own name and its own use. There was "spoon" and "fork" and "knife." They were much harder than chopsticks, too, because she had to choose the right one with the right food. And most of the time Chun didn't have a bowl to eat from, but instead had a round flat thing called "plate" which she wasn't allowed to pick up and put to her mouth like with a Chinese bowl. And it was a long ways from the plate to her mouth because she had to sit up straight too. And not bend over. And the other girls would laugh when she picked up the wrong thing or used the wrong hand or when the food fell off her fork. But Chun soon forgot about trying to save food for later. Because every day she ate three times.

The day before the Jesus day when Mr. Chan yelled at them in the dark room downstairs was always a special cleaning day. Saturday. At Mama's place Chun had to pick things up from the floor and table every day. That was cleaning at Mama's place. But here Mrs. Kate thought everything was dirty. Everything. Even people. And all the time. At first Chun just thought white people were really dirty and that was why Mrs. Kate always had them clean things. But Chun soon found out Mrs. Kate thought Chinese people were dirty too. Like white people. So every time before they ate they had to wash their hands. And after pooping and peeing too. And after they ate they had to take their dishes and cups and eating things to the kitchen door near the stairs and put them in a tub for the big girls to wash. Then the little girls had to wash the tables and chairs and sweep the floor. And so everything had to be cleaned all the time. But especially on Saturdays.

On Saturday everything in the Home got "dusted" with a stick that had beautiful bird feathers on the end of it. Then the rugs got beaten and the floors got swept and the big girls would get on their knees and wash the floors with warm bubbly water. And afterwards they would have baths in more warm bubbly water to wash their bodies. Every Saturday. And Saturday was harder than any day at Mama's place. But all the girls did the work and nobody got hit. And at the end of all the work Mrs. Kate "inspected" everything. But she never hit anyone. Even if the girls had to do something again. And Siu called it "training."

"When we get bigger we might go out to American houses and do work for them. And they'll pay us money to do it. Lots of Chinese girls do that," Siu said.

But even when they cleaned things, the little girls didn't spend time with the big girls. And Chun missed talking to Ming and Moy and big girls like that. She didn't miss Mama's place. But there was a hole in her chest when she thought of Mama's girls.

Siu said Chun should stay away from some of the big girls. Like Won Cum.

"You can always trust Gracie. And Caroline. And most times Toi Sing. But not Won Kum," Siu said. "Gracie hates her. She wants Won Kum to find a husband and leave."

And when Chun asked why, Siu said it was because Won Kum did bad things to girls. Then Chun told Siu that at Mama's place Ming said to tell her if someone wanted to do bad things.

Then Siu said "Well Ming's not here is she?"

護

Chun could see forever from the room at the top of the Home where the girls would sit quietly in the evenings. And sometimes when she stood by the window she wished she could fly away across the water to the green hills where the big smoking boats went. Like the seagulls and crows that could fly wherever they wanted. But Chun was learning that places were sometimes bigger on the inside than on the outside. And that was true about the Home. This place was bigger on the inside than Mama's place was on the outside. Outside in the alley and in the streets where the Army people took her. Here there were all kinds of things to learn. Here there were books and pianos and songs and stories and pictures. And girls who knew almost everything about everything. Like Siu and Sau who could play piano and read and write in American and Chinese both. And Chun wanted to be like that. Big on the inside.

法

Chapter Seven

LAW

Muriel squeezed into the gallery of the small courtroom off the second floor colonnade of City Hall. She found an empty chair in the back row and sat down. The court clerk stood beside the bench a few rows in front of her, hovering over Judge Coffey in what Muriel guessed was a pre-hearing conferral. The clerk glanced up from time to time, turning toward a gray-haired, wrinkled Chinese woman seated by the door—the one Muriel had nearly tripped over moments earlier. Despite being a few minutes late, Muriel apparently hadn't missed anything. She unbuttoned her gray silk jacket, opened her satchel, and took out a pad of paper and pencil.

Muriel had been in the building only a few times since its dedication at the end of the Endeavorer Convention two years previous—the summer she met Maggie. And as on those previous occasions, she was impressed with the building's size. It seemed even grander on the inside than the outside—with its bronzed and stained glass dome towering three hundred feet above the open double columned rotunda. Most people spoke in hushed tones when they walked inside for the first time, as though they were in a holy place—some medieval cathedral—instead of stuck in the muck of city politics.

Office doors and hallways radiated out from the rotunda like sunrays—or in a more mundane simile, like the spokes on a bicycle wheel.

People scurried nervously about, the way Muriel did when attending Easter services at an Episcopal church. But perhaps only the ornate façade was important to the city fathers, Muriel mused. There were rumors floating about that contractors had cut costs by filling the walls with beach sand instead of concrete—and if true, it was an apt metaphor for San Francisco politics.

Since that Endeavorer Convention and City Hall dedication, scarcely a week had passed without Muriel thinking of Maggie and Kate's Chinatown work. It wasn't that she wrote about their girls often—it was just that her emotions had gotten swallowed up by their stories. She couldn't get them out of her head or heart. And it hadn't been long before she also had Harry involved in the girls' lives. So now here the two of them were—husband and wife—teamed together in a courtroom with Maggie and one of the Home's newest inmates. Muriel was proud of Harry. But it was still surprising to see him in his element—in a setting quite foreign to her. This is what he must be like every day, she mused. The way most people see him. And yet she rarely had a similar opportunity—except when they argued at home and he put on what she called his "courtroom airs." But in this setting she was simply a newspaper reporter in a county courtroom, watching a lawyer work his craft. Muriel sat back in the uncomfortable wooden chair to watch the drama unfold.

Maggie was there too, of course, seated in the front row, facing Harry. Grace, the Mission's Chinese interpreter, sat next to Maggie, with the recently rescued Chun on her lap. All Muriel could see of the little girl was a little cornucopia boater hat poking over Grace's shoulder from time to time. There were a few other ladies whom Muriel vaguely recalled as being connected with the Salvation Army or the Rescue Home. Those she didn't recognize were probably the Board members Harry occasionally spoke of. From Harry's description, Muriel assumed Laura Williams was the somewhat frowzily dressed, overweight elderly woman perched uncomfortably on the edge of a chair to Maggie's left.

Everyone's attention seemed to be focused on Harry. He sat at a narrow table near Judge Coffey, surrounded by a plethora of papers, thumbing through a thick book. Harry had a cigar in hand and tapped it against the dull metal ashtray next to the book. Ashes fell onto the pages, and he hastily brushed them off. He marked a page with one of the papers, then snapped the book shut.

Judge Coffey was also smoking, and the room already smelled of Harry's Dick Custer cigar and Judge Coffey's Cuban, with its distinctive damp barnyard odor. If the hearing lasted more than an hour, people would have to cut their way through the blue haze.

An appalling sneeze forced Harry to raise his head, and he slowly scanned the room. It was the shriveled Chinese woman Muriel had stepped over when she entered. The way the woman cleared her throat made Muriel look for a spittoon. She didn't see one nearby.

Muriel fluttered her fingers at her husband in what she hoped was an unobtrusive greeting. Maggie, who had apparently been watching Harry, turned to see at whom he smiled.

"In the petition of guardianship for the Chinese girl called Chun." The clerk had begun the hearing. "Does the petitioner wish to make an opening statement?"

Maggie stood. "We do, sir. Our counsel, attorney Henry Monroe, has prepared an opening statement."

Harry stood and faced Judge Coffey. "Thank you, your Honor. I'm here this afternoon on behalf of Mrs. Laura Williams, Secretary of the Oriental Bureau of the *Woman's Home Missionary Society* and President of the Board of the Methodist Rescue Home at 916 Washington Street in this city; and on behalf of Miss Margarita Lake, deaconess of the Oriental Bureau, assigned to said Home. Miss Lake was responsible for arranging the rescue of said child on the afternoon of May 31.

"Secondarily, I am here on behalf of Mr. Frank Kane, Secretary of the *Pacific Society for the Suppression of Vice*, whom Miss Lake retained for conducting the rescue, and who is presently temporary guardian of said child.

"I intend to show that when the child was rescued, she was neglected and in poor health, living in a house of prostitution without parental oversight, and having frequently been seen begging on the streets of Chinatown. In view of the evidence I shall put forward today, I will ask you to grant Miss Margarita Lake guardianship of said child, and ask that the child remain under the care of Mrs. Katherine Lake, matron of the Methodist Rescue Home."

Muriel settled into a writing posture, scrunched in the constricted space of the four-row gallery. The chairs were bolted to the floor, and she pressed her knees against the chair in front to form a makeshift desk.

The respondent—speaking on behalf of Chun's alleged mother—was a swarthy, brushy-browed lawyer named Millard, whom Muriel recognized from the papers as someone often retained by the Chinatown tongs. He claimed he could prove Chun was, in fact, the brothel-keeper's child, born in the Palace Hotel on Jackson Street; that two witnesses would give sworn testimony they were there at the girl's birth; and that the girl was only on rare occasions in the brothel.

Harry spun the book on the table and took a pair of glasses from his vest pocket. "Your Honor, I have with me this afternoon a copy of the *Codes and Statutes of the State of California.* Page 87 of California Statutory Law—Section 309 reads as follows: 'the Penalty for Begging: Any child, apparently under the age of sixteen years, that comes within any of the following descriptions named: One. That is found begging, or receiving, or gathering alms (whether actually begging, or under the pretext of selling or offering for sale anything), or being in any street, road or public place for the purpose of so begging, gathering or receiving alms; Two. That is found wandering, and not having any settled place of abode or proper guardianship, or visible means of subsistence.'" Harry looked up from the book. "I'm skipping number three which does not apply to this case, and moving on to number four: 'That frequents the company of reputed thieves or prostitutes, or houses of prostitution or dance houses, concert saloons, theaters and varieties, or places specified in the first section of this Act, without parent or guardian, shall be arrested and brought before a court or magistrate.'"

Harry closed the book and tapped its binding. "The Methodist Mission believes these three descriptions fit the case of Chun—this Chinese girl—this street arab, seated before you. First: The girl was often seen 'begging, or receiving, or gathering alms' for the disreputable *God's Regular Army,* with whom Mr. Kane has had many dealings. In this regard, your Honor, I wish to call Mr. Kane to the stand to speak to this so-called 'Army.'" Harry returned to the other side of the table, sat down, and picked up his cigar.

Mr. Kane stood and addressed the judge. His handlebar mustache was thickly waxed, and pinned to the collar of his rumpled blue topcoat was a shiny six-pointed deputy's star. Muriel was curious as to how the man would comport himself. He had a reputation among newspaper reporters for occasional irascible, irreverent outbursts, dating back a few years to a series of confrontations he had had with the police during the Mid-Winter Exposition—over the sale of pornographic materials.

Mr. Kane began by drawing attention to his brass star—proving he was authorized to conduct the type of raid Miss Lake had requested. He said he had been retained by the Methodist women on the recommendation of Miss Cameron of the Presbyterian Occidental Home, for whom he had conducted a successful rescue.

"I have been following these religious imposters—this so-called *God's Regular Army*—ever since they appeared in the city two years ago, from their native Portland, Oregon. They were driven from that state due to their nefarious schemes, as shown by this article from a Portland newspaper." Mr. Kane reached inside his topcoat, pulled out a folded paper, and gave it to Harry. Harry handed it to the judge.

Mr. Millard, the attorney for the alleged mother, seized the moment to offer a rejoinder. "Your Honor, I wish to remind you that the Oriental girl's mother is as ignorant of the differences between various Christian sects as Mr. Kane and these Christian ladies are no doubt ignorant of the varieties of Oriental religions. All the Christian denominations in Chinatown use schools, food, and music to attract potential converts. We cannot expect ignorant heathens to understand the fine distinctions between higher religions that, frankly, confound even most Americans."

Judge Coffey put on his glasses and scanned the newspaper clipping before returning it to Harry. "Thank you, Mr. Kane." The judge turned toward Mr. Millard. "And I will take note of your comments, sir. But in the future you will do well to remain silent and seated until I give you permission to speak. You will have ample opportunity later to dispute the petitioner's claims."

Muriel was impressed with Mr. Kane's deportment under the circumstances. If Mr. Millard had been attempting to disturb Kane's composure, the tactic failed.

"Mr. Kane, you may proceed."

Mr. Kane went on to talk about his own past dealings with *God's Regular Army*, which he called a "fake religious order"—how it had opened a barracks near Chinatown and begun begging on behalf of the poor, and how its leaders canvassed merchants for money, provisions, and clothing—with everything ending up in their own pockets. "That's all, your Honor." Mr. Kane bowed toward Judge Coffey.

Harry stood and addressed the judge, gesturing toward Maggie and Gracie. "If it please your Honor, I wish to call upon little Chun over there—to sing something *God's Regular Army* taught her as a means to collect money for themselves. You will observe the presence of a court translator, because the child does not understand one word she sings."

Grace spoke to the girl in Chinese and set her on the floor.

Chun wore a white dress with a broad, blue line trim, and a dark blue satin bow collar. From the way she walked on the edges of her feet, her buckle shoes must have pinched her toes. Her boater hat was tied under her chin, and as she faced the judge, she tugged on the hat strings from time to time. She glanced twice over her shoulder at Maggie and Gracie, then belted out:

> "At the cross, at the cross, where I first saw the light,
>
> And the burden of my heart rolled away;
>
> It was there by faith I received my sight,
>
> And now I am happy all the day!"

When Chun finished, she turned and faced the courtroom. She smiled and bowed, and the courtroom observers burst into a round of spontaneous applause—including Judge Coffey himself. The little girl paused and surveyed the room as though searching for some sort of additional affirmation. When she turned toward the door, she froze. The old Chinese woman Muriel had nearly tripped over earlier was staring at the girl with an unearthly scowl. Muriel understood immediately who the woman was: The brothel keeper—the girl's supposed mother. Maggie told stories of how girls reacted when testifying in front of their abusers, and Harry was currently working with a group of lawyers who wanted to change California state law so children wouldn't have to face their tormentors in court.

Maggie leapt forward and swept Chun into her arms. The little girl shuddered and buried her face in Maggie's neck.

法

Chun closed her eyes. But she wasn't tired. It was because she saw Mama in the room and Mama stared at her like she was a ghost. Chun didn't know how Mama got into this place or how Mama knew she was here. But Chun knew if she held on to Miss Lake, Mama wouldn't touch her.

And Chun didn't know why Miss Lake and Gracie wanted her to sing. Because no one gave her money when she was done. People just smiled and clapped. Except for Mama who was like the wolf in the picture book Siu read to her. The one with big teeth that wanted to eat little girls.

In the old place where Mama beat her, Chun would sometimes climb out of her body and go to a different place where nothing hurt and where no one could make her afraid. And because Mama was in the room staring at her, Chun found a cable car for herself. Because she had liked the ride on the way over. So she got on it and went up into the sky like a bird. And it took her back to the Home where she could lie down for a nap in her own room. Where she was as far away from Mama as she could be.

法

Mr. Millard jumped out of his chair to protest Chun's singing. "I wish to call the petitioner's attention to the fact that Section 309 of the Code—"

Judge Coffey slammed his gavel on the bench, but Mr. Millard ignored its staccato drumbeat.

"Which the petitioner just quoted, explicitly makes exceptions 'for children used as singers or musicians in any church—'"

"Mr. Millard, you will sit immediately, or I will hold you in contempt of this court."

"Yes, your Honor. I apologize." But as Mr. Millard shuffled his papers and took his seat, he managed to finish his point: "And *God's Regular Army* is a religious organization. Thank you."

"Mr. Millard, you will remain silent until called upon by the bench, or I will adjourn this hearing and bar you from ever entering my courtroom again. Do you understand?"

"Yes, your Honor."

Harry seemed unruffled by Mr. Millard's second outburst. He leaned back in his chair and gazed at the ceiling fan slowly turning, droning overhead. He took a final puff from his cigar, then stood and walked in front of the table to face Judge Coffey. "What the respondent said is true." Harry crushed the cigar stub in the ashtray. "But children may be used as singers and musicians only on the written consent of the mayor of the city. If Mr. Millard can produce a document showing *God's Regular Army* is a church or has the written consent of Mayor Phelan to use child musicians in fundraising, then his point should be allowed to stand as evidence in this hearing. But as Mr. Kane has shown, the group is not a church. Nor is it listed as a legitimate charity in Charles Jenness's *Directory of the Charities of San Francisco.*

"Now, your Honor, I have two additional arguments." Harry tapped the thick volume on the table with his index finger. "May I continue?"

Judge Coffey nodded. "You may proceed. And that, Mr. Millard, was your last disruption. Do you understand?"

Harry waited for Mr. Millard to acknowledge the judge's warning. "Thank you, your Honor. Now my second point has to do with paragraph two of the *Codes and Statutes of the State of California.* Page 87 of California Statutory Law—Section 309: 'This child was often found wandering, and not having any settled place of abode or proper guardianship.'

"I call on Ah Quai to make a statement."

The Chinese woman Muriel recognized as Old Mary stepped forward hesitantly to face the judge. "That girl over there stayed with the Sing family sometimes." Old Mary wore the regular Salvation Army uniform of cadet blue and kept pushing back her oversized drooping hallelujah bonnet—apparently so she could see the judge.

"When she got sick last year, the keeper there, Kim Yook, was afraid the girl might die at her place and bring bad luck to it." Old Mary paused and pointed at the gray-haired Chinese woman slumped in the chair near the door. "So she sent her to the Sing's place. After that I saw her in the alley lots of times—by herself. With no adult. When I asked about the girl, the keeper told me she adopted her. That the mother was dead."

Harry thanked the Chinese Salvationist, then began his final argument. "My third point, you Honor, has to do with paragraph three of *Codes and Statutes of the State of California.* Page 87 of California Statutory

Law—Section 309: 'The child frequents the company of reputed thieves or prostitutes, and houses of prostitution without parent or appropriate guardian.'"

After calling upon Captain Thomas of the Salvation Army to describe her encounters with Chun in Spofford Alley, Mr. Leong, the young China-man whom Muriel had interviewed a few months earlier, during the last quarantine, approached the bench.

"I used to see a girl at that place." Mr. Leong stuffed his hands deep into his pockets, his flexed fists bulging at the thighs of his thin black pan-taloons. "One time I ask about Chun, the little girl there." He turned to-ward Chun. "Because she a baby then—and just show up one week.

"The girl I used to see there—Yet, she say Chun—the little one there, sell by mother to keeper of that place—that woman." Mr. Leong pointed at Kim Yook, who glowered at him and began to push herself out of her chair. The Chinese translator sitting next to the old woman poked her in the ribs and said something, and she sat down—but not before doubling over in another fit of coughing.

Mr. Leong eyed Chun, whose head lay on Maggie's shoulder.

"The girl I was with, say—" he paused and tilted his head back as though he had just discovered the ceiling fan. "She say when keeper buy girl it make her keeper's baby—her slave—like Ye—" Mr. Leong's voice faded to a whisper and his head slumped forward. "Like everybody in that place."

"Mr. Leong, can you tell us when you first saw the girl in the brothel?" Judge Coffey emphasized the word "first."

"Maybe two year—in summer. About Moon Festival time."

"Did you see her there more than once?"

"Only Saturday. Every Saturday. Maybe six month. She almost always there."

Judge Coffey pressed home his point. "Did the owner try to keep her away from the other girls there?"

"No. The girl just there. Do chores."

"Did the child show any signs of abuse or neglect?"

"Don't understand." Mr. Leong turned toward the interpreter, but Judge Coffey waved him off.

"Did the girl have cuts or bruises? Was she dirty or in rags?"

"She sometime clean. Sometime not." Mr. Leong's hands were thrust deep in his pockets again. "She always wear same thing. A thing pull over head." He lifted his arms and mimicked pulling down a smock. "That's all." Mr. Leong glanced at Harry. "One time she want show me a place on her body where she say someone hurt her. But I don't look." Muriel leaned forward in her chair, straining to hear his final words. "But that woman there hit all her girls—so I think she hit Chun too."

法

Chun was tired and her feet hurt. She didn't know why she was still in this hot room full of smoke that made her eyes burn. She didn't know why Ti was here. And why people were talking, talking, talking, like Sunday with Mr. Chan. She wondered if she was going to sing again. She yawned and looked over Miss Lake's shoulder and saw an American lady with a big pretty hat that was even bigger than hers. And the American lady was writing in a book like when Siu and Sau and her played school. And she wished she was back at the Home with the other girls.

Then Chun heard Mama. Mama said Chun is my daughter. And that it's hard to raise a daughter without a man. And that she's always careful to give her daughter food and a safe place to live. And that she wants her daughter to go to school in China to become a famous singer. But she needs money and that's why she has the other girls. To make money so she can send Chun to China to go to school.

Then there was an American man talking. "Let the record show that the mother of the child seated there has in her possession the child's official County of San Francisco birth record. It proves the child was born to her at the back of the Palace Hotel on Jackson Street. Number 614.

"And now I call upon two Chinese witnesses who will swear to this court they were present in the Palace Hotel when the child was born to the mother seated before you."

法

Chun closed her eyes again to make Mama go away. She buried her head in Miss Lake's shoulder and was soon up in the sky again in the cable car that she was riding before. She took off her shoes and threw them out the cable car window and watched them float in the sky. She wiggled her toes. This time Gracie and Miss Lake were with her and Gracie told her she was going to sing again. This time for money. Some place far away. Maybe across the water.

But now she was holding on to Miss Lake's neck again and Miss Lake smelled like sunshine and white fluffy clouds. And she wouldn't look at Mama. And the people in the room were talking and talking and talking some more. Then Chun fell asleep. With her arms tight around Miss Lake's neck.

法

After a brief recess, Judge Coffey reconvened the hearing. He tapped his gavel on the bench, and the clerk rose. "Order in the court!"

Judge Coffey cleared his throat. "Thank you. In the guardianship hearing of Chun, the alleged daughter of Kim Yook. The court decides in favor of the Methodist Mission and Mr. Kane. Although Mr. Kane has expressed privately to me certain reservations about leaving the girl in the Methodist Rescue Asylum, it seems best under the present circumstances, and for the child's sake, not to make any changes in her living arrangements. Therefore, Mr. Kane shall retain guardianship of the girl, but she shall remain under the care of Miss Margarita Lake, her mother Mrs. Kate Lake, and the Oriental Board." The judge tapped the gavel on the bench once more. "This court is adjourned."

Muriel dropped her pencil and paper into her satchel, and threaded her way from the gallery's narrow aisle toward the front of the courtroom where Maggie stood. By the time Muriel managed to squeeze around Mr. Millard, the translator, and Kim Yook huddled near the door, Mr. Kane had taken aside Maggie and the frowzily dressed fat woman, and was making some point about the dangers of mixing young girls like Chun with older rescued brothel girls and steamship detainees. Mr. Kane's black bowler hat was tucked under his arm and he jabbed a forefinger perilously close to Maggie's breasts. "I prefer to place the rescued children under my guardianship with trusted families," he was saying. "And as you know, I have no qualms about relinquishing my guardianship rights to any child left in the Presbyterian Home. Miss Cameron and her Board keep those two types of girls separate from each other." The man's handlebar mustache wiggled nervously as a fly buzzed about his large nose. He swatted at the insect, but missed. "Now, the day I came to see Chun in your Home, you intimated the inmates' current living arrangements were only temporary. Are you any closer to purchasing a site for a new Home?"

Maggie shrank from Mr. Kane's probing finger, and the fat woman whom Muriel supposed was Laura Williams, stepped forward. "You'll be happy to know, Mr. Kane, that we've purchased a lot across Trenton Street from our present Rescue Asylum. We hope to begin construction next month."

Mr. Kane stepped back, smiled, and donned his hat. "Well, ladies, that is indeed good news. I congratulate your Board on securing a property so close to your present Mission. I look forward to touring the building when it's completed. At that time I will determine whether it meets the specific moral requirements stipulated by my organization. If it does not, I may have to explore other options for Chun's care."

Muriel watched Maggie's neck and shoulders stiffen. "You should also know, Mr. Kane, we Methodists have a different understanding of human nature than the Presbyterians do—or than you Catholics, for that matter. We don't believe it's necessary to separate our girls into different classes of people based upon their former lives. And our Board doesn't think our older girls contaminate the younger ones. With proper training, our little rescued slave girls are prepared to receive God's sanctifying grace regardless of their surroundings. You need look no further than Grace there, as an example of what our work can accomplish." Maggie pointed to the girl chasing a giggling Chun through the maze of courtroom chairs. "With God's help."

Muriel momentarily abandoned her attempt to talk to Maggie and returned to her seat to retrieve her satchel. She had just witnessed a classroom debate in medieval philosophy. Mr. Kane seemed to think of human vices as a sort of bacteria—almost like Dr. Kinyoun's plague bacillus—

something children were especially susceptible to; something that would destroy the moral fabric of society if not isolated and quarantined. That, coupled no doubt with Mr. Kane's typical American view of the Oriental propensity toward immorality and duplicity, compounded the problem of leaving a young girl with naïve Methodists.

By the time Muriel retrieved her satchel and jacket, Maggie was gone. And Harry, now with Laura Williams at his side, was deep in conversation with Judge Coffey. Muriel caught her husband's eye, waved goodbye, and hurried down the stairs to catch Maggie. She found her with Grace and Chun at the corner of Eighth and Market, waiting for a streetcar. She touched Maggie's arm as one of those strange new horseless carriages whizzed by scattering a group of gawking pedestrians.

"I see you finally got away from Mr. Kane."

Maggie pursed her lips. "Yes, he was quite annoying. I've never met an American so concerned about our accommodations. And I don't understand why. There's really very little difference between our Home and the Presbyterians. But he seems to think there's a world—and perhaps a few extra planets, between us." She waved at an approaching streetcar, and it rumbled to a stop a few yards in front of them. "But I think my comments at the end satisfied him and Laura. Time will tell, I suppose."

"Speaking of accommodations, Maggie, I've been meaning to ask you—how much does it cost to support a girl?"

"Fifteen dollars a month." Maggie stepped onto the streetcar behind Grace and Chun. "And thanks again for coming today, Muriel. Keeping cases like Chun's in the papers is a real help in putting a stop to this awful trafficking."

"Harry and I've been thinking." Muriel shouted at Maggie as the streetcar conductor collected his final fares. "We'd like to help with Chun's monthly support." But she wasn't sure Maggie heard her last sentence.

法

True to Laura Williams's word, on Wednesday, July 17, 1901, on the twenty-first anniversary of the *Woman's Missionary Society of the Pacific Coast*, a new Oriental Home was dedicated at 912 Washington Street, across Trenton from Reverend Gibson's original 1870 Mission building. It was a two-floor former cigar factory with a high, windowed basement, added to and remodeled with a faux-Spanish style façade.

The *International Epworth League Convention* was in San Francisco the same week, with over twenty-five thousand young people attending various meetings at Mechanics' Pavilion. More than a thousand visitors came through the Home that week alone, and the Mission girls sang almost daily for their Epworth and *WHMS* guests.

Maggie spent all day Wednesday at the hospitality events, greeting guests and leading tours of the Oriental Home. At noon she found Mr. Kane in line with what she assumed were two of his *Society for the Suppression of Vice* underlings. They were sandwiched between five starry-eyed Epworth girls from Pennsylvania and Chinese Consul-General Ho Yow and his family.

Mr. Kane approached Maggie and tipped his hat. "You haven't been answering my letters, Miss Lake." He spoke quietly, in the practiced, authoritative voice Maggie recognized as belonging to an officer of the law. "So I thought I'd come over in person." Mr. Kane straightened and quickly moved into the parlor.

Maggie felt her face turning red. "As you can see, folks, we've been very busy preparing for today's dedication ceremony." She found herself speaking to the back of Mr. Kane's head. "I'm sure you'll be pleased with our new Home—and with the little ones' accommodations upstairs."

After greeting a few more guests and leaving the welcome table to Grace and Caroline, Maggie led Mr. Kane, the Pennsylvania Epworth Leaguers, and the Chinese Consul's family through the front parlor with its large stone fireplace, to the girls' classroom directly behind it. The girls had written a list of spelling words on the blackboard, as though a lesson were in progress. "You can see we still need rugs and curtains, and a few more desks for the classroom."

Maggie pointed to her right as they walked through the classroom to the back stairs. "Down that hallway is a small reception room, the matron's kitchen, and two rooms for the Japanese missionary. Our basement has a sunny room facing Washington Street," she said when they got downstairs. "That's our Chinatown kindergarten classroom. To the left are the kitchen, dining room, washroom, and storeroom."

Maggie climbed the two flights of back stairs to the second floor, just as her mother was leading another group down the central stairs to the parlor. "Here we have the matron's room, six dormitory rooms, a sick room, and two bathrooms. You can see the rooms are quite spacious, with only two or three girls per. But each room can accommodate six inmates. And if you look out the windows on that side—" Maggie pointed north, "you can see we're building a tall fence around the back of our property to protect the girls from those who would try to kidnap them and return them to lives of slavery. All the windows on the ground floor have heavy iron screens on them, and all our doors are constantly locked. They can only be opened by a responsible adult."

Mr. Kane had taken a notebook from his coat pocket, and he stopped his scribbling to peer into one of the bedrooms. "But what are you doing to protect the girls on the inside from each other? It seems both types of girls are kept on the same floor—the babies and little rescued slave girls right next to the older girls—those who have lived lives of ill-fame." He stepped across the hallway. "And they all use the same bathrooms?"

There was a moment of uncomfortable silence as the little tour group turned toward Maggie and awaited her response. "We have a different philosophy from Catholic organizations—or from the Presbyterian Occidental Home around the corner." Maggie surveyed her audience, smiling at each person as she caught their eye.

"Miss Lake, *The Society for the Suppression of Vice* is not a Catholic organization." Mr. Kane's comment had an edge to it—a certain testiness Maggie could taste on the tip of her tongue. The upstairs hallway suddenly seemed cramped and warm. The smell of fresh paint stung Maggie's eyes, and she wished she had had the girls open some of the upstairs windows earlier. "I know the *Society* isn't officially Catholic, Mr. Kane. But you— and your former *Society*—the *Youth's Directory* are."

Mr. Kane ignored her remark and wandered down the hall, away from the little tour group.

"My point is," Maggie raised her voice so Mr. Kane could still hear. "We don't believe our older girls are bad influences on the younger ones. In fact, we think by keeping our Home more like a family—with a wide variety of different-aged girls, and with the older girls caring for the younger ones—that they lose the effects of the brothels more quickly, and learn how to be good older sisters and mothers. We take the Home part of our name very seriously. And we do not take it lightly that we call ourselves a family. The babies call my mother—our matron—the same name I use for her—'Mama.' Family, home, and mama are not idle words to us." Maggie managed a lop-sided smile at Mr. Kane, who apparently had finished his private inspection and returned to the group.

"Yes, I understand all that." Mr. Kane pursed his lips in what Maggie thought was a condescending manner. "But as you know, Miss Lake, there are many kinds of families in this world, and we need to be sure the homes where we place our children are safer than the ones we take them from."

"Well, thankfully we have the testimony of our girls, the ones who have left here and married, and are now raising families. And if you care to stay for a few minutes after the tour, you'll all have a chance to hear from some of them. I do hope you can stay." Maggie meant the invitation for everyone. But she was staring straight at Mr. Kane as she spoke.

法

Later that evening Mr. Kane sauntered up to the Oriental Home entrance just as Maggie, Kate, and the girls finished planting two beech trees alongside the new sidewalk. Maggie's fingernails were caked with dirt and she held a trowel in one hand, but she stood to greet him.

Mr. Kane reached into his topcoat and pulled out a fat envelope. "Here. This is for you and your mother." He thrust the letter into Maggie's empty hand. It had the stamp of San Francisco Superior Court in the top left hand corner.

"What's this?"

"The kind of letter you can't afford to ignore, ma'am. A court summons. A writ of habeas corpus. For Chun."

Without awaiting her reply, Mr. Kane tipped his bowler hat, spun, and marched up the street.

Maggie's body shook in a barely controlled rage. She turned toward her mother. "Mama—?"

法

After they finished planting the baby trees Chun asked Siu if she would help her make a sign. Chun had been in school long enough now to know her alphabet but she wasn't very good at putting letters together to make English words. And she knew she wanted a special word to print on a sign for their bedroom door in the new Home. After she told Siu her word, Siu said she would help. So they asked Mrs. Kate for paper and a pencil and Mrs. Kate said, "What are you going to do?" So Chun told her and then Mrs. Kate said they could do it. But not to use glue or pins on the door. And Siu said, "Well how will it be a sign if we can't put it on the door?" And Mrs. Kate said, "Well maybe you can put holes in the paper and put string through the holes and then loop it on the doorknob." And so that's what they did.

Chun wrote the word "Best" on the sign for their door. And she wrote the word about a hundred times. Enough to cover the whole sheet of paper. And at the end she wrote: "Home ever." Because that's what she thought. That it was going to be the very best place in the whole world.

法

Muriel sat at the dining room table after supper, sipping absinthe mixed with sugar water from a fluted champagne glass. Wisps of smoke from her Dick Custer cigar hung in the air above the ashtray on the table beside her. "So how exactly would a writ apply in a case like Chun's?" She felt lightheaded, and she wasn't sure how much longer she would be able to concentrate on her husband's response.

Harry was in the parlor, and when she heard him clear his throat, she knew he was working himself into a professorial mode. Harry stuck his head into the dining room, an empty shot glass in one hand and a cigar in the other.

"Well, dear, I assume Mr. Kane has tried to get Chun on other occasions, and Maggie and Kate have refused to let him see her. But if that's so, I know nothing about it. They haven't said a word to me about Mr. Kane since Chun's guardianship hearing last summer." Harry tapped his cigar on the rim of the shot glass.

"Now, if he's following the approach of the law, and I assume he is—I know he's taken out writs of habeas corpus in other cases—then he's also already written to Maggie and Kate, stating his reasons for wanting Chun. He's still her legal guardian, so of course he has a right to take her. The court established that last summer. I suppose he thinks he has a good reason for taking her out, and that he's acting in her best interests. Obviously, he doesn't have easy access to Chun, since she's living in the Home and men aren't allowed to roam the building. So as a last resort, he can only get to Chun by filing a writ." Harry took a long pull on his cigar and blew a thin, roiling smoke ring in Muriel's direction. It was a skill she hadn't yet mastered.

He strode into the dining room and braced his hands on the edge of the table. He stared over Muriel's head as though he were at a podium, addressing a lecture hall of devoted students. "Class, the writ of habeas corpus is as follows: It is a summons with the force of a court order. In this case it is addressed to the custodian or custodians (our example shall be Kate and Maggie Lake), with the demand that the 'prisoner' (our example shall be the little slave girl, Chun) be taken before the court, and that the custodians present proof of their authority to keep the child. The court then determines whether the custodians have lawful authority to detain the prisoner. If the court determines the custodians—Maggie and Kate— are acting beyond their authority, then the prisoner must be released."

"Oh stop it Harry." Muriel put a finger in her drink and flicked a bit of absinthe in his direction. Harry pretended to jump back toward the parlor, but in the process, he scattered a line of glowing ash across the hardwood floor of their Oakland bungalow.

法

Chun and Won Kum were in the downstairs parlor looking out at Washington Street on a summer day when Won Kum told Chun that American August was Hungry Ghost Month. "See those men burning incense and paper money and setting food out on tables, and others marching around, banging those gongs and things? They're either feeding their favorite ancestors and giving them money, or trying to chase away the evil ones." Then Won Kum turned away from the window and looked at Chun. "Yue

Tschi says people who want to get married should do that too—to have good luck in life."

A few days after Won Kum said that, Miss Lake told Chun they had to go to court again. To see Mr. Kane. Chun wondered why she had to see the man in the blue coat again. And she wondered if her old Mama would be there too. She asked Won Kum if Mr. Kane could be a ghost trying to take her to a bad place under the earth. But Won Kum said no, he was a white devil. And she didn't know how Chinese things worked with them. She only knew how things worked with Chinese people. And since no one in the Home was allowed to burn money for their ancestors, bad things could happen to them all. And that made Chun even more scared. So she decided to ask Siu about Mr. Kane and ghosts.

"You don't need to worry about any of that," Siu said when Chun asked her about Hungry Ghost Month and Mr. Kane.

They were doing their Saturday chores in the downstairs parlor and Chun was holding a picture of some old Home ladies. It had glass on the front so she had to be careful when she picked it up. She wiped it with her dust cloth then set it gently on the wooden whatnot.

"Me and Sau are getting the Holy Ghost pretty soon." Siu frowned at Chun. "You should move that picture more the other way. You're sup-posed to put things back in exactly the same place you found them. That's what Mrs. Kate says."

Chun moved the picture further to the right.

"The Holy Ghost's more powerful than any Chinese ghost. Or white devil too. Everybody knows that. So when we get it we'll be able to keep you safe."

Chun had heard Mr. Chan talk about the Holy Ghost but he never said what it was. So she asked Siu because Siu knew almost everything.

"It's like this." Siu sat on the parlor couch and threw her dust cloth on the floor. "You get the Holy Ghost when you get baptized." Siu rolled her eyes at Chun. Like Chun didn't know anything.

"Does getting the water on your head turn you into a ghost?" Chun stopped dusting and turned to look at Siu so she could think about Siu's words.

"No, dummy. You only turn into a ghost when you die.

"And you need to keep dusting. There's other pictures on that lower shelf."

Chun went back to the whatnot and pretended to dust.

"After you get baptized you go around helping people," Siu said. "That's all. Then later you get regerspected."

"What's regerspected?" Chun was getting more confused by the minute. All she wanted was the Holy Ghost. She didn't care about the other things that came along with it. She moved a picture so it made a noise. So Siu would think she was still dusting.

"It's when Jesus comes back. Like Easter with the colored eggs and everything. You remember that, don't you?"

Even standing backwards Chun could tell Siu was cross. So Chun just said yes. She knew she had asked too many questions.

"When me and Sau get baptized, you'll understand."

Chun turned around in time to see Siu's eyebrows go up like when she had a secret to tell. "We'll get American names too. I already picked one. I'm going to be Susie."

"I like that name," Chun said. "It's like you already have part of it."

"That's why I picked it," Siu said. "Are you finished dusting already?"

"Yes." Chun folded her dust rag like Siu showed her, then sat on the parlor couch next to Siu.

"Anyway, having the Holy Ghost inside you makes you stronger than any ghosts or devils on the outside. That's why I want it."

"I want the Holy Ghost too," Chun said. "Before I go to court and see Mr. Kane."

"Well, you'll have to talk to Miss Lake and Mr. Chan about that. It might take longer for you because you're littler.

"And after we get baptized we're going to be King's Daughters. Just like the big girls. Only Junior. I've already asked Miss Lake and she said we can." Siu frowned and took Chun's rag.

"I want to be that too," Chun said.

Siu rolled her eyes again. "You don't even know what it is."

"Well what then?"

Siu sighed. "When will I ever stop explaining things?

"King's Daughters is learning about Jesus. And singing. And the most important thing is standing up in front of everybody and saying this."

Then Siu walked to the other side of the parlor and stood under the arched doorway to the classroom. She turned to face Chun and fluffed her dress.

"Look up, not down:

Look forward, not back:

Look out, not in:

Lend a hand."

Then Siu turned sideways and stretched out her hand. "Thank you, Reverend Chan." She pretended to take something from him and put it on her dress. When she finished she came back and sat on the couch. "I already know those King's Daughter words. Gracie taught me. And the other part I did was getting a cross to pin on my dress. That's the most important thing. Because that's how the bad ghosts know if someone's a King's Daughter or not. When they see the cross they run away. So now you know, and you won't have to ask again."

Later Chun found out she couldn't be baptized before she saw Mr. Kane. As usual, what Siu said was true. Miss Lake and Mr. Chan wouldn't even talk about baptizing her until long after Christmas. And maybe not even then.

"You need to be in Sunday school for at least a year more. Then we can talk about it," they said.

But the good news was, everybody said they would pray for Chun when she went to see Mr. Kane. And every night before bed they did. And Siu's prayers were always the best. They went on and on and talked about Jesus and God and the Holy Ghost and the father. And sometimes she added things about Mary and Joseph and angels too. It always made Chun feel good when Siu finished.

法

On August 26, 1901, Maggie appeared in Superior Court, holding Chun's little hand. And once again Muriel was in the gallery—pencil and notepad poised; nose pointed at Harry's backside as he faced the judge.

Maggie had told Muriel how angry Laura Williams was when she discovered Maggie and her mother had received letters from Mr. Kane and hadn't told her. Laura said at least they should have told Harry, since he could have provided them with legal advice. She couldn't believe after five years in the work, Maggie and Kate still didn't trust her enough to tell her things. "Now we're back where we started, and who knows what the man will try next," Laura had fumed.

Muriel's newspaper account the next day summarized the hearing, and at the same time, deepened her suspicion of Mr. Kane's motives in Chun's guardianship. Muriel suspected his motives were less than honorable. But what they were, exactly, she was unsure. Harry seemed to think the man had been promised a monetary reward for placing out the girl. Muriel, however, wondered if Kane's interests were prurient. But she kept that theory to herself. She didn't want to risk losing what little professional credibility she still retained with her husband by raising the possibility that Mr. Kane liked to touch little girls.

But Mr. Kane claimed he had two reasons for serving the writ of habeas corpus. First, he was merely following the same philosophy he used in the past when placing out American children. His preference was always to find a reputable family. Institutions—whether religious or otherwise, were always secondary options. In this case, Mr. Kane claimed to have found an honorable Chinese merchant at 754 Washington Street. A Mr. Wing Hong. Mr. Hong, with his wife and two children, wished to adopt the six year-old Chun. As with his placements of American children, Chun would be with Mr. Hong's family on a trial basis only, and if it didn't work, Mr. Kane would return Chun to the Home.

Mr. Kane's second reason for serving the writ was based upon his original understanding that the new Home, when completed, would have separate floors to keep younger children, like Chun, away from the contaminating influences of older, former brothel girls. That was the only reason he had agreed to keep Chun temporarily in the old Methodist Home. But when he visited the Oriental Home a little over a month ago, on the day of its dedication, he was surprised and shocked to find the living arrangements in the new building were no different than what they had been previously. Both types of inmates were still living together on the same floor.

Mr. Kane rested his case. Chun should be taken from the Home and put with a Chinese family. It was the only morally acceptable thing to do.

Harry, however, argued Mr. Kane's reasons for taking Chun from the Home were complicated by additional facts. For example, Harry discovered Mr. Kane's "Chinese merchant" was in reality a saloon keeper, and his alleged wife was actually Kim Yook, the brothel keeper at 11 Spofford Alley. Harry drove home the point that Mr. Kane had no understanding of the Chinatown economy or how valuable girls were to it. It was naïve of Mr. Kane to assume his merchant, Mr. Hong, wanted to raise a daughter when Chun could be sold for nearly five hundred dollars the very next day—or if kept until the age of twelve or thirteen, sold for three times that amount.

At the end of the day Judge Cook determined that regardless of Mr. Kane's intentions, the Chinatown economy would ultimately dictate the girl's fate. And that meant the girl would likely end up with her former owner if Mr. Hong's family was awarded custody. With that in mind, Judge Cook rejected Kane's writ and returned Chun to the Oriental Home.

法

Chun spent a whole boring long day listening to Mr. Kane talk about her. And at breakfast the next morning she told Siu what happened.

"There were three empty chairs in the front row next to Mr. Kane. Just like what Won Kum said. For Chinese ghosts. And Mr. Kane kept looking at the chairs like there was somebody sitting there. But nobody was. And then he looked at me like he wanted me to go with him."

Siu snorted. "That doesn't mean anything. You need to stop listening to Won Kum. You're still here, aren't you?"

"Yes. But Mr. Kane got Haw didn't he?"

"That was different." Siu rolled her eyes like she always did when she knew the answer. "That's because Haw has a real mama, Miss Lake said. And you don't."

And as usual, Siu was right.

法

Not long after Hungry Ghost month when Chun saw Mr. Kane, Miss Lake said she could start piano lessons.

"These are called keys." Miss Lake sat beside Chun at the piano. "Every key has a name—like your ABC's. They're called notes. And you can learn to read notes to make a musical story—like in your Grade Two reader with Mrs. Kate." Then Miss Lake opened a book that was on the piano. "These funny looking things are the notes. A-B-C-D-E-F-G—and then it starts again.

"This note is called middle C." She took Chun's thumb and placed it on a key below two black keys.

"I know that one," Chun said. "Siu told me." And she showed Miss Lake where to find other C notes.

Miss Lake liked that Chun already knew about the piano, so she showed Chun how to find middle C in the book.

Before long, Chun could play songs. Like "Twinkle Twinkle" and "Jingle Bells." But Siu said, "Why are you playing those? It's not even Christmas."

Chun was bigger now both on the outside and on the inside. And before long she was almost as good as Siu at piano. "That's because you like it more," said Siu. "If I liked it as much as you I could be better too."

After that Siu and Sau got baptized. Which meant Siu got the new name she was waiting for. "You have to call me Susie now," she told everybody. "If you call me Siu, I won't answer."

法

Muriel sat at her *Examiner* desk in the Hearst Building at Third and Market, reviewing the day's Superior Court calendar. For some unknown reason, the news cycle was typically light in the weeks before Christmas, and she had learned over the years to scan the daily calendar for possible stories when things slowed. Muriel gasped when she saw Laura Williams's name on the docket. She read aloud: "Oriental Home petition to revoke guardianship of *Pacific Society for the Suppression of Vice.*" No one had mentioned to her any new developments in Chun's case.

Until now, Harry and Maggie had been good about keeping Muriel apprised of changes in the girl's status—still somewhat worrisome a year after the court had rejected Mr. Kane's writ of habeas corpus, yet preserved his role as Chun's guardian.

Muriel checked the time of the hearing: 9:15. If she left immediately, she might make it in time. She would call her husband when she returned, and scold him severely for failing to mention the court date.

When Muriel arrived in the courtroom, the hearing was wrapping up. Laura was without counsel, and apparently making her final remarks. "This is one of the placards Mr. Kane posted in Chinatown to warn people against sending their children to the Mission." Laura waved a yellowed half-broadsheet in the judge's face. "He's written here that the Mission is merely a place to barter marriage proposals. His actions show a total lack of regard and respect for our work, and they damage the Mission's reputation." Laura folded the broadsheet and put it under her arm. "Instead of coming to us, Mr. Kane is simply trying to defame us. I ask that you revoke his guardianship of Mei Chun Lai. Mr. Kane has never once attempted to visit his ward. And the placards reveal his true character. He's irascible and quick tempered, unfit to have possession of the child."

The judge shuffled through Chun's thick file for a few minutes, then pushed it aside. "Normally, a minor whose custody is challenged has only a minimal role in the proceedings, and the court won't consider the ward's personal wishes until the minor is fourteen years old. But sometimes we ask children of tender years whom they wish to live with, and depending on the situation we might side with them over a guardian's desires. If you think the girl in question understands the gravity of her situation, I'm willing to schedule the hearing in probate court. Perhaps this time the girl can speak for herself, and put an end to this ridiculousness." The judge sent Laura away with a hearing tentatively set for Friday, January 9, 1903.

Much to Harry's and Maggie's consternation, Muriel's telephone call to them later that day was the first they knew of Mrs. William's petition. The woman had acted entirely on her own.

法

It was the second day of January, and Maggie had missed her monthly. She knew it was probably the stress of Chun's guardianship hearing, so she wasn't particularly worried. She had missed monthlies in similar situations. But this time there was the additional concern of Won Kum's upcoming marriage to Yue Tschi.

Maggie and Mama had opposed it from the beginning. They had heard from Leong Ti and others that Yue Tschi was a highbinder in the Hop Sing tong—and heavily involved in buying and selling girls. But Laura had friends in Chinatown who vouched for the man's morals, and the woman trusted their judgment. On top of this, Laura had gotten Grace on her side, and poisoned the girl. Now Gracie was wildly enthusiastic about the marriage, refusing to listen—or even speak to Maggie and Mama. With Gracie as her ally, Laura had stepped up her meddling in the Home's daily affairs, planning Won Kum's wedding and trying to control all aspects of Chun's hearing.

But Maggie had other personal health concerns. She wasn't eating properly, and was losing weight—more than usual under such conditions.

"Maggie, you should make an appointment to see Uncle Ben again," Mama told her more than once. "You can't afford to get any thinner. I know you think it's the stress, but maybe it's something else. And whatever the cause, you simply have to stop worrying about what Laura thinks. You've always done what you thought was right, and whatever is going on between Grace and the other girls, you need to forget about it and concentrate on Chun's case. Once that's over, you can work on mending fences with Grace and Laura."

法

"Thanks for bringing so many documents."

Maggie plopped everything Harry requested on the classroom table in the Home. She was exhausted. It was only nine o'clock, but it felt like two in the morning. Either way, she wouldn't be sleeping if she were in bed. She had probably slept only three or four hours a night for the past month.

"This all could prove useful." But the way Harry's eyes searched her face told Maggie he was more concerned about her than he was with anything she had brought. Maggie gripped the table and pretended to ponder the collection of notes and journals; the daybooks, the letters, and the committee minutes, all stacked in front of the Oriental Home's pro bono attorney.

Harry went back to sifting through the materials. From time to time he pulled a document from the pile. "These show your interest in Chun began long before Mr. Kane was involved." He slid a couple of pages of scribbled committee minutes toward Maggie. "That's good. The other major issue, of course, is Mr. Kane's concern that the Home's not a morally safe place—perhaps not even a physically safe place for Chun. The law centers on what's in the best interest of the child with respect to the child's physical, mental, and moral welfare—"

"You know we have a different philosophy than Mr. Kane's organization on that." Maggie hoped her voice didn't reveal her irritation. "It's what started the problems last year. I don't know if we can add anything to what we said then."

"Yes, I understand. So I'd rather not focus on issues that can't be proven in court. Judge Coffey respects your work, but it will be better if we can make this about Mr. Kane's character—and not about yours or the Home's. For example, the law states a guardian might be removed for any of the following reasons." Harry flipped open a notepad and began to read from what appeared to be a hastily copied summary. "First, for abuse of his trust; Second, for continued failure to perform his duties; and third, for having an interest adverse to the faithful performance of his duties.

"I think Laura covered the first two issues in her petition last month. But more importantly, last week Muriel finally heard back from a reporter at *The Call* who has followed Kane's rescues over the past few years. What she found pertains to the third reason: The guardian's adverse interest."

Maggie sat down, suddenly alert, despite the pounding ache in the back of her neck. Harry flipped another page of his notepad.

"It seems that five years ago, Kane was charged with contempt of court for allegedly kidnapping a girl—after the court had already granted custody to her mother. The prosecution contended Kane had become the catspaw of a private detective who lay claim to the girl's deceased father's property. And I've found recent evidence of a similar sort. A situation linking Kane to suspicious financial arrangements—the type that fits perfectly with what we tried—but couldn't quite pin on him last year—of being promised a reward if he turned over a girl to a particular Chinese guardian."

"Harry, I appreciate all your work on this case." The pounding in Maggie's neck subsided somewhat. "I'm sure we wouldn't have Chun now without your tireless work. I just hope and pray we still have her after Friday."

"So do I. And before I forget, Maggie, you and I need to sit down with Chun tomorrow and go over the kinds of questions the judge might ask."

法

Friday's hearing was a lengthy one, which was appropriate, Muriel supposed, since it was the culmination of two and a half years of legal wrangling with Mr. Kane and his gaggle of attorneys. Muriel could remember at least four different ones. Ironically, the attorney he had secured for this hearing was Mr. Millard. The same Mr. Millard who had opposed Kane and Harry the first time.

Through all the various hearings, Harry had countered Mr. Kane's antics and audacious charges with patience and measured logic. And Muriel herself hadn't been silent. She had followed up each hearing with articles that were the pride of her editor—besides garnering for herself a bit of professional jealousy among the pool of *Examiner* reporters. But it wasn't professionalism that drove her passion—not the mere love of words, nor the satisfaction of crafting a perfectly turned phrase. It was rather the feeling she had when she saw her articles in print, with people reading them on the morning ferry ride into the city; talking about them with fellow passengers on the way home at day's end.

Take this morning, for example; when she overheard two gentlemen discussing yesterday's court proceedings.

"Have you come to the article on page six? The one about that little Oriental at the Methodist Home? That rascal Kane is at it again, trying to take her from the Methodists. He's apparently claiming Chinese quarter highbinders patronize the Methodist Home just to traffick in human chattel."

"Haven't gotten to it—but I remember some of the other ones dealing with those Christian missions. If you ask me, something's got to be done about this awful trafficking in girls. But I don't think Kane's the one to do it. Miss Lake and Miss Cameron are more honorable and braver than Kane or any fifty politicians in Sacramento. It's too bad they can't run for the State House."

As the gentlemen disembarked at the Ferry Building, Muriel made a point to tell the men that if they were really concerned about the trafficking problem, they should write their state representatives. Then she gave them each her *Examiner* calling card, and said she was the reporter who had written the article they had been discussing.

法

The final arguments in Chun's guardianship hearing were scheduled for today, Saturday afternoon, in San Francisco Probate Court. That was why Muriel had been on the ferry in the morning.

Muriel wore the winter mink turban her mother had sent for Christmas. It was the perfect complement to her gray pleated dress trimmed in a light mauve lace, even though her leather satchel—full of notepaper and pencils—matched neither. Not that she cared. This was simply one of the rare times she was early for an appointment and noticed the incongruity of the accessory.

Muriel jumped to her feet when she saw Maggie enter the courtroom. Muriel hadn't talked to Maggie the day before, since she had to rush out immediately after the hearing to draft her article. She thought yesterday Maggie seemed thin and pale, and uncharacteristically anxious. But now when she saw Maggie up close, Muriel was shocked.

"Maggie, whatever is the matter? You look exhausted. Are you all right?"

"I'll be fine." Maggie scratched at her neck. There was a red rash-like patch above her collarbone. "I need to make it through the day, that's all. Just today."

The courtroom door opened again, and Maggie and Muriel turned toward it. Maggie's body recoiled and stiffened, and she spun back toward Muriel, her jaw clenched tight.

Laura Williams, filling most of the doorway, marched into the room as if she were a general on dress parade. Two elderly women looking like her lieutenants followed on her heels. Muriel assumed they were Home Board members.

Whatever color remained in Maggie's cheekbones drained away. "It's been a difficult few weeks." She tried to smile at Muriel, but her entire body shook with the effort, and she put her hand out to find the armrest of the chair. She sat down awkwardly.

"What is it?"

"I can't talk about it right now. Come by the Home later. Maybe then." Tears filled Maggie's eyes and she turned toward the door again.

"Where are Gracie and Chun?"

法

Just as Muriel hoped, her husband kept the focus of Saturday's hearing on the topic of Mr. Kane's character. Besides recalling Kane's previous history of confrontations with the police and the courts, Harry described to the judge a more recent case where Mr. Kane had taken twenty dollars from a certain Mrs. Young to pay for a hearing, then remitted only one dollar of the amount to the court, arguing Mrs. Young was too poor to pay the normal fee. Mr. Kane then pocketed the remaining nineteen dollars.

After Mr. Kane's lengthy attempt at rebuttal, the hearing closed with an unusual conversation Muriel captured in shorthand.

Judge Coffey: "What were you planning to do with this child?"

Mr. Kane: "Keep her in my own home until certain things occur, and then place her in a school or with a responsible fam—"

Coffey: "That's enough. I don't want to hear anymore. You said yesterday you were going to care for her and bring her up yourself. Now you—"

Kane: "I have a reason."

Coffey: "What reason?"

Kane: "May I speak to your Honor privately?"

Coffey: "No sir. I am a public servant and have no private business in this courtroom. Your reason must bear the light of publicity or this Court wants none of it. That's all."

Kane attempted an elaborate apology, but the Court would have none of it. At this juncture Attorney Monroe asked the Court to grant Mrs. Williams's petition, and remove Kane from the guardianship of the little girl on the showing that he was unfit to be her guardian.

Coffey: "Let's hear what the girl says. Come here, little one."

The child was brought forward.

Coffey: "Do you want to go home with Mr. Kane, my child?"

Chun: "No."

Coffey: "He has a nice home in San Rafael, and he has some nice boys and girls of his own. Wouldn't you like to play with them?"

Chun's hand clasped the Judge's hand and she forced herself under his arm until she rested her head in his lap. Then with her eyes filled with tears and her lips quivering, the girl begged not to be sent to Mr. Kane's.

Coffey: "Do you want to stay with me?"

Chun: "No, I want to go home. I just want to go home."

Further questioning drew from the child that "home" meant the Mission and Miss Margarita Lake and Mrs. Lake—those whom Chun loved because they were good to her.

Coffey: "Let the child remain at the mission. I am removing Mr. Kane from his role as guardian effective immediately, and awarding Mrs. Laura Williams guardianship of the girl."

Muriel put down her pencil and rushed out of the gallery toward Maggie. Laura had Chun by the hand, and glancing over her shoulder, pulled the girl toward the door.

Muriel and Maggie were alone in the far corner of the courtroom. "What great news, Maggie. But Laura? Why her? What in God's name happened?"

Maggie crumpled on Muriel's shoulder, her sobs washing over Muriel in waves. "The Board—Laura—fired us. Mama and me. Two days ago. For behavior unbecoming of a Christian and a deaconess, she said."

才

Chapter Eight

GIFT
(1903)

Chun had got a beautiful doll for Christmas. Just for herself. And the other girls did too. And Mrs. Kate also got everybody *The Wonderful Wizard of Oz* book. Which all the girls wanted since almost forever. And every night except Sunday nights when they were at church until late, Mrs. Kate read them a chapter or two in the parlor by the fireplace. Chun knew they were close to the end of the story because Dorothy just got to Glinda's castle. And everyone thought she was the kind of witch who could help Dorothy get back to Kansas. But Susie Siu thought for sure the winged monkeys could fly Dorothy home too. And she wondered why Dorothy didn't use them. Then Chun said Dorothy already used the three wishes of the golden cap.

"I knew that." Susie sniffed loudly. "But maybe there's an extra wish no one knows about."

Miss Lake never stayed for story time. But tonight she did. She sat cross-legged on the rug with the girls all around her. Chun hadn't seen Miss Lake since Mrs. Williams said Mr. Kane would never bother her again. But now Miss Lake looked sad. It even looked like there were tears in her eyes. But she turned away fast and Chun couldn't be sure. Chun wondered why a big person would cry.

Chun always sat close to Susie when Mrs. Kate read. But this time she snuggled close to Miss Lake and pulled Miss Lake's arm around her waist. Then she folded her hand inside Miss Lake's hand. Miss Lake put her cheek on Chun's hair and Chun could hear her breathe in deeply.

"Do you remember what happened in the story last night?" Mrs. Kate asked. And all the girls nodded.

"Chapter twenty-three: The Good Witch grants Dorothy's wish," Mrs. Kate read. Then she held up the book for everyone to see the picture. "Aunt Em had just come out of the house to water the cabbages when she looked up and saw Dorothy running toward her.

'My darling child!' she cried, folding the little girl in her arms and covering her face with kisses. 'Where in the world did you come from?'

'From the Land of Oz,' said Dorothy gravely. 'And here is Toto, too. And oh, Aunt Em! I'm so glad to be at home again!'

Mrs. Kate repeated the last line and then closed the book. She was silent for a few moments. "What did you think of the story?"

Each girl had a different idea. And when they finished talking Mrs. Kate said "Those were all good thoughts about the book. But now, before you girls go upstairs to bed, Miss Lake has something to say."

Miss Lake got up and stood in front of them. "You remember how Mama told you girls *The Wonderful Wizard* is a fairy tale? That there really isn't a land of Oz or witches?"

Chun nodded, and the other girls did too.

"But there are some things in that book I think of often." Miss Lake turned her head slowly and looked at each of them. There were wrinkles and black shadows around her eyes. "To me, you—all you girls—Ethel, Josephine, Jennie, Susie, and Chun—you're all like Dorothy. And what the Wicked Witch said about Dorothy not knowing her power—is like each of you." Miss Lake's eyes found Chun's eyes and rested there for a moment. "No one can make you a slave when you know your power," Miss Lake said. "And you all have power. It's nothing magical. But it's a gift that's in each of you." Miss Lake paused and rubbed the corners of her eyes like she had pieces of dust in them she couldn't get out. "It's your voices," she said. "Don't ever forget that. Each of you has a voice. You only have to learn how to use it." Then Miss Lake looked down at Chun and smiled. "Last week, Chun used her voice in court when the judge asked her if she wanted to go with Mr. Kane. Chun said no, she wanted to go home—to stay here with you girls. And the judge said she could stay here forever. The judge granted Chun's wish because she used her voice. Some people use their voices by writing things—maybe stories, the way Mrs. Monroe does when she writes newspaper articles about you girls. And some of you use your voices by singing. There are many ways to use your voices, and that's why Mrs. Kate and I have been here for so many years. To teach you how to use your voices."

才

"I'm so glad I caught you before you left. You're not really leaving already, are you?" Muriel had gotten off the cable car and turned the corner at Powell and Washington Streets just in time to see Maggie standing pensively on the steps of the Oriental Home.

"No, I'm just going out for a walk." It was late afternoon on a chilly January day, and the low angle of the sun cast an amber glow on the cobbled street, giving Maggie's skin a ghoulish orange tint. There were dark circles under her eyes, as though she hadn't slept since Chun's hearing a week ago.

"Did you read my articles about Chun's hearing? I brought extra copies for you." Muriel reached inside her coat and pulled out the three copies of Sunday's *Examiner* she had set aside.

"Thank you." Maggie took the newspapers. "I haven't had a chance to read anything yet. As you probably heard, tomorrow's our last day." She rolled the papers and tucked them under her arm without so much as a glance at them. "I'm all packed—not that I have much. Only the one room to empty. No furniture. It didn't take long." Maggie wouldn't meet Muriel's eyes.

"Can I walk with you?"

"No. I really want to be alone. We can talk here, if you wish."

Muriel was breaking in half. One part of her was standing in front of Maggie, asking a reporter's probing questions. The other part was inside her friend's body, feeling Maggie's heart pound. Her struggle to breathe.

She wished Maggie would tell her the whole story of what had gone wrong, but she knew Maggie would never divulge the politics of the

Home. Muriel had tried to get her to talk about the Board on other occasions, and gotten nowhere.

"Harry was at the meeting last night." Muriel's words came in a rush. She wanted to keep Maggie poised on the front steps as long as she could. "As an ex officio member, he has no vote, but he supported you. He couldn't believe the things Mrs. Williams—"

"I don't want to hear about it."

"I know." Muriel shifted her feet and stared at her hands. Finally, she raised her eyes, searching Maggie's face. "Harry thinks you should fight the dismissal. He says you have supporters."

"I know. I've already thought about that."

Muriel sensed a narrow opening. "Harry probably couldn't do much. He doesn't know the members very well. But he was thinking about Mr. Henderson. We've already talked about it. Mr. Henderson knows the history of the Home—from back before you came, Harry says—and being a retired lawyer and all, it wouldn't take him long to put a strategy together—"

Maggie raised her hand to stop the flow of Muriel's words. "I fought so hard for the girls over the years—especially for Chun. Maybe I cared too much." Her silhouette on the stucco wall of the Home entrance was ghostly gray in the fading light of the day. It seemed to Muriel as though something of Maggie, too, was slipping away with that passing shadow.

"Maybe God's teaching me a lesson. Maybe I've put the children first, somehow, and lost sight of something more important. I don't know."

Maggie sat down on the steps of the Oriental Home. She leaned forward and clasped her knees. Muriel took the silent cue from her friend and sat too. One small victory, she thought. She pulled her shawl close around her shoulders. "Aren't you cold?"

"I'm fine." Maggie turned her face down Washington Street, away from Muriel, and tugged at the sleeves of her coat.

Muriel didn't say anything for a long time. A cable car clanged. Horse hooves clopped. Maggie took a deep breath.

"I'm sure this will sound strange to you, Muriel, but I was so convinced God was calling me—back at Cazadero. It's a Salvation Army Camp. In 1894. I said then, 'Whatever you will—wherever you want—I'll go.' And even though I was young, I meant it.

"So I went off to the *Chicago Training School,* then came here. It wasn't my first choice, you know. I really wanted to go to China. But by the end of the first week I knew it was the right place—that it was God's perfect choice for me. Every step of the way—" Maggie sat straighter, and there was a fierceness in her voice Muriel hadn't heard in a long time. "Every step of the way, I prayed and asked God to lead me. And every step I've felt God's presence. I can understand Mr. Kane being against me. I could take losing Haw to him last year. But it's the fighting of Christian women—the awful accusations—I don't understand. And it's gone right down to the girls themselves. Now even they feel obliged to take sides." Maggie turned to face Muriel, her mouth quivering. "Gracie won't talk to me anymore. I can't put the rest of them in the position of choosing." She turned away again.

"Maggie—please. Let me say something."

But Maggie continued. "I decided last night not to fight it. And anyway, after Mr. Kane was arrested for impersonating an officer of the law with that stolen deputy's star, he had the audacity to turn around and appeal Chun's case to the California Supreme Court. I can't take this anymore. It keeps going on and on."

"I know. Harry's told me about that. He doesn't think Kane's got a leg to stand on." In spite of herself, Muriel smiled at her inadvertent pun. "The Supreme Court will surely reject the case."

Muriel stood and faced Maggie. She had one foot on the step below Maggie, so she leaned forward, placed an elbow on her knee, and gazed directly into her friend's eyes. "How can you not fight this—after what you've gone through? Those girls need you and your mother now more than ever. And it's a just cause. You know that. The Board can't dismiss you without a written statement."

"I know. But it's not worth it. It would be all over the papers. It has all the elements of scandal they love. The *WHMS,* the Methodist churches here in the city—the Home might not survive it. I can't put everyone through that simply for myself." Maggie paused and shook her head. Despite the chill, Maggie wasn't wearing a hat. Strands of hair were plastered to her forehead. "I'm sorry, Muriel. I shouldn't have said that about the papers. I'm not thinking straight today."

"It's all right. And you're right. Most papers would love the salacious side of the story. Except for me. But it's not only for yourself, Maggie. Think of your girls."

Maggie searched Muriel's eyes, and Muriel thought it was the saddest expression she had ever seen on a woman's face. The widening pupils of a lost child, asking a stranger for help. The sense of loss—of abandonment. She remembered Kate once telling her how difficult it had been to raise her daughter without a father. "Maggie, I—"

"They feel like my own flesh and blood, Muriel. But I know they're not mine. When Mama prays with them at night, she tells them they're God's children, and that they're in his hands. No matter what happens to their world, no matter how it crashes down upon them, they know God loves them more than I—or any human ever could." Maggie's voice was thin and shaking. "How can I not believe that too? I have to—or I couldn't go on living."

"Maggie, listen to yourself. How can you care too much for a child? Especially for 'the least of these'—to quote the expression from the picture your mother has hanging in the parlor."

"Muriel," Maggie made a move to stand up. "I have to go. I'm sorry. I really want to be alone."

才

Maggie walked slowly down Washington Street, past Portsmouth Square and the Hall of Justice, toward the bay. When she got to the water's edge she stood and stared at the swells sloshing against the pilings. Long clusters of mussels told her it was close to low tide. She wandered aimlessly, listening to the cries of swooping seagulls. Her mind as muddy as the bay itself. On a whim, she stepped behind a solitary warehouse. A stack of wooden crates piled with rotting fruit and vegetables leaned against the weathered clapboards of the building. Maggie held her breath and squeezed past the crates, onto the pier. A rat scuttled beneath an empty box, and a couple of seagulls eyed her suspiciously from the well-worn dock planking. Apparently deciding she was no threat, they went back to their tug-of-war with a fish head left by some inattentive fisherman.

Maggie had overheard Laura's words to Mama spoken earlier that morning as she packed her last things. And the words still echoed in her head. They had been as sharp as the edge of a fisherman's fillet knife. The way most of Laura's words had been lately.

"The workers fall, but the work goes on." And Maggie had seen Laura's smirk.

The wind blew a gust of salty, dank air into Maggie's face and she instinctively drew a deep breath. A burning sensation lodged in the back of her throat, and she swallowed hard. Maybe Laura was right. For all their disagreements, they had this in common: They both knew institutions lasted longer than people. But there was still the sting of failure to deal with. It clung to her skin like a cloying compound that couldn't be washed away. It was the feeling that at nearly thirty years old, she had let Mama down. That she had somehow missed her calling; suffering the curse of always being younger than Laura and the other Board women. Of being perceived as naïve.

Maggie still had the newspapers Muriel had given her, and she raised them to her forehead. The lights of Berkeley were beginning to twinkle across the bay in the growing dusk. Here at the water's edge is where the story had begun. The story she had told so often to new girls. About Reverend Gibson and Jin Ho, the first girl in the Rescue Asylum, over thirty years ago now. The girl had escaped from the life on Jackson Street, run to a pier like this, and thrown herself into the bay. A Negro who happened by saw her struggling in the water and fished her out. After he took her to the police station, she begged to go see the "Jesus man."

Maggie understood how Jin Ho could have gotten to the point of suicide. The darkness and fog closing in; of not being able to cut through it. But Maggie wasn't there yet. She didn't know what she would do next—or what Mama would do. But a premature death wasn't in the picture. Being a deaconess counted for something. It meant she had a place and a family of women who would find meaningful work for her. But what the morrow would bring—she hadn't a clue.

"Hey lady, whatcha doing here at this hour?" A shadowy figure approached her from the warehouse, nightstick held warily at shoulder height. "This ain't no place to be, dressed like that." It was a watchman, and his eyes scanned her body, slowly, head to toe, as though searching for a weapon of some sort—or perhaps something else. "You with someone?"

"No. I'm fine," Maggie forced a smile. "These are just newspapers. That's all." She waved the folded papers Muriel had given her.

"Well, these docks are closed, ma'am. You need to leave."

Maggie drew back her arm and threw the papers as far as she could. She stood for a moment and watched them sink below the surface.

"Listen. I said you need to leave." The watchman started toward Maggie again, this time with a more determined step, and with his nightstick menacingly stretched out in front of his body.

"I'm going."

The watchman glowered as Maggie brushed past—pressing closer to the man than she intended. He trailed her back toward East Street, stopping only when she turned away from the docks. She began the slow, steady walk up the uneven cobblestones of Washington Street, to the Oriental Home. She was starving. She felt like she hadn't eaten in weeks.

Institutions might outlive people, but Maggie was a lot younger than Laura. And the least she could do was ensure she outlived that woman and all the other members of the Oriental Home Board.

Tomorrow there would be photographs of the girls with her and Mama, and then a farewell program the older ones had planned as a going away present. They needed her tonight and tomorrow. And that was enough.

才

"As of nine o'clock this evening, Laura Williams is no longer Secretary of the Oriental Home." Harry walked in the front door with a bow and sweeping arm gestures Muriel recognized as his mock courtroom behavior. "She resigned tonight, officially for 'health reasons.'" Harry made quotation marks with his index fingers, then bent to kiss her. He took off his coat and hat.

"Harry, those things are soaking wet. Don't leave them here." Muriel set down *The Examiner*'s "Society Page," got up from the parlor sofa, and went into the kitchen to heat her husband's dinner. "When you're done hanging them on the porch, you can come back and tell me what happened."

Harry's damp stocking feet made squeaking noises on the hardwood floor when he returned. "Carrie Davis was officially voted in as Superintendent—that new position the Board has been designing since the last quarterly meeting—and it was agreed that she'll move into the Home." Harry twisted his squeaky wet stockings on the floor a few more times and grinned at Muriel. "Carrie'll have the authority that neither Maggie nor Kate had—to make all day-to-day Home decisions. Christ, Muriel! Maggie was so stressed the last few months with Chun's case—and she's young and energetic—I have no idea how Carrie'll last more than a year. She must be in her late forties at least, and she seems so tense and nervous around children.

"And that Miss Gillette"—Harry rolled his eyes. "The girl who's been filling in— she's only about to finish her training at the Deaconess School. But the Board voted to keep her on as matron anyway, taking over for Kate. She can't be over twenty—and she has no experience with Orientals whatsoever—let alone with those kinds of inmates." His voice trailed off. "I don't know. At least the new Secretary of the Chinese Bureau—Lizzie Piatt, will take over all the fundraising duties. But still—"

Harry plopped himself on a dining room chair and began pulling off his stockings. Muriel glared at him as he arched his eyebrows, wadded the stockings, and set them carefully on the table beside the folded *Examiner*.

Muriel stepped back toward the kitchen, hot pad in hand, and searched for a match to light the burner. "And Harry, if you don't get those damn things off that table this instant, you'll be eating them for supper."

Muriel had a habit of taking off her dress, petticoats, and corset as quickly as possible after a day's work. Tonight she had on a simple muslin chemise and slippers. Harry squeezed past her on his way back from the porch where he had hung his stockings. He brushed his hand across her bottom as she leaned over the stove.

"What's for dinner?"

"Not that, if that's what you're thinking." Muriel watched him pick up the evening paper. "I never could understand exactly what was happening behind the scenes over there, beyond the power struggle between Kate, Maggie, and Laura." She turned back to the stove and lit it. "I mean, I can understand Kate and Maggie's argument with Laura—she was always doing things out of the blue without consulting them. But why didn't Laura like them? Do you really think it was about authority—that she didn't feel she could control them?" Muriel didn't wait for Harry's response. "From my problems at *The Call*, wanting to control things seems like such a male trait. I can't help but think there was something more to their dismissal." She bent to check the flame under the frying pan, setting it as low as possible without letting it sputter out. She turned and leaned against the dining room doorframe, with a spatula in hand.

"Well, here's what I now know." Harry tapped the newspaper. "What I didn't have at hand during Chun's final hearing. A lot of this the Lakes only shared with me a few days ago, after they received their official severance letter from the Home Board. Apparently for some time, a highbinder, Yue Tschi—a member of the Hop Sing tong, has been using the missions to rescue girls he wanted for his own prostitution business. It seems when he wanted an underage girl, or one who was owned by someone else, he would arrange for a prospective husband to contact a mission to rescue her. Which mission didn't matter to him—Baptist, Presbyterian, Salvationist, or Methodist. He used them all. Once the girl was at a mission, a 'marriage'"—Harry set the paper down and made air quotation marks with his fingers once again—"would be arranged to get the girl out of the place. Then, when the girl was married and out, Yue Tschi would move her into one of his brothels—without ever having to pay the original owner the one or two thousand dollars to buy out the girl's contract. It was quite a ploy." Harry opened the paper again, and paused for a moment before continuing his analysis of Yue Tschi's scheme.

"It took a while for the missions to catch on. Apparently Maggie and Kate had—but not Laura. And she was working behind the scenes, against the Lakes, to have one of the rescued girls in the Home marry the scoundrel. Somehow, the girls who did the interpreting in the Home ended up taking sides in the affair. Grace was on Laura's side, with Caroline on Maggie and Kate's side. Exactly why they were divided, I don't quite understand." Harry pursed his lips and shook his head.

"There was quite a lot going on at the Mission behind closed doors. Things I was never privy to. And had I known, it may have made my case against Kane more difficult—perhaps even impossible. If Kane or his lawyer had gotten a notion of the way Yue Tschi was using the Methodists, the papers would have been all over it—even more than they already were. And the reputations of all the missions probably would've been ruined. Chun's case may have been lost, too. So many people already think the missions are dupes of the tongs—and this would have confirmed it." Harry rattled the newspaper. "I think I've about had it with the Methodists. And every other religious organization, for that matter. I don't mind supporting Chun financially like we've been doing, but the other connivings I can do without. Mind you, I don't have any sympathy for Kane's methods either—impersonating an officer of the law with a star that didn't belong to him. But maybe his heart was in a place not that far removed from Laura's. Or the Lakes."

Muriel took the frying pan with the reheated steak off the stove. The spatula fell and hit the floor with a splatter. "Damn."

"Muriel, what are you doing in there? Did you hear anything I said?"

"Yes, I'm listening. I'm trying to warm your dinner. And unlike you, I can do more than one thing at a time." Muriel surveyed Harry warily as he got up from the table and walked toward the kitchen. "Did you really have any other choice, Harry? If you had been easy on Kane, and lost the hearing, Kane would have gotten Chun, and then what? Where would she be now?"

Harry leaned into the doorway as Muriel manipulated the hot pad and frying pan. "All I'm saying is, I don't know how this new information will affect my association with the Board. I feel a bit like I've been duped in this thing too."

"Harry, sit. Your supper's ready."

"You know I've been offered that job in DC with the new Department of Commerce and Labor." Harry cut into the steak. "And right now, that's looking pretty good. I could still work on immigration issues, but without all these religious people butting in. They're all so sure they're doing the right thing. But in the end they seem such hypocrites."

"Harry, eat your dinner—before it gets cold again. I'm not heating it twice." Muriel took off her apron and sat down at the opposite end of the table, watching her husband slop half a pound of butter on his potato. "And I don't appreciate you calling one of my best friends a hypocrite. Maggie may be naïve and idealistic—but she's no hypocrite."

"I didn't call *her* a hypocrite."

"Well, you may as well have. You said all religious groups. And if that doesn't include her, I don't know what would."

Muriel watched, incredulous, as Harry added one more knifeful of butter to the last sliver of potato skin. "Wouldn't you be interested in moving to DC, Muriel? They have papers there too, you know. It could be great for your career. You should think about it. Roosevelt has so many Progressive ideas important to us both—and all without having to deal with religious organizations."

"We don't have to decide tonight." Muriel picked up what was left of the butter, and shaking her head, left the room.

才

Muriel put the ceramic butter dish in the icebox on the back porch. It was almost eleven o'clock, and she wanted to go to bed. Harry's talk about the job offer in Washington only added to her weariness. She couldn't imagine leaving the newspaper position she had worked so hard to obtain. No matter how often she talked about her job, Harry really had no clue of the difficulties she faced. If she left *The Examiner* and followed him to Washington, it could be years before she found a comparable position— and perhaps she never would. And she had no intention of ending up as her husband's legal secretary. She puttered about the kitchen, waiting for Harry to finish.

Finally, Harry set down his fork and pushed his chair back from the table. "You know what breaks my heart, Muriel, is how the children got caught in the whole thing. They're the innocent victims here. No matter how much everyone wants to protect them—they're the ones hurt in the end. Miss Gillette thought it would be really nice if the girls wrote Valentines to the Lakes—which they all did—then yesterday they sent them over to the Lakes' new place on Powell. But I had to be the monster telling Maggie and Kate, that for legal reasons, they couldn't respond to the children. Their connections to the Home are completely severed—as if they'd been accused of some heinous crime. Think of it, Muriel.

"Take Chun, for example. Maggie and Kate are the closest thing to parents she's ever had—maybe the first time she's known real love in her life. She wrote such a tender Valentine to Maggie and Kate—they showed it to me. 'I'm so lonesome without you,' she wrote in perfect cursive. She's not even eight years old. No child that age should know the meaning of 'lonesome.' And Chun will never get another card or hug from them. It does no good for me, or Miss Gillette, or Carrie to tell the girls that for legal reasons Maggie and Kate can't contact them. All they know is the people who loved them the most over the past few years are gone and won't speak to them. The children can't help but think they've done something awful to make the Lakes leave."

"I know Harry. I feel for them too. But it's late and you can't solve that problem tonight." Muriel had taken down her hair, and now stood in the doorway between the kitchen and bedroom. "Why don't you finish cleaning up in there and come to bed?"

Muriel was drifting off to sleep when Harry came in. His rustling about the bedroom woke her, and when she stirred, he began talking again.

"I'm sorry, Muriel. I still have the Board meeting on my mind. I forgot to tell you the State Supreme Court rejected Kane's appeal. So that means Chun's case is really over. Laura will be her legal guardian until she's eighteen—or until she's married."

Muriel fluffed her pillow and sat up. "Well that's good news. Why didn't you tell me earlier?"

"I guess I kept the best news for last." Harry smiled crookedly and climbed into bed.

"Now that you have me fully awake, here's the question that's bothered me ever since the hearing. Why do you think Kane fought so hard to retain guardianship of Chun? Do you really think it was about the money? I can't help thinking he was in it for something more. Do you think he would have abused her? Or purposely sold her back to the brothel keeper?"

"I don't know." Harry rolled over toward Muriel and propped himself on one elbow. The only light in the room came from the street lamp across the way, and although the rain had stopped hours earlier, the remaining puddles in the street reflected the lamplight into their bedroom window. It was bright enough for Muriel to see each whisker on her husband's unshaven face. "We managed to paint an ugly picture of him for the judge. I know that. And his arrest later with that stolen deputy's star seemed to confirm my arguments." Harry paused. A tree branch scraped across the eaves. "But maybe the Home isn't a much better place for Chun than what Kane had planned. Tonight the Board approved a list of rules for the upstairs. Things like, 'Bedrooms must not be used as sitting rooms.' And, 'No two girls in the bathroom at the same time.' What real home has rules like that?" Harry shook his head, and the bedposts rattled. "Apparently Gracie had been saying vicious things about one of the girls. And since no one could verify her claims, no one felt the need to tell me anything. But the fact that the Board will print and post a list of rules makes me suspicious about what they knew before Chun's hearing."

"It's raining again." Muriel listened to the patter of raindrops on the windowpane. The ripples in the puddles caused a loss of luminosity, and the room darkened. "If we don't get some sleep, we'll be sniping at each other in the morning."

才

Sleep or no sleep, Harry and Muriel began the next day sniping. Harry cut himself shaving, which set him stomping around the house, cursing. Then, as Muriel was about to walk out the door, she realized she had left her umbrella at work. She asked Harry if she could borrow his—only a moment before she noticed he was still scowling and dabbing his bleeding chin. "I wouldn't be so peeved if it was the first time," Harry scowled. Then he practically threw the umbrella at her.

Even though Harry's long hours of pro bono legal work on behalf of the Oriental Home were behind him, he still came home no earlier than he had before Chun's hearing. He simply seemed to have transferred his energy to a different project. And his new project was convincing Muriel that the Department of Commerce and Labor job was best for both of them. As a result, Muriel became more and more irritated. Before long their sniping turned to snarls. They were a couple of stray dogs fighting for the same bone.

The bone of contention was, on the surface, Harry's job offer. But if Muriel was honest with herself and dug below the surface, she would have admitted the sharp point poking in her side was that she knew her husband would take the Washington job—regardless of her feelings. Finally,

Muriel caved in. "All right, Harry," she said one morning as he was leaving for work. "Just go. But don't expect me to follow you."

"What's that supposed to mean?" Harry had stooped to kiss her goodbye, but stopped in mid-motion, his lips hovering above her cheek. "What about you—about us?"

"I don't know, Harry." Muriel's face was hot and flushed, and her shoulder muscles coiled tight—like wagon springs about to break loose. She turned her head away. "I need time to think, that's all." She walked back into the house, slamming the porch door.

Muriel returned home much later than usual that evening and found a note on the kitchen table. Harry said he had purchased a single, one-way train ticket to Washington DC, that he was leaving in a week, and he hoped she would join him—when she was ready.

"P.S. Home late. Don't wait up."

Not even a "Love, Harry" or "Out with the boys," scrawled at the bottom.

Muriel went to the bedroom, and in a flurry of pent-up rage, stuffed a few changes of clothing into two large suitcases, then dragged them to the front porch. She purposely left the bedroom in a mess; thoughtfully draping a few of her delicate underthings over his pillow as a final effect. Then she left her own hastily scribbled note on the dining room table.

"Staying in the city with friends. Have a safe trip."

By the end of the month, Muriel herself had quit her job, broken the lease on their Oakland rental, and packed her belongings. She never told Harry she was coming to DC. They would have to decide whether they could still live together when she got there. But she had a job offer from the *Washington Evening Star* tucked in a pocket of her suitcase, and the offer was at least as good as Harry's—if not better.

才

Muriel hadn't seen Maggie in the months following her friend's dismissal from the Home. But she sent Maggie a note telling her of the DC job offer, and listing the time her train was leaving Oakland.

Much to Muriel's surprise and pleasure, Maggie was standing on the Oakland Mole platform when Muriel arrived breathless and late, laden with bags and packages.

"I'm 'Traveler's Aid' now, so I'm at the station almost every day." Maggie smiled, seemingly her cheerful self once more. She had put on some weight, and her cheeks had a natural, pink tone again. "And I have one more thing for you—but I don't know where you're going to put it. Your arms are already full. It's a memento. For your faithfulness to my mother and me—"

"And for our friendship." Muriel felt tears forming at the corners of her eyes. "It's that too—isn't it?"

"Yes, of course." Maggie stuffed a small flat gift box into Muriel's coat pocket. "It's not much—just something to remember us by. Don't open it until you're on the train." A whistle blew two long blasts. "You'd better get on board."

Muriel picked up her suitcase and stepped onto the slow moving train. The porter took her extra packages and pulled her into the car.

"Muriel, wait! Your satchel!" Maggie held it high and ran alongside the locomotive, trying to hand it to the porter. He lunged for it with one hand, but the engine had picked up speed. Maggie pulled her arm back, still clasping the leather satchel.

"It's all right," Muriel shouted. "Keep it. I'll write you." But she wasn't sure Maggie could hear her above the sound of the lumbering steam engine.

Hours later, as the train climbed into the Sierras, Muriel opened Maggie's gift. It was a simple, foldable leather case with two photographs of Chun—the typical before-and-after sequence Muriel recognized from Mission magazines. The photograph on the left showed Chun in traditional Chinese clothing. The photograph on the right showed her in American clothes—the same purple plaid dress she had worn her last day in court. In between the photographs Maggie had slipped a thin piece of paper on which she had written: "Thank you for all you've done for us—and for Chun. I trust you won't forget us. You and Harry will always be in our prayers. Love, Maggie."

When the train stopped in Reno, Muriel wandered about the station. She was surprised to find picture postcards of Glen Alpine Springs, the resort near Lake Tahoe where she and Harry had spent their honeymoon nearly five years previous. It seemed a lifetime ago. She bought three, and some stamps, then returned to her seat.

Muriel wasn't particularly sentimental about places or things. She had little interest in mementos. Her life was changing; her future was open, unknown. And so it was an appropriate time to discard her past, along with certain things that reminded her of it—like her father's old satchel, for example. When she got to DC she would buy something new and more suitable for the changes in her life. Something proper to the new place. What that would be, she had no idea. But she was looking forward to the adventure, and perhaps even to seeing Harry again. She missed his sarcastic wit, the mental repartee. His stomach curling into her back at night. The hardness of his body inside her. The way his arms wrapped around her—almost without thinking, squeezing her buttocks as the widow across the street peeked through her curtains.

She picked up a postcard and wrote:

"Maggie,

"Thanx for photos of Chun. Won't forget her, you & y'r mother. Ab't satchel. Mail contents only. c/o Wash. Eve. Star. I don't need it. M'be you or someone there does. Muriel."

Chapter Nine

DAUGHTER

The girl stood in the middle of the upstairs hallway, shaking. She stared at the carpet's twisted flowers and vines. She was naked except for her drawers. And they were wet and cold.

No one had hit her like this since Mama at the old place. That was over two years ago, and she had forgotten the pain of it and how she used to control it. She remembered now how she would pretend it didn't hurt. How she would go to magical places—sometimes even flying off with the seagulls high above the alley. But this was different. And it was too late for that. She couldn't stop the hurting. And the hurt inside her body was worse than the hurt on the outside of her body.

Here in the Home the big people said they loved her and that God loved her. And she believed it. Until now.

She hadn't thought of getting away from any place for a long time. But she was thinking about it now. Of Dorothy in *The Wonderful Wizard of Oz*. The last book Mrs. Kate read to her and the other girls before she left.

If there was a cyclone—or maybe if she had magic shoes—she could fly away. But it was a sunny day and she was barefoot. She wanted to fly away to Mrs. Kate and Miss Lake. But she didn't know where they were.

"You've been punished because you've been bad." The woman bent over the girl.

The girl could feel the woman's eyes like needles poking in the back of her neck.

"Do you understand?"

The girl nodded but didn't look up or say anything. She stared at the flowers and vines in the carpet, trying to see how they connected. It was all very confusing. Even a winged monkey might get caught there and never get out.

"Look at me, Maud." The woman took the girl's chin in the palm of her hand and forced it up.

The girl remembered her name. It was her new Home name. The name Mrs. Williams gave Chun a month ago when she said she believed in Jesus and Mr. Chan put water on her head and baptized her and all the little girls grinned. Especially Susie. And even some of the big girls smiled. And Mrs. Williams gave her a gold and jade necklace that she could keep all for herself.

Miss Gillette the Home's new Mama was talking to her. Her mouth was inches from Maud's face. "No matter how much it hurts now, it's better to learn these lessons when you're young, than to die in your sins."

Miss Gillette hung the rug beater back on its hook in the hall closet. "'Faithful are the wounds of a friend,' the Bible says." Miss Gillette looked like she was trying to smile. She patted Maud on the head. "And Jesus is our friend who gives us rules to abide by. Isn't that right?"

Maud nodded again.

"Now go to the bathroom and get washed up. And put on some clean underclothes. The dinner bell will be ringing shortly, and you don't want to be late and get into trouble again."

女

"See, it's no different here on the inside than out there." It was Won Kum. The big girl. Standing in the hallway outside the bathroom.

Won Kum came in to where Maud was and closed the bathroom door behind her. She walked to the sink and took a washcloth off the wall rack. "Only here, the Jesus god does the hitting instead of the old keepers. But it doesn't feel any different than in the places where I used to work. That's why I want this month to be over. So Yue Tschi can marry me and get me out of this place. I'll never come back. Ever."

"Miss Lake and Mrs. Kate never hit."

"That's because you weren't baptized." Won Kum ran the washcloth under the faucet and rung it out. "But now that Mr. Chan poured water over your head and gave you that new Christian name, you have to be perfect." Won Kum snorted. "So people like me will see what a good little girl you are and want to be Christians too.

"Come here. Let me help you." Won Kum knelt beside Maud and began to untie the strings on her drawers. The drawers stuck to Maud's bottom and she had to wiggle and push to get the wet things to drop.

"But this isn't the same as those other places." Maud's drawers rubbed against the welts on her bottom and thighs, and stung as she slipped them down and stepped away from them. "At the old place I used to get hit all the time. For nothing. But it's not that way here. This is the first time. Miss Gillette said I shouldn't yell when I'm mad at someone." Maud felt her face grow hot and she rubbed her eyes with her fists. "I'm never going to do that again."

"Spread your legs," Won Kum said. "Let me clean you off."

The cloth was soft and warm on Maud's skin, and Won Kum's hands were soft and gentle. The big girl's breath grew heavy as she bent over Maud. It was a sound Maud hadn't heard since the old place. Her body stiffened and her heart began to pound like she was running as fast as she could. But she wasn't moving even an inch. She felt the air going in and out of her nostrils and Won Kum's panting. They were both running. One getting closer. The other trying to get away. They were the only sounds in the room. Won Kum traced her fingers up between Maud's legs. To her bellybutton. Round and round. Then to her nipples. Round and round. Then back down. "Such a beautiful little thing," she whispered.

Maud stopped breathing. She forced the feelings away. As if they were another kind of beating where she could climb out of her skin. Then somewhere in the back of her head she heard a slow thumping in the hallway. And it was getting closer. "No." Maud grabbed Won Kum's hands and pushed them away from her body. "No."

"Maudie, are you still in there?" It was Gracie's voice. "Who are you talking to? Is someone with you?"

"It's Won Kum. She's here." Maud's voice was high and squeaky. Like a rat trapped by a dog. Unable to get away.

"I'm helping her get cleaned up." Won Kum stood quickly and moved away.

"Maudie, are you all right?"

Maud swallowed the dry thing stuck in her throat and tried to control her shaky voice. "Yes. I'm coming out."

Won Kum scowled at her. "I just wanted to help you."

Maud pushed the big girl away and opened the bathroom door. She was naked and shivering and Grace was staring at her.

女

Maud didn't feel like eating supper. As soon as it was over and she cleared her plate and cup and silverware from the table and threw away her left-over food, she went to her room and crawled into bed. She was still lying there like a ball of yarn when she heard someone creeping across the floor.

"Maudie! What happened?" It was Susie. Maud opened her eyes and moved further away from the edge of the bed. But Susie leaned over and began shaking her. "Maudie, how come you looked so sad at supper? What happened? Everyone said you got a spanking. Is it true? You know I won't leave your room until you tell me."

Susie sat at the edge of the bed for a long time before Maud said anything. There was nothing but the sound of their breathing—and Ethel and Jennie arguing about something in the room across the hall. Maud's eyelashes were sticky from crying and she rubbed them with her fists and sat up.

"I got baptized," Maud whispered. "I'm supposed to be a better girl now. And good for all the other girls to see. But Miss Gillette says I wasn't. And then I wet my drawers and when I went into the bathroom to wash myself Kum followed me."

"Oh no." Susie's voice changed to almost crying. But it wasn't even her that the thing happened to. "I told you to stay away from her. Why did you let her in?"

"I didn't. She was just there. Then she started to help me."

"Oh no." And Susie's voice was a shaky, whispery cry. Like Maud's before with Won Kum. "She helped me once too. A long time ago. That's why I stay away from her. And why I told you to stay away from her."

"I know. But Gracie found us before anything bad happened."

"That's good." The crying part of Susie's voice went away, and she sat straighter. She reached over and pushed the sticky hair out of Maud's face. It was like she was Mrs. Kate. "That's why Gracie can't wait for Kum to get married. To get her out of here so she can't hurt anybody else. Gracie hates her."

Susie was Maud's best friend. And ever since they got baptized and got their American names and started planning for King's Daughters, Susie called her sister. And they always told each other everything.

"Why did Mrs. Kate leave, Susie? And Miss Lake? What did I do to make them leave?"

女

Carrie Davis didn't feel particularly called to the work of the Oriental Home. She was different from Margarita in that regard. Margarita knew she was called, and could pinpoint the hour and minute. And Margarita had a passion for the work Carrie never would. But Carrie did feel as though God had laid his hand upon her and drawn her into the work—step by imperceptible step—until she reached a point where she couldn't imagine her life differently. And now that she had been in the work a year, Carrie could look back and see God's guidance at each crossroad.

Take marriage, for example. Carrie had never married, and for that she was now grateful. She had had her opportunities, but in the end, she had felt men weren't worth the trouble. They had always seemed disorganized and uncontrollable. You never knew what they might do, or where they might put things. And wherever they put things, you were guaranteed it would be the wrong place. Carrie had brothers, and they were enough to show her what men were like. The older a man got, the less likely he was to change. She'd seen that with her brothers and with her sisters' husbands.

But Carrie had always loved and wanted children, even though she hadn't been particularly interested in the method by which they were normally acquired. And so she was quite happy to obtain a family miraculously, as it were, without the pain of childbearing. It was like St. Paul said in Galatians 4:27: "For it is written, Rejoice, thou barren that bearest not; break forth and cry, thou that travailest not: for the desolate hath many more children than she which hath an husband."

Carrie's most recent "travailest-not" child was a boy, the first in the Home in five years. On the day of his arrival, Carrie wrote in her daybook: "July 12th 1904. Wong Bok Lum born June 5, 1899. Lived with his father, Wong Bing Leung. Store name, Fong Yuen. A pawnbroker at 1008 Dupont Street. Mother dead. Father pays $12.00 per month."

Lum was followed in quick succession by a girl, then by two sisters, and finally, by a set of three sisters. Carrie wrote in the Home daybook: "October 7th 1904. Moy Lut or May brought from Los Angeles by Miss Mayo as I couldn't leave the Home to go get her. May is five years old. She is the child of Sam Yo Ching and Sau Ying of Bakersfield. Born May 31, 1899. The mother ran away from home taking the five children with her and $1,050.00 that her husband had put in the bank in her name. She hid herself in a brothel in Los Angeles with a woman she had formerly known.

"October 28th 1904. Ruby and Pearl were brought to the home by their father, Tsang Wan, former cook of the old Home, after he found it impossible to live with his wife.

"November 14th 1904. Woo Jung Sing brought three little ones to the home at 10 AM. They were the youngest children of Qui Fah, who had been raised in the Home from the age of seven. She was the beneficiary of Howard St. Sunday school. She had seven children, and died shortly after giving birth to little Ida Alice. The oldest of the three, Sue Yung or Lydia Esther, born February 6, 1900. Suie King or Mamie, born March 17 1902. Sui Hong or Ida Alice, born March 29, 1904."

Thus, within a few months' time, there were seven new children in the Home. And each addition tested Carrie's organizational skills. She ended up moving Susie in with Josephine and Ethel; and the three oldest new girls—Ruby, Pearl, and May—she put in with Maud. The three littlest—all sisters, shared the nursery next to the matron's room; and the boy, Lum, Carrie put temporarily on a cot in the corner of her own room.

In the end, Carrie felt doubly blessed. She had no husband, but she had all the children a body could want. And the children were certainly easier to control than men. The children could be organized and made to fit into patterns and routines. Carrie knew that, because she had the new matron, Lois Thorn, post schedules on the bathroom doors for daily tasks. And to Carrie's delight, Lois kept the children to them—much more rigorously than Miss Gillette ever had. And without having to discipline the children nearly as often.

女

Muck Shee hadn't been back to Number One City in seven years—not since Foon had made her pawn her baby to the brothel keeper in New Spanish Alley in the Year of the Dog—1898 in American numbers. Since then Foon's business had flourished in Fresno—and Muck Shee didn't worry any more about what the American police might do to him or his partners.

"My business is legitimate now," Foon said. "No more police."

All Muck Shee knew was his store in China Alley sold things from the Celestial Kingdom—clothing and furniture, Buddhas and incense, and plates, tea cups, and bowls. No more opium or lottery tickets, and no girls in the back. And Muck Shee's two sons were now house servants to a rich American family. They brought money home every week.

Muck Shee hadn't forgotten that Number One City was large and built on steep hills, but the difference between it and Fresno still surprised her. Her cough made it hard to breathe, and as a consequence she felt much older than when she had last been here. She had to lean heavily on her sons in the walk up "Waystation to Prosperity Street"—the one Americans called "Washington Street."

Foon had business to attend to in the city, and Muck Shee had her own plans. She had with her the red paper receipt she had kept in a small cigar box beside her bed all those years in Fresno. When she took it out two days ago, it looked as new as the day the brothel keeper had given it to her. Now it was next to her heart, in a pouch strung around her neck— along with American paper money worth two hundred dollars. At least that's what Foon said. She had brought it all to the city to buy back Chun and take her with them to China.

Every few minutes Muck Shee touched her blouse in the place where the pouch was hiding. Its softness reassured her, as though she held at her breast the daughter herself.

Muck Shee couldn't get rid of her cough. It had been getting worse over the past year, and no Chinese herb seemed to help. She could feel in her bones she didn't have long to live. But Foon had promised he would build a big house for the family in the Celestial Kingdom, and when she died, her daughters—if they were still unmarried—would care for Foon.

Muck Shee knew Chun was alive because her eldest son, Seu Ho, had seen her in the brothel a few years ago, when he came to the city with Foon, on business. Seu Ho had returned with the news that Chun was still there and healthy. And that made Muck Shee happy. She had done the right thing. But Seu Ho was sad Chun didn't remember him.

"She was a little girl when you last saw her," Muck Shee told him then. "But when we go back to get her, it won't take her long to start thinking of you as her big brother again."

Muck Shee tried to reassure her son, but he wasn't easily convinced. And now she had the dark fear Chun wouldn't remember her either. But not a day had gone by without her thinking of her daughter. And she still wore on her wrist the bracelet Chun had twisted that day long ago. Muck Shee hadn't taken it off since then. Her sons teased her about it. They sometimes saw it when she rolled up her sleeves to scrub clothes. "No thief will ever find it there," one would say. Then the other would add, "And even if they did, they couldn't get it off. They would have to take you with them, just to get the bracelet."

女

"I'm looking for a girl named Chun." Muck Shee wheezed and coughed, then apologized to the old keeper. She had left the children with their uncle on Clay Street, then gone alone to find the red-letter sign she remembered from long ago. But the sign had disappeared, and Muck Shee had to ask several men where the place was before she finally knocked on the right door. "You took her as pawn seven years ago."

The keeper hobbled up to Muck Shee and squinted in her face, breathing heavily. She smelled as though she hadn't washed herself in months. "What? Who? Who are you?"

"The girl Chun. I gave her to you seven years ago—for one hundred and two dollars. I've come back for her."

"That girl? Chun? I don't have her."

"What do you mean, you don't have her?" Muck Shee's heart jumped into her throat and she swallowed hard to force it down. But that started a fit of coughing, and a few moments passed before she could speak again. "Where is she? You were supposed to write and tell us if you planned to do anything with her." Muck Shee's voice was unsteady, and she couldn't control its rising shrillness. She leaned against the doorframe and peered into the darkness of the foul-smelling room. The darkness began to seep into her lungs and choke her. The black phlegm gurgled up again, and this time she couldn't force it down. She closed her eyes and stopped breathing. She turned and spit the blackness out, into the alleyway.

"An American came and stole her. A long time ago," the screechy voice said.

"Where is she? Is she alive?"

"I don't know. All I know is, she brought me bad luck. A few months after I bought her, my best girl was beaten and then got sold. That girl broke my ghost screen when she left. My luck hasn't been good since. Chun was sick all the time after that. Then she was stolen from me. I think those Jeezachrise white demon women up the street have her. But I'm not sure. It was a long time ago, like I said."

"White women stole her? Whatever for?" Muck Shee felt lost again. All she could do was foolishly repeat the keeper's words, hoping they would lead her to a path out of the darkness.

"I never should have bought her." The voice ignored Muck Shee's questions. "I went to court to try and save her, but I lost. And I couldn't replace her. Now all my girls are Japanese whores. And I can't make money with them."

"But Chun—you say she might be up the street. Where?"

"I don't know the name of the place. Ask anyone about the Jeezachrise place for girls. They can tell you."

"Do you still have the paper I sold you?" Muck Shee opened her eyes and stared into the keeper's sunken sockets.

"What paper?" The old woman pushed Muck Shee into the alley and scraped an iron bolt across the door.

女

"Maudie!" Susie yelled down the classroom stairs. "Maudie! Come quick! Miss Davis wants you! She says there's people in the parlor to see you. She wants you right now!"

Maud was in the middle of practicing her piano scales. She had finished F major perfectly and was about to start D major. But she could tell from Susie's tone there was someone important upstairs. She closed the piano book. "I'm coming!"

An old Chinese woman with two boys and two girls sat nervously across from Miss Davis in the parlor. Maud looked at them and frowned. Then she took a seat on the couch next to Miss Davis. Maud pulled her skirt below her calves and crossed her legs at her ankles. The way young ladies were supposed to. The way she had been taught. "I wasn't finished with my practice Miss Davis."

"I know. But that'll probably be all for today. These people want to talk to you."

The old woman held something in her bony hands and twisted it. She gasped and groaned when she saw Maud. Like something inside her was broken and wouldn't let her breathe. "Mei Chun. It's me, your mother. Oh, my daughter." The old woman bent over and began to cough.

"Who are you?" It was strange to hear someone use her old name—a name nobody had used in over two years.

"I'm your mother," the old woman repeated. "And these are your brothers Ho and Moon, and your sisters Oy and Gum."

Maud held on to the edge of the couch. Her knuckles were white. Her stomach turned upside down. Maud shook her head. "I don't have any brothers or sisters."

"Yes you do," the old woman said. "You're my daughter." The old woman began to cough again. Like there was something big inside her that needed to come out.

Maud's mouth was dry and open wide. She looked at Miss Davis. "Is it true? Is she my mother? Are those my brothers and sisters?" Maud and Susie and Josephine talked sometimes about mothers—whose hers might be, and whether she might still be alive. And what it would be like to meet her. Susie knew because she met her mother once. And she told Maud about it. But Maud never really thought she would meet her own mother. Or imagined she had sisters besides the ones in the Home. And now that this old woman and her children were here Maud didn't know what to think. And she couldn't stop staring.

Miss Davis nodded. "Yes, it's true."

"We've been living in Fresno." The old woman began talking faster. "Not very far on the train, but—I've wanted to see you—every day I—"

"I don't know you." Maud looked at Miss Davis again. "What's her name?"

"Her name's Muck Shee—Lai. Like your last name." And Maud's heart almost stopped beating.

"I have papers." The old woman pulled something from her blouse and gave it to one of the boys. She pushed the boy toward Miss Davis. "And this is your big brother. He remembers you. Tell her, my son."

The boy the old woman called her son frowned at Maud and then put his head down and started talking fast but soft. Maud had to lean forward almost off the couch to hear.

Maud covered her ears. "I don't have any brothers do I Miss Davis? Why are these people here?"

The old woman began talking again. Coughing. Then talking. Then coughing some more.

"What did she say?" asked Miss Davis.

"She said she's come to take me to China. In a few days. She wants me to go with them." Maud whispered. "Miss Davis I don't want to go." Maud felt hot tears come up in her eyes. She shook her head to make them go away. The old woman wouldn't see her cry. "She can't take me can she? I won't go."

"It's all right, Maudie." Miss Davis smiled. "Remember when Miss Lake took you to court? That made Mrs. Williams your guardian. Now it's against the law for anyone to take you from the Home without Mrs.

Williams's permission. But I want this woman to hear your wishes, from your own lips. And you need to tell her."

The boy brought the papers to Miss Davis. Then Miss Davis showed them to Maud. There was a photograph of a little girl dressed in Chinese clothing wearing a Chinese hat and a strange necklace.

"Who's that?"

"It's you," the boy grinned. "When you were a baby. I was there."

"That may be our Maudie," Miss Davis said, "But it doesn't mean you can take her away. We have papers too."

"Tell her we know she sold you to a bad woman, and that Miss Lake found you in a bad place. That when she sold you to the bad woman, that was the end."

And so Maud told the old woman. That she had a new family. That she wanted to stay in America. And that the old woman had done a bad thing.

"But I didn't want to." The old woman held her arms to her sides and rocked back and forth on the couch like she was trying to keep herself from falling apart. "Your father made me. I've lived seven years with that photograph beside my bed. I've never taken off this bracelet since that day your father made me go to that brothel." The old woman pushed up the sleeve of her black silk blouse. "I prayed every day I'd live to see you again."

"Here, I have money." The old woman dipped her head and lifted a string over her neck. There was a thin red silk pouch on it and she fumbled with the pouch trying to untie it. "I'll pay for everything." The old woman coughed and put the silk pouch to her mouth. "How much do I owe? I can pay." She took some paper money from the pouch and gave it to the boy to take to Miss Davis.

"Tell her we do not buy and sell girls here." Miss Davis's eyes were shooting sticks of fire across the room.

"No. No." The old woman shook violently and stood up and Maud thought the old woman would fall over. But one of the boys jumped up and grabbed her arm. Another long cough started and the old woman's cheeks turned red. She took off the gold bracelet. "This is all I have. Please. I want her back. She's my daughter."

"Tell her she gave up all rights to you when she sold you," Miss Davis said. "That the American law says a parent who leaves a girl in a Home like ours for one year without saying anything, loses the girl. We've had you almost three years now. And this is the first time anyone's come to see you."

"I'm sorry." The old woman panted like she had just run up the basement stairs. "I didn't know—I thought if I saved enough money we could get you back. That's what your father—Foon—said—what everybody said. The red piece of paper—"

"You need to leave now." Miss Davis stood and moved toward the front door. "There's really nothing more we can do."

"I want you to have these photographs, my daughter. Of us—your real family. And this bracelet. Please, to remember us. Promise me you'll keep them." The old woman set the things on the lampstand beside the couch. She kept rubbing her wrist like she was scratching an itch or a scab that was ready to fall off. But there was nothing there. Just a wrinkly almost white mark.

"Mrs. Lai, it's time to go." Miss Davis sounded like she was talking to baby Ida.

Maud stood by the door shaking like a leaf about to fall from a tree branch. She watched the old woman stumble down the steps and into the street. The old woman's sons and daughters were on either side of her and she leaned on them. She was bent over and shaking like she was a tree too. A tree with one last leaf on it. And the leaf was falling off.

女

"Maudie, look! The door to the roof is open. Let's go play up there." Susie's eyes were big and sparkly. The way they always got when she had an idea for an adventure. It was almost Christmas. 1905. Six months since that strange day in June when those people came to visit Maud in the Oriental Home parlor. Leaving photographs of themselves and wanting her to go to China with them.

Sometimes Maud would think about those people suddenly for no reason. Mostly she thought about them when she was by herself and quiet. And it always made her feel like she wanted to take a bath. The way those people she didn't even know gave her things just so she would go to China with them. So she always liked it when Susie had a game to play or an adventure to do. Even if some of them were a bit scary. Like this one promised to be.

"I don't know Susie. Do you think it's all right? Miss Thorn—"

"Oh, I'm sure Miss Thorn won't mind. The skylight wouldn't be open if it wasn't, now would it? And we've been up there before."

"But only with Miss Thorn—or Miss Davis."

"Well, you can go ask them if you want. But I'm going up there. Is anyone coming with me?" Susie was already halfway up the ladder. And Maud could see up Susie's dress—all the way to the back of her chubby knees.

Ethel and Lily climbed the ladder behind Susie, without a word.

"Come on, Maudie. You're always such a spoil-sport."

So Maud climbed onto the roof with the other girls.

The first thing she saw even before she was on the roof was the blue, blue sky. With no clouds at all. It was like looking straight into heaven. It was windy and cold. But there was a large square place for playing and if she stayed in the middle it was almost warm. Some men must have been there earlier because of the large buckets of smelly tar and the long brooms leaning against one of the chimneys.

There was a little wall that went all around the edge of the roof. And because they had played up there before Maud knew it was safe. Even if Miss Thorn wasn't there. As long as they stayed away from the edges.

Maud wished she had a ball. She went to the edge where the tallest part of the wall was like stair-steps. Where they put the American flag on the Fourth of July. She looked down over Washington Street, and then off toward the bay. She thought about the first time she was in the old place across the street and looked out and thought she could see all the way to China. She now knew China was far across the ocean and took weeks to get there. And since that time years ago she had been to the Ferry Building and had ridden across the bay to Oakland and Berkeley. Just like Gracie said way back then.

A gust of wind caught her dress and sent it swirling around her bare legs. And even though the day was sunny it felt like what it really was—the first day of winter.

Susie shouted and Maud turned to see her best friend running in circles in the middle of the roof with Lily and Ethel chasing her.

"I'm a monkey! Whoosh. A winged monkey! Just like in Oz! Whoosh. Whoosh." Susie flapped her arms like they were real wings. And the wind blew her dress and Ethel and Lily laughed and said it really did look like Susie had feathers. Because they could see the lacey bottom part of her drawers.

Then Susie ran to the back edge of the roof where the wall was only three bricks high and she stood on the ledge and flapped her arms.

"Look, Maudie, I'm a winged monkey! Watch me fly."

Susie laughed and leaned backwards. There was a scream and then she was gone. There was a squishy crunch of something soft and heavy hitting the ground. And then nothing.

Maud and Ethel and Lily stood staring at each other. They couldn't move. Then finally Maud found her voice.

女

Carrie dipped the coarse bristle brush in a small tin bath of soapy carbolic water. She shook off the pink suds and returned to scrubbing the back steps of the Oriental Home. It was only a few hours since Susie's death. After Carrie had helped the undertaker take Susie's body away.

Carrie worked alone and on her knees. Her hands were red and raw. But the pushing and pulling seemed to ease the hard knots lodged in her neck and shoulders. When Carrie finished scrubbing, her shirtwaist and skirt were wet and bloodstained. But she couldn't find it within herself to change her clothes. She wanted to carry with her whatever part of Susie she could, for as long as she could. And if she only carried the girl's life-blood smudged on the breast of her blouse and hem of her skirt, so be it. She would change her clothes after supper and then take them downstairs to the laundry to soak in a tin bath of cold water and vinegar.

Death wasn't an unusual thing for anyone in the Home—for either the older girls or the younger ones. But until Susie's death, all the deaths had been the result of illness. And those were often long, drawn out affairs. They were losses the Home could prepare for. Not that a person was ever prepared for a child's passing.

Also, most of the deaths happened to girls who had only been in the Home a short time—girls already at death's door, rescued from the

"Chamber of Tranquility" as the Chinese called their mortuary. In such cases the Home girls had little time to develop attachments to the dying.

But that wasn't true in Susie's case. Susie had been in the Home over ten years—from the age of a year-and-a-half. She had been baptized across the alley in the Mission chapel, and she was a shining testimony to the younger girls—ones like Maud—who admired her and counted her as a best friend and sister.

It was Susie's idea to start the Junior King's Daughter Circle, and Maud and Josephine and Ethel had been her enthusiastic compatriots— and in any other project or idea Susie proposed. And that was the difference. Susie's was the first death in the Home that mattered to the younger girls. It was sudden, and Susie was loved. She was family.

女

"Where is Susie now?"

The girls were in their nightgowns, sitting cross-legged on the parlor floor in front of the fireplace. Their evening devotions were finished—and it had been a lengthy prayer time. Normally only two or three older girls would pray out loud. But tonight every one of the Christian girls—from the oldest to the youngest—had wanted to pray. And all their prayers had been heart wrenching.

"You know where she is, Maudie," Carrie said.

"But she disobeyed the rules, Miss Davis. And I did too. Susie always wanted to do adventures, and usually I stopped her if it would break the rules—but this time I didn't." Maud began to sniffle, and that started everyone's tears flowing again.

"We've been on the roof before, and it's been safe. But I should've stopped her. Because we didn't ask first. Most of the time she listens to me, even though I'm not as old."

No one said anything. There was just the sound of the crackling fire and the ticking of the mantle clock.

"Miss Davis, could Susie still have the Holy Ghost, even if she disobeyed the rules?" Maud's eyes were focused on the flames in the fireplace. There was a loud pop and the girl stiffened, arching her back away from the flames. A spark shot out and landed on the hearthrug near Lydia. Carrie leaned forward and flicked it onto the hearthstone and watched it turn from bright red to black. Maud moved a bit further from the fire and sank into Gracie, who was behind her. Maud's little body moved in rhythm with Gracie's as she breathed in and out.

"No Maudie, Susie didn't lose her salvation. If people lost the Holy Spirit so easily, no one would be in Heaven." Carrie had noticed long ago, that Maud and Susie had a peculiar preference for the expression "Holy Ghost" instead of "Holy Spirit." She had no idea why. And Maud always emphasized the first word—"*Holy*" rather than the second word, "Ghost." It was almost as though the girl thought of the Holy Ghost in contrast to something else—some other type of ghost, perhaps. Who knew for sure what went on in the minds of girls like her. Girls who had spent their early years in brothels with who knows what wild superstitions and beliefs floating about. So Carrie made a point of only using the word "Spirit" around the girls, hoping eventually, Maud—and others like her—would develop a Christian understanding of things, instead of Chinese.

"I'm sure Susie is in Heaven now," Carrie added. "She's looking down at you—at all of us, and smiling."

"But she didn't have time to confess her sins."

"Maudie—girls, remember about grace?"

Everyone but Maud turned toward Gracie, and Gracie sat up straight, solid as stone behind Maud.

"Tell us again, Miss Davis," Ethel said.

"No, I'm going to let Gracie tell you what her name means.

"Will you do that, Gracie?"

Grace wrapped her arms around Maud and took the girl's hands in hers, weaving her fingers into Maud's. "It means getting something good—having something good happen to you, even when you don't deserve it."

"Yes. 'Undeserved favor,' the dictionary says." And although Carrie wanted to say more, she didn't. It was enough on this longest and darkest of nights—the night of the winter solstice—that their world end in silence.

女

Maud followed the other girls up the stairs to bed. Slowly. Without saying a word. There was nothing good about today she thought. No "undeserved favor." No grace anywhere—except for the girl in the Home with that name. And even though Maud knew Gracie was good—far better than she was—she knew Grace wasn't perfect. Gracie was different from Susie that way.

Until today Maud always thought Susie was perfect—except in playing piano of course. Already Maud was much better than Susie in that. But Susie was still the one who knew practically everything about everything. Grace wasn't perfect like that, but she was bigger than Susie. And her arms were long enough to wrap around Maud. Gracie was always there when Maud needed her—like tonight downstairs when she held Maud tight. In front of the fireplace.

Maud wanted Susie to tell her things would be all right. Before she went to her room and closed the door and climbed into her bed and said goodnight to Ruby and Pearl and May.

Maud tried to pray after she got in bed, but she couldn't. Ruby was snoring, and then when Maud tried to say the word God, it got stuck in her throat and wouldn't come out. She lay awake for the longest time staring at the ceiling. At the blackness she couldn't see there. But finally, after the downstairs mantle clock struck two, she fell asleep.

And then she was wide-awake. There was a girl standing in the middle of the room. The girl had her back to Maud, and her black hair was long and shiny and tied in a ponytail—not the way Ethel or May or Ruby or Pearl did. And Maud could tell by the way her shoulders shook the girl was crying.

"Susie? Is that you?"

The girl nodded and turned to face Maud. Her face was perfect again. Like in the morning, when they first went onto the roof. Not bloody purple, cracked open. And she wasn't crying, even though her eyes were shining. They were full of life, and she was laughing.

"Maudie," she said. It seemed like she wanted to say more. But then she was gone. And Maud knew then what Susie said was true. That there were holy ghosts. And Susie was one of them.

"I saw Susie last night," Maud whispered to Gracie at the breakfast table in the morning.

"Sometimes that happens in dreams," Gracie said.

"But it wasn't a dream Gracie. I was awake and she was in my room and she was laughing. And she said my name."

"Christians don't believe in ghosts," Caroline said.

"But Susie was there. In my room. And I know it was her."

Gracie and Caroline raised their eyebrows but said nothing. And Maud vowed if Susie ever appeared to her again—and she hoped she would—she wouldn't tell a soul.

女

Tuesday, April 17, 1906. Two days after Easter. The day Maud had been waiting for forever since Susie first told her about Junior King's Daughters over four years ago. Now Josephine and Ethel were going to join too. The three of them would start a "Whosoever" Junior Circle at the Chinese Mission church that would be like the Circle Caroline and Gracie had. And Maud would get a silver cross like the older girls had. And she would wear it every day Miss Davis said she could. Because it was one more thing to keep her safe. Just like the Holy Ghost—which she already had. But that was inside her and invisible. And she needed something on the outside too. Something everyone could see. Something Susie didn't have the day she went up on the roof. The silver King's Daughter cross.

Miss Davis had picked this day—actually this night—for their "induction."

"It's a fancy word for joining something," Miss Davis said.

It was because a huge revival at Mechanics' Pavilion had started the day before. But tonight the main preacher would be Reverend Bulgin, who everybody knew. And he wanted the Oriental Home girls to sing when he took an offering for foreign missions. Because he thought Oriental children singing Christian songs would be something special.

All the girls were dressed in white. From top to bottom. Even the parts no one could see—like drawers. And after that there were white stockings to put on, and white petticoats and white dresses and white shoes. And white bows in their hair. The big girls even got white gloves. But not her or Ethel or Josephine.

Mechanics' Pavilion was the hugest place inside that Maud had ever seen. Not the tallest—that was City Hall across the street where she had been lots of times with Miss Lake. This place wasn't tall. Just long and wide.

The singing and the "induction" came at the end. After the preaching. Which was long and loud. Longer and louder than anything Reverend Chan ever did. But it was interesting because there were so many people there. Maybe three thousand, Miss Davis said. And because Maud knew what was going to happen at the end.

Maud and Lydia and Ruby and May and Pearl with Lum who was the only boy, marched up on to the platform and stood in a line. With Lum in front of them waving a baton. And Maud looked down at Miss Davis who was in front of everybody. And Ti was in the front row too. And Mrs. Williams with a bunch of even older ladies. And then there was Caroline and Gracie. And Jennie with Ida and Mamie. But try as she might Maud couldn't see Susie anywhere. Even though Susie was the one girl Maud wanted the most to be there. Susie wasn't.

Maud and the four other girls sang three times before they were allowed to sit down. And that was good because they didn't know any more songs. The last one was *Come Over and Help Us*, which Miss Fish the music teacher was only starting to teach to them. But people didn't seem to care when Lydia mixed up some of the notes and words. And Miss Davis and Mrs. Williams smiled the most when they got to the part about "coming into the land where the weak are oppressed," and "where the races in bondage cry out to be freed."

People clapped and cheered after each song. And some people even stood and stomped their feet after the last one. It was the loudest sound Maud had ever heard. And she liked the feeling inside when she looked out at all the people clapping and cheering.

After that Reverend Bulgin called Ethel and Josephine and her up in front of everybody. And the three of them stood beside Reverend Bulgin and faced the crowd.

"These children have completed a two-year program of Bible study." Reverend Bulgin reached down and put his right hand on Maud's head and his left hand on Josephine's head. "And they have a Christian service project they have faithfully contributed to for three years. This is all part of their commitment to become the first Chinese Junior King's Daughters Circle in the United States."

The project Susie decided on long ago was to bake cookies every month and sell them after church on Sundays. And they did. And in two years they saved five dollars to give to missions in China. Just like American girls. And because tonight's offering was for foreign missions, Maud said they should put the five dollars in an envelope with their names on it and give it to Dr. Bulgin. And they did. And Maud handed the envelope to Reverend Bulgin.

Then after he read their names and opened the envelope, Reverend Bulgin held up the five dollars for everyone to see. And he coughed loudly and rubbed his eyes. Then he said, "I consider this blood money. I'll always keep it. After what you all have seen and heard tonight from these dear Oriental children, you should know missions pay."

Then Miss Davis came up and had Maud and Ethel and Josephine repeat Bible verses they memorized. And recite the books of the Bible in order. With saying what parts of the Bible had what books. Like Law and History and Poetry and Epistles, and things like that.

Then finally Reverend Bulgin got to the part that made Maud's heart pound. "We're gathered together here, in love and Christian service, dedicated to helping others. Maud, daughter of the King, do you wish to become a member of the Order, and in the presence of the Almighty God, dedicate yourself in service to your King, in His name?"

On the outside Maud only had to say one yes. But on the inside she was saying a hundred of them.

Then Maud went to the big piano in front of the thousands of people and sat down to play the song she had been practicing for months. And everybody sang:

> "Take my life, and let it be
>
> consecrated, Lord, to Thee;
>
> Take my hands, and let them move
>
> at the impulse of Thy love.

Take my feet, and let them be

swift and beautiful for thee;

take my voice, and let me sing,

always, only for my King."

When Maud was done, everybody in Mechanics' Pavilion stood and clapped and cheered. And Reverend Bulgin came over to the piano and took Maud's hand and led her to the center of the stage and raised her hand in the air. Then he bowed so low that Maud's hand came down too and she bowed too. And Reverend Bulgin said in front of everyone, "Can you believe what you just heard? This little Oriental girl playing hymns like that? What a testimony to Christian missions."

And Maud felt inside herself that she had found something she had lost somewhere long ago. A something she didn't even know she had until this moment when she played the piano in front of all these people. A song she loved because it reminded her of Susie. And when she played the song, it was like Susie was sitting beside her on the piano bench pointing at the notes and saying, "Yes, yes." And so Maud was playing for Susie. Not for the people cheering who thought it was a song for them to sing to. And if people wanted to clap and cheer, that was fine. But Maud wasn't playing for them. Or for missions. Or even for Jesus. It was for Susie.

Then Maud and Ethel and Josephine repeated by heart the King's Daughter's motto. The one Susie had told her years before when Mr. Kane was trying to get her away from the Home. When Miss Lake and Mrs. Kate were still there:

"Look up, not down:

Look forward, not back:

Look out, not in:

Lend a hand."

Then Reverend Bulgin took out of his pocket three little boxes and gave them to Miss Davis. And Miss Davis opened them and pinned the silver crosses on the collars of their dresses, with Maud being last. A cross like the ones Gracie and Caroline wore only smaller. It was the "sign of the Order," Reverend Bulgin said. "And should always be worn as an outward symbol of your inner dedication to the King."

And Miss Davis bent down and whispered in Maud's ear that she would remember this day forever. And Maud knew it was true.

女

"It was the most beautiful and wonderful thing I have seen since I left DC," Mrs. Street said to Miss Davis after the revival was over and the King's Daughter ceremony too. Mrs. Ada Street was an important *WHMS* lady Miss Davis said. Who came out especially to see the Home, and then decided to stay an extra day so she could hear the children sing, and Maud play piano, and see the three girls get their King's Daughters silver crosses. They were sitting in the parlor of the Home drinking lemonade and eating cookies after riding the cable car back to the Home. And Mrs. Street said she wished everyone on the East Coast could hear what good singers they all were, and what a good pianist Maud was. Then Mrs. Street said she couldn't stay long because she was taking the late train east. "I should have been home two days ago," she told Miss Davis at the door. Then she hugged each of the new Daughters. "Such a wonderful work."

And Ti couldn't stay long either because of having to get up really early to get fruit and vegetables at the produce stalls down on the docks for Jew Ho's grocery store. But he told Maud it was the best piano playing he had ever heard her do too. And that's what Mrs. Williams said. And Mrs. Piatt too who was the Secretary of the Chinese Bureau. And other old ladies who Maud couldn't remember their names. They all said the same thing. And even though Susie wasn't really sitting next to her on the piano bench when she played Maud knew Susie would have said the same thing.

女

Just before she climbed into bed, Maud unpinned her silver Junior King's Daughter cross and put it under her pillow. Then she laid her doll beside the pillow and climbed into bed. She pulled the blanket tight under her neck. She put her arms under her pillow and found the cross. She clasped it in her hands and fell asleep.

Maud awoke while it was still dark as tar. A horse screamed somewhere, and then all the neighborhood dogs started barking. It sounded like maybe the noises were coming from Dupont Street. But she wasn't sure. But they were scary noises, and made Maud shiver and hold her cross and doll more tightly. She lay awake listening for another scream, but that was the only one. And before long Maud went back to sleep. She dreamed she was on the roof of the Home again, watching Susie balance on the ledge. Susie held Maud's new silver cross in her hand.

Susie looked at Maud and laughed. "See Maudie! I'm a monkey with a cross! A winged monkey! Whoosh! Under his wings! Whoosh! Under his wings with a magic cross!"

"No!" Maud screamed. "No Susie no!"

The whole building suddenly tilted on its side and Maud got thrown toward the edge where Susie was. Then Susie lost her balance and grabbed Maud's arm and pulled her so hard her shoulder felt a sharp pain.

"Susie! Let go!" But it was too late. Maud rolled to the edge and fell over the side with Susie. But she didn't fall far. She hit something hard and stopped. And she was still very much alive. She lay wherever she was, and felt around in the dust and darkness for Susie. And for something to hold on to as the building crashed down.

Maud choked and coughed, and then realized it wasn't a dream.

She was under her bed, and the entire Home was falling apart.

Chapter Ten

FIRE
(1906)

The fish and produce men were beginning to arrange their stalls at the foot of Washington Street when Ti drove Jew Ho's wagon up to his favorite fruit stand. Jew Ho's horse was unusually skittish, and Ti pulled the reins tight to stop the nervous animal. It snorted and shook its mane.

Ti hopped off the seat and patted the horse's neck. "Shhhh."

"Wats amatta yo hoss today, Mr. Leong?" The grizzled, bristle-cheeked Italian farmer stood up and grinned. He wiped his hands on his red-stained apron, and pulled a handful of bruised strawberries from the pile of wooden crates stacked beside him. He put them to his nose and sniffed. "Perfeck ripe, deese are."

Two fishermen—Greek brothers whom Ti sometimes bought from, were setting up a table next to the Italian man. They often fought with the Italian over the space, but this morning the Italian had gotten there first and managed to establish a long row of berry crates as a dividing line. The Greek boys glared at Ti and the Italian, then leaned their sign against the Italian's crates.

"Fresh shrimps and crabs. Ask about our prices," it read in large, hand-printed black letters.

"Don't buy from dose guys today." The Italian kicked the sign. "Dose fish stink. Same as yesterday."

"You gotta no money ta feed dat ting?" The Italian took a step towards the horse.

"Here, I give him somma deese. Soft ones like dis free today. For hosses only."

"You see. Very sweet."

The horse shook its mane, whinnied, and backed away from the fruit.

"Maybe he don't like those," Ti frowned. "Too early. Still too much white. Not ripe."

"No, no, your hoss just actin' funny today. Maybe misses his girlfriend. Like you. I find you new one. White, black, or yellow?" The Italian poked Ti in the chest and winked. "No matta. All same in da dark."

Ti and the old man had a well-rehearsed bartering litany, one they had developed over the past two years of weekly, predawn meetings. And they rarely strayed from their good-natured feints and parleys. Only the prices were negotiable.

"So how much you want for these?" Ti shook the top crate, burrowing with his hands to see if the farmer had hidden the hardest, unripe berries at the bottom—or worse, the overripe ones.

"I tell you, Mr. Leong. Dats aboudda da bes strawberry we pick. First ones. For you—special price—today only. Tomorrow who knows? Big box—twenty cent."

"Nah, Mr. Jew say he only pay five cent. He got another baby coming." Ti pulled his hand out and touched it to his nose. His hand was clean, but the smell of strawberries was strong and sweet in his nostrils. The Italian was right. The berries were perfect.

"Always anudder baby. Mus have twenty now. You tella Mr. Jew he keepa his ting in his pants where it belong—den he can pay. My famly needa eat too.

"Can't do for under fifteen cent."

"No, eight. Eight cent, that's all."

"Oi! Maria! You tink we eat rice and mice like you?"

"All right. Ten cent."

"Ten cent." My chillin be hungry tonight." The Italian's shoulders slumped and he shook his head. "Not good."

As Ti reached out to shake the Italian's hand, Jew Ho's horse whinnied, panicked, and bolted. Before Ti could grab the reins, the wagon crashed into the Italian's produce stall, knocking over the row of strawberry crates and the fishermen's sign.

There was a tremendous jolt. It was the feeling Ti got when Jew Ho's dray went over a large pothole—one he hadn't anticipated. Like the bottom dropping out of something.

Whatever was left standing after Jew Ho's horse bolted was now in shambles. The Italian farmer, the two Greek fishermen, and Ti stared at each other, slack-jawed. Ti looked up Washington Street in the direction Jew Ho's horse and dray had fled. The street was buckling and rippling like great ocean waves.

It was Wednesday, April 18th. Three days after Easter.

火

At the Oriental Home, the downstairs pianos sounded like the babies were pounding on the keys and there were no big girls around to tell them not to. It was the same way with the church bells. Clanging and clanging, but no song.

From Maud's place under her bed she heard crashing glass and cracking walls and the thud of falling plaster and chimney bricks. She heard Pearl and Ruby scream from across the room. And then she closed her eyes and covered her head with her arms. When she opened her eyes, white plaster dust swirled around the room like smoke.

Maud was just about to crawl out from under the bed when there was another huge crash right over her head. Then she screamed too. The mattress on the bed sagged low and squeaked and groaned like somebody really fat sat on it. Dust filled Maud's eyes and nose. "I'm going to die," she thought. "Just like Susie." Maud choked and coughed and rolled out from underneath her bed in time to see Pearl and Ruby crawling toward the hallway door. May sat up in her bed and rubbed her eyes. "What happened?" she said.

The closet door opposite Maud was ajar and the dresser next to it had fallen over—but not before emptying everything on the floor. Dresses and shoes and underclothes were everywhere. The shaking had seemed to last forever. But now that it was over Maud knew hardly any time had passed.

"Earthquake," Maud said.

"Miss Davis! Miss Davis!" All four girls were standing now, staring at each other. Their hands over their noses and mouths to keep out the choking dust. Maud turned back toward her bed. She saw a hole in the ceiling above it with a gash of pink morning sky showing through. A big wooden beam lay on her bed where she had been sleeping moments earlier. Then someone yelled. It was Miss Davis.

"Girls! Are you all right? Come here!"

Miss Davis was in the hallway with baby Ida in her arms. Everyone was in the hallway now. All the girls in their nightclothes. Rubbing their eyes and jabbering.

"Is everyone out of their rooms? Anyone hurt?

"Hurry, we've got to get outside."

Soon everyone was huddled in the street, shivering. Their bare feet on the cold paving bricks wet with the morning. Then another tremor hit and part of the Home roof collapsed. And everyone screamed again.

After a few minutes Miss Davis told Gracie and Caroline to stay with everyone while she checked out the backside of the Home. Before long Maud heard Miss Davis shouting for everyone to come inside by the back door.

Miss Davis was throwing clothes downstairs from the upstairs hallway.

"Don't worry about what you put on. You can change later," Miss Davis yelled as she tossed another pile down the stairs. So everyone grabbed something and dressed with the door open to the pale cold dawn. So they could rush into the street if another shake came.

When everyone was dressed, they ran into the Mission building across the alleyway. Maud was wearing one of Ruby's dresses she thought—it was too small and tight across her chest. But she didn't have time to find one of her own.

Reverend Chan was downstairs in the chapel inspecting things when everyone tumbled inside. Miss Davis told Reverend Chan how not one of the girls had been hurt in the quake. "I don't know how we all escaped from the Home alive—let alone unhurt and without a scratch." Miss Davis shook her head. "It's truly a miracle. Thank God for his protecting care."

"Other than rooms in a mess and broken windows, this building seems to have survived well." Reverend Chan wore Chinese slippers and a long thick robe over his pajamas. His hair was uncombed and stuck out every which way. "I haven't checked the basement yet, but the wife and girls are fine. Just scared. They're upstairs, cleaning the kitchen. Broken dishes everywhere, spilled flour and things. It'll take them a while.

"That was a monster."

火

When the shaking ended, Ti instinctively looked up at the Ferry Building clock tower. Although chunks of stone had fallen from the facing and had exposed parts of the skeletal metal frame, the tower itself remained standing—for the moment, at least. It cast an early morning shadow over the market below. But its hands had stopped. Frozen at 5:12. Incongruously, the Oakland Ferry was at that moment steaming toward the dock. In a few moments the day's first businessmen would be disembarking—and then start walking up Market Street—to who knew what.

Ti shaded his eyes from the brightness in the eastern sky and scanned the breadth of East Street for Jew Ho's horse and wagon. He finally saw them, a block up Washington Street. The horse was penned in by a wall of brick and rubble that had fallen across the street and blocked it. The horse was rearing and whinnying nervously, unable to turn around.

By the time Ti managed to control the horse and return to the store on Stockton Street, Jew Ho was already there, surveying the damage. A crowd milled about, clamoring to get inside. A boy had managed to climb through the broken storefront window and was now trying to crawl out with fruit and vegetables stuffed in his pockets.

"See if you can pull the wagon up on the sidewalk." Jew Ho directed Ti with one hand while grabbing at the boy with the other. "Maybe that'll keep people from stealing anything more."

"I was about to buy some cases of strawberries when the quake hit." The horse was still full of nervous energy—*chi*, and Ti had to pat its neck and whisper soothing words in its ear to calm it. "But the horse was gone in an instant. We're lucky to have the wagon back in one piece, the way the horse was whipping it about." He jumped down and tied the reins around a shattered telephone pole.

Within a few minutes, Ti and Jew Ho had the broken window blocked by the wagon. And within the hour they had sold every edible thing—including ripped bags of beans and rice, and broken boxes of dried fish and mushrooms. People took anything—at any price.

Ti sprawled in the dray alongside Jew Ho, exhausted, even though the sun had been above the Oakland hills for barely an hour. Suddenly Ti sat up. He had no idea whether the building where he lived was still standing. In the morning's trauma he hadn't thought to stop by his own place. He was about to ask Jew Ho if he could check on it, when an American came toward them and tapped the side of the dray.

"What do you want?" Ti eyed the man suspiciously.

"How much to take the wife and family from Mission and Fifth to Van Ness and California?" The American had a gash on his forehead. Half-congealed blood oozed down his cheek. "The wife has a brother there, and our flat's been destroyed. There's a fire south of Market, and everything's in real bad shape. A lot worse than here. I need to get them out of there."

Ti looked at Jew and raised his eyebrows. He could tell Jew Ho was thinking the same thing.

"Two dollar each person." Ti looked back at the American. "Ten dollar more for heavy stuff in house."

"You bastards. How about half that amount? One dollar a person, and five dollars for belongings."

"No. Two dollar and ten dollar. Take or leave."

"Pissy yellow Jew chinks. All right. I guess I don't have a choice."

"Must pay now."

The man spat at one of the wagon wheels and pulled out a fistful of gold coins from his pocket. He counted out the agreed upon amount. "Jesus Christ Holy Ghost!

"Well, let's go. I don't have time to waste."

"You take him," Jew Ho said to Ti. "I need to stay with my wife and family."

By the time Ti got back to Chinatown, Jew Ho had another panicky American waiting for the wagon. "Don't worry about coming back," Jew

Ho shouted. "If you see someone who wants the wagon—just make them pay, and then take them wherever they want."

Ti found himself moving further north and west with each trip. People were clogging the streets now; everyone moving like gray ghosts, away from the fires on the waterfront and Market Street. He was on Jackson Street near Sullivan Alley when he passed a group of girls headed toward him from the shadowy, dead-end street. Two girls were dressed in thin nightclothes. Two had nothing more than blankets clasped over their shoulders, their bare legs showing up to their thighs as they picked their way around a collapsed balcony and a jagged gap in the boardwalk. None of the girls walked with the gentle sway-step of bound-footed women, and Ti knew they belonged to a brothel.

The girl in front seemed older than the others, and as she walked she turned back toward the smallest one—a girl perhaps ten years old. The lead girl wore what must have once been an expensive jade green cheongsam. She was barefoot. Her black hair was long and matted, and hung below her waist like dry, pressed seaweed. Like something brittle that would break if touched. The girl turned toward Ti and stopped in mid-step. Her face was flecked with soot and red brick dust except for the sunken places around her bloodshot eyes. The girl behind her was walking with her head down, and she stumbled and cursed when she bumped into the lead girl's shoulder. But the lead girl didn't move. She stared into Ti's eyes, and then shouted.

The instant the girl said his name, Ti knew who it was: Yet. It was Yet, the girl he had kept in his heart for the past seven years. Instinctively he reached into his trouser pocket and felt for the thing he kept there. The cool, smooth piece of porcelain he had found on the floor of Yet's room not long after she had been beaten. It was still there, and he rubbed the charm between his thumb and forefinger as though offering a prayer of thanksgiving to a god—which one, he didn't know or care. Only that the girl now running toward him, arms spread wide, face red from the heat and dust of the day, was Yet.

"Ti!" she cried again. And he was on the ground waiting for her; and then she was collapsing into his arms and he was lifting her onto the seat of the dray.

"Come with me," he said. And she motioned to the girls behind her to climb into the wagon. "I have a place where you'll be safe."

How had this thing happened? That the horror of the earthquake had brought to him the one thing he most desired, but despaired of ever finding?

"I never forgot you," Ti said. "I've looked for you and asked about you—"

"I've been gone," Yet said. "I came back to Number One City two days ago—with these girls. From a place far away."

And that was enough for Ti. Without thinking more, he drove around the corner to the Mission and jumped off the wagon. He ran up the steps and knocked on the door. When Reverend Chan opened it, Ti told him he had some girls who needed a place to stay. "Please, take care of them until I get back."

"Don't worry, it's safe in there." Ti reached for Yet. And then he remembered Maud. "And Chun's there too. Remember the little slave girl from the place where you used to be? She's a big girl now, with a new name. But she's there. You'll see."

There was a choking sound. "Chun? That baby? She's alive? Inside?" And then Yet fell into Ti's arms. Her arms wrapped around his neck and she sobbed in between deep, gasping breaths.

Ti put his hands on Yet's waist and helped her from the dray. "Yes, she's there. Stay with her, and I'll come back for you tonight."

Later, as Ti drove the dray down Stockton Street toward Market, he turned and glanced back at the Mission. Yet's body was framed in a cracked upstairs window, her eyes following him; her mouth open, in the shape of his name. Her eyes were large and full of fear—and filled with something else he couldn't quite name. And Maud stood beside her.

Ti's hand was in his pocket again, and he squeezed the porcelain stone nestled there as if it were the girl herself. He was headed back into the angry mouth of the fire. But it was different now. In all the chaos and destruction of the morning, the demon earthquake had inadvertently spit out a treasure in jade silk. And Ti knew he would never relinquish that treasure.

火

Maud tried hard to remember the girl standing beside her who was Ti's friend. But her mind was blank. She could only think of a girl named Ming who used to carry her places. But Ming wasn't beautiful like this Yet. But like magic, this girl hugged her like Miss Lake did long ago. Only this wasn't a goodbye. This was hello. And the girl burst into tears when she saw Maud, and wouldn't let go. She said over and over, "Chun. Chun. I can't believe it's you." It was a name Maud hadn't heard since the time her own mother used it when she came to the Home. But now here was a girl beside her. Yet. Ti's friend. And they were both watching Ti look back at them as he drove away.

And even though there was no order on the street below, there was order in Maud's heart. A feeling that even with people running every which way and the street with huge cracks and bumps and things fallen down into it, that nothing would stop Ti from coming back for this girl—and for her. Because she heard Ti say to the girl, "Stay here with Chun until I come back and get you." And even though everyone seemed to be desperately searching for something or someone—maybe brothers or sisters or parents—Maud wasn't. Because she knew Ti would come back—for the two of them.

There were Japanese ladies with their strange thin flowing dresses. And muscly half-naked American men with hair all over their bodies. And tiny bound-footed Chinese ladies in black pantaloons. All kinds of people heading up the steep hills away from the bay and Chinatown. But Maud wasn't among them. And neither was the girl Yet. They were together. They had a place. And it was here. Upstairs in the Mission. Together. The two of them, waiting for Ti.

火

Between the occasional seismic spasm, Carrie, Lois, and Reverend Chan began to make raids into the groaning Oriental Home to collect whatever clothing, blankets, food, and water they could find. The front of the building had now collapsed. Chimneys had fallen through to floors below; and because the parlor's major structural beams had splintered, they couldn't get through the front door. They had to use the back entrance and the back stairs. The Home seemed to be alive—like an elderly man or woman trying to get out of bed in the morning, complaining about all their aches and pains. Like her parents used to do on cold, Canadian winter mornings.

On one trip Carrie found an old leather satchel fallen from a seldom-used shelf in the upstairs closet, and she took it downstairs into her office where she stuffed it with everything from the safe—gold coin, government files on detainees, guardianship and insurance papers, and the Home's daily logbooks. The Home was uninhabitable for the near future. Not even her office was salvageable. It would be months before the family could move back into the building—and it was likely they would have to tear it down completely and start over from the foundation—this, for a building not quite five years old.

By noon Carrie and the other adults had cleared a path through the hallways and stairwells to the upstairs rooms, and Carrie let the children return briefly to collect a favorite thing or two to comfort them through their coming nights away from the Home. Carrie and Reverend Chan had decided the family could sleep on the Mission chapel floor for at least the first night.

火

It was Maud's turn to go back into the Home, so she left Yet in the Mission chapel and ran with Josephine and Gracie across the alley, and through the back door into the parlor. She wanted to get two things. Her doll and her cross.

The bookcase beside the fireplace had fallen over and thrown things every which way. The knickknacks she and Pearl and Ruby so carefully dusted each Saturday lay shattered on the floor, and Maud had to step over the sharp broken pieces. She was glad Miss Davis had found shoes for her earlier in the day, and that she was finally wearing them after having gone barefoot for most of the morning. The house shook again, and Maud tried not to scream. She didn't want to scare Josephine or Gracie. But the instant it stopped, she saw another bookshelf tip and spill everything onto the floor. There, on top, was *The Wonderful Wizard of Oz*. Without thinking, she grabbed it and tucked it under her arm. Then she ran upstairs to her room. She found her doll still lying on the bed where she had tucked it in the night before—her little head on the pillow.

But the long piece of wood that fell across the bed also fell on the doll's face and cracked its cheek. And now the doll's left eye and the left side of its mouth were crooked.

"My dolly," Maud cried. "Gracie help me." Gracie came running, and together they pushed on the mattress just enough to get the doll out from under the piece of wood. Maud held the doll close to her chest and brushed the doll's hair back and soothed her. "I'm sorry," she said over and over.

Then she remembered her new King's Daughter cross that she put under her pillow the night before. It was the one reason the wooden beam didn't land on her during the earthquake. She found the cross and pinned it to the collar of her dress. She would wear it forever. It saved her life.

Maud found her Bible in the middle of the floor where it had fallen off something. She picked it up too. Then she helped Josephine find her things.

When the three girls got back into the alleyway, the sky was getting dark with smoke from the fires and small white things were fluttering from the sky. Maud had never seen snow before. But she had read about it and Miss Davis told them about it. What it was like to grow up with cold snowy winters in Canada. This is what snow must be like Maud thought. Except it wasn't winter.

"You've got ash on you," Miss Davis said when the girls walked into the chapel with their things. And then she brushed the white off Maud's books and doll and clothes. "I'm glad you girls found your King's Daughter crosses. But you need to be careful when you're outside. The bright red embers are the hottest and can burn holes in things."

火

By late afternoon everyone was exhausted. The babies could sleep through anything if their little tummies were full. But there had been no milk delivery that morning, and with only a little left from the previous day, the babies had been getting fussier. Their cheeks and eyes were puffy and red from crying. They seemed to sense everyone's distraction and worry. But there was nothing Carrie could do for them. Apologizing to Reverend Chan's wife, Carrie left the babies upstairs and made her way back to the chapel.

The older children were a different story. Along with everyone else, they heard every rumor that made its way through the parlor doors. No one tried to shield them from anything. And like everyone else, they had been on a cable car ride of ups and downs all day. Carrie was putting Maud and the others down for a rest on their makeshift beds in the chapel, when she heard what sounded like Reverend Freeman Bovard's voice in the parlor. He was the Superintendent of the Methodist Chinese Conference and lived in Berkeley. But why would he be here now?

"I don't think you'll be able to spend the night here. It took me the entire morning to work my way from the Ferry Building along East Street— to the Presidio. The good news is, there aren't any fires to the north and west of here. But the bad news is the soldiers I talked to said their plan is to try and hold the fires at Powell. If they do that, Chinatown will be destroyed, and you'll have to move somewhere to the west."

It was Reverend Chan who replied. "Someone told us they're dynamiting on Kearney right now—using Giant Powder. So maybe they hope to hold the fire below there."

"I know, but they're not sure they can." The man's deep bass convinced Carrie it was Reverend Bovard.

"If we leave, where will we go?" It was Reverend Chan again. "We're over forty people—nearly fifty—with the girls someone brought in this morning."

"It's a lot of people, I know—but that's why I checked the churches on the way over. To see if there was a place you people could get to—if need be. California Street seems to have the least damage."

"That's two miles away." Reverend Chan's voice became more agitated. "Up the steepest hills in the city. And we have children—and babies."

Carrie stepped out from the chapel, into the parlor. The heavily bearded Freeman was huddled next to Reverend Chan. Their two parlor chairs faced each other; their knees nearly touching.

"When—how?"

"About half an hour ago." Freeman stood and wiped a hand on his black suit pants. They were knee-high with reddish brown dust. "You were upstairs, I guess.

"I left Berkeley about eight this morning when I saw the smoke in the city. From the other side of the bay it looked like all of San Francisco south of Market through Chinatown was on fire. I didn't know whether the Home was still standing, or the Mission building—or whether anyone was even alive. I feared the worst."

"I can't imagine the fires getting this far north." Carrie reached out to shake Freeman's hand. "Please, sit down.

"I know this may sound ridiculous, but a verse from Psalm 34 has been running through my head all day: 'The angel of the Lord encampeth round about them that fear him.'

"Not one member of our Home family was hurt in the quake—and on your way in I'm sure you saw what the Oriental Home is like. If God's kept us safe thus far—without a scratch, surely he won't let his work be destroyed."

"Well, it'll take a miracle to stop the force of the fire." Freeman sat again. "Or a strong change of wind direction."

"You must be exhausted." Carrie scowled in Reverend Chan's direction. "Have you had anything to eat—or drink?"

Freeman shook his head. "I think I was about to be offered something, but then Reverend Chan and I got sidetracked by our stories of the morning's events." Carrie thought she detected the shadow of a smile at the corners of Freeman's mouth, but his eyes and voice betrayed his weariness.

"I don't know what we have to offer—as you can imagine. But I'm sure I can find something."

It was fifteen minutes before Carrie made it back to the men. They were exactly as she had left them. She carried a small pitcher of warm lemonade from the King's Daughters celebration the night before, a glass, some crackers and sardines; and cookies—also left over from the night before.

"I hope these will be all right."

"Thanks. Anything will taste wonderful after my hike today. I think I must have walked about nine miles total."

Reverend Chan stood and offered Carrie his chair. "I need to check on my wife and children. From the sound of the chapel, the Home children must be sleeping."

Carrie took the vacated chair and poured Freeman a glass of lemonade. "When you're ready, I'd love to hear the rest of your story."

Freeman emptied the glass in one swallow. A sudden roar shook the building. The parlor windows chattered and the lemonade pitcher skipped across the mahogany lamp table. Freeman jumped to his feet. "They've been dynamiting all over the city, but that one was close."

Carrie heard whimpering coming from the chapel. "I'd better check on my children too."

"While you're doing that, I'll see what's happening down the street."

Carrie found Maud in the far corner of the darkened chapel with little Ida and Mamie on her lap. She had her arms around them, trying to comfort them.

"What was that noise, Miss Davis?" Maud asked. "It woke us all up."

"Just more dynamiting, like before. The soldiers are doing it to keep the fire out of Chinatown. I know it sounds scary, but it's actually a good sound."

Carrie picked up Ida and carried her into the parlor just as Freeman came back inside.

"A policeman out on Stockton Street says he heard some soldiers were blowing up buildings down on Clay and Kearney. With black powder, no less. I can't believe they're that foolish."

火

Ti was on Clay, not far above Dupont when he heard the roar. He stopped Jew Ho's dray and watched a flaming mattress fly over his head. He touched the horse's hindquarters with his whip, and at the corner of Clay and New Spanish Alley, he saw the mattress again. It was lying beside a pile of broken crates and shattered bottles—the contents of which had spilled across the alley. Ti jumped down from the wagon to pull the smoldering mattress away from the crates, but then caught the telltale odor of alcohol. Within seconds flames were shooting ten feet in the air. Ti ran across Clay Street and watched from the seat of the dray as the fire began to creep up the walls of a dilapidated storefront.

"It's the beginning of the end," he whispered to Jew Ho's horse. "And I've got nothing but this wagon and the clothes I'm wearing."

He patted the horse's hindquarters, then scanned the street, looking for a family—anyone—with enough gold to make it worth his while to cart them to safety. A solitary woman hobbled out of the blazing New Spanish Alley storefront, weaving her way through the alley and onto Clay Street. Her clothing and hair, already smoldering. Maybe the old keeper from the place where Yet used to be, Ti thought. But he couldn't see her face. The woman had a bottle clutched in her right hand, and as she lifted it to her lips she stumbled and fell. The bottle broke and spilled its contents on her clothing. Within seconds her body was engulfed in flames. She lay there for a moment, then began crawling up Clay, one dusty gray cobblestone at a time. She could have been an old newspaper set on fire by a bored band of boys. And he was the curious bystander, watching the wind blow the burning thing up the street. And the thing didn't make a sound.

There was nothing Ti could do. He had nothing to stop the fire except his hands and Jew Ho's wagon. And he couldn't put a ball of flames into a wooden wagon. If it was the old keeper, she was finished. And her fate had found her at last. How strange he should find Yet alive that morning—and perhaps be watching the death of her tormentor the evening of the same day.

Ti looked further up Clay Street and saw an American running toward him. The man was waving his arms frantically.

"Let's go." Ti shook the horse's reins. "Maybe we'll make enough money tonight to get me a new apartment—and you a new stable."

Ti pulled the horse beside the man who had paused to catch his breath.

"How much?" The American spoke reasonably good Chinese. "How much for the wagon?"

"Only one?" Ti answered in English, suspicious of who might be hiding around the corner.

"No. A lot of people. At the Mission around the corner."

"On Washington Street?"

"Yes."

"How many—and where to?"

"A full load." The American ran his fingers through his mustache and beard. "We want to go west—I don't know where. We haven't decided for sure."

Ti thought about Jew Ho. How the wagon and horse belonged to someone else. How they had already changed the prices twice. "My boss say one hundred dollar for whole wagon." Gold only. Otherwise ten dollar gold for each one."

"It's a mission—a church. Not a business. We don't have that kind of money. Can't you do it for less?"

Ti thought about Yet and Maud. About getting them away from the fire.

"My boss, he make rules, not me. His wagon. But since you're Mission—half price. Fifty dollar. Only tell me where you go."

火

Carrie passed around the remaining crackers and cans of sardines she had found and waited with Reverend Chan for Freeman's return. They still had a little milk for the babies—but not much water. And the milk wouldn't last much longer. And they had a few cold rice balls. But she wanted to save those for later. There was no telling where they would be tomorrow, or if they would find more food.

It was after seven o'clock, and night had fallen. But the world had turned upside down. Washington Street was brighter now than it had been at noon. It had been dusk six hours earlier, with thick, billowing towers of smoke blocking the sun. But now, after sundown, a flickering, reddish-orange monster ruled the sky.

There was a hard pounding on the Mission door. "Open up!" More pounding. "Open up I say! Everyone must evacuate. General's orders."

"We're almost fifty people here," Reverend Chan told the soldiers when he opened the door. "Women and children. And a number of babies. I have someone out right now looking for a wagon. We can't leave until he gets back."

"Listen, mister. You've got no choice. It's a federal order."

"Please. Give us half an hour."

Carrie came up behind Reverend Chan and peered over his shoulder. A flame-tinged, smooth-faced boy stood there—not a day over nineteen, she guessed.

"You may be dust and ashes by then, ma'am."

"We'll trust God in that case."

"Then their blood'll be on your hands—and God's—not mine. If I can get back here in a half hour, I will—but if you're not gone by then, by God I'll use my bayonet on you all."

The little band of half-men marched up to the next building and repeated their well-rehearsed lines. Carrie leaned against the doorframe and squinted into the stinging smoke rolling up Washington Street. A horse-drawn dray had turned the corner of Stockton, heading toward her. Leong Ti was at the reins, and Freeman sat beside him.

火

"We can have it—but it's going to cost," Freeman told Carrie when Leong Ti pulled the horse to a stop in front of the Mission steps. "It's this or nothing. And I don't think we can out-walk the fire if we have to carry the babies."

Carrie ran inside and came back with the satchel. "How much?"

"Fifty dollars, he says." Freeman paused. "His first price was a hundred."

"It's not my price, Miss Davis." Leong Ti tilted his head back and stared off somewhere above Carrie's head. She followed his gaze, but saw nothing. "It's the boss." Leong Ti grimaced.

"I know. You've been good to us over the years—what you've done for Maud. We can pay." Carrie knew she had no choice. The only way out of the fire's path entailed climbing some of the steepest hills in the city. And the children couldn't do that. They wouldn't get more than a few blocks without a wagon. Carrie rummaged around in the satchel until she felt the heavy bag of gold coin. At least one of the five dollar gold pieces in the bag had come from Leong Ti himself—for his support of Maud. Carrie swallowed hard and counted out the coins. "Here's the fifty dollars." She handed over the money. The other forty-five dollars would have paid a month's room and board for three women.

"I'll leave the wagon here to get ready." Leong Ti hopped down from the dray's seat, and was gone.

"We'll have to move fast." Carrie led Freeman into the chapel. "Lois and the older girls can collect the clothes we brought from the Home and put them in the back of the wagon—along with these blankets. We won't have room for pillows." Carrie wiped her brow with the back of her long-sleeved shirtwaist. She had the fleeting feeling she was good at this sort of thing. Knowing what needed to be done during a moment of crisis.

"The children can bring their one or two special things. That may help comfort them. Any tins of food we have left—any water—we should bring that, too. Am I forgetting anything?"

Leong Ti returned with a box of oranges balanced on his shoulders. "This all we have in store." He set it atop a pile of blankets in the back of the dray. "For children and girls. Don't worry about pay."

"Thank you." Carrie managed a smile at the Chinese man. "I don't know what we would have done if Freeman hadn't found you."

The women and children crowded onto the steps of the Mission and spilled out into the street. "We'd better count how many people we have," Reverend Chan said. "We don't want to lose anyone." They began to lift the children onto the piles of blankets and clothes in the wagon.

"We keep adding more." Carrie shook her head. "We had thirty in the Home when we started the day. I count forty-eight now—with the folks from the church and the new girls Leong Ti brought earlier. Is that what you have?"

Reverend Chan finished his counting. "Yes, forty-eight."

"Where you go?" Leong Ti climbed onto the driver's bench and took the reins.

"I keep thinking about the Methodist Church on California—up on Broderick," Freeman said. "I was there earlier today, and the area looked relatively undamaged."

"Long way." Leong Ti leaned forward and frowned. "Most Chinese going Beach Point. But Americans go Presidio. That about same."

Carrie was too tired to argue. "I'm sure Broderick will be fine. It's far enough from the fire for the night, and we can sleep on the pews. We can decide in the morning what to do next."

There would be no need for streetlights on their journey. The city in flames was more than enough to lead them out of Chinatown. Leong Ti shook the reins, and the refugees headed up Washington Street toward the grand mansions on Nob Hill. Carrie could already see their bizarre gingerbread turrets silhouetted against the southwestern sky.

At Mason Street Carrie turned and watched the wall of flames slowly moving toward the shattered Oriental Home. Her mind was a jumble of thoughts and feelings. A fevered dream—a mix of imagination and memories—and the ever-present reality of the fire. She felt as if she were Lot's wife looking back at Sodom. Or maybe a pilgrim, leaving John Bunyan's City of Destruction.

火

"Miss Davis, may I sit by Ti?" Maud tugged on Miss Davis's skirt. She was trying to keep up with Yet and with Ti's wagon but her feet hurt. They scrunched up against the front of her shoes in such a way that she had to curl her toes under just to walk at all. Lydia and Mamie and Ruby and May were already sitting in the wagon. Maud wanted to be with them.

"Yes, you may," Miss Davis said.

"Mr. Leong, we need to rest for a moment." Miss Davis and even Reverend Chan and the big girls were gasping for breath. Their shoulders moved together like they were one big animal pulling an invisible load up the steep hill.

Ti reached down and lifted Maud onto the wagon seat. Its worn softness held her there. Ti's arm muscles were strong and tight holding the horse's reins. Shushing it. Then guiding the wagon once again up and up the steep hill.

Ida was half asleep in the wagon. Her head bumping on her sister Mamie's knee and Mamie's spine digging hard into Maud's back. No one could move in the wagon. They were packed tight like the little fish in the tin Miss Davis opened for them earlier in the evening. Maud looked at her shoes and tried to straighten her toes. And that's when she saw what she had done. The shoes she had weren't hers—at least not her newest pair. In her hurry to help pack the wagon she put on her old shoes—the ones that didn't fit anymore. The pair she gave to Ruby a month ago. They were Ruby's shoes. And Maud really hoped Ruby was wearing hers.

To the left the city was all in flames lighting the night sky. Reds. Yellows. Orange. Sometimes stray cinders falling from the sky like tiny twinkling stars. Maud knew now to brush them off before they burned her dress, like Miss Davis said. Her eyes and nose and throat and lungs burned like the fire had gone right down inside her.

Ti's horse panted and pulled hard up the hill that was getting steeper and steeper. There were people all around them. Everyone walked silently carrying anything they could. They didn't talk because of the hard gaspy breathing. And everyone had to keep looking down because there were holes and bricks and wires and poles and other things in the street. And sometimes people stopped and looked back to catch their breath in huge gulps. But Maud didn't because it was too bright, and because she knew if she was in this wagon with her silver King's Daughter cross pinned to the collar of her dress and seated next to Ti with Yet walking, breathing hard beside her, at least while she was in the middle between the two of them then for this night—maybe for once in her lifetime—she was safe. And then after that, maybe forever.

Sometimes people around them prayed. She heard "Jesus!" and "Oh God!" Sometimes babbling gibberish. Sometimes only lips moving in silence in the flickering light. Then almost at the top of the steepest hill she saw a body in the rubble. Only pant legs and one bare foot. But it was a person. And then there was an arm twisted with a white bone sticking out. It was like seeing Susie all over again. Lying on the back steps of the Home with her head broken open and everybody screaming her name. But this time there was nobody screaming. Nobody rushing up and falling on the body and feeling it oh so warm, but not moving, and crying like your whole insides were coming out. Oh no, no, no. There was none of that here. Only the creaking of wagon wheels and the panting of climbing a hill to get away from a fire. And when Maud looked away, she saw Yet's mouth open wide too.

Ti stopped the horse to let it catch its breath at the top of the big hill. Then when they dropped over to the other side the dull roar of the fire faded away. And they were almost in another world.

火

When they finally got to Gough and the top of the second hill, Carrie could see the Presidio with its cypress and eucalyptus trees green against the yellow sky. Leong Ti turned south at Laguna, following Freeman's instructions, toward the California Street Methodist Church. But as soon as they turned on California Street, Carrie knew it was a mistake. There were hundreds of people picking themselves along, and it was extremely slow going.

"I'm going to scoot ahead and see if there's any room in the church," Freeman said.

The wagon was still two blocks away from the church when Freeman returned. "There's no room there. I couldn't even get to the front doors."

"Shh." Leong Ti pulled on the reins to stop the wagon. "What now?"

"Laura lives around the corner," Carrie said. "Maybe she can put up the children, at least."

火

It was only ten o'clock, but Ti was exhausted. He had been moving people and belongings since early morning. And there were many times when he walked almost as much as he drove. Moving things out of the streets so the horse and wagon could get through. As he turned toward Sacramento Street, Miss Davis said, "I think this is it." It was a little yellow house with a jade-green leafed tree of some sort towering above some porch stairs.

The street was relatively clear of debris, and the houses on the block seemed to have sustained only minor damage. Ti lifted Maud down from the dray, then turned toward Yet.

"I have to go back and get more people." He held her against his body for a moment longer than perhaps he should have. She clung to him wordlessly, and he didn't care who saw.

"Stay with these Mission people. Do whatever you have to, but stay with them. I know how to find them. But if you don't stay with them, I'll have no way to find you. And I don't want to lose you again."

火

Reverend Chan and Freeman were sitting on the back porch steps of Laura Williams's house, watching the red sky to the east when Carrie and Laura found them.

"We've got everyone down for the night. But I don't think many of them will sleep—no matter how exhausted they are. They're packed in like sardines." And suddenly Carrie was hungry, thinking about the last time she had eaten—of Reverend Chan's precious hoard of canned fish and crackers.

"Who would've thought I had a house that could sleep over forty people?" Laura rattled on, oblivious to Carrie's silence. Her hunger and exhaustion. "Well, we're happy to put you all up for the night. Who knows what the morrow will bring."

"We've been trying to determine if the fire is moving north or west." Freeman turned away from Carrie and Laura and faced the neighbor's yard. "But we can't tell because of those trees blocking the view. There's been a steady stream of refugees heading this way all night. And the dynamiting seems to be getting louder."

"The latest bunch we talked to out front said they live a few blocks west of Powell and were told to leave," Reverend Chan added. "They say the new fire line's going to be Van Ness. I can't believe it could get that far west."

"We need a plan for the morning, regardless." Freeman paused and turned half around to face Carrie and Laura. "We can't stay here tomorrow."

"Well, you're welcome to stay as long as you need to," Laura said. "I'm sure I can find other Methodist folks to help."

"Thanks for the offer." Carrie managed a half-smile. "But I'm all for trying to get out of the city. What do you think, Freeman? You've seen more of the devastation than anyone."

"I've been thinking the same thing." Freeman's voice had regained a measure of the vibrancy Carrie was used to hearing from the pastor. "I didn't see any fires in Berkeley or Oakland when I left—and that was about eight this morning. So I think maybe we should try for the Ferry Building first thing. We could probably put everyone up in a couple of churches in the East Bay for a few days while we work out a plan from there. I don't think it's worth staying here just to see if we can get back to the Mission House. Even if it survives the night, we can't live there. There's no water or sewer. And won't be for weeks—maybe months."

No one spoke for a long time. A baby stirred and cried somewhere in the house, but someone rustled about and shushed it.

"Well, if we're going to try that, I think someone should go on ahead to try and arrange places for the family to stay." Carrie felt again the weight of everyone's deep aching weariness. "Otherwise we'll have nothing if—when we arrive."

"I can do that." Reverend Chan stood and squared his shoulders. "In fact, I may as well leave now. I'm not going to sleep anyway. And the sooner I get across and make arrangements, the better."

"Then why don't you take the Home records with you?" Carrie turned back toward the porch door, trying to remember where she had set the satchel full of documents. She thought it was on the dining room table. "I'll have enough to worry about in the morning without carrying those."

"You'll have to go by way of Beach Point," Freeman said. "If the Ferry Building's still standing, the north side will be the only way to get to it. We'll keep an eye out for you tomorrow. Hopefully, we won't see you. But if we do, we'll know that way across the bay is closed, and we'll have to make other plans."

Reverend Chan followed Carrie up the porch steps. "Let me go inside and say goodbye to my wife and girls."

It was a little past midnight and bright as an overcast winter day. But it wasn't the sun burning through a late morning, low-lying fog.

"It feels like the wind's shifted, and maybe's coming from the west now." Reverend Chan had returned to his sentry post on Laura's back steps. "If that's so, it could be a godsend for us—and the rest of the city—so long as it doesn't chase the fire north."

There was a hopeful tone in his voice Carrie didn't share. She and Laura followed Reverend Chan and Freeman around the side of the house to the front yard. Carrie scrutinized the pink-blossomed camellia next to the front stairs but couldn't see any evidence of a breeze. She simply nodded. "We'll be praying for your safety."

"Thanks. And you'll be in my prayers, too." With the Chinese pastor's words echoing in her head, Carrie watched the man disappear down Sacramento Street and into the Valley of the Shadow of Death.

Freeman, Carrie, and Laura sat silently as an endless stream of people struggled up Sacramento Street on their way to the Presidio—or who knew where.

"I feel like we've reached the House Beautiful." Carrie stood to stretch her back, and as she did, her eyes swept down the street toward the city in flames. Her lower back ached from the bending and lifting of the day. Because of that, she hadn't been able to walk all the way to Laura's house. And the rough ride in the wagon had made things worse.

"Bunyan's *Pilgrim's Progress* keeps coming back to me." She put her right hand on her spine below her waist. She exhaled, then straightened as though she were one of the Presidio soldiers they had seen guarding Powell Street earlier in the evening. Freeman remained silent, bent and brooding, a gargoyle on the porch steps, protecting the house.

"The City of Destruction we left—the Hill of Difficulty we came up tonight—this house—" Carrie looked at Laura and tried to smile. "This house—thanks to you, tonight, is our own House Beautiful. It seems as much God's leading as Bunyan's story.

"Finding the wagon, getting here safely—I feel we've had our own Shining Ones watching over us, despite the horror of it all."

"The fire's incredible." It was as though Freeman hadn't heard a word Carrie had said. "It's likely we'll all be fighting Apollyon's fiery darts later today. And unfortunately, we won't have any of Christian's holy armor to protect us."

"Yes, but we have prayer."

"Well, prayer alone won't get you to the Ferry Building," Laura grimaced; her pudgy face tinged orange by the flickering shadows of the bile-colored sky.

"True. And if we're not going to sleep, we might as well make a plan." Freeman turned toward Carrie again. "We have those babies to think about. They're my biggest concern."

"Mine too," Carrie nodded.

Freeman talked faster now. "People will have to carry them all the way.

"Now, I think forty-eight people are too many for one person to lead by himself. But if we divide everyone, we can put adults in charge of smaller groups, and that'll make it easier to keep track of any stragglers." Freeman stood and resumed the posture of a pastor, directing his faithful parishioners from the foot of Laura's front porch.

"Carrie, you and I can both head groups. Maybe we should be at the front and rear. And Mrs. Chan and Lois can be in charge of the middle groups. That's the four adults."

"I think we can put Caroline in charge of a group too, and probably Gracie," added Carrie. Freeman's burst of energy had renewed her strength. She brushed a tickling cinder off her upper lip and forced herself to stand taller. "That would make six groups of eight. We can put a baby in each group and make the leader responsible for it. That'll make things a bit more manageable. Then we can divide the next youngest children among the groups, since the adults will probably have to carry them part of the way, too. The older children will have to carry whatever they brought with them. And we can divide the older inmates among the different groups. We can't afford to lose any of them, or they could be kidnapped and sold again.

"I'd better keep those new girls with me—and maybe Maud." Carrie thought out loud. Her shoulders tensed imperceptibly at a sudden explosion of light and sound down east of Van Ness somewhere. "Maud can translate for me, and one seems to know her from her former life. There may be tongs on the lookout for those new girls. Who knows what we'll find tomorrow."

"I came down Divisidero on my way to the Mission this morn—yesterday, I guess now. I've lost track of time already." Freeman stopped pacing and smiled sheepishly, stroking his ash-flecked beard. "But I don't want to start out that way, if we can help it. It's much too steep for the children, and they'd be exhausted before we got a mile."

"Fillmore's flat," Laura interjected. "You could walk that route all the way to Broadway, if you wanted, with hardly a rise anywhere."

"I was thinking the same thing," Freeman said. "Coming up tonight, Fillmore seemed pretty clear. Not much rubble in the street, at least as far as I could see. And if it's like that all the way to Broadway, it would be the perfect route.

"From there we could probably get to Van Ness all right."

"Yes. It's a gradual slope to Van Ness from there, as long as you don't try and go down through Cow Hollow." It was Laura again.

"From Van Ness it would be a straight shot to Beach Point," Freeman added. "We'll probably have to stop there, check the time, talk to people, and see whether we can get to the Ferry Building or not." "Can you go over that again?" Carrie was tired and bewildered. "Perhaps someone could write it out for each group—in case we get separated."

火

"Girls! Time to get up."

It was Miss Davis's voice. But Maud didn't want to open her eyes. She was hot and sweaty and could barely move. She wanted yesterday to be a bad dream. She wanted to wake up and find she was in her room in the Home on Washington Street. Or at worst—that there was an earthquake and she was under her bed. But she didn't want to wake up in a strange house. She didn't want the ride in Ti's wagon to be true. She didn't want the fire and the burning and the body under the rubble to be true.

Then she remembered Yet. And how Yet found her in the Mission. Maud opened her eyes and her doll was lying beside her. And Yet was sitting close by running her fingers through her long black hair.

"*Jo sun*, Chun." Yet smiled down at Maud.

Maud couldn't tell if it was still nighttime or the middle of the day. The brightness seemed no different than when she fell asleep. But she propped herself on one elbow anyway, and said good morning to Yet. "*Jo sun*. But my name's Maud now. Not Chun. That's my old name. Before I got baptized."

"Girls, we have to be on our way soon." Miss Davis called from the steep crooked stairs. "Mrs. Williams has a little breakfast for everyone downstairs, but there's no water for washing up. You may use the toilet, but please don't flush. We don't want to use any more water than necessary."

When Maud got downstairs, Miss Davis saw her carrying her doll with the cracked face. "And you girls who brought your dolls—Mrs. Williams says she'll keep them and take care of them until we have a permanent place. We have a lot of walking to do today, and we need to carry as little as possible. Your clothes are the most important things."

"Miss Davis, do you think the Mission is all right?" Maud finished lacing her new shoes—the ones Ruby had worn the night before when Maud had accidently put on Ruby's. And the question about the Mission was the one Maud wanted to ask Miss Davis all morning.

"We don't know, honey." Miss Davis sat at the dining room table and ran her fingers through Maud's tangled hair and tried to smooth it. But it pulled instead and hurt.

"Honey." Maud never heard Miss Davis call anyone that before. Maud looked up at Miss Davis. She tilted her head because there was another question about to fall out of her mouth. "I prayed last night it wouldn't burn," Maud said. "God will answer our prayers. Won't he, Miss Davis?"

火

Miss Davis told everyone the plan for the day as soon as their little breakfast was over.

Maud got to be in the group where Miss Davis was the leader. And Yet was in her group too. And Ida and Lydia. Maud saw that all the girls who were King's Daughters had their silver crosses pinned to the collars of their dresses and that there was at least one King's Daughter in every group for protection.

Everyone had their clothes and things tied in bundles. And they put them over their shoulders in the way Yet showed them. She said it was an old Chinese trick for carrying things. One her grandfather showed her long ago in the Celestial Kingdom. Then Reverend Bovard prayed they would get safely to the Ferry Building and that they would get across the bay. And that no one would get hurt or lost. And Miss Davis prayed because she was thankful no one got hurt the day before. And that the angel of the Lord protected them before and that it would do so again.

At the beginning of the walk the way was smooth. Then later they had to look down to see where they were going so as not to trip over fallen bricks or cracks the earthquake had made in the street. And they also had to look up so as not to bump into people going the other way. And there were lots of them. Then they had to look far ahead to make sure they didn't lose sight of Caroline's group which was ahead of them. And Maud had to look behind to make sure Gracie wasn't too far back.

And every two or three blocks they stopped for the littlest children to rest. Then they started again. They passed dead horses in the street with flies buzzing around their nostrils and their legs sticking straight out like they were standing only they were on their sides. And sometimes they passed by houses with the fronts fallen off. But with everything else still standing and you could see right inside where people lived. Like seeing someone with no clothes on. You could see dining rooms with dishes still on the table or bedrooms with things fallen on top of the beds like her room in the Home. And sometimes there would be people scurrying about collecting things. And then they would disappear and suddenly you would see them again only on the next floor down—or up. Like a rat poking its head out of a hole in a wall. But of course there were stairs somewhere you couldn't see.

Then when they got to Broadway they turned right and the wind came up over the top of the hill from the bay and blew in their faces cooling them off. And it smelled all salty and alive. Not like the city behind them that was burning and dying. And Maud could see the silver blue water and *gum moon*—the Golden Gate—beyond. And all the way across to where there were green hills with no smoke or fire.

Then they were on Van Ness and there were loud booming sounds behind them. And Miss Davis said it was dynamite and soldiers were blowing up buildings like yesterday when they were at the Mission.

火

Jew Ho's horse was exhausted. Its head drooped almost to the ground and it barely lifted its fetlocks as Ti guided it to a patch of grass near the water's edge at Beach Point. The wagon's front axle had been squeaking badly ever since it hit a deep hole on Columbus Avenue about an hour earlier. Ti had been able to nurse it the last few blocks, but it had gotten worse and he was afraid it was cracked and in danger of breaking.

Ti jumped down to help his latest refugees—a wealthy Chinese merchant and his family (a little bound-footed wife with four children)— all seated on three ornately carved mahogany trunks stuffed with their belongings. Their faces were pale, and they clutched at their trunks as though it was the first time they had ridden in such a crude form of transportation.

Ti had worked Jew Ho's horse hard all night and into the late morning, climbing the hills to the Presidio, loaded with people and possessions—then turning right around and doing the same thing again. The horse wasn't used to climbing such steep hills with heavy loads. And then there were obstacles everywhere—collapsed store fronts and houses bleeding their belongings into the streets. Corpses, fallen telegraph lines, splintered posts, dazed people wandering. All this, with a dray that didn't turn sharply. The typical load for the horse was stacked crates of vegetables—five high—on a typical trip of less than a mile along some of the flattest if not smoothest streets in Chinatown—Washington, Dupont, and Stockton—and all in straight lines.

Despite the difficulties of navigation, Ti had made nearly two years' wages in a little over twenty-four hours. But if he didn't give the horse a few hours' rest and find a way to repair the dray, he would lose everything to Jew Ho's temper. The man wouldn't tolerate the loss of his prized possessions. Today—and probably for the next few days—the horse and the wagon would be worth their weight in gold.

Ti had just crawled out from under the wagon when he saw a group of Mission people straggle into the makeshift camp of refugees near the water's edge. He couldn't believe his luck. He waved at them and shouted, searching the group for Yet. But she wasn't there. Without thinking, he reached into his pocket and rubbed the porcelain charm.

"We saw the wagon from across the way, and hoped it was yours." The Mission man who had first found Ti the day before strode up to him and clasped his hand in a fierce grip. "Everyone else should be here shortly." It was the answer to Ti's silent prayer. The man turned, and Ti followed his gaze. He saw Miss Davis. And then Yet and Maud slowly making their way through the jumbled crowd.

Their faces were splotchy red. Sweat dripped from their foreheads and across their cheeks, and they didn't even try to wipe it away. Everyone was breathing hard.

"Come. Sit in the shade of my wagon. I think I have enough food and water for all of you." Ti had been hoarding some tins of crackers and a bag of oranges he had found in an abandoned store on Columbus. Now he reached under the seat of the dray and pulled them from their hiding place. Then, awkwardly, he thrust the cracker tins toward Miss Davis. "Take this. It's for you."

Ti went to the back of the dray where he had hidden a stoneware jar of water under a blanket, and he brought that out too, along with one tin cup.

"Drink this. All of it." And he poured cupful after cupful and passed them around until the jar was empty. And although the little ones wanted more, they were too exhausted to whimper.

Lastly, he brought out the oranges. "I think there's enough for everyone to have a few pieces." He peeled the first one and divided it between Yet, Miss Davis, and Maud. And then everyone else followed his example. And even though Ti didn't have much, the Mission people were overjoyed. And there was enough for everyone to have a little.

When they finished eating and drinking, the Mission people slumped in little clumps on the small patch of green grass beside the wagon. Their faces were dust-streaked; their eyes, bloodshot and sunken; barely open. The babies lay on blankets under the wagon where there was a bit of shade. Then Miss Davis said a prayer of thanksgiving. She said it was a miracle they found Ti—and with food—in that fiery furnace of a place.

After some time, the Mission man Ti didn't know stood and approached him. "We'd better be on our way soon, or we'll be spending the night here. Do you think we can we get to the Ferry Building?"

"If that way, the worst part coming." Ti pointed east. "I don't lie. The wind is blow from hills and people say only narrow path between water and fire. Last I see, East Street still open to Ferry. But I don't go that way. Americans go to Presidio. So I take there. Chinese come here. All night. All morning."

"Well, we haven't seen Reverend Chan anywhere, so we can only hope he got to the Ferry Building all right. And if he got there, then we need to try."

"I wish I take you—but wagon not good. I fix before I go anywhere. And that not easy."

Ti glanced over at Yet, seated against one of the wagon wheels. Everyone had been resting for over an hour. Their heads drooping, their eyes half-closed. But the girl was surprisingly alert. Her knees were pulled tight to her chest, and her arms were wrapped around her ankles. Her jade green cheongsam was speckled with dark pinpricks of cinder and ash. Yet's chin rested on her knees, and her eyes fastened onto Ti's and wouldn't let go. Ti felt a sudden sharp pain of recognition. Of the last time he had seen her—like this—on her cot in her little room, in the Merchant Association Club in New Spanish Alley. And as he gazed into Yet's eyes now, he saw the same fire he had seen then. It was burning as brightly as the fire he knew was in front of her. And he knew she would get safely across the bay.

"Until we meet again." They had all had assembled and broken into their smaller groups, preparing to leave. Ti's eyes wrapped around Yet as though they were his arms lifting her, holding her, carrying her through the last part of the perilous journey. He put his hand on her shoulder, and she reached up to touch it. "On the other side."

"Yes," she replied. And the girl spoke more with her eyes than with her voice. "On the other side."

火

The little meal Leong Ti had offered the Mission people would have to sustain them for the remainder of the journey, which now lay through the burning and burnt part of the city. They had no more provisions.

The heat from the fire and sun were intense, and many times different ones fell by the wayside. But there was a rhythm now to their walking, and when one person collapsed in exhaustion, another was there to lift them up. They walked for a block—sometimes less—until the group ahead stopped. Then they would rest and turn to see if everyone was still following. They would wait for everyone to catch up. Then after a few minutes they would start moving again. It was slow, tedious work, but the way was open as far as Carrie could see. Wharves, ships, and water on the left. And on the right, the ever-present fire creeping down Telegraph Hill toward East Street where they walked. And always the acrid smoke burning their eyes and lungs.

East Street was wide and flat, and relatively free of debris. And there were fewer people than there had been on Fillmore and Van Ness. Since most refugees were walking in the opposite direction, toward where the

Mission people had come from, it was also easier for Carrie to keep track of the groups behind her. And for that she was grateful.

火

Every time Maud looked back, Gracie's group got further and further behind. Gracie was still in the lead but she was limping now. Like Maud hadn't seen in a long time. So Miss Davis stopped and told Maud to go back and check on Gracie. Grace was bent over, rubbing her right hip. "Are you all right?" Maud said.

Grace looked up. She wasn't smiling like she always did. Maud could see Gracie's teeth. All straight and white. Like a dog somebody kicked all the time and was about to snarl. Gracie was ashy gray and her eyes were red and puffy. Sweat dripped down her face and she wiped her dirty dress sleeve across her cheek. "Does Miss Davis know how much further to the Ferry Building?"

Maud lied. "I talked to her a little ways back. She says not far now."

"I'll be all right then. I just need something to lean on. Maybe that over there."

Maud's squinting eyes followed Grace's pointing finger to a broken broomstick lying by a pile of bricks. She ran over and brought it back. It was perfect.

Miss Davis's group started again, and Maud had to walk fast to catch up, even though her feet and legs were tired and achy. Her back and shoulders too. From carrying a blanket tied up with the clothes she brought from the Home. Which was hardly anything. Along with her Bible and *The Wonderful Wizard of Oz* book.

It was the end of the world, Maud kept thinking. What hell was like in the Bible when Reverend Chan preached about it. With fires burning and flames shooting into the sky so hot you felt like you were going to melt. And they were marching straight into the hell. Not away from it. Into the bloody heart of a city on fire.

But no one cried or complained. Not even Ida, who Miss Davis was carrying all the time now. With sweat dripping down all salty and stinging their eyes, even though no one felt like wiping it away because they were too tired to. No one could spare the strength. And Maud began to think only about something to drink. And nothing else. Then Lydia started saying softly, "Water water," almost like it was a song they would sing in church only it wasn't. And then they all said it. One word at a time. One step at a time. Another then another. Then "Water!" Then they started over again. But after a while Miss Davis wanted them to say Bible verses instead. And Miss Davis started first. With Psalm 23. "Yea though I walk through the valley of the shadow of death." And when she got to the part about "thy rod and thy staff they comfort me," Maud thought about the stick she had found for Gracie. Then everyone else said a Bible verse too. And when it was Maud's turn she thought of the one where Jesus said, "I thirst." So she said that one. After that Miss Davis said, "That's enough." And no one had to remember anything more.

Then suddenly after what was almost forever, Maud saw the Ferry Building clock tower. Through the billowing smoke. The same tower she saw so many times from upstairs at the Mission. Stuck on 5:12. And she knew she could make it there. And that it wasn't the end of the world after all.

And then they were at Washington Street, and she knew it was Washington Street because she recognized the two big buildings that were still standing and hadn't burned. And then she looked up the street beyond the two buildings to where the Mission and the Home should be. But there was nothing there. Only smoke and ash.

It can't all be gone, Maud thought. It can't be. And she turned away to find Gracie.

But just then a boy ran past her carrying something under his arm that was maybe a piece of meat in butcher paper. And Maud saw a soldier in front of them that was running too. And he had his gun out and was yelling, "Halt! Halt I say!" Then the soldier knelt in the middle of the street, right in front of them almost and rested his elbow on his knee. And there was a loud cracking sound like firecrackers on Chinese New Year's, only with one loud boom and with smoke coming out of the gun. And everyone jumped and Gracie who was behind Maud screamed, "Oh God he shot him. Oh my God." And the soldier stood up and started running and shouting, "Stay where you are everybody! Stay where you are! Keep moving people! Keep moving."

And Miss Davis said, "Keep walking, children. Keep walking. We're almost there." And she took Maud's hand and yanked her hard, but she didn't need to because Maud knew what it would look like. She didn't need to see.

火

Before long they were all sitting on the curb in front of the Ferry Building. And Gracie was still saying, "I can't believe he just shot that boy. I can't believe it."

They were in line for a ferry. Like thousands of other people in the slow snaky line. And Maud looked up Market Street to where City Hall should be, but there was only a black smoking skeleton. And where Mechanics' Pavilion should be—where she had been two nights before and had gotten her King's Daughter cross—the one that at this very minute was pinned to the collar of her dress—there was nothing. And then again she looked back to Washington Street and to the Home and to the Mission—hoping from this side she would see something. But there was still nothing. Except for the boy that she couldn't see, but knew was dead in the middle of the street.

Maud poked her elbow into Gracie's ribs. She pointed toward the hills they had climbed the night before. "Gracie. Look." It was more like a croak than a whisper. "Everything's gone. Everything. And we prayed. And we wore our crosses." And at that moment the world really did end.

"Come." Gracie leaned on her stick-cane and stood. She pulled Maud with her. She pointed in the opposite direction. Toward the bay. "We need to get on the ferry. Before it's too late."

"But what are we going to do, Gracie?" Maud began the slow shuffle like everybody else. Following the snaky line to the ferry. "Where are we going to live?"

"I don't know, Maudie. All I know is what I know right now. That we need to get on that ferry. Everything else comes later."

火

By three o'clock the whole Mission family was on the ferry. And Miss Davis counted everybody, and there were forty-eight of them. Just like at the beginning.

They found the drinking water line, and stood in it forever. But it was worth the wait, and they could drink as much as they wanted, almost. Nothing in Maud's whole life tasted better than her first swallow that day.

Afterwards, they all sank into the seats. Along with the hundreds of other people trying to get away from the fire.

"You were the bravest children I've ever seen," Miss Davis said to them. "'The Angel of the Lord encampeth round about them that fear him.' Surely God was with us today. We have much to be thankful for."

Maud watched Miss Davis's lips move and heard her words, but they didn't sound right to her. What was there to be thankful for? The Mission and the Home were gone. Where would they live now?

She had some clothes and a Bible and *The Wonderful Wizard of Oz* book all tied in the blanket on her back, and the silver King's Daughter cross pinned to the collar of her dress with little burnt holes in it everywhere. But nothing else.

The ferry slowly pulled out into the bay, and Maud turned and stared at the black city with the flames and smoke rising high above it. Above all the nothing that was once Washington Street.

火

Within the hour they were on the other side of the bay. In another world, it seemed. At least one not on fire. The Golden Gate Oakland. Reverend Chan was there at the dock, waving at Carrie. He had a place for them, he said, and after they gathered and were accounted for, they all went to Trinity Methodist Church in Berkeley. They spent one night on the floor of the sanctuary, then Carrie divided everyone into smaller groups so they could be cared for in various East Bay homes.

It took a frantic week of searching, but finally Carrie—with generous help from The Oriental Bureau Secretary Lizzie Piatt and Reverend Bovard's wife, Sallie—found a house for the family to rent in Berkeley, at 2116 Spaulding Avenue. The girl who knew Maud and Leong Ti—Yet, the one with the jade green cheongsam, was still with them. Carrie had no idea how long the girl would stay, as she had no support. But there was no place for her to go, and she seemed content to stay with Maud, awaiting Leong Ti's return.

At first the family slept on mattresses on the floor of the new place. Wall-to-wall people in every one of the house's ten rooms—except the bathroom, of course. Not that Carrie hadn't considered turning the tub into a bed for the two smallest babies. But after more thinking, she decided against it. They ended up using the kitchen floor instead. No one had pillows, and the little ones had to share blankets. They needed towels, sheets and blankets, napkins, and every sort of cooking and eating utensil one could think of—forks, spoons, knives; pots and pans.

For meals, they stood in long lines at a temporary commissary set up in a park a few blocks to the east. They were alive. And they were together as one family. And for the moment, that was enough.

火

It took Ti almost two weeks to find the Mission people. He kept thinking, what if Yet was afraid to stay with them, and ran away? What if she accidentally got separated after he left her in the city? What if a tong man found her and kidnapped her? He couldn't bear the thought of losing the girl again.

It was a Sunday afternoon when Ti finally found the Mission people. They were in west Berkeley, at the edge of town, in a house surrounded by bean fields. And Yet was there, waiting for him.

When Yet came to the door, Ti drank her in hungrily. Yet's eyes were no longer red from the smoke of the burning city, and her face was no longer black from the cinders. And although her eyes still burned with the fire, everything else from that day had disappeared. Ti smiled at her, and her eyes turned liquid, like a young child's. They were the eyes Ti had been dreaming of for the past seven years.

"I want to take you out of this place for a few hours." His voice sounded as if he was still wandering through the smoke of the burning city. "Will you walk with me? I want to talk to you."

They left the house on Spaulding Avenue and walked east, toward the hills at the far edge of town. It was spring. The charred city of San Francisco was at their backs, and before them lay the Berkeley hills covered with orange poppies and yellow mustard. "*Gum Saan.*" Ti smiled shyly. His arms swept in two wide arcs. "Not quite the reason our people first called this place 'Gold Mountain,' but gold nonetheless. Sometimes the treasure isn't where you expect to find it." He was afraid to look at the woman beside him—walking so close he could reach out and touch her. They walked in silence for a long time, skirting the center of town and the University, heading higher into the oak-covered hills.

They were wet with sweat and their breath came in measured gulps. Ti stopped in the shade of an enormous tree and then turned toward Yet. "Now, look back where we came from."

As Yet shaded her eyes and faced the blackened city, Ti reached into his pantaloons and took out the small piece of porcelain, its sharp edges worn smooth from the years he had carried it in his pocket, absentmindedly rubbing it in his fingers like a good luck charm. The painting was still distinct.

"*Gum moon.*" Ti clasped the porcelain fragment in his hand, pointing across the bay and beyond the city in ruins. To the golden gate. "What a beautiful passageway."

Then he said, "Here, Yet. This is for you."

火

When Yet turned toward Ti, he was smiling and looking straight into her eyes. She glanced down at his outstretched palm.

She gasped. She recognized the thing instantly. It was from the porcelain ginger jar in her room on New Spanish Alley. She took it from Ti's hand and pressed it to her cheek. "Where did you get this?" She examined the fragment more closely and saw part of the mulberry tree and half of the lute-playing girl's downcast face. "Where did you find it?" Her heart pounded and her body shook. Then Yet could see and say no more. Her legs crumpled, and Ti caught her before she collapsed.

"Come, sit in the shade."

She was lost in a jungle of bright green and gold. But she didn't notice the beauty surrounding her. She cradled the broken thing in her hands, her body still shaking. "Where did you get this?" she choked. "How?"

"I was at that place the Saturday after you were beaten and taken away." Ti's voice was tight and thin. "I saw this piece of the jar under your bed. I knew what it came from, so I took it. I thought, perhaps foolishly, if I kept it, it would mean your eyes were on me—no matter where I was. And that whenever I looked at the fragment, my eyes would be on you—wherever you were. It was a childish thought—but there were many times when I touched that broken thing—sometimes even accidentally—and my heart would tell me I was touching you." Ti's voice broke, and Yet looked up, off into the shimmering brightness of the bay. A soft wisp of a breeze caught in her hair, and she swallowed the dark fragrance of crushed mustard and poppies, savoring the sun, warm on her shoulders. She turned toward Ti. His eyes were glistening. There are oceans there, too, she thought. Waves gently washing. And the silence—the space between them—was no longer a deep sadness. It was full, pregnant. Expectant.

"If it wasn't for Chun—Maud's poor sweeping, I would never have had that—that heart-stone." Ti's voice lightened and he smiled down at her.

"That was the last time I was in the Merchant Association Club.

"I've kept the broken thing in my pocket all these years. Always thinking of you, looking for you; hoping I would see you—that maybe I would hear your voice from some window as I was driving Jew Ho's wagon around Chinatown—but I never did."

火

Ti reached out and pulled Yet to her feet. He could feel her body lean into his. He took a breath, swallowing the musky scent of her dark hair. He felt the mist-like moisture clinging to the back of her neck. It had been so many years since he had been alone with a woman—with her. He wondered what she remembered about him—if she could recall anything. She had so many men forced on her—so many years. How had she survived?

He knew there was a strength in her yet—something rooted deep; still, unbroken. True. He wanted to nourish that strength and give it life.

Make it grow. He wanted to hold her tenderly, to make a child with her—one that would bring hope out of these ashes, out of this brokenness and burning.

"Some people are saying God was in the earthquake and fire." Ti stared down at the dark indigo shimmering of her hair. "That it happened because there were bad things and bad people in the city. At first it was all I could think of. Fate got the bad ones. But there was a lot of good in that city too. It wasn't all evil. You were the good of that place." He held on to her to keep from falling; his weight bearing down on her. His shoulders were shaking, his lungs burning; her hair, now wet with his tears. "Without the earthquake and fire I never would have found you.

"I keep wondering why I'm the lucky one."

Ti fell hard against the gnarled old oak, and Yet fell against him, breathing in rhythm with him. "I don't know if I believe in God the way those Mission people do. I was just beginning to believe their way, and then you were taken from me." Yet shivered, and he held her more tightly. "I couldn't understand why, if there was only one God, and he was good, why he would take you the moment I had a plan to save you.

"After that, I decided there were either many gods—some good—without much power, and some bad—who had more power, or no gods at all. Perhaps—if there is a good god or goddess—it's smiling down on us now. Or perhaps it's just blind luck we're here."

火

Yet heard Ti's voice not as distinct and separate words, but as intertwined sounds—a kind of music. Something she imagined the girl with the lute would have played, seated cross-legged beneath the mulberry tree.

Ti's voice was rich in rising and falling tones. His voice was calm and reassuring. It was filled with longing, and she had never heard anything like it before—a voice without anger or bitterness or rancor. And Yet wanted the music to go on and on. But she had lost the melody somewhere beneath the loud pounding of her heart.

"I have something to tell you, too," Yet said. She pressed her body into Ti and into the tree. "Do you remember the cheongsam I was wearing when you found me?"

She could feel his belly tense, his breath, quickening and warm on her neck. "It was the one you gave me," she said. "And that was only the third time I wore it. The first time was to see if it fit—I told you that the day I was beaten. And the second time was the day before I was taken out of *kwai po*'s place. I hardly slept those days after the beating. I was in a lot of pain. And when Ming told me she saw Yue Tschi talking to *kwai po*, I knew someone would be coming for me. So I put the cheongsam on underneath my normal clothes. I didn't want to lose it. Luckily, no one ever found it." She paused and stared off into the distance. The watery sky at the edge of the world was the same jade-green as the cheongsam lying hidden under her blanket at the new place down the hill.

"When the earthquake came, I took the thing closest to me and ran. I always slept with the cheongsam beside me, but I didn't even think of what I had in my hand until I got outside. It was the only thing I had besides my sleeping clothes, so that's why you saw me wearing it.

"The fire burned holes in it—and it has stains I don't think will come out."

"I don't care what it looks like. I want to see you wear it again." Ti's voice was deep and muffled, and Yet heard it more in her bones than in her ears.

She stood. "We should be going."

When Yet was a little girl walking home from the rice fields in the evenings, her grandfather would sometimes take her hand and hold it tightly. She turned and gave the piece of porcelain back to Ti. Then, taking his hand, she closed his fingers over the porcelain, and closed her hand over his. The back of his hand was soft. The hairs, fine and feathery, like what she imagined a newborn baby's might be.

"Come. We should be going back. Chun—Maud and Miss Davis will think you've kidnapped me." She looked into Ti's eyes and smiled. He stood, and Yet's heart lifted.

A sudden breeze sent a golden wave of mustard blossoms and poppies dancing ahead of them, and they slowly walked down toward town. A startled flock of quail took flight, heading for a far off hiding place. And Ti did not withdraw his hand.

行

Chapter Eleven

JOURNEY

Ti agreed to pay Yet's room and board at the temporary Home in Berkeley. He signed a piece of paper for Miss Davis, and faithfully gave her the money he owed, every Sunday. The expense wasn't burdensome, for Ti was content knowing where Yet lived, and that she was safe from whoever owned her body.

Ti visited Yet nearly every day—even if only for a few minutes after a long day of backbreaking work. And after the earthquake and fire, everyone wanted men who could work hard clearing rubble in the city. No one cared if they were Oriental. They just wanted workers. And Ti was a hard worker. Most days he returned to Oakland so exhausted, he simply sat with Yet on the front steps of the overcrowded Berkeley house. His shirt was often stiff from dried sweat. His shoulders, stooped and sore from heavy lifting. But those few moments in the evening were enough for him. To be with Yet and feel her body leaning into his put breath back into his lungs. Made him come alive. Sometimes Maud would sit with them, and together they would watch the sun sink slowly into the jade-green bay.

But on Sunday afternoons Ti had Yet to himself. He would lead Yet up into the Berkeley hills where they had gone the first time, when he had shown her his porcelain talisman, and they would make love in the wild mustard beneath the old oak tree. She gave herself to him willingly, completely.

Passionately. And when Yet kissed him, she touched him deeply, where no one had been before. At the very heart of his being.

One Sunday, as they walked down from the Berkeley hills, Ti told Yet how he and Jew Ho had become rich from the fire, by carting people and possessions out to the Presidio. "We made more money in those few days than we made in two years," Ti said. Then he told her he wanted to marry her. With the money from the fire, and the money he had saved from before the fire, he said he could open his own store in a different city—far away from Number One City. He would take Yet to a new place, where no tong could find her and kidnap her and sell her.

She smiled up at him and said, yes, he could take her there. Wherever it was to be—she didn't care, as long as it was with him.

Theirs was the first wedding at the 2116 Spaulding Avenue house in Berkeley, surrounded by bean fields. It was a simple affair, an American wedding. Two months after the earthquake and fire, things were still scarce. But much to Ti's delight, Yet wore the jade green cheongsam he had given her so many years before. The Home girls worked long and hard to get out the smoke smell and soot stains. And they carefully patched all the holes the burning cinders had made.

Maud was the flower girl. And Yet wore a wreath of golden poppies in her hair, and held a bouquet of dark red peony blossoms close to her breasts. Ti promised to be loyal to her, and he promised no matter how hard times got, he would never sell her. And when he looked into Yet's eyes, he knew she trusted him, for his promise was strong and true.

Three days after their wedding, Ti and Yet were gone. No one but Miss Davis knew where they were, and at first she didn't tell anyone. A Methodist woman from the East had been out visiting the Home during the time of the wedding, preparing an article for *Woman's Home Mission* magazine about the desperate needs of the Home. Miss Davis had arranged for the Methodist woman to take Ti and Yet to Philadelphia where Ti had a kinsman. There, in a city with a fast-growing Chinatown, he opened his own grocery store. And above the store, he and Yet lived in a one-bedroom apartment.

行

There was no way to separate the older girls from the children in the over-stuffed house in Berkeley surrounded by bean fields. For weeks after the earthquake and fire the inmates suffered from nightmares. Often the little ones awoke in the middle of the night, screaming. And if a tremor shook the house—as they often did in those first weeks—everyone froze as if they were animals sensing a predator. They got so they could almost smell an aftershock before it struck. And they were jittery and cross with one another.

The rules that had been posted in the upstairs hallway of the old Home in San Francisco were impossible for Carrie and Lois to enforce in a house not intended for so many people. And privacy of any kind was impossible. As a result, the older girls, especially, were stony-faced and sullen.

Carrie felt sorry for the girls—particularly the little ones—most of whom were just beginning to discover what it was like to be a child in a real family, when the earthquake and fire destroyed everything. So she could understand when they reverted to childish behavior—as some might call their angry outbursts. If they never had a chance to be children in the first place, you couldn't use the word "revert" to describe their actions now. Most were experiencing for the first time in their lives what Americans took for granted—a loving family. And so regardless of age—whether five or fifteen—they often responded as young American children would.

"There is still no gas or electricity, and little or no prospect of getting it," Carrie wrote to a national board member in one of her more desperate moments. And then the last straw. "Our matron, Miss Lois Thorn, broke down because no one could be found to relieve her of the work."

行

It seemed to Maud that the moment she was beginning to belong to some-one, the someone would disappear from her life. First it was Miss Lake and Mrs. Kate. Then Susie. And now it was Ti and Yet.

Miss Davis told her Ti and Yet moved far across the country to a city called Philadelphia. And that she had to keep it a secret, because if a tong found out they might try to get Yet back. It was for Yet's safety, Miss

Davis kept telling her. But Maud had an empty feeling in her stomach that went right through to her bones. And she couldn't get rid of it. The cook they had in the Berkeley house wasn't as good as the old one in San Francisco. And Maud began to eat less and less. She wondered if she could live on only air. That if she took really big gulps and held them inside, she wouldn't need to eat anything. But her clothes were getting bigger, and they flopped around on her body when she walked.

One day Miss Davis called Maud into her bedroom. "I have something for you." She smiled and pushed an envelope across her desk.

Maud saw her name in the middle, and in the return address place it said, "Ti Leong" and "Philadelphia."

Maud's heart skipped a beat and she grabbed for the letter. "For me?"

"Yes, for you." Miss Davis was still smiling.

Maud tore it open and out fell a five-dollar silver certificate. "This is for your care at the Home," she read aloud. "Please give it to Miss Davis. Even though Yet and I have moved far away, we still think of you often. And we will continue to send five dollars every month.

"There are not many Chinese here in Philadelphia, and already we have the biggest grocery store in Chinatown. But we miss our old friends. Most of all, you.

"Your friends, Ti and Yet."

Maud held on to the edge of Miss Davis's desk. She felt her face grow hot and her shoulders get tight. And then everything poured out. "I miss them," she said. "I miss everybody. Susie. Miss Lake. Mrs. Kate. Everybody. Everybody leaves. And no one says goodbye. I thought maybe Ti and Yet would be different." Maud's shoulders shook and the tears came again, and it felt like they would never stop.

Miss Davis came around the desk to where Maud stood and put her arm around Maud's shoulders.

"I'm so sorry, Maudie. I knew something was bothering you—but with the stress of the move and everything—I haven't had time to ask.

"I didn't know you missed them so much. I'm sorry." And then Miss Davis began to cry too. The two of them in front of the desk silently holding on to each other. With their bodies shaking. Their tears mixing together and soaking each other's clothes.

"We needed that, didn't we?" Miss Davis finally said. And all Maud could do was nod.

"I have a feeling they'll be writing every month. Will that make you feel better?"

Maud nodded again. "And Miss Davis?"

"Yes, Maudie?" Miss Davis was still holding her.

"I miss piano too. I want to play again."

"I know. I've been trying to arrange a place for you girls to practice. I wish we had room for a piano here. But you know that's impossible."

行

Gracie and Caroline enrolled that fall at Berkeley High School and they were the only Chinese girls there. And Maud and May and Ruby and Pearl were the only Chinese girls in Washington Elementary School. And Lum was the only Chinese boy.

Leaving the Home for school was a new thing for everyone. In San Francisco Maud just went downstairs to the basement for school. But now she and the other girls and Lum walked seven blocks to school every day. And Caroline and Gracie were their chaperones who dropped them off on their way to high school and then picked them up on their way home.

In San Francisco Maud never spent much time outdoors. The parks and playgrounds were far away, and Trenton Street between the old Mission and the Oriental Home was too narrow and crowded even to bounce a ball—although sometimes she did that with Ruby and May. But now she was getting used to the warm sun on her face and neck and arms. And she loved the feel of the wind in her hair, blowing it every which way. The smell of different green things growing. The dust that turned her black shoes orange. Even though Miss Davis made everyone wipe their shoes before they came inside.

And just like Miss Davis said, she did finally do something about piano lessons. Before long Miss Davis was giving Maud a dime for a round trip ticket on the University Avenue trolley. She rode it up to Trinity Methodist Church for lessons with Miss Fish, her old piano teacher from San Francisco.

Sometimes after school Maud also got to play the organ at Trinity Methodist, and sometimes the pastor came out of his study and stood at the back to listen. "You play with so much feeling," he told her once. "Where does a child of your size and race get such passion? How old are you?"

Maud turned around on the bench. "Eleven and a half."

"Amazing." He shook his head. "Just amazing."

One day the pastor told Maud she could stay and practice longer if she wanted. "But make sure the side door is locked and pulled tightly shut when you leave."

After that Maud hardly ever knew when he left. She just practiced alone in the cold and dark with no idea of what time it was. And she began to use her body like a big clock. She played until her shoulders ached and she could feel bruises on her fingertips. That's when she knew it was time to stop and take the trolley back to the Home.

Without really thinking about it, music was now a mysterious magical place for Maud. A world of beautiful sounds that filled the emptiness she often felt inside. Music gave her a way to get away from the house at 2116 Spaulding Avenue. The crying babies. The silent angry girls who couldn't get away.

No one wanted to stay in that house for long. And most of the girls had no way to escape. But Maud had a way. She loved piano lessons with Miss Fish. And she felt dead if a week went by without one.

行

Carrie never forgot the children's performance at the E. J. Bulgin revival, the night before the earthquake and fire. How Ada Street, the *Woman's Home Missionary Society* representative from Washington, DC, had gushed so over the children.

And although the move to Berkeley had put a temporary stop to the children's practices and performances, within a few months they were singing for Oriental Home Board meetings, *WHMS* quarterly meetings, and a variety of other evangelistic and missionary events. Every time Lum lifted his baton, every time the children lifted their voices, and every time Maud lifted her fingers to play the piano, audiences would rise to their feet and cheer. So perhaps it wasn't too surprising that in the summer of 1908, Carrie lay before the quarterly meeting of the *WHMS* Oriental Bureau a seemingly outrageous proposal.

A few days after that meeting, Carrie called the family together in the parlor to share her idea.

"I don't need to tell you how difficult the past two years have been, living in this house." Carrie slowly scanned the faces of the thirty girls crowded into the room and hallway, and waited for them to quiet down. "So I called you together tonight to share with you the good news the Bureau gave me a few days ago." The house was suddenly silent.

"They've approved the rental of a new place on University Avenue. It's larger than this house, and more like our old Home in San Francisco. And it's closer to Mrs. Piatt's house. That'll make it easier for her to help you older girls care for the younger ones when I'm called away.

"We'll be moving as soon as possible." There were broad grins all around, and Lum let out a whoop that made everyone laugh.

"In the meantime, the Bureau has decided to send me back east to Philadelphia, to the annual *Woman's Home Missionary Society* meeting. It's in October. I've also asked the Bureau for permission to take some of you with me, to share with the *WHMS* ladies our need to rebuild our Home in Chinatown." Carrie paused.

"And the Bureau's given me permission to do so. We'll use the trip to raise money for a new Home by singing in churches along the way. And since I'll be taking some of you out of school for a few months, we'll also use the trip to learn about America. God willing, we'll find a deaconess to be the matron while I'm gone. To take Miss Thorn's place.

"Until then, Mrs. Piatt will be in charge of the Home. I've also asked Caroline and Gracie to help Mrs. Piatt with the younger children. Gracie will be the teacher while I'm gone, and Caroline will be in charge of the babies."

行

Carrie was a no-nonsense woman, and she had been working on the details of the trip for weeks. Long before she brought the idea to the *WHMS* Oriental Bureau Board.

Her first job after graduating from high school had been postmistress in her hometown of Flesherton, Ontario. It fit her personality perfectly. Everything that came to the post office had a place. And Carrie was good at putting things in their proper places. But the job wasn't a calling. And she had yearned for something more.

Back then Carrie had no idea what that something more might be. But when her parents passed away and left her with a small inheritance, San Francisco beckoned. It was about as far away as her imagination could carry her. She had a sister in central California, and a cousin who offered her a job as a clerk in his San Francisco grocery store. So she had come to the city in 1890 to keep the books at her cousin's store, order goods, and stock shelves. Like the Flesherton Ontario post office, everything in the store had its place. And she learned how to keep track of things.

But then Carrie met the Lake women and their rescued Chinese girls, and she began to volunteer at the Home, helping in whatever way she could. And when the Lakes were dismissed and she was offered the Superintendent's position, Carrie thought of it at first as being another clerk—only with a Christian emphasis. But the past two years of shortages had tested her organizational skills to their limits. She kept careful inventories of everything in the Home and kept track of each penny spent. And because of the overcrowding, she made sure every child had a schedule, right down to which girls got to use the bathroom first in the morning and which ones were first in the evening. And Carrie's system worked. She typed schedules and posted them on every bedroom door, and the children were expected to keep them. And they did.

Children could be trained in ways adults couldn't. In the words of Proverbs 22:6: "Train up a child in the way he should go; and when he is old, he will not depart from it." Carrie believed that Scripture, and like the trains they would be taking to Philadelphia, she believed together they would be a perfectly synchronized team: the trains and the trained. And because Carrie had come to know each child and their habits in ways she hadn't in the old Home, it was easy to choose those for the trip. She planned to take eight. Six of them had been on the stage of Mechanics' Pavilion two and a half years ago, when Ada Street had been so impressed. They had sung in many situations since then, and there wasn't a shy child among them. They were precocious, gregarious, and outgoing. They would have no problems meeting new people on the cross-country fundraising trip.

Eight fewer children in the Home would also make living arrangements easier for those left behind. With the eight children gone—all between the ages of four and thirteen, there would be no young, impressionable children to separate from the older, "rescued" girls in the Home. Those girls whom Board members viewed as the cause of "disturbances."

"Here are the ones I'm planning to take with me," Carrie said after her plan had begun to sink in. "Maud, May, Ruby and Pearl, and Lum. And lastly, Lydia, Mamie, and Ida."

Maud was the oldest child in the group, and would be the musical accompanist, Carrie told them. She had already talked this over with Miss Fish. Maud was also old enough to care for Mamie and Ida, the six and four-year old Woo girls, when Carrie was busy with other affairs.

Lum was nine years old and the only boy in the group. He would be the conductor for the little choir. May, Ruby, Pearl, and Lydia were all between the ages of eight and ten, and would do most of the singing. But even Mamie and Ida could sing some of the songs and could recite short Bible verses. And Ida could speak English as well as any four-year old American.

May and Maud had once been little *mui tsai*—slave girls—whose rescue stories Carrie would tell on tour. And most importantly, all eight children had been in the Oriental Home during the earthquake and had made the long trek through the fire to safety. They were living testimonials to God's miraculous grace, and Carrie was convinced their winsome ways would attract crowds and donations, as on that Mechanics' Pavilion stage.

"Do you remember the lady from Washington who visited the Home the night before the earthquake? The night Maudie got her King's Daughter cross, and some of you sang for that huge crowd?"

The children nodded.

"Well, that lady's husband knows President Roosevelt, and she told me she might be able to have us sing for the President. It's not settled yet. But it's our hope."

"The President of the United States of America?" Lum jumped up and made circles with his fingers, then put them around his eyes.

"Yes, the very one. With glasses, about like that."

行

The departure date was finally set. For the first day of fall. Monday, September 21. For weeks Carrie had been working on their itinerary, and it was now completed through early November.

Carrie made three copies of their scheduled stops—two she would take with her, but would keep in separate places in case one got lost—and one she would leave with Lizzie Piatt in Berkeley. Each one listed the dates, and the names of the towns and cities they would be in, along with the names and addresses of the contact people—usually *WHMS* women—and telephone numbers, if they were available.

The first stops would be Salem and Portland, Oregon, where Margarita and Kate Lake were from, and then Denver. Then after some small town stops in Kansas and Nebraska, on to Ohio, and finally Philadelphia and Washington, DC. Even if they arranged additional stops on their return trip, it was likely they would be home by Thanksgiving.

Most of the larger cities had Deaconess Homes where they could stay. But in the small towns she had no idea where they would eat and sleep. They would be dependent on the travelling mercies of God—and anonymous Methodist women at those stops.

Then there were the lists of personal items they would need for the trip. Carrie thought they could manage with three large travel trunks—one for her clothes, and two for the children's clothes. One of the children's trunks would have all their performance clothing. Their Chinese costumes and their white outfits. And anything else related to that—like Maud's music books and Lum's baton. The other trunk would have the children's everyday clothes. Carrie hoped they could manage with three sets for everyday, plus extra underwear and socks, since she had no idea how often they would be able to do laundry. Most performance places were simply overnight stops, with no time for washing and drying clothes. It might be two and a half weeks before they could do the wash.

Carrie decided each child should have a personal overnight bag to carry on the train. For a change of underwear or two, toiletries, and a few special items. Besides their Bibles, each child would be allowed to bring a small book of their own choosing. Or if Ida wanted, her small rag doll.

Carrie also would require the older children to keep daily journals, so they would need pencils and notebooks. Then Gracie had the idea that train timetables could be used for geography and arithmetic lessons. Gracie said they could keep track of how many miles they traveled each day, whether the train was on time or not, and what states they were traveling through. So the older children would need those timetables too.

Finally, besides her own overnight bag, Carrie would take the old leather satchel she had found in the upstairs closet the day of the earthquake. She hadn't thrown it away, and now she thought it might be useful for keeping snacks. And perhaps washcloths and hand towels, her small emergency medicine kit, and any other odds and ends she might need without digging into their baggage car trunks.

行

A few days before they were to leave, Carrie glanced up from her desk to find Maud leaning against the bedroom door, a thoughtful expression on her face. Carrie put down her pencil and pushed aside her "to do" list with its multiple checkmarks denoting "task accomplished."

"What is it, Maudie?"

"Miss Davis, if we're going to Philadelphia, do you think we can see Ti and Yet?"

"That would be wonderful, wouldn't it? We'll have to see what our schedule is like once we get there. Right now we don't have many commitments, but that could change quickly. It's hard to know who'll ask for us.

"That reminds me. I have a letter for you. From them. It came yesterday, and I forgot to give it to you in the rush of getting ready." Carrie pushed her chair back from her desk and rummaged through the stack of correspondence at the far end of the desktop.

"Here it is."

Maud ripped it open and scanned it silently. "Miss Davis, Ti says they want to see us. And that they might have a surprise waiting for me when we get there." The girl's eyes shone with excitement. Carrie contemplated telling Maud she too had received a letter from the couple, but decided against it. The pleasure of waiting for an anticipated surprise was a rare gift in itself, and Carrie didn't want to take that good thing from the girl.

"I wonder what it could be?" Carrie drummed the desk with her fingertips and feigned ignorance. "Do you think they might have a baby?"

"No, they would've told me if that's what it was." Maud spoke with the conviction typical of a thirteen-year-old. "They probably have a book for me. Or maybe some clothes."

"Maybe. I guess we'll just have to wait and see." Carrie sat again at her desk and picked up a pencil.

"And Maud, I've been thinking. I'm going to be depending a lot on you over the next few months. Especially to be an example for the younger children, and to watch them when I'm having meetings or when I'm busy talking to people. You're the oldest. I'll have no Josephine or Gracie or Caroline to fall back on."

"I know, Miss Davis. I'll do my best."

"Thank you. By the way, have you decided what book you're going to take?"

"I think *The Wonderful Wizard of Oz.* "

"Really! Haven't you already read that a number of times? Most other girls at thirteen are reading *Anne of Green Gables.*"

"I know, but you said we could take whatever we wanted. And it's something I can read to Mamie and Ida. They haven't heard it. And besides, you said we're going to Kansas."

"Well yes, that's true. But it won't be like the Kansas in the book. That's only make-believe."

"I know. But Miss Lake said some parts of the story are true."

"Miss Lake said that?" Carrie had no idea what Maud had in mind. But she had loose ends to tie before they left, and she had no time to pursue the girl's line of fanciful thinking.

"Well, it's your choice. I hope you won't be bored. We'll be spending a lot of time on trains." Carrie pursed her lips and picked up the trip's checklist to review one more time before supper. "I know you're capable of reading books more suitable to your age. And I don't want your reading skills to slip while you're away from school."

行

Maud and Ruby sat on the front steps of the Oriental Home in Berkeley and looked up the street. The evening shadows were growing longer, and Maud got the feeling she was on the edge of a really big adventure. Maybe one as big as Dorothy's in Oz. Which was one reason she decided to bring that book along on the trip. And now sitting next to Ruby waiting for something big to happen made Maud think about Susie and how much she would've liked this trip. The biggest adventure ever.

Finally, Maud and Ruby saw a baggage wagon turn the corner onto Spaulding Avenue. They waved to the men seated on the wagon bench.

行

It was 6:30 in the evening, and just a short ride to the new Stanford Place Station on Shattuck. The sun was sinking into the Bay, and the pink and white brick train station glowed from the streetlights being turned on.

"Those trunks will have to go in baggage, ma'am. You can pick them up when you get off." The blue-suited baggage man stared at Carrie and then at the children. He took off his hat and scratched his head.

"And what about these?"

"They're with me."

"All eight? And Oriental? Where'll you all be going?"

"Yes, they're all with me. And we're on our way to Salem, Oregon." Carrie showed him their tickets.

The baggage man scribbled on some green-colored tickets and tied them to the leather straps of the trunks. He tore each ticket in half and gave them to Carrie.

"Is there a problem here?" A tall Negro porter stepped down from the train and strode over to where Carrie and the baggage man were talking.

"No, I think we have everything straightened out." Carrie pulled the children to her side. "I have a missionary pass, and the children here have excursion passes." She waved them in the air. "The type that allow us to travel anywhere in the country for the year—with open destinations."

"I see." The porter put his fingers to his tongue, then flipped through the tickets. He looked over at Maud and the rest of the children. "So these here must be charity cases."

Carrie nodded.

"Orphans?"

"Some, yes—and half-orphans."

行

"Salem. Next stop, Salem, Oregon." The conductor turned on the electric lights and came marching down the aisle. It was a little after four o'clock in the morning, and still pitch black outside. They had been on the train for a day and two nights, and only a stop near Mt. Shasta had allowed them time to get outside and stretch.

"How many miles from Berkeley, Miss Davis?" Carrie saw Maud's head peeping around the sleeping berth curtain across the aisle.

"When you get up and dressed, you can check your train timetable. It'll tell you, if you add all the numbers between Berkeley and Salem."

Carrie stood and tried to stretch. Her shoulders and lower back were stiff, and a nagging pain had settled in her back soon after they left Berkeley. She knew it would linger for days if she didn't start walking the aisle regularly. She was constipated, too, but walked toward the toilet anyway. She grabbed the seats and pulled herself along. And then without warning, a hot flush. She had been experiencing them more frequently since her forty-eighth birthday not long ago. The sudden heavy perspiring soaked the armpits of her dress. Thankfully she would have access to her trunk before long, and she could change out of her travel clothes—and perhaps even have time for a bath. And this is just the beginning of the journey, she thought in a moment of panic. How would she survive the next leg? Three full days and two nights on the train from Portland to Denver.

"Almost six hundred miles from Berkeley, Miss Davis. I added it all up."

行

First Methodist in Salem wasn't a big church like Trinity in Berkeley. But it was completely full on Thursday when Maud played the piano and they sang three times and everybody clapped and cheered. After that Maud and Ruby and May and Pearl recited Bible verses like at a King's Daughter induction. Then Miss Davis talked about the earthquake and fire. Some of the things Miss Davis said about it weren't true Maud decided. Like saying a strange Chinaman gave them crackers and water on the walk to the ferry. Maud knew it was Ti who did that. And for her that was the biggest miracle on the long day of the fire. That it was Ti that found them. And Maud also remembered how Yet looked when she saw Ti. And now they were all on their way to see Ti and Yet again. In Philadelphia. And that was almost another miracle Maud thought. That she was going to see them again.

And then there was the part where Miss Davis said everyone ran into the Home to get their Bibles first. After the earthquake. But Miss Davis didn't know because she didn't follow everyone. And anyways Maud knew she got *The Wonderful Wizard of Oz* first.

But after Miss Davis talked the old ladies seemed to like the way she told the story. They smiled and shook her hand and said how lovely. What wonderful work you're doing with all these orphan children. Then they came over and hugged everybody and said how beautiful they were in their exotic clothes and their long black hair and how good they spoke English and how well they sang and how old are you and how amazing that you play piano. Especially for an Oriental.

All the old ladies promised to give them money to rebuild the Home so it was probably all right for Miss Davis to say whatever she did about the earthquake and fire. And maybe Miss Davis didn't really remember anyways. She was getting old and sometimes she forgot things. Like old people did.

The last thing was there was a bunch of old ladies who came up to Maud and said "You must be the one Maggie called Chun."

But Maud didn't say anything to the old ladies or even to the girls about her own age who were standing beside them staring. Until another old lady said "Oh you wouldn't know her that way. You probably know her as Miss Lake."

Then Maud said she knew her both ways. And even one more. Margarita. And they said "Well we're Maggie's aunties and these are her nieces and here are her nephews. And Maggie's mother is our sister." And Maud said you mean Mrs. Kate. And they said "Yes that would be her."

And then they told Maud how Maggie told them all about her whenever she came to Oregon to visit. That her Chinese name was Chun. That she got sold by her parents. How awful how very awful. It must be so hard knowing that. And for one hundred and two dollars. And to a brothel keeper no less. How could anyone sell a baby! And how wonderful Maggie was to rescue her and how wonderful it was to meet one of Maggie's little rescued slave girls that they read about and heard so much about. And then all those dreadful court hearings. Three was it? Or four?

And Maud didn't know what to say. But to just stand there and listen and try to smile even though inside her stomach was as unsteady as if she was trying to walk on a train for the first time. And she was hearing things about herself that she had forgotten. And even some she never knew. But it was strangers telling her the things as if they had been in Chinatown themselves. Only they hadn't.

行

The thing with trains Maud found out was everyone on them had a story. And when you're sitting with people for days at a time like they were from Portland to Denver everyone wanted to know everything. Especially when you're Oriental and people say you're exotic. Which is a word Maud had to ask Miss Davis about because it wasn't the first time someone said it.

People asked her where they were going and why and then they would ask Miss Davis how she could do it. And Maud wondered what they meant by that. "How she could do it."

And Maud was also finding out how good it was to know two languages. Like how she could talk to Lum or Ruby or May in Chinese right in front of people but the people would have no idea what they were saying. Most times the people would just smile at them and say things like "Chinese is such a musical language." Or "We love to hear you talk." When they were actually saying bad things about the people and they didn't even know it.

The train chugged across the dry desert of eastern Oregon and southern Idaho then along the Bear River Mountains and down to Granger, Wyoming where it picked up the original Overland Route. That's what the train booklet said anyways. How the pioneers got to California before there was a railroad. By covered wagon.

行

They got to a town in Wyoming that nobody could say right because it was spelled all wrong. And Miss Davis said you should just remember a bashful girl and say it that way. Shy Anne. Which didn't help because it only made Ida keep asking Maud where was the girl and why was she shy. And finally after leaving Wyoming there started to be more clouds in the sky. Big huge fluffy ones in all kinds of amazing shapes. And then a little later the sky below the clouds turned dark blue. Almost green. Like jade. And then the clouds got really bright and then dark again. It was like there was electric lights inside them turning them on and off. Which Miss Davis always got mad at Ida for doing at the Home in Berkeley.

"Lightning" Miss Davis said. "Watch carefully and you'll see the lightning bolts. Like bright jagged tree branches. If the storm gets closer you'll hear thunder too."

And sure enough that's what happened. At first the thunder was sort of a soft rolling sound like a baggage wagon on cobblestones. But when the storm got closer or maybe it was when the train got closer to the storm Maud couldn't tell which one, the thunder was more booming. Like the dynamite during the fire that burned down the Home. Then huge raindrops started hitting the train windows and even little white ball things that sounded really loud when they hit.

"Hail" Miss Davis said. And Lum had his face stuck to the window and he was pointing. Then he said "Ah hail." Like it was a bad word. And Miss Davis looked at him crossly and told him not to say it again. But he did anyways. Really softly under his breath. And grinned at Maud. But Ida and Mamie put their heads on Miss Davis's lap and covered their ears.

Then there was a huge flash right outside the window and a huge crash that shook the whole train and Maud and Ruby and the rest of the girls screamed. Though Maud had learned about lightning and electricity in science at school in Berkeley and about Benjamin Franklin and his kite it was still a lot different in person with it happening right outside your train window.

But before long they were out of the thunderstorm and the sun came out and there was a rainbow and water flowing everywhere outside. And there was a buggy that almost turned over on a muddy road with the people standing around it with their clothes all drenched and their hats still dripping. And the ladies throwing their arms in the air.

Then a line of mountains started that stretched off into the distance mile after mile after mile. They were green at the bottom then golden yellow towards the top where the sun was about to dip behind them. And Miss Davis said it was because it was autumn and the yellow was trees far away turning colors before winter came. Then after a while Maud traded places with Ruby and got to look out the other side.

The land on the other side was flat as a griddlecake—the kind their old cook in San Francisco used to make sometimes on Saturdays. It stretched off into the distance until the dark blue sky touched the long line of flatness. The earth was all reddish-brown furrows with yellow stubble that Miss Davis said was leftovers from the wheat harvest. Which was used to make bread. And from time to time Maud saw roads that went straight off to the edge of the world. Like the Yellow Brick Road. No houses or trees or hills or anything. But the roads had to go somewhere Maud knew.

Sometimes there was a farmhouse out in the middle of a field all lonesome by itself. Like Dorothy's house in Kansas. And once she even saw a lady that could have been Auntie Em bringing in clothes from a windy clothesline.

"The edge of the Great Plains" Miss Davis said. And she made them all write about it in their journals.

行

After Denver where they sang it was three hundred miles to Oakley. That's what the train booklet said when Maud added all the numbers. That was their next stop. In Kansas. And as soon as they got on the train everyone fell asleep again from the jostling that they were used to now almost like it was home. Everybody's heads bouncing around like Ida's rag doll. But

Maud sat up with her journal on her lap writing whatever she thought of. And one thing she was thinking was if she kept this up she would need another journal for the trip home. Unless she used Ida's or Mamie's which were pretty much empty anyways.

When everyone woke up Maud asked Mamie and Ida if they wanted to hear more of *The Wonderful Wizard of Oz* which she hadn't finished reading to them. Which was perfect because they were almost to Kansas and Dorothy in the book was still in Oz but getting close to returning to Kansas. It was just like when Mrs. Kate read it to Maud a long time before. Except on the train everyone stared and said can you believe that Oriental girl is reading to those little ones in English and they actually look like they understand it. With everyone going on and on. And now the girls wanted her to go back and read the part again about the cyclone that picked up Dorothy's house. And they wanted to see one. And Maud said well you almost did in Wyoming with the big thunderstorm and remember how nobody liked it. But they said it wouldn't be the same if it was Kansas.

Finally the conductor said "Last stop in Colorado." And then not long after that "Kansas state line." And Ida squealed "We're in Kansas Ruby. We're in Kansas!"

Then all the passengers around them stopped talking and stared at them like they were Winkies or something. But some men with cigars peeped over the tops of their newspapers like they weren't really looking only they were. Then Miss Davis told everyone why Kansas was so exciting to an Oriental girl. Because of the cyclone in *The Wonderful Wizard of Oz*. And everyone laughed. Then a man sitting in front of them turned around and flicked the ashes off his cigar onto the floor and said well we sure hope you don't see any cyclones on this trip. And anyway it's pretty much past tornado season. Those mainly come in spring and summer.

And Maud wrote down the word tornado in her journal without Miss Davis even telling her to.

Then when Miss Davis had them line up to get off the train in Oakley like they always did a white boy they hadn't seen before who was about Lum's size laughed and pointed at them and said look at those little Munchkin Chinks. And the man with the boy laughed too and said it was a good thing they don't know English.

But Lum said "Oh but we do." And Maud could tell he was about to start a fight with the boy right in the middle of the aisle if he found the chance. Because he got into fights before at Washington Elementary School in Berkeley. So Maud just scowled at Lum and reached back and grabbed his arm and yanked it.

The sun was beginning to set when they got off the train and the wind almost blew Ida off the train steps. And Miss Davis had to drop her satchel and grab her hat. And Maud's hair whipped around her face and got all tangled and stung her cheeks.

"Is this a cyclone?" Lydia yelled. And you could hardly hear her at all and it did no good to yell no.

And when Miss Davis got inside the station she said "My I had forgotten about the wind on the plains." And how she couldn't even hear herself think outside. And Maud laughed at the idea. Of hearing a thought stuck in your head from before.

行

After they sang in Oakley the Methodist ladies sent them off to the next place with lunch boxes full of boiled eggs and tiny little tomatoes that would be perfect for Ida's rag doll and cheese and apples and different kinds of cookies. And they had thick ham sandwiches with mustard and lettuce and bad tasting black bread nobody liked. So everyone took the ham out and used the bread to wipe the mustard off the ham and threw away the black bread and ate the ham all by itself. And Miss Davis didn't even say anything about starving children in China.

Everything was griddlecake flat Great Plains again until Wilson when there was hills again. And wind too. But this time Ida held on to Miss Davis's hand so it wouldn't blow her off the platform. And the day after they got to Wilson they sang at the Northwest Kansas Conference *WHMS*. And Miss Davis wanted to wash their clothes there but all the Methodist ladies could do was wash their underwear and socks. But Miss Davis said can you at least hang out our clothes and air them because the tobacco smoke on the train makes everything stink. So the Methodist ladies did that too. And because it was sunny and windy they were lucky to dry out their underwear and socks before they packed for Lincoln Nebraska. And Miss Davis put her nose to their clothes and said they were somewhat better too. And that she hoped they could wash them when they got to Nebraska.

Nebraska was the same as Kansas. Flat as a griddlecake. Only in Nebraska you could see everything when you came into a town. Nebraska people didn't even close their curtains. If they had them. And lots of people didn't. But even if they did it didn't matter. It was as if Nebraska people thought the train was empty or everyone that rode them was blind. Maud saw husbands and wives arguing and kissing. People eating and praying at their tables or washing dishes or hanging clothes. Sometimes when it was nighttime people would have a light on and a curtain open or no curtain at all and they would stand in front of the window completely naked.

Then they were in Omaha. "Where the wizard lived before his balloon took him to Oz" Maud told the Woo girls. But the train tracks went right next to the stockyards and it stunk so bad their eyes watered and everyone held their noses. Maud wrote in her journal the word "stockyard." And drew a picture of cattle everywhere.

Then Lum said "No wonder the wizard left Omaha." And "I would too if it smelled like this all the time." And everyone laughed. Even Miss Davis. And the fat man sitting behind them who had been poking at his pocket watch until Lum said it.

行

It was a long ways from Omaha and Council Bluffs where they crossed a river as big as the Columbia River in Oregon to Cleveland Ohio. Day and night. Day and night. And then day again. And barely time to stop and get off on their wobbly train legs to eat. And everyone was tired and stinky and bored.

Miss Davis knew Maud had been writing in her journal a lot lately so she asked Maud what she was writing about. And Maud said "Everything. What I see and what I think about. And sometimes what people say." And Miss Davis thought that was marvelous.

Not long after they left the little town of Warren which was the last place they sang in Ohio everything out the train window changed. Geography was the word for it. And Maud liked the sound of that word.

Gracie learned Greek at Berkeley High School and she said geography was a Greek word. Actually two words put together like rainstorm which was what it looked like was going to happen in a few minutes or miles. Only Greek. And Gracie said it meant land writing. Which was what Maud was doing right now. Writing about how the land changed when they went across the country. Like for the first time since Colorado almost three weeks ago there were hills again. Not quite mountains. But the biggest hills in a long time. And the trees that had come back after the Great Plains where there were hardly any at all were all sorts of different colors. And all beautiful. Red and orange and yellow. And when the wind blew the leaves blew off the trees everywhere. Sometimes filling the sky. Sometimes with greens mixed in. Who would have thought trees could be so many colors and so beautiful.

行

On October 20th the train finally got to Philadelphia. The place where Maud was finally going to see Ti and Yet and the surprise he promised so long ago in the letter in Berkeley. Which Maud hadn't forgotten.

Philadelphia Station was the most trains in one place anyone had ever seen. More than Portland or Denver or Cleveland or Chicago even. Trains coming in from all directions and long lines of them row after row. And more people squeezed together in one place than they had ever seen in their lives. More even than at the Ferry Building after the fire.

And Lum was as jumpy and excited as ever. And Miss Davis had to hold his hand to keep him from running off which meant Maud took both Mamie and Ida's hands.

As usual the deaconesses were there to meet them and they whisked them away in a carriage to their Home. And finally they got to have deliciously warm baths and sleep on parlor floors that weren't moving and had no train whistles blowing.

The first thing they did in the morning when they got up and ate breakfast was to go to the big church where the *WHMS* Conference was going to be and have their pictures taken for all the newspapers. In their Chinese clothes that everybody said were colorful and exotic.

Flash! Pop! Flash! Pop! Flash! Pop! One right after the other with lots of smoke. And standing and sitting all different ways. And always someone saying smile and look over here. And isn't the little one darling. And what is her name? Ida. And her English is just perfect. Like an American. And so you're here all the way from China? And always having to say no from California which might as well be China for the people taking the pictures who had been only as far west as Chicago. Which wasn't very far west at all.

行

The eight-day annual meeting of the *Woman's Home Missionary Society* was held at the Church of the Covenant, at Eighteenth and Spruce. And the children were on the program the very first day. Since the newspaper photographers and reporters had been there in the morning taking pictures, the children had to wear their traditional Chinese clothing all day. The children's bright blues and reds clashed with the grays, whites, and browns of the attendees—four hundred mostly middle-aged matrons like Carrie herself.

The children sang *God is Love* and *A Prayer for China* before lunch. And when they finished and had received their customary ovations, Carrie gave her talk about the earthquake and fire, and the present need to rebuild the Oriental Home in Chinatown.

When the morning program was over, Jane Bancroft Robinson, the National President of the *WHMS*, said grace and dismissed the delegates for lunch. Carrie was sitting behind the pulpit, collecting her notes from the empty chair next to her, when Lizzie Piatt rushed up.

Carrie stood and hugged the Chinese Bureau Secretary. "Well, what did you think of the children's program this morning?" It felt good to see someone from Berkeley among the crowd of women milling about the front of the sanctuary. Carrie had always thought of Lizzie as someone cut from the same cloth as Margarita Lake. Both women were diminutive in stature, and both shared a fierce determination for just causes—a determination that belied their size.

"Absolutely wonderful. Absolutely wonderful," Lizzie enthused. "I know the last few weeks on the train have been hard on you, Carrie, but it was the right thing to do—to bring them here." Lizzie turned and swept her arm across the sanctuary. "There's talk out there already of having the children sing again tomorrow."

"I hoped to take them to some of the historical sites around Philadelphia." Carrie frowned. "So far, they haven't done anything fun. And I promised them Philadelphia would be different. I thought maybe we'd go to Independence Hall." She stood and scanned the pews. She had told the children to meet her behind the pulpit as soon as the morning program was over. But they were nowhere in sight.

"I'm sure there'll be time for that when the Conference is over, Carrie. Don't forget you're here the entire week—actually a bit more than a week.

"We need to 'strike while the iron is hot,' as the proverb goes. There are women here from all over the country, and the more they see the children, the more opportunities you'll have to share their needs."

"I'm sorry Lizzie, but I told the children to meet me here, and I don't know where they've gone." Carrie started for a side door that led to the pastor's library, thinking the children might be waiting there.

"You don't need to worry about them. I told one of the Philadelphia deaconesses—she said she knew the children—to take them out to the foyer for a few minutes." Lizzie took Carrie's elbow and steered her back toward the pulpit.

"I brought the postcards with me from Berkeley—all colorized nicely with the words 'Chinese Children's Choir' at the bottom. A thousand of them. I told the deaconess to have the children stand out front with the postcards for a few minutes. They can go downstairs for lunch when the crowd thins out. There won't be a place for them to sit together now anyway. And they may as well do something useful while they're waiting."

"If we can get to the lunch line by the back stairs, we can eat quick and get back to take over for them."

The smell of chicken soup and fresh baked bread wafted up the stairwell before they were halfway down the stairs. Carrie had had nothing to eat since six o'clock that morning, and she was famished.

"And speaking of opportunities." Lizzie pushed open the door into the basement and paused as a cacophony of light and sound swept around them. "I talked to Ada at the break this morning, and she said your White House visit has been confirmed. For Thursday, November 5th."

"Well, that's certainly exciting news." Carrie surveyed the room. It was filled with rows of tables and chairs and women searching for places to sit. Lizzie was right. There was hardly an empty chair in the place. "Lum will be thrilled. He's been the only one convinced it would happen."

"Ada has arranged for all of you to stay at the Deaconess Home the week you're in DC," Lizzie smiled. "And the White House visit comes right at the end of the Baltimore Conference *WHMS* meeting."

"All as the Lord wills, Carrie. And as you have strength, of course." Lizzie squeezed Carrie's arm. "We don't want to wear you out. It takes a lot of stamina to travel with so many children, I know. If they were white it would be one thing. But when they're Chinese—I can imagine you've had to put up with a lot."

"The little towns in the Midwest were the worst." Carrie shook her head. "Unfortunately, I didn't know about 'sundown laws'—about all non-whites having to be out of town at sundown. But once we learned how to deal with those situations, things got better."

There was too much commotion in the food line to continue their conversation. But after a bit of wandering about they found two empty chairs at the far side of the room under an unfurled American flag. They sat there, where it was quieter, away from the clatter of plates, bowls, and silverware.

Lizzie set her purse on her lap and bent over it, rummaging around for something. "I almost forgot these. They're letters from the girls at the Home." She pulled out a fat one.

"This is Grace's. For Maud. She's been writing her almost every day. And she's gotten all Maud's postcards. It seems Maud's become quite the little writer on the trip."

"She's been really good about keeping her journal." Carrie took the bundle of letters and looked under the table for the old leather satchel— then remembered she had left it in the pastor's library upstairs.

"Most days I don't even have to remind her. She picks it up—usually in the afternoon—and scribbles away. I have no idea what she writes, but it keeps her occupied and can only improve her skills.

"Lots of times she doesn't get out at the stations." Carrie buttered a slice of bread. It was still warm. The smell reminded her of Saturdays baking with her mother. "Maud stays on the train with the older girls when I take Lum and Ida out. And when she stays on the train, she usually spends the time writing postcards.

"Even if it's only for a few minutes, Lum and Ida need to get out and walk around. To see something different and get some fresh air. And my back's been bothering me lately. All the sitting on the hard narrow seats." Talking about her back made Carrie aware of its stiffness. She forced herself to sit as straight as she could on the wooden chair. Stretching seemed to help.

"I know it hasn't been easy, Carrie." Lizzie reached across the table and rested her fingers on Carrie's wrist. "We pray for you every day. And for the children, too, of course. But every day you're away from Berkeley, singing and speaking, raising money, is less time we have to spend in the building on University Avenue. It's no more designed to be a Home than the place on Spaulding Avenue was."

"I know, Lizzie. I don't mean to complain, you know that. I—and the children too—believe in the cause. And we certainly understand the cost." They ate in silence for a few minutes. And Carrie was content to let the happy chatter of a couple hundred women swirl around her like the autumn leaves drifting into the basement window wells above her head.

"Did I mention to you Scranton wants you for their *WHMS* Conference the week after your White House appointment? That's November 12th and 13th, I think." Lizzie interrupted Carrie's reverie. "And then the beginning of the next week is the New York East *WHMS* Conference in Brooklyn. Perhaps you could head home after that, and still be home in time for Thanksgiving."

行

While the ladies were going downstairs to lunch Maud and the rest of the children followed the deaconess named Gertie out into the foyer by the front door of the church. Gertie said their new picture postcards were on a table there and they could stand there and try to sell them to people while she ran downstairs to find something for them to eat.

"A penny apiece" Gertie said. "Or six for a nickel." And she said Maud should be in charge of collecting the money.

The table in the foyer was piled high with little boxes of postcards. And it was the same picture that got taken in Berkeley before they left. But Maud had forgotten about it until a few minutes ago when the lady who was in charge of everything shouted at the ladies going to lunch "They're here! What we've all been waiting for and telling you about! The pictures of the Oriental children in their costumes!"

And the postcards were in color just like the Chinese clothes they were wearing right then. With Maud who was tallest at the back. And her and Lydia in dark blue. And Mamie and Ida in white with red and gold-braided hats that had long ribbons hanging down to bring good luck. And May and Lum in pink and Ruby and Pearl in light blue. And Ruby and Pearl and her in their jade-green Chinese shoes with the horse-hoof heels in the middle that made you wobble when you walked so it was like you had bound feet. Only you didn't. Which wasn't an easy thing to do. And Ruby and Pearl and her with their long hair tied in buns on the side because they weren't married yet. But May and Lydia with only one long braid because they were little girls. And Lum with a scholar's hat. Because he was a boy going to school.

And each one of them got sold for a penny. Like they were volcano mountains in California like maybe Mount Shasta. Or train stations which was the kind of postcard Lum was collecting. And he had about twenty of them by now. And some of the ladies wanted them all to sign the postcards. With their own names. Under their pictures.

行

The next day was Thursday and they sang at the Conference again. And Maud played the organ again. But this time they wore their white American clothes instead of their Chinese clothes. And they sang *Wonderful Love*. Then after that *America*. And everyone clapped and cheered like they always did.

When the evening program was over Maud went out into the foyer by herself to sell postcards again because it was late and Miss Davis wanted to put the littler ones to bed. And Gertie said she could bring Maud back to the Deaconess Home on the streetcar which wasn't very far.

And while Maud was out selling postcards in her white dress with the big white bow in her hair she saw a lady standing at the back by the door that went up to the balcony looking at her. With a baby holding on to her neck. And Maud thought it might be Miss Lake because she looked the same as she did the last time Maud saw her in the old Home. Which was a long time ago now. And the lady was wearing a black pleated dress with what could be a shiny gold cross pinned to it just like Miss Lake always did. With the little deaconess cap too. Then when everyone was gone the lady came over to the table and it was Miss Lake and she asked Maud if she remembered her.

And Maud said yes. Even though Miss Lake looked older than before. Not taller or fatter. Only older. And it looked like she had tears in her eyes. And there was a baby holding on to her neck.

"My how you've grown" Miss Lake said. "My little Chun. Does anyone still call you that?"

And Maud said no. Then she looked at the baby holding on to Miss Lake's neck.

Miss Lake saw her staring at the baby and said "Oh I'm sorry. This is Shizuma. She's Japanese."

And Maud said. "I know. I could tell."

Then Miss Lake turned the baby around so she could see Maud. "And Shimuza this is Maud. She's one of the special girls I found long ago." And she bounced the baby up and down.

Then Maud felt a sudden sharp pain in her side. Like someone had stuck a knife in her and twisted it around. Like after Susie died and she kept hoping Susie would come back but she knew she wouldn't. And seeing the little Japanese girl with her arms around Miss Lake's neck and Miss Lake putting her soft brown hair against the dark black hair of the Japanese girl made Maud wonder if she had ever been the little girl Miss Lake carried up the stairs in the old Home. On the top floor of the old Mission where she used to look out and think about flying away. Something she was thinking about right now. About flying away.

Then Maud gulped a mouthful of air and grabbed the edge of the table to steady herself.

And Miss Lake was staring at her like she asked a question Maud forgot to answer.

"Pardon me? It's so noisy in here. I didn't hear what you said."

"I said I watched you play the organ a few minutes ago. When you all sang *Wonderful Love*. It looks like you still enjoy playing.

"I always knew you had a gift. An amazing gift. From the first time I heard you singing with the Salvation Army."

"Thank you."

They didn't say anything for a while. Just looked at each other. And then a lady came up to the table and said how marvelously Maud played and how she wished her own grandchildren had kept up their lessons but they hadn't and now they could hardly play "Twinkle Twinkle." And then the lady picked up a postcard and said yes she could tell which one was Maud. It's that one right. Even though Orientals pretty much all looked alike with their black hair and almond shaped eyes and all. And even though she was wearing an American dress this time.

Then the lady asked about the postcards. How much to buy five. And Maud said a penny each. But you could get six for a nickel. So the lady bought three.

When the lady left Maud said "Lots of times when I play I forget where I am." She looked down and straightened the stack of postcards the lady had rummaged through trying to find ones where the corners weren't bent.

"That's mostly what I like about playing. It doesn't matter where I am or how many people are watching or listening. Because I'm not really playing for them. Everyone thinks I am. But I'm not."

"So who do you play for?"

"Oh I don't know." And Maud looked at her hands and felt tears coming up from the inside. But she stopped them before they spilled over the top. Then she looked up at Miss Lake again. At the baby. The one whose arms were tight around Miss Lake's neck like a starched ruffled collar when you want to take the uncomfortable thing off but you can't. And the baby kept pulling on the gold cross on Miss Lake's dress and Miss Lake had to hold the baby's hands so it wouldn't grab it again.

And without thinking Maud touched the King's Daughter cross on the collar of her own dress to see if it was still there. And then she quickly dropped her hand.

"I see you're a Junior King's Daughter now" Miss Lake said.

"Yes" Maud said. "For two years."

And Miss Lake said she was sorry to hear about Susie and how she was always so full of life just like this one and how she wanted to go to the funeral but it was Christmas time and she was in Oregon visiting her uncles and aunts. And speaking of aunts they had written recently saying how they met Maud and how she was such a beautiful gifted young lady.

And Miss Lake said she thought about Maud every day since she left. And that Mrs. Kate (and when Miss Lake said her name she smiled for the first time) and her still prayed for Maud every night. That she would know she was loved. Even though Miss Lake couldn't say anything after she left because her lawyer wouldn't allow her to write or call.

Then for some reason Maud thought about her doll back in Berkeley. Even though she hadn't played with it for years.

"Remember the doll you and Mrs. Kate gave me for Christmas that time?"

Miss Lake smiled again and said yes.

"I still have it. Only its cheek is cracked. And one of its eyes is sunk in and broken. And its mouth too. Because of the earthquake. A big piece of wood fell on it. But I still have it."

"I'm glad" Miss Lake said. Then she put the baby on the floor and walked around to the side of the table where Maud was.

"May I give you a hug?" Miss Lake said. And Maud said yes. And Miss Lake held her so tight it felt like she was squeezing out her last breath. And Maud thought she might faint.

"I'm so sorry about how everything turned out" Miss Lake said. "I loved you so much. And for a long time after we left Mama and I couldn't do a thing but think about you and how you must feel. And the other girls too."

But then the baby started crying and Miss Lake stooped to pick it up. "She gets jealous easily." And Miss Lake smiled at the baby and jostled it.

Then Miss Lake looked at the postcards on the table. "How much did you say they cost?" And Maud said the prices again. A penny each. Or six for a nickel.

"I'll take quarter's worth" Miss Lake said.

"You'll get thirty for a quarter" Maud said with sort of a question in her voice. Because she couldn't imagine why Miss Lake wanted so many. But Maud counted them out anyways and handed them to her. Then Miss Lake gave her a half dollar.

"You can keep the change" she said.

It was the most any one person bought all day.

行

The children's photographs were in the Philadelphia papers almost every day during the week of the Conference. And that meant whenever they went out and about the city, people recognized them. At times it seemed as though people would trample them or pull their limbs off. But they just wanted to get close to the children. To touch them and ask them questions. And once the children realized people didn't want to hurt them, they basked in the fame.

On Monday afternoon, Carrie wandered downstairs during the break to have a cup of tea. Jane Robinson found her alone and came over to sit with her. Jane talked about Monday's newspaper articles for a few minutes, then mentioned the Student Volunteer Union of New York meeting at Crouse College on the campus of Syracuse University. The Volunteer Union wanted Carrie and the children to perform for them. "There'll be over four hundred delegates, Carrie. Think of it. All young people, interested in missions.

"I told them you'd come. It's November 21-22. It's an opportunity you can't afford to miss."

A woman who sat down across the table smiled at Carrie. "So you're the woman with the little Oriental children." She leaned toward Carrie, gesturing enthusiastically, her hand nearly knocking over Carrie's tea.

The woman said she was from Rochester, and their District *WHMS* meeting was being held just down the track from Syracuse. The meeting was on Thanksgiving Day weekend. "Why don't you come over and see us while you're in the area? We would love to have you and the children."

Before Carrie could respond, Jane had told the woman it sounded like a splendid idea. She wrote the woman's address on the day's program, tore off the corner, and gave it to Carrie. "She'll be in touch." Jane smiled at the woman, and then at Carrie.

All Carrie could do was nod. And right then even that was a painful experience. A hard knot—more like a round, smooth river rock—had lodged in her neck, near her right shoulder. Ripples of pain spiraled out from it, sending a thousand little waves crashing against her skull.

On the last morning of the Conference, Carrie met Jane and Lizzie at the postcard table in the church foyer. The children were there too, offering attendees one last chance at a purchase.

"My calendar is getting crazy," Carrie told Jane. "With what you've lined up, it looks like we now have bookings through the first week of December. All across New York."

Lizzie looked at Jane with a raised eyebrow, then turned back toward Carrie. "My Indiana relatives are trying to organize a mass meeting of missionary societies for the first week of January, in South Bend. If they can do it, I want you to be there. And if you are, it means you'll be spending the heart of the winter in the Midwest. And none of you are prepared for that. You don't have winter clothes.

"So I'm thinking you should probably spend a day shopping for winter wardrobes before you leave Philadelphia."

"What do you think, Jane?"

"You could do that at Mr. Wanamaker's Store," Jane nodded. "It's an incredible place. The children really should see it.

"Mr. Wanamaker's well known for his interest in China missions," Jane said. "Even though he's Presbyterian, he supports any China mission work as long as it's Protestant. I'm sure he'd want the children to sing for customers under the eagle in the Grand Court."

Jane said she had an account at the store, and Carrie and the children could pick out winter clothes and put everything on her bill. "The *WHMS* will pay, of course," she smiled. "It's the least we can do, if we keep you back here that long."

Lizzie and Jane continued their planning of Carrie's afternoon at Wanamaker's. And Carrie was content to let their conversation float above her. She knew it would do no good to tell them how she was feeling. That her head was in a vise, squeezed ever more tightly.

"You now have us booked almost every night for the next month, Jane." Carrie hoped the pain and weariness in her voice wasn't too obvious. "And if we end up in South Bend in early January, it means we'll be somewhere between Rochester and Indiana for Christmas. Is there a chance we could take a break around Christmas—say in Buffalo, perhaps? I didn't take my vacation in August this year because of planning for the trip, and I have a sister in Ontario. I haven't been to the home place in twenty years. It's not that far from Buffalo."

Lizzie and Jane stopped their Wanamaker planning and stared at Carrie. They didn't say anything for about a minute.

Carrie hastened to fill the awkward silence. "I'm sorry I mentioned it." Her head was pounding and she could barely hear her own voice. "It's probably too much to ask."

"No, no, it's an excellent idea," Jane enthused. "I only feel badly it didn't come from me. We need to take care of you, too, Carrie. After all, you're the linchpin of the axle here. Without you, the fundraising cart would collapse.

"There's the Deaconess Home in Buffalo, so maybe I can arrange for the women there to care for the children while you spend a few days with your family."

And Carrie thought if she could get to Buffalo, and then slip across the Canadian border to spend a few days with her sister, she might be able to make it back to California without her head exploding.

行

When the big Conference was finally over Miss Davis took Maud and the rest of them to Independence Hall to see the Liberty Bell just like she promised. And Miss Davis said it was a place every American should see. Because they were as American as anybody since they were all born in the United States. And that made them citizens with rights. Then the caretaker opened the special metal cage that was around the bell to protect it and they all got to touch it. And Maud put her finger in the crack in its side. And so did everyone else. Which nobody ever did any more. Then the caretaker said they were the only Orientals to do that.

After that they sang *America* in their white clothes to the people in Independence Hall. And the crowd stood up and cheered. Even the care-taker. And everyone said the same thing that church people did. Even though they weren't in a church. "They sing just like Americans" and "Yes but they're from China. And it's wonderful what we're doing for foreign missions."

There were some people who wanted to talk to Miss Davis afterwards about what it was like to be a missionary in China. And to touch Ida who was so precious. Then Lum asked if he could go outside and Miss Davis said yes if Maud went along to watch him. So she did. When they got outside a white boy said to Lum "You speak English really good."

"So do you" Lum said. And Maud knew then there would be trouble. Because they were all tired of people saying that. Especially Lum. That and "You dress like little Americans. How adorable." And so on and so forth.

"Well of course I do" the white boy said. "I'm American. I was born in the United States."

"So was I" Lum said.

"Sure you were" the white boy said. "You're Oriental. A damn little Chink. From stinkin' China."

"Am not" said Lum. "I was born in California. In San Francisco.

"And you're a stinking little Dago." And Lum swung his baton at the white boy in a sort of pretend way because the white boy wasn't close at all.

Even though Dago was a word Maud hadn't heard before and she didn't know where Lum learned it she knew what was coming next. Lum had lots of fights with white boys on the playground at Washington Ele-mentary School. And Maud knew Lum had learned a lot from all that. The first few times he came in from the playground all bloody and scraped. And the teachers would have to send him to the nurse and then after she put on bandages Lum would go to the principal and then to the Home. But after a while it was the other boys who looked that way. Bloody and beat up. Sometimes with black eyes and torn clothes. Even if there was two of them against just one Lum. And if Lum came back to the Home with skinned knuckles or dirty pants he would tell Miss Davis he got that way from sliding into home plate in baseball.

"What did you say?" The white boy was rolling up his sleeves.

"Come on." Maud pulled on Lum's arm. "We're supposed to be waiting for Miss Davis."

But Lum pushed her away. "I said you're a little Dago."

Then the boys circled each other wary-like and Lum had his baton in his hand. He was swinging it like it was a sword and he was Peter Pan fighting Captain Hook. With the white boy being Captain Hook because he was bigger than Lum. And the Captain Hook white boy grabbed Lum's baton and pulled it hard. And Lum held on to it for a second but then he let it go and the white boy fell backwards.

Then Lum yelled "Give it back!" But the white boy shouted "Come and get it."

Then Lum ran at the white boy with his head down and his fists in front of his nose like he was a prizefighter you could see on page six or seven of *The San Francisco Call.* Which was the only part of the paper Lum ever looked at. The sports. And if there was a picture of Jack Johnson in the paper he always cut it out and put it on the wall by his bed. And he must have hundreds.

But the white boy whacked Lum on the head when he got close and the baton broke in half and Lum cried "Ow! Look what you did! You're going to pay now!" And he kept coming at the white boy. And then Lum tackled the white boy's legs right out from under him in front of Independence Hall with the caretaker of the Liberty Bell watching them. Which was something Maud knew Jack Johnson wouldn't do because she read page six and seven of the newspaper too. And boxers couldn't just knock people down without hitting them first. But she also read the Society Page which was actually more interesting than sports.

Then the Liberty Bell caretaker shouted at them and looked around for Miss Davis but he couldn't do anything because there were people beside the Liberty Bell and he was supposed to be telling them about it.

But the boys didn't care where they were. And anyways Lum was faster than the white boy and he jumped on top of the white boy and started hitting him everywhere. "Take that!" Lum yelled. "And that!"

And Maud had seen so many fights on the playground she knew not to jump in and try to pull them apart. So she just yelled "Lum! Lum!" Which is what she usually did even though it never did any good.

"Hey. Hey! Stop you two!" A man ran toward the two boys and leaned over them and pulled Lum off and pushed him away. "This is no place to fight" he said. And "Son you know better."

"That damn Chink broke my nose" the white boy cried.

"Did not" Lum shouted. "I barely hit you. You're just a big sissy.

"And anyways, you broke my baton."

"I'm bleeding, Papa" the white boy said. And his father led him away muttering some foreign language under his breath.

Finally Miss Davis and the others found them. "What happened Maud?" Miss Davis said. "I thought I told you to keep an eye on him." And Maud said that's what she did. Actually two eyes. But Miss Davis said with Lum sometimes you needed to keep a hand on him too. Then Miss Davis knelt beside Lum to brush off the dirt and grass.

"Oh Lum. Look at your white pants" she said. "Those stains aren't going to come out easily. Look at you. You have blood on your dress shirt."

But Lum just blew on his red knuckles. "Jack Johnson," he grinned.

Then Maud told Miss Davis what happened. That it was the other boy's blood on Lum's shirt. But Miss Davis shook her head. "And in front of Independence Hall and the Liberty Bell of all places."

But Lum said he didn't pick the fight. The Dago did. And Miss Davis said that was enough and to not ever use that word again.

Then Miss Davis said Lum could get a new baton the next day at Mr. Wanamaker's store if he promised never to use it as a weapon again. But if he did he would be directing the girls with nothing but his hands.

"These are Jack Johnson's." And Lum waggled his fingers. "They don't need a baton. They can do anything."

Then the next day they sang under the eagle in the Grand Court at Mr. Wanamaker's store which was the largest department store in the world. And they got to pick out coats and scarves and mittens and long underwear and boots for winter. And even though Lum got in a fight the day before he got a new red baton. And a new white shirt because of the white boy's red blood on his other one.

行

"Well if it's not the famous Chinese singers from California! I read all about you this week in the *Philadelphia Record*." It was Saturday. The day before they were leaving Philadelphia for President Roosevelt. And Ti was standing outside the entrance to the *Mei-Hsiang Low Restaurant* on Race Street greeting each one of them with a handshake and a big smile.

"When we heard you were coming to Philadelphia we decided to wait to have the red egg and ginger party." And Maud knew the instant he said red egg Miss Davis had guessed right. Long ago in Berkeley when they got the letters from Ti. That there would be a baby upstairs with Yet. And at the end where Maud was Ti hugged her and said "My how you've grown" and that he hadn't forgotten the surprise. And that it was upstairs with Yet.

Then Ti led them up some steep stairs above a Chinese laundry with Maud only thinking about the baby that would be at the top of the stairs. And whether it was a boy or a girl. But Ti was too far ahead to ask.

At first they only smelled the laundry with the steamy soap and starchy smells coming through the thin walls. But before they got to the top of the stairs they could smell steamed rice. And to Maud it was the most delicious smell ever. And it made her think of all the Chinese people in Berkeley and Oakland and San Francisco and how long it had been since she was just normal. Not some sort of exotic thing like a colored postcard that someone wanted to buy. And the rice smelled that way. Not exotic. But like Berkeley. Like home.

And then there were other smells she hadn't smelled since Berkeley with their Chinese cook at the Home. There was five spice and ginger and garlic and sweet barbecue pork and Chinese mushrooms and everything all mixed together. And it was enough to make you want to cry which was strange because it was only smelling food. But it was what Maud knew and longed for inside without always even knowing it on the outside.

Then Ti pushed open the door and the light poured down the stairs and it was noisy with everyone not speaking English but Chinese. And Lum turned around and grinned at her and Ruby too and none of them had to say anything because they were all thinking the same thing. But then Lum said it anyway. Like he always did. "I don't smell any fried chicken" he said. And then Maud said "And I don't smell any cheese or mashed potatoes or gravy either." And even Miss Davis laughed.

And the room was filled with Chinese people who they didn't know. And even though everyone in the room looked up and smiled not one of them acted like they were something strange from China that a missionary brought across the ocean for a show. To raise money for a Home somewhere far away. And suddenly Miss Davis was the exotic one because she was white and wore a silly floppy little woolen hat and gloves when no one else even had any kind of hat whatsoever or gloves on at all. And even though Maud knew she didn't know anyone there except Ti and Yet she didn't care because Ti and Yet were the only ones she cared about.

And then Maud saw Yet with the baby on her lap. And she had never seen a person in her whole life who looked so happy as Yet did right then. It was like her happiness was a Chinese spice that flowed right out of her and you could almost smell it or taste it even. And they all stood in line to greet Yet and the baby. From youngest to oldest. So Maud was last. And it seemed like forever. But finally she got to Yet and Yet looked at her and smiled and said my how you've grown. And Maud was suddenly too shy to say anything except I miss you. And that she loved the baby's tiny tiger shoes.

Then Ti stood in the middle of the restaurant in front of a table with a whole pig on a platter. And it was brownish red and huge. With its head and feet still on. And its eyes were sunk in and its ears had curled under and were crispy black. And Ti looked over to where Yet was sitting with the baby on her lap and said how happy he was the day his baby was born. And that he knew he had done one good thing in his life. And when Yet looked up and smiled at him Maud knew what he meant.

Then Ti said "Let's eat." And so they did.

And oh the food. Of course pig feet in black vinegar for Yet because she had carried the baby for so long and needed strong feet. And of course boiled eggs that were dyed red for good luck with pickled ginger. That's why it was called a red egg and ginger party. And then shark fin soup and pork buns and happy family vegetables and tea-smoked duck and scallops and squid and chicken feet.

And always rice which she had smelled earlier. And more rice. And all sorts of dumplings. And black bean spare ribs and bitter melon and steamed fish with the head and tail still on and winter melon and beef with broccoli and shrimp in red sauce and fish balls and sesame balls and lotus root and bok choy and mushrooms and bamboo shoots.

And even though Maud had been Chinese all her life most of the foods she had never seen or tried before. And almost all of them were delicious.

Then at the end a waiter brought out long life noodles. And Ti said it was because it was sort of like everybody's birthday. Not only the baby's. And he wished long life and good luck to everyone especially to the children for the rest of their journey.

Then Yet and Ti gave out little red envelope *lai see* gifts to all the children with a silver coin inside each one of them. And Ti announced the baby's milk name was Ming. And her American name would be Maud.

"Like me?" Maud asked—even though of course she didn't need to.

"Yes like you" Yet smiled. "Except our Maud was born in the year of the Monkey. She's an Earth Monkey."

"But I'm a Wood Sheep" Maud said.

"The Buddhist priest told us she would have lots of friends and be able to read people like a book" Ti said.

And Maud liked that idea. Of reading people like a book.

"Do you want to hold her?" Yet lifted the baby up to Maud. But all Maud could see was the baby's bald head.

"We shaved her head for the party because we want her hair to grow in thick and dark and beautiful—like yours."

But before Maud picked up the baby Yet put her finger under the baby's head and lifted up a thick gold chain.

"See what she's wearing?" Yet stroked the chain.

There was a little odd-shaped thing hanging from the chain. It looked like it had been made from a piece of a broken jar or something. Maud held it in her fingers and turned it over. There was a tree branch on it and half of a girl's face pointing down. Then Maud realized the thing was shaped like a heart.

"What is it?" Maud asked still holding it in her fingers. Then she let it drop against the baby's skin because she was afraid she might pull too hard and choke the baby.

"You probably don't recognize it" Yet said. "It's something from that place where I first knew you."

Maud frowned.

"From a jar I used to keep on a shelf in my room. It was my favorite thing. I used to look at it every night before I went to sleep to help me dream of another place. And this is a piece of that jar.

"Ti said he found it on the floor of my room after I was taken away. He said it was hiding behind a leg of my bed and that's why you missed it when you cleaned the room. And now finally I've made it to the place I used to dream of."

There were tears in Yet's eyes and Maud didn't say anything for a long time. She just stood there looking at Yet's baby with the fullest stomach ever of all the most delicious Chinese foods ever. And she could still taste them all mixed up in her mouth just like her feelings were here now with Ti and Yet and their baby. The bitter and the sweet mixed together. The feelings of long ago when they all found each other in the fire mixed in with their wedding so soon after everything. And then Ti and Yet leaving without saying goodbye. And then now. With Yet and Ti's baby so beautiful—even with no hair.

And Maud lifted it up and held it close. Rocking it and making silly sounds like it was a new baby that Miss Davis found and brought back to the Oriental Home. And the baby was soft and fat and warm. And when she wiggled she smelled like Chinese five spices.

"If I ever get married and have a baby I'll name it after you" Maud said.

"But what if it's a boy?" Ti said.

"I'll never have a boy" Maud said. Then Ti and Yet laughed.

It was late at night when the party was over. And Ti gave Miss Davis all the leftover pork buns and sesame balls in a big box to take with them on the train to Washington. And Lum pretended to be sad there wasn't any fried chicken to take with them. And they all laughed and told Ti why. About always getting fried chicken from the deaconesses and being so tired of it.

When they walked back downstairs to the streetcar Ti said he had a special gift for Maud. Then from under his coat he pulled out a package wrapped in brown paper and tied with a red string. He put it in Maud's arms like maybe it was something he didn't really want to give away.

"Unwrap it" Ti said. And when Maud untied the red string a piece of silk cloth that was jade green fell out. And Maud knew immediately what it was. What Ti said he bought for Yet many years before. The thing

Yet wore the day San Francisco burned. And then later on the day of her wedding.

"Yet wants you to have it" Ti said. And now there was a little bit of a smile on his face. And Ida and Mamie were jumping up and down to try and see it.

"Yet said after the baby came it didn't fit any more and that it won't be very long before it fits you perfectly. So she wants you to keep it and wear it on a special day."

Then without thinking Maud buried her face in the jade green cheongsam. And she smelled the two of them all mixed together again. The bitter of the smoky fire with the sweet of the flowers from their wedding day. Everything that made the baby sleeping in Yet's arms upstairs so special. The very one that shared Maud's name.

Chapter Twelve

CAPITAL
(1908)

"Union Station! Washington DC! Union Station, Washington! End of the line, folks. Everyone must detrain."

The blue-uniformed, handlebar-mustached conductor came marching up the aisle, tipping his little flat-topped hat at the ladies and smiling at the children. "All the way from San Francisco, eh?" he said when he got to Carrie. "Well, enjoy your stay in DC, ma'am. And don't lose any of those children while you're here. That's a lot for one woman to keep track of." He opened the vestibule doors to the next car, and as the doors slid shut behind him, he began the litany again.

Carrie stood and tried to stretch her back. "Make sure you have your coats, children. We certainly don't want those left behind. And give me your books. Your notebooks and pencils too."

She put their things in the satchel and checked the clasp twice to make sure it clicked shut. It was difficult to keep the old thing closed, with all the use it had gotten lately. She handed it to Lum.

"Maud, take Ida's hand, please—and Mamie, hold on to Ruby's hand. Don't let them wander off, girls. This is a huge, busy place.

"Now, line up behind Maud." Carrie checked each child twice to make sure they had their overnight bags. "I don't know if Mrs. Monroe will be here to meet us. But if she is, she'll probably look for you first by the *Philadelphia Line* sign."

As soon as Carrie walked into Union Station, she knew she had no need for concern. She recognized Muriel immediately. The woman was perhaps twenty feet from the children, smiling and striding quickly toward them. Despite the bustling crowd swirling about the high-ceilinged room, Muriel was head and shoulders taller than most of the women around her. She was still slim, and her striking auburn hair—Carrie remembered that from the first time she had seen the woman ten years earlier—spilled out from under a broad-brimmed, black merry widow hat.

Muriel wore the new style dress Carrie had seen at Mr. Wanamaker's store a few days ago. A form-fitting, straight-line ankle-length skirt in peacock blue, with a long tunic-like jacket the color of California acorns. Carrie waved to catch her attention.

Muriel saw her and hurried over, extending a gloved hand and grinning broadly. "Muriel Monroe. It's been a long time, but I remember you. We met a few times back in San Francisco. When I was writing for *The Call*, I believe."

"Yes, of course. You look as young and slim as when I first met you—in Spofford Alley, I think it was." Carrie suddenly felt old and plain. Thanks to Jane Robinson's connection with Mr. Wanamaker's store, at least her winter coat was stylish. But her hat—a simple woolen toque she had hoped would keep her head warm—was at least three years old. Not that she kept track of such things. But she knew it did nothing for her mousy, slightly graying hair.

"And thank you so much for your faithful support of Maud. Maud?" Carrie nudged the girl with the edge of Mamie's overnight bag.

"Thank you—Mrs. Monroe?" Maud's tentative smile expressed more doubt than gratitude.

"You were just a little girl the last time I saw you. That has to be over five years ago now," Muriel laughed. "I'm afraid I don't look much like the photograph I gave Miss Lake to give you back then. But look at you! You're a young lady now. I wouldn't have recognized you at all if it hadn't been for Miss Davis sending me pictures of you once a year."

"I do hope you'll be able to hear Maud play while we're here. She's so talented. And all the girls are quite fine singers." Carrie pulled the children in closer and introduced them. "And Lum here is a wonderful director."

"Seeing the children perform won't be a problem," Muriel said. "I managed to talk my editor at *The Star* into letting me write a Saturday feature about your fundraising efforts. So I'll be following you around most of the week. I think you said you'd be here that long?"

"Yes—we leave Tuesday next."

"Good. That should give me a chance to show the children some of the sights. This is such an amazing city—the Washington Monument, the Library of Congress, the Capitol building—"

"Where's the Capitol?" Lum tugged at Carrie's coat sleeve. "Is that where we're going to see the President?"

"Well, let's wait for the porter to get our baggage, first, shall we? Then we can find the Capitol." Carrie searched about for a uniformed Negro.

"It won't be hard to find the Capitol," Muriel smiled. "Just step out the main entrance to the station, over there, and look straight ahead." She pointed to her right, beyond the rows of wooden benches. "You can't miss it."

"But we're going to see the President in the White House, right, Miss Davis? Not the Capitol." Maud gave Lum a withering stare.

"Yes, that's what I was told," Carrie said.

"And you'll see that on the way to the Deaconess Home where you're staying." Muriel flagged a young Negro baggage porter wheeling an empty flatbed cart.

"George, can you take these things out to my auto? It's the Franklin parked out front—behind the red Packard. Be careful with the overnight bags. They shouldn't be crushed."

"Not every Negro porter is named George," Lum frowned. "We've met lots on our trip who have different names."

"What's that dear?" Muriel was staring down at the satchel Lum had picked up. "Let me carry that."

She gasped, then burst out laughing. "This looks exactly like my father's old satchel that I left in the Oakland Mole when I moved here five years ago. Who would have thought—"

"Oh, my! Is this what you used to carry around Chinatown?" Carrie felt her face growing unusually warm. But for once it wasn't a hot flush. "I found it in a closet after the earthquake." Carrie knew her cheeks must be beet red.

"At the time, it was the perfect thing for stuffing the Home records in—so that's what I did. The satchel kept them safe through the fire until we got to Berkeley. And it was my only file cabinet for months afterwards. Until we got furniture.

"I decided to bring it on the trip for our school supplies.

"It's funny what you grab in a moment of crisis." Carrie shook her head, remembering the day of the earthquake. "Your body does things without your mind thinking. I didn't even know it was in the Home until the quake.

"If it's yours, you're welcome to it."

Muriel knelt beside Lum and opened the clasp. "Yes, those are my father's initials." She pointed to three barely discernable letters embossed on the inside flap.

"I can't believe I never noticed them!" Carrie straightened. "Do you want it back?"

"No, no, that's fine. It looks like you've found a good use for it. This town's tastes are much too sophisticated for me to think of using it for work. I'm afraid it would simply sit in a closet at my house too."

"Ma'am, do you have anything else?" The baggage porter stood beside the flatbed cart, scratching his head. There was nothing on it except the children's overnight bags.

"We have those three large travel trunks too." Carrie pointed at the stack of baggage being wheeled into the main waiting room. "But I don't know if they'll fit in an auto. What do you think, Muriel? Perhaps we should have them delivered to the Deaconess Home later."

"I think we'll be fine. I borrowed an auto for the baggage. And Harry's driving our Packard. There'll be room for all the children in it, I think."

It was a gray afternoon when they exited Union Station with the baggage porter's squeaky cart hard on their heels. A chilly gust of wind caught Carrie's dress and whipped it around her legs, and Muriel grabbed the brim of her merry widow's hat. A man with a leather motoring coat stood with his foot on the running board of a cherry red Packard, grinning at them and tapping his fingers on the vibrating hood of the rattling engine.

"Carrie— you remember my husband, Harry?"

"Yes. We've met before. Once or twice, perhaps. You were doing some legal work for the Home at one time, I think."

"In a former life, it seems now." Harry looked over at Muriel with raised eyebrows and a tight-lipped attempt at a smile that gave Carrie the feeling she was somehow on the wrong end of a sensitive conversation. She smiled anyway and stretched out her hand. Harry grasped it in a strong, firm handshake. "Welcome to our nation's capital." The nervous edge in his voice seemed to dissipate with Carrie's touch.

"Are we going to ride in this?" Lum approached the Packard with eyes nearly as large as its spoke wheels. "Woohoo!"

"A boy? No one told me there'd be a non-girl on the trip!" Harry winked at Muriel who was directing the porter toward the black Franklin Landaulette parked behind the Packard.

"What a pleasant surprise!"

"The name's Lum." The boy thrust his hand toward Harry. "Lum Wong, sir. And we're here to sing for the President of the United States."

"So I've heard," Harry chuckled.

Carrie watched Lum run his fingers over the front fender of the Packard.

"Well, Mr. Wong, I'm pleased to make your acquaintance." Harry yanked at Lum's gray herringbone newsboy cap, pulling it over the boy's eyes. "And it's your lucky day—or perhaps I should say, your lucky week. Because you and your chums will be riding in this machine all week. So you might as well climb in the front seat there, and get comfortable."

Lum flicked his cap back and clambered up into the driver's seat, with a grin on his face wide enough to swallow the steering wheel.

"What's this?" And before Carrie could grab his arm, Lum had pushed in a knob he had found on the dashboard. There was an unearthly screeching "ahooga ahooga" sound and Carrie almost jumped out of her winter boots.

"That's the auto's horn—a klaxon," Harry laughed. "Pretty impressive, huh!"

A few serious heart palpitations and loud reprimands later, Carrie had Lum scooted grumpily to the passenger's side. She watched him warily for a few moments, then went to the back of the Packard to help Muriel open the tonneau cover. After Maud, Ruby, and Pearl climbed up, the women helped Lydia, Mamie, and May into the auto's middle seat.

When Harry and the porter finished arranging the trunks and over-night bags in the Franklin, Muriel wrapped herself in a balmacaan motor-ing coat and took the driver's seat. "Carrie, you and Ida can ride with me. I'll follow Harry. I'm sure the children will be fine with him. He's a very safe driver.

"With all the appointments you no doubt have scheduled this week, we thought it would be easier for me to chauffer you by auto." Muriel set the carburetor control and watched Harry crank the starting handle, then pulled away from the curb and out into the chaos of Massachusetts Avenue.

京

The next day was another *WHMS* meeting. Just like the one in Philadel-phia only not so many people. And also this one was called Baltimore which was funny because it was in Washington DC at the Hamline Meth-odist Church which was a long ways from Baltimore. And Maud played the organ again like in Philadelphia. But this one was absolutely huge. Big-ger than Philadelphia. So big her feet didn't even reach the pedals. So Miss Athey who was the organist at the church sat beside her and worked them.

It was a very strange feeling having someone beside you pump while you played. And Maud found it hard to think about the music. And she made lots of mistakes because of Miss Athey. It was like having a teacher there just waiting for something to go wrong so she could say no no not that. Look again. But at the end everyone clapped and cheered as usual. As if mistakes didn't matter.

On Wednesday night after they went to bed on the parlor floor of the Deaconess Home Maud and Lum and Ruby and the rest of them all talked about what would happen the next day when they went to see the Presi-dent in the White House. Lum kept saying he didn't care much for Mr. Roosevelt because most men he knew voted for Mr. Bryan instead of Mr. Taft. And Mr. Taft was the President's man and the men he knew didn't like the President for all sorts of reasons. Most of them about money.

But no one cared about what Lum had to say about Mr. Bryan. Maud said she only hoped she didn't get nervous in front of the President. Since he was so powerful and all. And Ida kept asking "What's a precedent?" And "Why do we have to see it?"

And Lydia said "It's not an it. It's a he. You'll find out tomorrow. Now be quiet and go to sleep."

京

By eleven o'clock on Thursday Miss Davis was finally done with her talk about the Oriental Home and the earthquake and the fire and Maud was finished playing the organ. And while the *WHMS* ladies were standing and cheering everyone ran off the stage and put on their coats and hats right over their colorful Chinese clothes as fast as they could and ran outside to the front of the church to get into Mrs. Monroe's cherry red Packard which Miss Davis said would be there on the corner. To go to the White House and sing for the President.

And Miss Davis looked up and down the street for Mrs. Monroe's cherry red Packard that she told Miss Davis would be there waiting for them. But she couldn't see it anywhere. And Miss Davis told them all to look for the cherry red Packard. And you could tell Miss Davis was getting more fretful by the minute because her hands were shaking. Which they always did when she fretted. And she said Mrs. Monroe was always late and she remembered how even long ago in Chinatown she would say nine o'clock or something like that and everyone would say yes yes and then she would be late. Or actually forget altogether. And you would think when you were going to visit the President of the United States for the very first time and you were a newspaper reporter you would be early if anything. And at least on time. But surely not late. Which was the worst possible time to do that. And Miss Davis's hands were shaking and twisting around her gloves which she pulled off. And she started yelling at them all to get out of the street and hold on to Ida and Mamie's hands and to look this way and that.

Then finally Miss Davis said you stay here and watch for her while I go inside and tell someone we need to get to the White House right now to sing for the President and can you please take us there this very instant.

And almost the minute Miss Davis went back inside the church to find someone to take them to the White House there was the cherry red Packard zooming down the street with its klaxon going "ahooga ahooga" at the very top of its lungs and people scattering every which way with ladies holding on to their hats trying to run away and men jumping up in the air and yelling out bad words really loud about a lady driving an auto which no one should allow.

And Maud told Lum to wave at the auto so Mrs. Monroe would see them standing there waiting in front of the church because she couldn't wave because of having to hold on to Mamie and Ida's hands to keep them from falling out into the street and getting run over by Mrs. Monroe's Packard. Which she was afraid of them doing.

And Mrs. Monroe finally saw them and made the klaxon go "ahooga ahooga" again and the auto squealed to a stop right in front of them with making Maud have to yank the girls away from the street where the auto was now making rattle-rattle putt-putt noises. And Mrs. Monroe hopped out with her big beautiful hat almost falling off her head and her red hair flying about in the air almost as cold as winter.

And Miss Davis must have heard Mrs. Monroe's klaxon and recognized the sound of it because almost as soon as Mrs. Monroe got out of the cherry red Packard Miss Davis was right there with the old satchel and you could tell she was still all fretful and even angry but trying not to show it. But Maud and the rest of them knew she was because her face was almost as red as the cherry red Packard only not as shiny. And it wasn't because of it being almost winter. And her voice was sputtering like she had an auto motor inside her too like in the cherry red Packard.

But Mrs. Monroe just smiled and said "Jump aboard children and we'll be on our way."

And Miss Davis was saying "Where were you? You said you would be here at eleven and we were all out here waiting for you."

And Mrs. Monroe said her boss gave her something to do at the last minute and she couldn't get away and then a trolley got stuck in the middle of the street not far from the church and she couldn't get around it until she drove up on the sidewalk with a policeman chasing her. But that here she was now and everything would be fine because they still had lots of time to get to the White House.

So Lum climbed into the front seat beside Mrs. Monroe and Maud and Pearl and Ruby and May climbed into the tonneau and Miss Davis and the Woo girls got into the middle seat with Miss Davis in between them and Ida on her lap. And they barely sat down and closed the doors and pulled their coats around them tight when Mrs. Monroe hunched over the steering wheel like Jack Johnson who was Lum's favorite boxer. And her left hand was on the knob on the klaxon and she pushed it in and the "ahooga ahooga" screech nearly made Miss Davis jump out of her new coat from Mr. Wanamaker's store even though Ida was on her lap holding on. And Mrs. Monroe scrunched over the steering wheel and steered with her right hand. Like she was afraid someone was going to hit her with a punch. And she made the tires squeal and Lum was in the front seat beside her. And he folded in half almost from laughing and even more when Mrs. Monroe made the auto stop suddenly so it wouldn't hit the lady with the parasol and a baby carriage who was walking almost exactly in front of them but to one side and had to hop up onto the sidewalk. And Lum almost fell out the front window but then he held on to it and didn't. But he was still laughing anyways.

And Mrs. Monroe shouted over her shoulder that it wasn't quite two miles to the White House from where the church was but it didn't matter anyways because she was going a different way and not by the trolley that got stuck. And the different way Mrs. Monroe drove was exactly the way Lum loved. With the top down on the cherry red Packard and the sun shining and everyone's hair blowing every which way and their ears about ready to drop off.

And Lum kept telling Mrs. Monroe about horse carts and trolleys and other blustery autos and where people were walking and how many and what direction and if they stopped to look at the Chinese children waving at everyone in the street. And sometimes Maud was sure Lum was making up things happening on his side of the auto just so Mrs. Monroe would swerve fast to miss something that wasn't really there and operate the klaxon. And even when Miss Davis told him not to Lum still did it and laughed. And Maud began to think maybe even Mrs. Monroe was having fun too and trying to make Miss Davis have a heart attack. Which she was almost having anyways.

And one time Lum shouted "Horse cart on the right, ma'am" even when it was at least fifty feet away. And Mrs. Monroe pushed in the klaxon again and the "ahooga ahooga" made the horse startle. And then Lum shouted out "Good job ma'am you just saved a Chinaman's life!" And then he burst out laughing again. And Maud was sure by now Miss Davis was praying to God in heaven to get them to the White House safely and with her eyes shut too. The same prayer she said every morning when they were going to ride on a train. But this time for real because of Mrs. Monroe's auto driving. And Maud could tell from Mrs. Monroe shouting "Ai yai yai!" that Lum was close to rolling out of the auto in laughter almost every minute. And finally Miss Davis told Lum to stop it but he said we might be late to see the President and what would that be like to come all this way from California and not to sing for him. So he did the "ahooga ahooga" sound without the klaxon really loud and it was almost perfect when a wagon came towards them. And Lum kept shouting "Woohoo. Woohoo!"

And now everybody was laughing and even Ida was squealing because it was the most fun ever with everyone on the street staring at them and the klaxon going "ahooga ahooga" over and over again. And Lum too.

And then Miss Davis found her courage to shout "This isn't a game Lum." And you could tell it was true because she was holding onto Ida so tight that Ida was turning blue in her ears. And then Miss Davis reached over from the middle seat and twisted Lum's ear until he said ow and that he wouldn't do it again. But not to blame him if they didn't get to see the President.

Then after that Lum settled back in his seat and didn't say anything anymore. And he tried not to laugh the same as Maud and Ruby and Pearl and May were doing in the tonneau. But they did anyways only not so loud. And besides they were sitting behind Miss Davis and she couldn't see them without turning around which she wouldn't do.

京

Just when Carrie thought she couldn't endure another minute of Muriel's driving, Muriel swerved into a circular drive near the north entrance to the White House.

"I think this is where we're supposed to be. It's the new Executive Office." The wheels squealed as Muriel pulled the auto to a stop in front of two glass doors where a uniformed man stood at attention.

Muriel set the brake, then hopped down from the auto. "Do you recognize any of those people?"

Carrie shaded her eyes and followed Muriel's pointing finger. She shook her head, trying to clear the high-pitched ringing in her ears. "Oh yes, there's Ada—Mrs. Street. She's the one off by herself. In the dark gray—a beaver felt hat is it? I can't keep up with styles. She's the Chairman of the Sibley Memorial Hospital and the one who knows the Roosevelts. Her husband Daniel's a doctor, and he and President Roosevelt are quite the outdoor enthusiasts, apparently."

Carrie lined up the children as though they were getting off a train. Tallest to shortest. Lum was in the middle, obviously still thinking about the ride in Muriel's automobile. He pretended he had hold of the Packard's steering wheel. He leaned as far as he could to the right, then to the left, all the while making dreadful squealing noises to go along with the awful sound of the auto's horn. Within a minute he had the younger girls mimicking him.

"Children! Children! Listen to me!" Carrie clapped her hands and walked to the front of the line where Maud stood quietly, teetering in her high-heeled, horse-hoofed Chinese shoes. Carrie turned and walked slowly toward the end of the line—to where Ida stood, still mimicking Lum. "Stand up straight girls. Straighten your clothes. And you all need to calm down. The auto ride is over, and we're here to sing for the President of the United States."

"That means you, too, Lum." Carrie pinched the boy's shoulder to get his attention. "This is what you've been talking about for the past two months. So mind your manners and stay with me until we're told what to do."

Ada led the procession up to the doorman.

"Passes ma'am?"

京

When they got inside a man sitting at a huge desk with an American flag behind it was frantically waving his arms at everyone. "Please, please" he said. "The President is ready to see you."

Then after Miss Davis straightened everyone's clothes again and complained about the girls' hair needing to be combed she said "Don't speak unless you're spoken to." And "You need to be respectful."

And Maud felt like she was Dorothy with the rest of them being the tin woodman and the scarecrow and the lion. And maybe Miss Davis being the Wicked Witch today. But all of them waiting to see the Wizard. Even the witch. And nervous about what the President would be like. And not knowing for sure. Which was like Dorothy before she met the Wizard.

Then Lum wanted to know if he should bow to the President. Like he always did after his directing. And then he bent down like it was a bow right in the doorway to the corridor and Ruby bumped into his behind sticking out and almost knocked him over.

And Miss Davis said "No. Now Lum straighten up." And then "You don't need to bow. It may be that he's the most powerful man in America. And one of the most powerful men in the world. But he's not royalty like King Edward."

京

Then on the right there was a door with an eagle holding arrows painted on it. And the door was open and a voice said "Come in." And it was sort of a high voice Maud wasn't expecting. But very human. And the voice said "Ah Mrs. Street. It's so good to see you." And "How's your husband." And then "Who have you brought with you today?"

And then after Miss Davis went in it was Maud herself going inside the President's office. Into a big room of the White House. And then everybody else with Mrs. Monroe last. And there he was. Theodore Roosevelt. The President of the United States. Wearing glasses like in all the photographs you could see. And they were like Miss Davis's glasses only his came with a bushy mustache which of course Miss Davis's did not. Standing behind his huge desk with all of them kind of in a circle line around the desk. With barely enough room to stand even though it was a very big office. Because there were eight children and three adults or four counting the President. And everybody stared at the President like he really was the Wizard. And even though Maud of course knew he was human he was even more so when you saw him up close.

And the President came out from behind his desk and walked up to everyone and shook their hands. With Miss Davis walking behind everybody and pushing them out a little ways and saying their names. Starting with Ida who was the littlest. And the President even bent over and shook Ida's hand so it looked like he was bowing to a little princess or something. Which most of the time she thought she was. And you could tell Lum wanted to bow too or do something foolish when the President got to him. But Miss Davis was standing too close and wouldn't let him.

And when the President got to Maud who was last in line it was a big hand and a warm one but not real rough like a farmer's or anything. Which she had a lot of hands like that. And he held it tight. But not too tight like some people did who squeezed your fingers together until they hurt. Then the President said "I hear you've been touring the United States." And nobody knew how he knew because it was almost the first real thing he said to anybody.

And Maud nodded and said yes that was true. But then Lum jumped in and started to name all the states. "California Oregon Colorado Kansas Nebraska Iowa Illinois Indiana Ohio Pennsylvania New Jersey. And Maryland."

And Maud said "You forgot Idaho and Wyoming." Which of course he had. With the President still standing right in front of her.

Then President said "That's quite a lot." And "Most American children haven't even been in three."

Then the President went back behind his desk and sat down and pulled open a desk drawer and poked around inside it. And Maud thought about the Wizard of Oz with his secret wires he used to do his pretend magic. And she wondered what it would be like if Toto suddenly appeared and did something. But of course it was the President and there was no dog nearby.

Then the President looked up and said "Mrs. Street tells me you're excellent singers." And when Miss Davis said yes that was true the President said "What are you going to sing for me today?"

And everyone said *America* all at the same time. Because it was the perfect place for it. Then Lum stood off to one side of the President's desk and blew the starting note on his little Hohner harmonica pitch pipe and Miss Davis gave him his baton from the satchel. And Lum lifted his baton in the air like he always did. And even though it was at least the millionth time they sang that song it seemed like it was the very first time because of the President of the United States of America being there. And Maud sang the harmony like she was the alto part on the piano. And she knew she would remember that moment forever. With the President of the United States sitting right there listening intently.

> "My country tis of thee
>
> Sweet land of liberty
>
> Of thee I sing.
>
> Land where my fathers died
>
> Land of the pilgrim's pride
>
> From every mountainside
>
> Let freedom ring.
>
> My native country thee
>
> Land of the noble free
>
> Thy name I love."

And so on and so forth. And when they finished singing the President stood up and clapped. A standing ovation. And from the President of the United States. His very own self.

京

"Mr. President, I'm the only person in this room who isn't an American citizen by birth." Carrie stepped toward the President's desk as he sat down. "I was born in Canada and became naturalized a few years ago.

"Every one of the children before you today was born on American soil." Carrie swept her arms out dramatically.

"And the mother of these three little ones," she pulled Lydia and Mamie and Ida out of the line and pushed them forward a step, "died in the United States.

"These proud little citizens have touched the Liberty Bell in Philadelphia. They've seen the forests of the Northwest, the Rocky Mountains, the rolling hills of Iowa and Ohio. So when they sing of 'freedom ringing,' of 'mountainsides,' of 'rocks and rills,' and of 'woods and templed hills,' they know whereof they sing."

"And they're marvelous singers! Such beautiful harmonies!" The President looked down at the desk drawer he had opened earlier and rummaged around, then pulled out some postcards and set them on the desk.

"Miss Davis, you may be hearing soon of something I've been working on for a month or so. I'll tell you about that in a moment. But first I have a gift for each of the children." He began signing the postcards and stacking them in a separate pile.

After a few moments of silence, punctuated only by the sound of the presidential fountain pen on postcards, the President looked up at Carrie. "I'm going to be sending out invitations for folks to join me in a National Conference on Dependent Care."

"What a wonderful idea." Carrie flinched at her overly enthusiastic response. "The nation needs a conversation like that. And you're the perfect person to lead it."

"I, myself, am in favor of placing out orphans or half-orphans and neglected children." The President handed an autographed postcard to Ruby. "I think the natural family unit is the ideal for any child. And so much better than institutional care. But we'll have a wide variety of positions represented at the table."

"We're not against placing out, Mr. President," Carrie smiled. "It often works well with American children. But not with immigrant children—especially not Orientals. The only people who want orphan Oriental girls are procurers, who masquerade as caring relatives. Then they turn around and sell the girls into lives of shame.

"The same goes for many other innocent girls who don't know English or our American ways. They're often taken advantage of.

"The only places where we can be sure such children are safe and cared for is in Homes like ours."

The President picked up another postcard and reached across his desk to give it to Maud. "I applaud your passion, Miss Davis. But I'm quite sure the focus of this initial conference will be on American families. We need to deal with that problem first before we can turn to the unique and more difficult issue of the Oriental in our midst. But I want you to know I am grateful for what churches like yours do for these children."

He winked at Lum. "And one for the boy, too.

"If ever the Orientals should become true Americans, it will be because of selfless Christian workers like you, Miss Davis."

Carrie watched Lum from the corner of her eye as he took the postcard and put it up to his nose, scrutinizing the President's signature.

"Mr. President, these children are also American citizens." Carrie turned toward Lum, who had set his postcard on the corner of the desk and was now staring intently at the President.

Although she had spoken for barely three minutes, Carrie was exhausted. She had rehearsed her lines numerous times over the past few weeks, hoping she would have a chance to speak what was on her heart. But her body was suddenly drained of energy. She wanted to sit, but there was no chair nearby.

Carrie put her hands on the President's desk to support her weight. As she did, Lum lunged forward.

"Mr. President?"

Carrie realized too late she couldn't reach Lum's arm from where she stood. She had no idea what would happen next—or what would come out of the boy's mouth.

Lum folded his arms and rested his elbows on the President's desk. "Mr. President, when I was down in Nebraska I was for Mr. Bryan. But since I came up here, I'm for Taft—because you are."

The President burst out in a roar of laughter that made everyone in the room jump. He stood and reached across the desk to squeeze the boy's shoulder. "Lum, you are a politician—and a mighty great one already."

京

Maud had been thinking about asking the President a question too but Miss Davis said not to say anything unless he asked them something. But if Lum could talk to the President without the President asking first then so could she. So she did.

"Mr. President?"

The President looked up from his desk.

"Do you like dogs?"

It wasn't the question Maud planned to ask. And the room was suddenly silent. It was as if her mouth wasn't even connected to her body and could do whatever it wanted to all on its own. And for a minute Maud stood there unable to move. She looked at her jade-green horse-hoof shoes poking out from beneath her blue silk pantaloons. She hated wearing the shoes. They made her walk like a dainty bound-footed girl. Something she wasn't. She wished she could twist the heels and sink through the carpet. Maybe to Kansas like Dorothy. Or to Berkeley.

She had made a huge mistake and knew Miss Davis would scold her later. How she was supposed to be an example to everyone else.

But the President was talking and so she lifted her head. The President was looking at her and smiling with a really big smile. "Well yes I do" he said. And "In all the years I've been President I don't think that question has ever been raised in this room. And I can assure you this room has heard many a question.

"In fact, my family has five dogs right now. My daughter Alice once had a little black Pekingese named Manchu the Empress of China gave her. And besides the dogs we have snakes and cats and a badger and all kinds of birds and guinea pigs and a one-legged rooster and a pony that once took a ride in the White House elevator. We even have a bear. But we don't keep it in the White House."

Then for a moment Maud thought what it would be like to live in a mansion like this with a whole circus full of animals and with a man who seemed almost as jolly as Santa. But not nearly so fat. And with someone who didn't think she said stupid things.

京

The following days sped by in a blur, with Muriel's driving improving exponentially. It was raining lightly on Tuesday morning when Muriel parked the Packard near the front steps of the two-story clapboard Deaconess Home where Carrie and the children were staying. Lum and Ida were standing at the parlor window apparently waiting for her, for as soon as she waved they disappeared. Harry squeezed the borrowed Franklin in behind the Packard. Before he had turned off the engine, Carrie and Maud were on the porch with four overnight bags to put in the borrowed auto.

Harry had attached the extension cape and car top on the Packard the night before, so its seats were dry. But that apparently didn't make any difference to Carrie. The woman made a point of asking Harry quite loudly if she could ride with him. That was fine by Muriel. She was a reporter, and she preferred a few minutes alone with the children.

京

After everyone piled into the auto Mrs. Monroe said Maud can you tell me why you asked the President whether he liked dogs.

And Maud felt her face get hot. And she thought about the way she felt at first. And she said it was a stupid question. That she was always saying stupid things. Like the time in Philadelphia when she told Miss Lake about the doll she kept after the earthquake. Even when its face was cracked and it couldn't be fixed.

Then Mrs. Monroe said she didn't think it was a stupid question. That she thought it was interesting. And how she saw the President's face light up when she asked it. So Maud decided to tell Mrs. Monroe the truth. About it being because of *The Wonderful Wizard of Oz*. About how she kept thinking almost everything in Washington was white. Just like the Emerald City after Dorothy took off her green glasses. How it wasn't an Emerald City at all. Just every-day normal. And how the way they waited for the President was like Dorothy and everybody waiting for the Wizard. And that when they saw the President he looked and sounded like an every-day American. How he didn't seem so powerful or special up close. And that was what she was thinking. But then everything came out wrong and it wasn't what she wanted to say.

Then Mrs. Monroe said she liked the question even better after Maud told her about it. And she said it was very perceptive. Which was a new word that Maud wanted to remember. And then Mrs. Monroe said she was going to write everything Maud said in a newspaper article. And with what Lum said that made the President laugh too.

京

Muriel found a copy of Saturday's *New York Times* on her desk Thursday morning, when she arrived at *The Evening Star* Building. There, on the front page, was a two-inch, single-column edited-down version of her article.

"Tiny Chinese See President," was the headline. And underneath, in a smaller font:

Each Gets a White House Picture and Roosevelt Autograph

WASHINGTON, Nov. 5—Eight Chinese children, ranging in age from 4 to 13 years, all inmates of the Oriental Rescue Home of the Methodist Church, in San Francisco, called at the White House Thursday. The President received the foundlings with great cordiality and sent them away with each hugging a photograph of the White House marked with the President's autograph.

The Chinese were on their way home from a missionary conference at Philadelphia, and were in the charge of Miss Carrie Davis, their matron. The only boy in the crowd was little Lum Wong. He told the President he had been in Lincoln, Neb. And that while in that town he had been a Bryan man, but now he was for Taft. The President congratulated him on his change of heart, laughing heartily at the frankness of the lad.

There was nothing in *The New York Times* article about Maud's question. There was no mention of Carrie's appeal to the President. It was as if the women and girls didn't exist.

京

Muriel met Harry for dinner at the Occidental Grill Thursday, after work. It was just a ten-minute walk from *The Star* building, and only a few stops on the trolley from Harry's law office near the Treasury Department.

It was already dark when they arrived, and after they ordered, Muriel told Harry about *The Times* article, how everything she had written about Maud and Carrie had been expunged.

"Maybe we ought to encourage Maud more when we send our monthly support." Muriel picked up her salad fork and poked at a piece of Romaine lettuce. "She has such a talent and passion for music. It's one thing for her to mention her lessons in an annual letter, but quite another to actually see her play. You should've heard her on Sunday—the way people clapped and cheered. And it wasn't gratuitous at all—because of being Chinese. It was because she's really that good. She plays and sings with incredible passion. And she's been doing that for over a month and a half now—sometimes three or four times a day. She may as well be on a professional tour."

Harry had ordered oysters on the half shell, and he noisily slurped one after the other—a behavior Muriel found particularly crude, and one Harry loved to taunt her with. She ignored his gurgling. His arched eyebrows.

"I was thinking—what if we promised to pay for her college education—providing she keeps up her lessons? Carrie told me she pretty much gets all A's and B's in school.

"As a woman she may never be able to vote for the President of the United States—but I'd like to ensure her music is at least as loud and well known as Lum's mouth."

Harry choked on the last oyster and set the shell down with a clatter on the blue and gold hors d'oeuvres plate. "Now look what you made me do." He wiped his mouth with his table napkin and cleared his throat. "Simply having Lum in the front seat of the auto that one time, was enough to make me think that if you can find someone to compete with his mouth, you'll have accomplished a minor miracle.

"I'm in. Let's do it."

"And one more thing, Harry." Muriel toyed with her fork, coyly balancing it between two fingers as if it were a playground seesaw. "Last week was the most fun I've had in years—not counting Carrie's nervousness over my driving." She paused for a moment and set down her fork. She looked up, searching her husband's eyes.

"Those children have such *joie de vivre*." Muriel saw the trace of a smile playing at the corners of her husband's mouth. She felt her cheeks grow warm, and she stared down at her plate.

"Their exuberance is contagious," she added somewhat hurriedly. "And that little one, Ida, is such a doll—the way she held on to me so tightly when I picked her up—"

"Muriel, is this going where I think it is?"

"You know I'm not getting any younger." Muriel leaned across the table and rested her fingers on her husband's wrist. The restaurant was cold, and she wore a black embroidered evening cape over her simple shirtwaist ensemble. She caught the cape in the palm of her other hand and pressed it against her chest a moment before it would have drooped into the remains of her salad.

"But there were eight of them, dear. Surely you're not suggesting—"

Muriel sat up quickly. Her hand moved to the top button of the cape. Then to her collarbone. "Oh Harry. Of course not. But one—perhaps two, might be nice."

"Well, I'm all for trying for one, at least. And if we're successful, maybe we can proceed further. You're in luck, too, because I believe I understand the basic mechanics to get us started."

"Really!" Muriel dropped her jaw in an act of feigned shock. "What they teach men in law school these days! It never ceases to amaze me."

"No more French letters, then?"

"You're really serious about this, aren't you?" Harry picked up his glass of *Loire Muscadet* and tipped it towards her *Côte d'Or* chardonnay, and winked. "Well, if you insist. A toast. To the testes—and to tossing away our French letters."

The foursome at the table across from them had just finished their assorted desserts of thick chocolate cake and crème brûlée. They stopped their animated speculations about a Taft presidency and gawped at Muriel and Harry, their silverware poised on the edges of their fluted glass dishes.

Muriel bent over her empty salad plate. "Shush! Harry, everyone can hear you."

Chapter Thirteen

HOME
(1909)

From Washington, DC Carrie and the children traveled further north and east to Brooklyn and New London, Connecticut. At that point they finally turned back west—toward home. Their first westward stop was at Syracuse, New York, and they arrived in the midst of a snowstorm. It was the children's first, and Carrie's first in nearly twenty years. Even though it was late in the evening, the children's noses were pressed against the steamy train windows; their eyes as large as teacup saucers. The fluffy flakes fell pell-mell, spinning around the lampposts as though poured from a giant sugar bowl. And when the train finally wheezed to a stop at the station, the children couldn't wait to get out into the swirling white world.

By Advent they had snuggled down in snowy Buffalo, New York. Carrie left the children there at the Deaconess Home while she traveled north to visit her sister Mary Ann near Owen Sound, Ontario. It was eight degrees the morning she said goodbye to the children. She had forgotten how cold northeastern winters could be, until she stepped outside at dawn and felt the tingle of ice crystals in her nostrils and heard the snow crunch beneath her boots. But as soon as she boarded the train she could think of nothing but being with her sister.

家

After Miss Davis went to Canada Maud and everyone else went to school for the first time since June across the alleyway from the Deaconess Home. And Maud had almost forgotten what it was like to sit cramped up in a desk all day that didn't move and listen to a teacher she didn't know try to get her to learn things that she already knew. And that made her feel stupid. But some days the deaconesses showed them maps of the United States and where things were. And on those days Maud told everyone Oh yes I've been there and here's what it's really like.

On the day before Miss Davis was supposed to get back from visiting her sister the deaconesses took everyone on the trolley to Niagara Falls. And they got to ride in a sleigh too. And people stopped on the road and stared like they always did except now it was because of eight Chinese children sitting in a sleigh singing *Jingle Bells* like they were in a one horse open sleigh. Only it was a two horse and the horses had the jingle bells not the sleigh. And they could all sit in it at once with thick blankets wrapped around them and their hats and mittens from Mr. Wanamaker's store and their breath making big clouds like they were smoking pipes or cigars which Lum loved to pretend he was doing. And it was amazing how you never knew horse poop was so warm until you saw one lift its tail and saw a bunch of steamy poop fall out onto the snow on a really cold winter day. And how it froze into little piles of rocks that Lum tried to kick like they were mud balls. But of course they weren't and the deaconesses had to scold Lum about what he was doing.

And they all sang loud in the sleigh with barely their mouths and eyes showing and still it was so cold their eyes almost froze shut because it was a sunny day with a blue sky and with snow so white their eyes watered like they were crying but they weren't really because you couldn't believe how beautiful the world could be. With snowdrifts so high it looked like houses and trees and carriages were clean white sheets draped over clotheslines. But of course they weren't. And when they got out and walked to the falls they sank so far that if you were Ida you almost disappeared. And dogs really did. Which was the most fun to watch how they seemed to have as much fun playing as humans.

And nobody could believe there was so much water anywhere in the world the way it kept coming over the top of Niagara Falls. With a sound like thunder in a Wyoming thunderstorm. Which is what the deaconesses said the word Niagara was. An Indian word that meant thundering waters. And at the edges the waterfall was frozen into the biggest icicles ever. So much so it looked like a huge organ with silver pipes. Only the pipes were icicles and the sound wasn't very musical. Just loud. And the waterfall made its own mist that was so thick it was like rain in the middle of winter. And when it landed on you it turned to ice. So when everyone walked back to the sleigh they were all big clinking icicles that kept breaking off when they walked. Like they were little tin woodsmen trying to walk without being oiled.

家

Carrie and the children celebrated Christmas at the Buffalo Deaconess Home, gathered in front of the parlor Christmas tree. Carrie brought out a big package from Berkeley and handed out gifts the Home girls had wrapped and packed. Each child received a little notebook-journal, hand-decorated and personalized with the child's name written in fancy letters on the inside. There were also new pencils for everyone, and photographs of the girls sitting on the front steps of the Home on University Avenue.

A *WHMS* group in Buffalo gave the children hand-knit mittens and scarves, and a woman from a farm outside Buffalo made woolen stockings for everyone, spun from the wool of her own sheep.

The deaconesses themselves had purchased books for the children. May, Ruby, Pearl, and Lum each received a *Five Little Peppers* book. The Woo sisters got *The Tale of Peter Rabbit, Benjamin Bunny,* and *Miss Tiggy-Winkle.* And Maud got *Dorothy and the Wizard in Oz.*

"Someone told us you love *Wizard of Oz* books" one of the deaconesses said, after Maud opened her gift.

"Oh yes," Maud grinned. Her eyes were as bright as the silver garlands on the Christmas tree behind her. "They're my favorites."

"Well, this one's about Dorothy's latest adventure. It starts with an earthquake in San Francisco. We thought you'd like it."

家

On December 30th, after nearly a month in Buffalo, Carrie and the children once more boarded a westbound train. And although they had performances scheduled through February that took them only as far west as Utah, it seemed to Carrie that they were finally homeward bound. By New Year's Day, Carrie and the children were finally back in the Midwest, in South Bend, Indiana for a mass meeting of missionary societies. From there it was on through snow and ice to Chicago, Des Moines, Kansas City, and then to Topeka, where in late January, the children performed on the vaudeville stage of a Midwinter Exposition.

家

In Topeka there was a huge organ Maud got to play that looked like it was made out of gold. And almost as big as Niagara Falls. And it was in a huge building that was about as cold as Buffalo too. And Maud had to put her fingers right next to her lips and blow on them to warm them before she played. And she still made mistakes. But it didn't matter because people just wandered around talking about farm equipment and things like that which is the main thing there was there. Because it wasn't a church at all. Or even a revival like Reverend Bulgin's. But just a big place to go and look at mainly big boring machines that made Lum happy to wander off so everyone had to go looking for him when they weren't singing. And when Miss Davis found him in front of a giant iron tractor and dragged him back to the main stage where other people were doing things that hardly anybody was watching they all sat down and got to see the end of an acrobatic act with men who were almost naked twisting their bodies into shapes that you wouldn't believe anyone could do. The way Lum played with Ida's rag doll sometimes to make her mad. With the arms where the legs should be and the legs where the arms should be and Ida saying stop you're going to break her. And Lum of course always laughing and saying how can you break a rag doll. At which time Miss Davis would get mad and take it away from him and tell him to not ever play with it again. But of course he would anyways.

And then after that the best thing ever. Which was a moving picture show Miss Davis said they could watch because there was a sign that said it would be the story of Jesus. But when they were in the middle of watching Jesus do his amazing miracles and the organist was playing really beautiful on the huge gold organ Miss Davis said she needed to take Ida to the toilet and for Maud to watch everyone else while she was gone. Which wasn't going to be a problem because they were all sitting together on a wooden bench watching the moving picture show anyways.

But when the picture show was over Miss Davis was nowhere to be found and Lum was starting to walk away to go find another big farm machine. So Maud grabbed onto Lum's arm and told him to stay but he tried to get away and yelled "Ow!" and "Let go of me!" Then finally Miss Davis came hurrying back almost dragging Ida and said some ladies in the washroom were talking about a big storm moving down from Montana. And that it could be the worst storm in twenty years and that they needed to find their hosts and leave immediately. Without even giving Maud a chance to say anything about Lum and how she had to grab on to his arm so he wouldn't run off like at the Liberty Bell.

家

After that everybody was cooped up in the Lowman Methodist Chapel where they were staying with the wind and snow blowing every which way. So cold you couldn't go outside and play. Which you didn't want to do anyways because it wasn't the first time anymore and you couldn't even see anything that wasn't white from the snow. But just to stay inside in the cold and dark and try to read and write in your journal with your mittens on. Which wasn't easy to do.

And the wind kept howling and moaning all day long like it was a real ghost trying to get inside. Which is what Lum told Ida and Mamie and Lydia so it made them scared. So Miss Davis made Lum go off by himself in a corner of the church and read. And not to bother the girls anymore.

And the church shook like they were in an earthquake all over again. Only it wasn't. Because Miss Davis said it was only the wind.

And when the pastor came over with their breakfast on the second day of the storm looking like a snowman with his moustache more icicles than hair he brought a newspaper too which Miss Davis read to them. About it being a real blizzard with wind gusts as high as sixty-six miles per hour and with temperatures hovering around fifteen degrees and all the rail lines closed. And how the roof of the State Capitol building that wasn't very far away at all got its roof blown off in the storm. But not all of it. Only part. But it was still exactly almost like in *The Wonderful Wizard of Oz.* Where Dorothy's house got blown away by the cyclone. Only this time it wasn't a cyclone but a blizzard that did it.

But it was Kansas. And that part was the same. And the other part that was the same as in Oz was about wanting to be home again. Like how Maud wanted to be back in Berkeley with Gracie and Caroline. And with Josephine and Ethel. Where it surely was warm and green.

家

The morning they left for Salina Ida and Mamie and May were sniffling and Miss Davis said Ida seemed to be teetering on the brink of a serious cold. And the *WHMS* ladies of Topeka had box lunches for them. And it was fried chicken and boiled eggs and cheese and bread and pickles. And there was dried apricots and dried pears and raisins and nuts. And two different kinds of cookies. Which they couldn't tell what they were and Miss Davis wouldn't let anyone try one until after they got on the train. And if Lum didn't stop teasing the Woo girls Miss Davis might eat his all by herself. Which made him stop everything for a while.

And even after the blizzard everything was still grayish white. Not even any blues anywhere. And it was amazing how when they were in Kansas the first time everything was green and there were leaves on the trees and green grass and the biggest blue sky anybody could imagine. But now it was just gray and brown trees with no leaves.

And now even Miss Davis was turning gray. Like a tree that lost its leaves too. Only the leaves would be her blood maybe and it was like there was no blood in her anymore. Not even in her lips that were gray like the stone pebbles Lum was always kicking when there was no snow on the ground.

And Maud had never thought about it before. About how a white person wasn't really white at all. Not until you saw one without any pink in their skin. Like Miss Davis right now. Sitting there beside the window on the train to Salina but not really looking anywhere or at anything. Really really white. Or maybe more grayish white like the Kansas sky. Or like ashes in a fireplace after the fire has gone out.

And all through the gray of everything the train went to Salina where they stopped and sang as usual. And Salina was as boring as ever but now even worse because everyone felt sorry for Ida and said oh the poor dear she has such a runny nose and have you tried sassafras tea for her or fried onions or boiled cockleburs. And Miss Davis said she was just as much a princess as ever or maybe even more now that she was sick and pretending to be worse than she really was so people would stimpasize with her. And lots of times after Salina Miss Davis couldn't carry Ida at all when she was crying because of complaining about her back which she said was getting worse. And so Maud had to carry her now. And one lady on the train after Salina said have you tried *Lydia Pinkham's Vegetable Compound* which surely cures all ailments. And Miss Davis said no so the lady gave her a new bottle for free and Miss Davis started to drink it more often than not and put some in water to give to Ida to help her sleep at night on the train and not wake up everybody in the car.

And the last part of the gray Kansas prairie lasted almost forever. On and on. All so boring. Flat. White. Gray. Griddlecake. White. Flat. Oh and then a little hill. The first one in over a day or maybe a century. And nothing but the train's clickety-clack, clickety-clack going on and on. And Maud was so bored and Lum was too. So much that he said he wanted to go back to Berkeley and not ever use his baton anymore. Maybe throw it in the ocean and watch it float away like a stick.

家

Then when they got to Colorado Springs where they sang again there was finally mountains and Maud felt like maybe they would eventually get home to Berkeley. And the morning the train left Colorado Springs Maud put her face to the train window as usual and had her journal on her lap as usual. With the pencil stuck in the place where she was writing. And there was Jack Frost on the window. All beautiful ice jungley shapes that appeared from nowhere. As if there was a fairy world made for her when she wasn't looking. And if there was an ice-butterfly which there probably really isn't such a thing but if there was you could grab on to its wings and fly right inside and go exploring until the sun comes out and melts Jack Frost's world into nothing again.

"Mombi" is what Maud called Miss Davis now. The Wicked Witch of the North. But only in her journal. Of course not to Miss Davis herself. As if Miss Davis would know who that was anyways.

家

The train arrived in Ogden a few hours before another blizzard blew down from Canada and across the Rockies. The conductor told Carrie the trains behind them were already stuck in the Colorado mountain passes. No one had any idea how long the trains would be snowbound.

Carrie was grateful they had beaten the storm. It was why people asked for "journeying mercies." And that was something she prayed for daily, with the children. Journeying mercies. One day at a time. She couldn't imagine being snowbound on a train after so many months of travel. She knew she would have gone stark raving loony. Would probably have walked straight off the train and disappeared into a Rocky Mountain snowbank. Not to be found until a late spring thaw.

Without thinking, Carrie gathered the children into line and paraded them into the station. It was a routine they knew well. Like lemmings marching to the sea.

家

"I think one of the girls—the littlest one here—might have the measles." A deaconess stood at the front door of the Ogden Deaconess Home, holding Ida, when Carrie stepped off the streetcar. Carrie had spent the day in Salt Lake City, without the children, visiting a wealthy, enthusiastic supporter of the Oriental Home. The brief trip had been worthwhile. Carrie had in her purse a promissory note for three hundred dollars dedicated to the building of a new Home.

The deaconess held Ida out to Carrie, but Ida clung to the deaconess's neck and wouldn't lift her head from the deaconess's shoulder. When

Carrie spoke the girl's name, she finally lifted her head and stretched out her arms. "Carry me Miss Davis."

Ida's mouth opened just wide enough for Carrie to see the telltale signs of the illness—small red spots with blue-white centers everywhere. "She's had a cough the last few days—and a runny nose for a week or so." Carrie shook her head. "But I thought it was a cold. We've had such bad weather the past few weeks—and everyone's had sniffles and coughs."

Carrie turned toward the deaconess. "Do you know how long the incubation period is?"

"A week to two weeks, I think."

"She must have caught it in Kansas. That seems so long ago, now."

"Trains are awful for that sort of thing." The deaconess smiled down at Ida, who had buried her head against Carrie's breast. "People sit so close together. Smokers coughing. And the washrooms!"

"Have any of the other children had the measles?"

"I think so," Carrie frowned. "But I'm not sure about Lum. I suppose we'll know in a few days."

"Well, regardless, it looks like you'll be staying here until this one's better."

Carrie stroked Ida's forehead. Ida's illness wasn't something she would have wished for. But under the circumstances, it could be a gift. Especially if no one else took sick. It would give them ten days of respite from the journey. A chance to relax in one place and draw strength for the final fundraising push in southern California.

Carrie wanted the trip to be over. To stay in one place without having to talk to strangers every night. To put her clothes in a chest of drawers and wardrobe, and know they would still be there when she went to look for them in the morning. Maybe Dorothy was right after all, Carrie thought. Maybe there was "no place like home."

Maud had finished reading *The Wonderful Wizard of Oz* to Mamie and Ida a few days earlier—for at least the third time on the trip. It seemed as though Maud hoped the magical story would somehow rub off on them with her reading. And how ironic the book the Buffalo deaconesses gave her was about a San Francisco earthquake. The San Francisco Home wasn't the first place the poor girl had lost. But it certainly was her most painful displacement—for all of them. And now they all wanted to be home. In Berkeley—in the place on University Avenue they had hardly set foot in before leaving on the fundraising trip.

But Carrie knew when Lizzie heard about Ida's illness, she would be busy rescheduling their southern California appointments. And as soon as Ida was well enough to travel, Carrie knew they would be on a train to Los Angeles. Lizzie had written saying the *WHMS* women were expecting them. And God would grant Carrie and the children the strength they needed for the journey. At least that's what Lizzie Piatt and Jane Robinson claimed.

家

Maud tapped on Miss Davis's door on the second floor of the Ogden Deaconess Home. "It's me Miss Davis. Maudie." She whispered because she didn't know if Miss Davis was awake. But she really wanted her to be. "I can't find my King's Daughter cross." There was some noise on the other side of the door that made Maud think of a mouse scurrying about.

"Did you check the dress you wore yesterday? Sometimes you forget to take it off." Miss Davis's voice was muffed like she was taking off her nightgown or something.

"Yes. I already looked. It's not there." Maud pushed her forehead against the door like there was a peephole she could see through. But there wasn't. "I know I wore it yesterday. I can still see the pinhole in the dress."

"Did it fall off onto your bed? Did you check there?"

"Yes. I even had Ruby help me. I can't find it anywhere."

"Well if you can't find it, we'll get you a new one when we get back to Berkeley." Then Miss Davis opened the door and brushed her hair out of her eyes with one hand. And she had a bottle of *Lydia Pinkham's Vegetable Compound* in her other hand. And she was wearing only her corset cover and petticoat. Maud didn't often see her that way. With Miss Davis's skin almost rosy pink. With only a little gray left over from Kansas. And it made Maud think maybe she shouldn't be calling Miss Davis "Mombi" anymore like she did in her journal in Kansas and Colorado. That maybe the icy whiteness and grayness had left her for good.

"But I always wear my cross." Maud kept staring at Miss Davis's almost pink face. With only little patches of gray mixed in. "I don't want to leave without it."

Maud was a faithful and true King's Daughter and she wore her cross wherever she went. Ever since the day of the earthquake. Which had saved her life that day. Even though she was older now and knew the cross wasn't magic. But still it reminded her of how God kept her safe through the earthquake and fire. And every day since then. Even in the Kansas blizzard that shook the church like it was an earthquake or cyclone.

"You know we can't miss the train Maudie." Then Miss Davis looked at the *Pinkham's* in her hand and put it on the little table beside the door.

"Maybe one of the deaconesses will find it and can send it to us in California."

"I hope so. But I really want it now."

"I know. But I have to finish getting dressed. And you need to go get Ida ready."

Maud wasn't happy about leaving her cross behind in Ogden. She sighed loudly and went downstairs to the parlor where everyone was getting up. How could a Junior King's Daughter lose her cross? It was the best thing she had to remind her of the promise she made to Gracie and Caroline the night before she left Berkeley. How she would wear it every day until they were together again. And now she knew she had broken that promise.

家

Because of staying so long in Ogden because of Ida being sick everybody at the Home sent their letters there. And it was lucky for them because the letters all came the day before they left. Which was almost the middle of March. And Maud had three from Gracie and two from Caroline that was just about her beau and the wedding she was planning that would be the most beautiful ever. And how she hoped for sure Maud would be home in time for it because she wanted Maud to play *The Wedding March* which was her favorite song to get married to. And Gracie was still writing about how all Caroline talked about was her wedding and how oh so much she wished she had a beau too but probably never would because of her leg that was crippled. Which was all she wrote about last time too. And was she still wearing her King's Daughter cross. Which of course Maud wasn't because she lost it. And for a while on the train Maud read the letters again—all twenty-six she had in her overnight bag. Going back to the first ones Mrs. Piatt brought with her to Philadelphia from Berkeley.

And looking out the train window now was beautiful because of the blue skies of Utah and Nevada that were so much better than the gloomy gray winter days in Indiana. And Illinois and Iowa and Kansas too. And probably at least one other state she couldn't remember. But not most of Colorado. And you might actually learn to like winter if you knew you would see the sun from time to time.

And then finally a day later the train slowed to climb into some mountains. And it was Cajon Pass Maud's railway booklet said. Finally in California again. Since almost forever it seemed like. It was night and everyone was sleeping except her. With her head poking out of the curtain of the sleeping berth to read the booklet with the little light shining in the aisle. And even Miss Davis was snoring as usual. And everyone knew what she sounded like. And even with the train windows closed Maud could suddenly smell some kind of beautiful flower. And there must have been thousands of them to smell them on the train with the windows closed and everyone sleeping. Like the poisonous poppy fields Dorothy and the lion fell asleep in.

And when the conductor came walking down the aisle and said San Bernardino softly Maud whispered to him what the smell was.

"Orange blossoms" he said. And "It's just the start."

家

The day after they arrived in Los Angeles Carrie had a lengthy interview with a reporter from the *Los Angeles Daily Times*. The conversation seemed to drain from her whatever energy she had built up during the forced delay in Ogden. And now all she could think about was her speaking engagements for the next two weeks: Riverside, Redlands, Colton, Upland, Pomona, Ontario, San Bernardino, Pasadena, Whittier, and Redondo Beach. And that was just the churches. Who knew how many last minute ladies' teas and monthly *WHMS* meetings she would be asked to speak at—and of course, there were always the children. No meeting was ever complete without their singing and Maud's accompaniment.

Carrie and the children boarded a Santa Fe train heading east to Riverside and Redlands a few days after the *Times* interview. The papers advertised the route as "seeing the snow while riding in summer comfort through orange groves," and when the conductor came through their car, he told Carrie she ought to be sitting on the left side of the train. "Then you can see the mountains." He smiled down at Ida who was sitting on Carrie's lap. "When we get east of here a ways, you'll be able to see Mount Baldy still topped with snow."

But Lum told the conductor he had seen so much snow in New York and Kansas and Colorado, he didn't care if he ever saw any again.

"It sounds like you've had quite a trip," the conductor chuckled. A little later he came through their car again. "Put your windows down, ladies and gentlemen. Take a whiff of pure southern California sunshine. That's our orange blossoms." He winked at Carrie. "I'll bet that boy of yours didn't smell that in Kansas."

"What a beautiful world." Carrie nuzzled Ida's thick hair and forced a smile at Lum and Ruby who sat across from her. But the smell drifting in the windows from the orchards was overpowering. Carrie felt light-headed and nauseous. She had survived the past two months by taking one day at a time. But now, the thought of a week of performances with only one day off made her heart pound. She laid her head back on the seat and tugged at the collar of her dress. She groped for her handkerchief, and mopped her brow. She felt a telltale hot flush moving from her chest to her throat and face. She needed the *Pinkham's*, but it wasn't in her overnight bag, and it would have been impossible to pour a dose on the swaying train.

Thankfully, Redlands was much cooler than Carrie expected. And the children's Riverside performance the night before had gone well. The forced break in Ogden seemed to have revived the children's enthusiasm for singing. Even Ida had shown a bit of her old sparkle.

"We're over a thousand feet high here," the pastor said to Carrie, when he met them at the Redlands station.

Regardless of elevation, the scent of orange blossoms was still thick in the air. Heady. It's what being drunk must feel like, Carrie thought. Her head in a fog, with what her brother-in-law would call a hangover.

家

There was nothing any different about what they did at First Methodist in Redlands from any other place. First Ida and Mamie came out dressed in their Chinese clothes and sang *God is Love* then everyone else came out in their Chinese clothes too that everyone called exotic. But in California where everybody should know what Chinese people looked like.

Then Lum held up his baton and they sang *Come Over and Help Us*. And of course Maud was all the time playing the piano. Which she could do if she was blind by now. And the church was pretty much full of people and everybody clapped and cheered like they always did. And it was boring all over again even though it was only the second time since Ogden where they hardly did anything because of Ida being sick with the measles.

And then Miss Davis gave her speech about the earthquake and fire and about Maud and May being little slave girls that got rescued. And they went into one of the Sunday school classrooms and changed into their white dresses. Then Lum changed into his white suit which he always did. Then they all came back on the stage and sat cross-legged on the floor behind Miss Davis because there was no place for them to go. And Maud had to keep pulling Ida onto her lap and wrap her arms around her to keep her from standing. Then when Miss Davis was done Maud and Ruby and Pearl and May answered the questions about the Bible that Lum asked. The same old ones they always did. The kind Junior King's Daughters needed to know before they got their crosses. Except of course Maud didn't have hers which made her feel peculiar. But at least not naked anymore. And as usual everybody thought they were geniuses. And then everybody stood and sang *America* with Lum leading everybody. And Maud played the piano again of course.

家

"I'm taking everyone to help set up the sleeping arrangements and get ready for bed" Miss Davis said afterwards. She was standing in the doorway that went downstairs. And Maud thought Miss Davis was starting to look like Kansas all over again. Already white and tired. Like Mombi had come back.

"But I want you and Ruby to stay here with the postcards" she said. "And watch Ida until we have her bed made."

Maud spent at least half an hour with Ruby selling postcards at a table by the front door to the church and answering the same old boring questions about how long have you been playing the piano? And how old are you? Really. You're so small. And are all Oriental girls short? And your hair is so thick. What do you do to it? Can I feel it? And your English is so good. You talk as good as an American.

Always the same questions. And Maud was really really sick of it all.

But Ruby had gone downstairs and most of the people had left when Ida started screaming.

"Stop touching me!" she said. "Stop touching me!"

Maud turned in time to see an American girl trying to run her fingers through Ida's hair who had been sleeping on a pew next to where you walk into the sanctuary. But not any longer.

"Leave me alone! Leave me alone! Maudie carry me." Then Ida stretched out her arms and Maud ran over and pulled her away from the American girl and shook Ida by the shoulders. But not very hard. And she said "Ida. Stop it!"

Then Maud said "I'm sorry Miss. She's been sick. I think she needs the toilet." But she really didn't. Maud just wanted to get Ida away from the girl.

Then when Maud went out into the hallway with Ida to get away from the girl Miss Davis was standing there panting and pressing her hand against her back by her waist. And she had Maud's overnight bag in her other hand and the old leather satchel was at her feet. And she started yelling as soon as she saw them.

And she said "Ida you were awful to those girls tonight. We only have a few more weeks. And Maud you have to keep a closer eye on her. That's all I ask of you girls. Just a few more weeks."

Then Maud said exactly what she felt like and she didn't even care how it came out at all. "She's not just my responsibility" is what she said.

Then Miss Davis said "No Maud she's not. But I told you and Ruby to carry these things to the Sunday school classroom before the program. And people were tripping over them in the foyer all evening." And Miss Davis set Maud's overnight bag down so hard a latch came unfastened. And Maud watched it tip over. Her underwear spilled out on to the floor. Then Yet's jade green cheongsam Maud had folded so carefully. Then her precious journals. All of them. And after that *The Wonderful Wizard of Oz* and all her souvenirs from the trip. Everything scattering every which way.

And Maud said "Now look what you've done! You've dumped my things everywhere." And she stooped to stop a Liberty Bell souvenir pin from rolling under the edge of the church carpet that was old.

Then Miss Davis said "Shush Maud. Just clean up this mess before someone comes along and trips."

But Maud said "I'm not your slave." She said it under her breath. And not very loud at all. Not to anybody really. Maybe mainly to herself. But it was exactly the way she felt. And if Miss Davis was there to hear it she didn't care anymore. Then she bent over and picked up one of her journals that had fallen. And the page was torn.

"What did you say?"

"I said I'm not your slave." And Maud said it louder this time. And this time she didn't care if the whole world heard. "You think that's all we're good for. To do what you want." And Maud stood tall and stared straight into Miss Davis's eyes. For no one could make her a slave if she knew how to use her power. And that was from *The Wonderful Wizard of Oz* that Miss Lake told her long ago. The same thing Maud read to the Woo girls not so long ago. And she remembered it now. That she had her own power too.

Then Miss Davis's face was suddenly red like a tomato from a Kansas farm. Maybe in Oakley or somewhere like that. Where there was a line of sweat dripping from her forehead like it was raindrops on the tomato only it was Miss Davis's face. And Miss Davis said "You have no idea of what you're talking about." Then she leaned forward and shook a finger in Maud's face. "And don't you ever—"

Maud had never seen Miss Davis look like that before. With her eyes like there were sparks jumping out from them that would catch anything on fire that got too close. "Don't you ever accuse me of treating you like a slave" Miss Davis screamed. "You don't know—"

And Maud said "Yes I do." Then she stepped back from the fire. And now she was shaking too. Her voice all trembly and screechy like it came from someone else's body. But she didn't know whose. Or if it was really her own self talking this way. Only that she was tired of everything and wanted to get away. Away from everything. From the trains and the people and the singing and the playing piano. From always having to do something. Of having to be somebody for someone else. And she did remember some things about being a slave girl long ago. The feeling of never being her own self for herself. The feeling of always having to do what someone else wanted her to do. The very same feeling she was having right now.

So Maud didn't move. She didn't care how many times she had to say it. And she would say it as loud as she wanted. "I do Miss Davis. I know exactly what it's like."

And Miss Davis stood there too in the hallway with her breathing coming more gaspy every second like she was running a long ways. And then her body swung backwards and forwards like she was trying to balance in the vestibule of a train. Only there was no train. And she picked up the satchel and threw it. Then she screamed again.

家

Maud ducked and spun around. The old satchel flew over her head toward Ida who was right behind her. The fat satchel hit Ida in the face and the clasp broke. Then she fell backward and twisted like her rag doll Lum sometimes tossed in the air for fun.

Ida's head hit the washroom doorknob and there was a sharp cracking sound. Like Susie. Then Ida crumpled on the floor. Like Susie lying on the back steps of the old Home. Like a pillow with the feathers inside of it falling out all over. Only what poured out of Ida was red. Like with Susie.

"Look what you've done!" Maud had the satchel in her hand and now she was staring right back at Miss Davis's red face. "Look what you've done to her!" Then before she thought of anything she threw the satchel at Miss Davis.

The satchel fell at Miss Davis's ankles without doing anything. But Miss Davis kicked it anyways and everything spilled out. "I can't take it anymore. I simply can't take it. I've had to carry your things—you children—everywhere. For six months. All by myself. And I'm at the end of my rope with you. With all of you." And now there were tears pouring down Miss Davis's cheeks.

"You're not babies anymore. Least of all you, Maud. You've got to stop all the complaining and grow up. And start taking some responsibility for things."

Miss Davis only cried like this once before. In Berkeley. When they were remembering how things were in Chinatown before the earthquake and fire. But this was different. This time Miss Davis was crying like a baby that didn't get its way. And Maud wasn't about to give Miss Davis what she wanted.

Maud turned back towards Ida who was moaning and trying to get up. Maud dragged Ida away from the door and then turned to see where Miss Davis was. She was sitting in the middle of the hallway with her legs spread wide apart. She was staring at the ceiling with her wire glasses stuck crooked on her runny nose and her mouth open wide and her spikey gray hair every which way. With the fire gone out of her and with nothing left in her but gray and white ashes. Like she was Mombi in Kansas again. The Wicked Witch of the North melting away to nothing.

Maud lifted Ida and pulled her to her chest. Ida's head was bleeding all over the place and her eyes were rolling around in her head. All white. And then the black pupils. And then all white again. "Maudie. Maudie" Ida moaned. And then her face went empty. And it was Susie all over again.

The wail started deep inside Maud's belly. Like everything inside wanting to come up and out and spill into the dark of everything. Onto the hallway carpet that was old and frayed like everything else in that place.

"Help! Somebody! Oh please. Somebody help!"

Then the front door of the church burst open and there was a rush of cool air and the sweet smell of orange blossoms. And there was the sound of footsteps in the dark hallway. And out beyond the door and the shadow of someone running Maud could see a star-filled night sky. And beneath that the lights of the town ringed with snowcapped mountain peaks were shining.

"Who is it? What happened?" the voice said.

家

It was much later that night when the church people finally let Maud go back to the Sunday school room where Lydia and Mamie were sleeping on a mattress on the floor. Maud undressed by starlight with the pointy edge of a silver moon shining through a classroom window smudged with little handprints. And even in the almost nothing light she could see blood on her white dress. And she knew it was from Ida. From holding her.

Maud was almost fourteen. And everything she had ever cared about was either broken or gone. People carried things far too long and then the heaviness of everything broke them and they fell apart. People like Miss Davis. Who was like her doll with a broken face from the earthquake.

Everyone had parts of their bodies that spilled out. Things their skin and bones couldn't keep inside. That burst open and needed to be picked up. Like the old leather satchel and the overnight bag lying on the hallway floor.

Maud didn't want to be the one gathering the scattered and broken pieces anymore. But whenever she looked around there was no one to do that. No one to pick up the brokenness.

Maud took off her drawers and put on her nightgown. And that's when she saw it. More blood. She gasped so loudly that she was afraid Lydia and Mamie would wake up. But they just turned over and went on snoring. Maud wadded her underwear in a ball and looked for somewhere to put it. How could she be bleeding down there? She didn't remember Miss Davis hitting or kicking her.

Maud wished Gracie was there. That she could talk to her about the bleeding. Gracie would know what to do. Maud had heard Gracie and Caroline talk about bleeding down there and maybe that's what this was. But she didn't know for sure. And there was no one to talk to.

Finally Maud took the ball of bloody drawers and hid them at the bottom of her overnight bag. Then she crawled onto the mattress on the floor of the Sunday school classroom. She hated sleeping on church floors. But she fell asleep rolled in a ball beside Lydia and Mamie thinking about her soft bed in Berkeley and hoping she wouldn't see any more blood in the morning.

家

The next morning at breakfast in the church kitchen the pastor told everyone that Miss Davis and Ida were nearby in something called Loma Linda Sanitarium. "Ida suffered a concussion last night" he said. "The doctor needs to watch her carefully for the next couple of days. And he says Miss Davis is not well and will require complete bed rest for a while." Then the pastor said he sent a telegram to Mrs. Piatt in Berkeley to tell her what happened and to see what she wanted to do about the singing tour.

The next evening the pastor came into the church parlor where Maud was reading and told her a Missions lady from Los Angeles named Mrs. Humphreys was on the telephone in his office and wanted to talk to her about going back to Berkeley. Maud had never talked on a telephone before but she had seen Miss Davis and other people do it many times. So she was willing to try.

"You can stand on that chair by the phone if you need to" the pastor said.

Maud picked up the earpiece and stared at the wooden box on the wall. The voice on the other end sounded far away. "Maud you probably don't remember me but I met you once or twice before when you played the piano at *WHMS* meetings in San Francisco and Oakland. I know Miss Davis and Mrs. Piatt and I've been talking with the pastor there where you are and he told me about Miss Davis and about the little girl's accident. We're so sorry—" The line was crackly and scratchy.

Maud didn't remember meeting anyone named Mrs. Humphreys. She had met hundreds of ladies over the past months but there were only two she cared about. Mrs. Piatt and Miss Davis. Maud climbed on the wooden chair to get closer to the mouthpiece. "Mrs. Humphreys it wasn't an accident with Ida. Miss Davis threw something and that's why Ida fell."

The line crackled and went silent.

"Mrs. Humphreys?"

"I'm still here Maud. I know all you children are tired right now. You've had a wonderful trip up to this point and we thank the Lord it's gone so well. Now all we need to do is get you home safely to Berkeley."

"I was there Mrs. Humphreys. It wasn't an accident."

"This is no time to be putting the blame on people dearie. Least of all Miss Davis. She's done so much for all of you. You know she wouldn't do anything to hurt anyone."

Maud could barely hear the lady. She stood as tall as she could on the chair and shouted into the mouthpiece.

"It wasn't an accident." The chair started to tip and Maud grabbed the mouthpiece and managed to step off the chair before it fell over. She discovered the mouthpiece was jointed and could be pointed down and if she stood on the floor on her tiptoes she could speak into the mouthpiece easily.

"Miss Davis threw something and that's why Ida fell and got hurt."

The lady went on talking as if she hadn't heard a word. "Maud we're so thankful there's a doctor there to help Miss Davis. And that you all have a place to stay for a few days. But I need you to listen carefully to me right now. Do you think you can do that?"

"Yes."

"Mrs. Piatt sent me a telegram today and she thinks it would be best if you and the rest of the children go back to Berkeley as soon as possible. I could meet you there in Redlands and bring you back as far as Los Angeles. But you might have to be in charge of taking everyone from Los Angeles to Berkeley if I can't find someone to go with you."

"Miss Humphreys? What did you say?"

"Do you think you could take the children back to Berkeley?"

"Why? What about Miss Davis? Why can't she do that?"

"Miss Davis will be staying in the hospital there until she gets better and that may be awhile. In the meantime Mrs. Piatt thinks it would be best for you and the children to return to Berkeley. You know what to do on the train don't you?"

"Yes, I think so." But Maud's heart was flip-flopping like Ida's rag doll was alive and stuck inside her.

"Good. I can meet you there in Redlands as soon as the little one's out of the hospital and bring you back to Los Angeles. If I can get you on the early *Limited*, you would be home late that same day. You wouldn't have to change trains at all. The conductor could help you but you would be in charge. Do you think you could do that if I can't find a Methodist lady to go with you?"

"Yes Mrs. Humphreys." And Maud knew she could.

"We're all so proud of what you children have been doing. Miss Davis told me a few days ago that people have promised over five thousand dollars to help pay for building the new Home. And that's all because of your hard work. You've truly been a King's Daughter these past few months she said."

"Thank you Miss Humphreys." But Maud didn't feel much like a King's Daughter right then. She didn't even have her cross. The lady didn't know Maud had lost it somewhere in Utah. Maud hung up the phone and thanked the pastor for letting her use it. She wished she had magical shoes and could knock them together and be wherever she wanted. But she knew that only happened in storybooks.

家

Just like Mrs. Humphreys promised, she came out to Redlands and rode back to Los Angeles with Maud and the children. Mrs. Humphreys told Maud she had telegrammed Mrs. Piatt with the train schedule and when it would arrive in Berkeley. Then Mrs. Humphreys's friends gave Maud and the children boxed lunches for their trip. And even though they could smell it was fried chicken again, they didn't care. Because they knew it was the last time they would have to eat it. Maybe forever. And while they waited in the Los Angeles train station Mrs. Humphreys told Maud she hadn't found anyone to go with them to Berkeley. And so Maud would have to take everyone back by herself. Then Mrs. Humphreys handed Maud a list of "how to ride home on the train alone" instructions, and read them to her three times. And when Maud and the children were ready to board, Mrs. Humphreys found the conductor and gave him a copy too.

A couple of hours after the train left Los Angeles, the tracks turned east, back toward the hot desert they had passed through two weeks earlier. Everything was dusty brown. The mountains, just pointy piles of rocks and brush poking the bright blue sky. Lum had read about the great train loop near Tehachapi in his railway booklet, and two old ladies who had been watching them asked Maud if they would like to trade places so Lum could see the train do the double loop. Maud said yes, and so they all switched seats for a while.

As usual, whenever the train stopped and new passengers came aboard, they walked past the children and stared. When the two old ladies who had traded places with them found out this wasn't the children's first train ride, the ladies wanted to know everything—where they had been, how long they had been gone, and why.

"Can you sing something for us?" they asked.

Maud said yes, and Lum stood in the aisle and directed them as he had so many times before. He took out his little Hohner harmonica pitch pipe, blew into it for the girls' starting note, and then they sang *America* and *Come Over and Help Us*. Maud rummaged through the old satchel and found a handful of the color picture postcards of them, and the two ladies gave Maud a dollar for two postcards even though Maud told them they were a penny apiece. Maud dropped the dollar into the satchel to give to Mrs. Piatt when they got back to Berkeley. Then other people in the car came over and bought postcards too.

"My, my! Just imagine. Eight little singing orphan Oriental children—traveling alone on a train—" is what everyone said.

Then Maud took her postcard of the White House out of the old leather satchel to show the passengers who crowded around her.

"And singing for the President of the United States! Such wonderful examples of Christian missionary work."

Their journey was almost over, and Maud was anxious for it to end. She wanted to see familiar faces. To sleep in the same bed for more than two nights in a row. To eat normal Chinese food.

There was nothing interesting about the trip from Los Angeles to Berkeley after the Tehachapi loop—not even the singing part. And the day seemed to go more and more slowly the closer they got to Berkeley. Desert. Then miles of vegetable fields. Then a dusty little farm town or two. Then desert again.

Maud rummaged through the leather satchel, searching for something to take away the boredom. Her two *Wizard of Oz* books were there of course. *The Wonderful Wizard* was missing a couple of pages now from a time somewhere in Kansas or Colorado when Ida and Mamie fought over it. Maud had read the books to the girls so many times she didn't even want to look at the covers.

Then there were their journals, and Miss Davis's fat envelope of pledges that Mrs. Humphreys put in the satchel and told Maud three times not to lose it—and another envelope of newspaper clippings of their performances Miss Davis was saving.

Finally, Maud found a magazine of word puzzles and leafed through it. But most of them had already been filled in. Half of them by Mamie. Maud recognized her penmanship. She still printed most of her e's backwards. She did the same thing with her threes.

Maud was about to close the satchel when she pricked her finger. "Ow!" she said. She pulled her hand out and saw a little drop of oozing blood, so she put her finger to her lips and sucked off the blood.

She put her hand back in the satchel, this time more carefully. Her hand found the sharp thing again. It was small and one side was smooth.

"My cross!" She looked quickly around the car, embarrassed at her childish outburst. But no one seemed to notice. Ida was still asleep, curled in a ball next to her on the seat. The men with newspapers across the aisle and in front of her didn't look up. The mothers across the aisle were still scowling at the children tugging at their legs, and the old ladies behind them were still staring out the window at the speeding by emptiness. Maud looked over her shoulder at Lum and the other girls. Lum was reading his *Five Little Peppers* book for the hundredth time, and Mamie and Lydia were playing with Ida's rag doll. May and Ruby and Pearl were talking about something—but Maud couldn't tell what. Nothing had changed.

Maud held her King's Daughter cross up to the on-again-off-again afternoon sunlight streaming through the train windows. It had some scratches that hadn't been on it before. If the cross had been sitting at the bottom of the satchel for two weeks with things being dumped on top of it, that's probably how the marks got there. But Maud had no idea how the cross got into the satchel in the first place. Maybe it had fallen there when she bent over to carry it that time in Ogden. Or maybe Miss Davis had found it on the floor of the Ogden Deaconess Home and tossed it into the satchel—but then forgot to say anything with all the *Pinkham's* she was drinking.

Maud sucked at another little drop of blood and then felt around for the pinhole she knew was on her dress collar. All her dresses had them somewhere. She found the slight dimple and pushed the pin through and then secured the clasp. She was happy to have it back. Not because she thought it would keep her safe. She didn't believe in magical things like that. But because of Gracie. And because of Caroline. But mostly because of Gracie. Who she knew would be waiting for her at the end of the journey. A journey now almost over.

Maud closed the satchel as best she could, then set it on the floor between her legs. Ever since Miss Davis had broken the satchel's latch, it had been almost impossible to carry. It flopped open all the time. Like Miss Davis's mouth when she slept on the train. With her head flopped back over the seat and snoring away with everybody noticing.

Maud couldn't wait to get home and empty out the satchel—and then throw it away. She hated it. It was old, ugly, and broken, and she didn't need it anymore. Maud rested her head on the back of the coach seat and in a few minutes she was fast asleep.

She awoke when the conductor shouted, "Berkeley. Stanford Place Station, Berkeley! After that it's the Oakland Mole and the end of the line. All out for Stanford Place!" The conductor paused when he came to where Maud was sitting. "You slept a long time, Missy. This is your stop. I'll help you and the other children off after everyone else deboards. So sit tight until I come back to get you."

Ida had been sleeping next to Maud, and she sat up, startled, when the train's brakes began to screech.

"Maudie, are we there yet? Are we home?" She yawned and snuggled under Maud's arm.

"Yes, we're finally home. Exactly where we started from. See?" After seven months and eight thousand miles, they were back in a familiar place. There was at least one other part of *The Wonderful Wizard of Oz* that was true, Maud thought. The part where Dorothy says, "There's no place like home."

Maud pulled Ida to her feet and pointed out the window. There was still a thin line of pink daylight in the sky above San Francisco. Together they scanned the crowd on the Shattuck Avenue platform in the gathering darkness. "Do you see anybody we know? I don't. Let's go look on the other side. Maybe we'll see them there."

Maud picked up the leather satchel one last time, and took Ida by the hand. She crossed the aisle to an empty seat and motioned to the girls opposite her. "Come over here everybody. We're home! Let's see who's here to meet us."

She patted the seat beside her. "Lydia, May, Mamie, Pearl, get your things. And Ruby, put on your shoes. You too, Lum. Over here."

A crowd of people stood on that side of the platform, looking anxiously at the train as it squealed and hissed, blowing steamy amber clouds into the glow of the street lights and the spring night. The crowd disappeared, and for a brief moment only the moon was visible. It was the first week of April, 1909, and the moon was huge and full. A golden hot air balloon, untethered, floating free above the Berkeley hills.

Then, amidst the billowing clouds of steam, Maud thought she saw Susie—off to one side, searching for her. Susie looked just as she had that day on the roof of the old Home. Her eyes seemed to find Maud's, and then she laughed. And Maud realized that at nearly fourteen, she was a full year older than Susie was when she died. But as quickly as the face appeared, it was gone. It was only Ruby's reflection in the coach window, turned strangely translucent by the rising moon. Maud shook her head to clear her mind, and this time she saw Mrs. Piatt with fat old Mrs. Williams beside her. And then the girls she had known so long. Caroline and Josephine. Helen, Ethel, and Lily. Nearly the whole family.

Maud pulled Ida and Mamie closer to the window. "Look!" she said. "Who do you see? Almost everybody's here. Let's wave."

Maud stood, and that's when she saw Grace. At the back of the crowd, behind everyone, with a baby's arms wrapped tightly around her neck like a heavy necklace. Gracie wore a loose-fitting white dress, and her hair was bound in a topknot bun. She had never looked more beautiful. Gracie's face was shiny like fine porcelain, as if she was one of those goddess statues Maud would sometimes see in Chinatown storefront windows before the earthquake and fire.

Gracie lifted her head and waved—one arm free. Open wide and welcoming.

Grace was there, and Maud knew she would lead them up the last little hill, through the shimmering moonlight, to Home.

GLOSSARY OF NAMES AND TERMS

AGE OF CONSENT: Prior to 1889, the legal age of (sexual) consent in the state of California was ten years old. In 1889, it was raised to fourteen, and eight years later, in 1897, it was raised to sixteen. In traditional Chinese culture, children were considered to be a year old at birth and they turned a year older during the Chinese New Year festival, which falls between January and February. So it was entirely possible for Chinatown brothel keepers trying to comply with California law to consider their girls legally "of age," when by Western reckoning they were nearly two years *under* the age of consent (that is, girls barely twelve by Western reckoning could be "fourteen" by Chinese accounts, and girls fourteen could be "sixteen" by Chinese accounts). In 1897, when the California age of consent was raised to sixteen, San Francisco newspapers ran numerous articles about Protestant missionaries rescuing twelve- to fourteen-year-old girls from Chinatown brothels.

AH QUAI: See "Old Mary."

ASYLUM: The fourth-floor of the Methodist Mission House at 916 Washington Street; also known as the "Gibson Rescue Home." Founded in 1871, it was dedicated to the rescue and protection of Chinese women and girls.

BAILEY, MURIEL: A San Francisco newspaper reporter, 1896-1899. Apparently never married. For the sake of simplicity in the novel, she is married to The Oriental Home's attorney, Henry (Harry) Monroe.

CHAN, HON FAN (REVEREND): Pastor of the Chinese Methodist Church in San Francisco, 1901-1906.

CAROLINE: a rescued *mui tsai*.

CARRIE: See Davis, Caroline G.

CHINESE SOCIETY FOR ENGLISH EDUCATION: Founded in 1897, the group was involved in the rescue and financial support of trafficked Chinese women and girls.

CHUN: (Mei) aka Maud (Lai), a rescued *mui tsai*. The author's children's great grandmother, whose Chinatown childhood is the basis for most of the novel's plot.

DAVIS, CAROLINE G: aka Carrie. Superintendent of the Oriental Home, 1903-1913.

ENDEAVOR: (*Young People's Society of Christian Endeavor*) An interdenominational Christian youth society founded in 1881. It held its annual meeting in San Francisco in July 1897. In the novel, this event is moved forward a year, to 1898, because that was the year the San Francisco Ferry Building opened—an event San Francisco historians know well, and a building mentioned several times in the novel.

FRENCH LETTER: A nineteenth century term for a condom.

GOD'S REGULAR ARMY: Founded in Portland, Oregon, March 8, 1898. Active in San Francisco Chinatown by August 1898. Frank Kane called *God's Regular Army* a "fake religious order" run by "George Spurgeon Duggan" who "was five years in the Salvation Army. Then he branched for himself and started the *Army of Jesus Christ*, in which he was the General. In fact the whole organization was himself. He said the reason he left the Salvation Army was he saw it was an easy way to make a living and money." At five years old, Chun (Maud) raised money for Duggan by singing on the streets of Chinatown.

GRACE/GRACIE: aka "Ying," a rescued *mui tsai*.

GUM MOON: (Cantonese) "Gold Gate/Door."

HARRY: See Monroe, Henry.

JEW HO: A Chinese Stockton Avenue grocery store owner who brought a legal challenge against the quarantine of Chinatown during the bubonic plague (*Jew Ho v. Williamson, 103 F. 10 [C.C.N.D. Cal. 1900]*).

JO SUN: (Cantonese) "Good morning."

KANE, FRANK J.: Roman Catholic layperson, Secretary of the *Pacific Society for the Suppression of Vice*, 1893-1903. Aided Presbyterian women in Chinatown rescues from 1900-1902, and Methodist women from 1900-1901.

KIM YOOK: Brothel keeper at 11 Spofford Alley, fictitiously named the "Merchant Association Club."

KING'S DAUGHTERS: Founded by Margaret McDonald Bottome in 1886. The Christian spiritual development and service organization is structured into groups of ten, for self-improvement and Christian service. The organization's magazine is called *Silver Cross*.

KINYOUN, DR. JOSEPH J.: Head of the Marine Hospital Service in San Francisco 1899-1901. In March 1900 his research led to the discovery of the bubonic plague in San Francisco.

KWAI PO: (Cantonese) (brothel) "keeper."

LAI FOON: Mei Chun's (Maud's) father.

LAI SEE: (Cantonese) "good luck." Little red gift envelopes with money inside, given to children on holidays and special events.

LAKE, KATE: aka Mrs. Lake. Matron and schoolteacher in the Methodist Rescue Home, 1896-1903.

LAKE, MARGARITA J.: aka Maggie, Miss Lake. Methodist deaconess, daughter of Kate. Responsible for much of the Chinatown rescue work on behalf of the *WHMS*. 1896-1903.

LEONG TI: Yet's lover.

LIZZIE: See Piatt, Julia Elizabeth.

LUM: The only boy in the Oriental Home, 1903-1909.

MAGGIE: See Lake, Margarita.

MAUD: See Chun.

MILK NAME: Whatever name Chinese parents give to a newborn, before they have settled on the baby's official name. The "milk name" may be abandoned, but is often continued as a nickname.

MING: aka "Ugly One." One of the trafficked girls in the Merchant Association Club.

MONROE, HENRY: aka Harry. Occasional attorney for the Oriental Home. For the sake of simplicity, in the novel, he is married to Muriel Bailey.

MUCK SHEE: Lai Foon's wife, mother of Mei Chun (Maud).

MUI TSAI: (Cantonese) literally, "little sister." A term used for Chinese debt slaves.

NEW SPANISH ALLEY: The Chinese name for Spofford Alley, just east of Stockton between Washington and Clay streets, known for its many brothels.

OLD MARY: aka "Ah Quai," a Salvation Army Chinatown Corps volunteer, instrumental in Chun's rescue. Committed suicide in 1903 after being constantly threatened by Chinese tongs because of her rescue work.

ORIENTAL HOME: Opened by the *WHMS* in 1901 at 912 Washington Street, it was destroyed by the 1906 San Francisco earthquake and fire.

PACIFIC SOCIETY FOR THE SUPPRESSION OF VICE: founded October 21, 1893. Its mission was "the suppression of all kinds of vice, including illicit literature, obscene pictures and books, the sale of morphine, cocaine, opium, and tobacco and liquors to minors, and lottery tickets." Active in the rescue of abused and abandoned children.

PIATT, JULIA ELIZABETH: aka Lizzie. *Bureau Secretary of the Oriental Home* 1903-1919.

SALVATION ARMY: Founded a San Francisco Chinatown Corps in 1886, whose women officers often worked with the Methodists in identifying and rescuing abused children.

SIU: aka Susie, rescued as a baby from a San Francisco Chinatown brothel. Maud's fictional best friend.

SPOFFORD ALLEY: aka "New Spanish Alley," just east of Stockton between Washington and Clay streets, known for its many brothels.

STREET ARAB: A homeless child, wandering city streets.

SUSIE: See Siu.

TI: see Leong Ti.

WHMS: *Woman's Home Missionary Society* of the Methodist Episcopal Church, founded in 1882.

WILLIAMS, LAURA P.: *Bureau Secretary of the Oriental Home* 1893-1903.

WON KUM: A rescued trafficked girl.

WORLEY, DR. MINNIE G.: Chinatown doctor. Buried in the Chinese Christian Cemetery, Daly City, CA

YET: aka "Pretty One." A trafficked girl in the Merchant Association Club. Leong Ti is in love with her.

YING: aka Gracie, a rescued *mui tsai*.

YUE TSCHI: A procurer of Chinese prostitutes.

DR. JEFFREY STALEY is the author of three academic books and the editor of three others. He has taught at the University of Portland, the University of Notre Dame, Pacific Lutheran University, and Seattle University. He is the historian of Gum Moon Women's Residence in San Francisco.